ABOUT THE AUTHOR

Annamarie Jagose was born in
New Zealand, in 1965. For the last ten years
she has lived in Australia where she teaches
in the Department of English with Cultural
Studies at the University of Melbourne.

Also by Annamarie Jagose

In Translation
Lulu: A Romance

Slow
Water

Annamarie Jagose

VICTORIA UNIVERSITY PRESS

VICTORIA UNIVERSITY PRESS
Victoria University of Wellington
PO Box 600, Wellington

Copyright © Annamarie Jagose 2003

ISBN 0 86473 450 6

First published 2003, reprinted 2004

Cover design by Darian Causby/Highway 51
Typeset in 11/13 pt Bembo by Midland Typesetters, Maryborough, Victoria
Printed and bound by Griffin Press, Netley, South Australia

For Lee

Tera Kopu, ka heke i te pae. See there, the last star on the edge of morning's sky.

Like the sad mamaku, I sit outside the mission fence at Waimate. My sweet-throated bird is gone and nothing remains for me. All the night, from the darkness of my blanket, I watch the dead houses, Mr Clarke's house, Mr Williams's house, Mr Davis's house, all dead. Still dead, in the first curve of daylight. A dream comes on me in the heart of the night, a warm spirit visiting me from death. It is yours, Wiremu. I know it at once. Your scent hangs in the ashen night air and in my dream you are laughing again and walking. Oho rawa ake, te hua-kore noa. Awake, sorrow chews me like a hunger. Your horse is dead and lies swelling in the grass, black legs in the air like a blasted harvest. The church roof points at the sky and you are gone from here. Sing, sing on, bird, your true song.

All my sadness cannot slow the netted sun that slides up the sky as it ever did when you lived here. Smoke climbs over my shoulder from the cooking fires at Okuratope but at the mission nothing moves, only the wind that shakes the leaves of the apple tree and blows the cold white ash of the fire. Three days gone Mr Clarke is in his house behind the curtains with Mrs Clarke and the children. Mr Davis is in his house, Mr Williams in his. The school is closed, the servants have run and the wind weeps through the grass.

Hei te wa te mate, hua ke te manuka. In this season of death the manuka is white with flower and tui swing in the sweet spikes of the harakeke. Many who were here when

1

you lived at the Waimate are dead, Tangiwai, Paitaro, the wife of your boy Toataua and Toa crying ever since. Cosmo is dead of a pain in the long bone of his back. Kohine Rangi who took the name Mere is dead, Richard and Abraham and Temorenga. Your friend Edward Hongi is dead. His mouth flowered pink spittle and he left us.

The sickness does not stick fast to the pakeha. Perhaps your God does not understand our native prayers and we are dying unheard. All your books are burned, your bed, even the picture of your sister. The fire is cold, ash-blown. Mr Davis shot your horse that I led to him from the stable and I knew you were dead. We prayed and sang. Mr Davis cried and hugged his musket. In the night your soul visits me and I wake in the dark thinking you are home. Ashes from the fire fill my mouth and again I cry.

Some say the mission men bring sickness and when we are all dead they will take the land for their children. Like the native rats, killed off by the England rats from the ships. I do not say this. I say Jesus Christ brings us to everlasting life. Remember our lessons in your room, the fire jumping at your hearth in winter, in summer the door open to Mrs Clarke's garden? It is my desire to have my lamp ready like the wise virgin, not the foolish virgin. Perhaps my thoughts are right, perhaps wrong.

See there the morning star. Alone and uncertain, it weeps as I do. Where are you now, who went so suddenly on a promise to return? You were my treasure, my window post, my one true book. God says every man must die but he has not said when. My skin is grey with ashes, my weeping heart will not lie still. Every house is closed and the people fled to Okuratope and Pukenui. Far is your canoe on an ebbing tide and I am left behind with my cheeks salted and my heavy heart. If only you could send once more your living soul to me in a dream. Kei te manu marama, korihi mai. Sweet bird of truth, sing to me.

William Yate, aged thirty-three, spark-eyed, pale-faced, with the hunched shoulder and high, cautious footwork of a wading fowl, had come aboard with his sister Sarah and the other missionary ladies, Miss Bloomfield and Miss Baker, carrying in his arms a one-inch deal box jointed and sealed with white lead, heavy with crocus roots, snow-drops, tulips, tiger lilies, amaryllis and ranunculi, all the bulbs his father had been able to collect for him, each one wrapped in separate paper and packed in dry chaff. He wore a pair of spectacles from Charles Tulley's shop at Islington that caught the light as he cocked his head about the ship. His eyeglasses acquired in manhood, he was rubbed through with the habits of his near-sighted youth, a crook-necked absorption in a universe of detail of which he had been always the constrained centre. Though he could see back without difficulty to the Gravesend wharf or out to the foreland where the land stubbed out to sea in a crinkle of foam, he favoured still the near particulars of his homuncular world, the shaggy coils of rope on the close-grained deck, the opalescence of his sister's glove buttons taking a marine tint.

He remembered this feeling of being on board ship, remembered it the moment he felt it yet could not have recalled it one second earlier. Not really a memory then, he supposed, but a knowledge, locked away in his body and only emerging in the form of recollection at the faint shiver of the deck's planking, the rush of the ship itself. What was it, this rush? An inkling of something, some checked

3

vitality, like the pale blindness of his bulbs husbanding their promise of growth and green. He felt it, too, that animal rush, not every time but on occasion, riding – Selim no fancy footer, yet at unexpected moments his steady tread and farmyard heat giving way to some rude force of life that caught his rider in its compass, causing him to throb beyond the limits of his skin. No stranger to ships and borne along now on the slipstream of their remembered pleasures, Yate felt painfully the gawkiness of his companions (his sister excepted, of course) who stared about themselves so wildly it seemed that until now the very idea of a ship must have been beyond their imagining. The grinning steward's boys had their measure, prying their mantles and reticules from them with a pretended courtesy to take below, where they pranced in gross impersonation, holding the cloaks to themselves as skirts: My dear, the ship is so very big; Yes, m'lady, so much bigger than I had thunk; So big, my dear, so big. Some wild compassion flared in Yate's chest so that he laid down his deal box and offered Miss Bloomfield one elbow and Miss Baker his other but yet they stood on deck as if they were fastened to it, blocking the passage of the handsome men as they went about their business and doubtless looking to them no less foolish than the steerage passengers now being unloaded, a fat old nurse called Mary Ford, and the Parkers with their rank troop of children.

Yate preferred to take his cabin from London. He had written as much in his letter to the Committee: that he preferred to take his cabin from London; that he wished to be equipped with a life preserver, the Mackintosh variety with a collar, and a complete set of tooth instruments; that, if his sister could be adequately instructed in raising the female character in New Zealand, he wished her to accompany him. Also, that he planned to take to New Zealand a swarm of bees in a patent glass hive. Later, he realised the Committee, accustomed to gulping down their knowledge of foreign manners from letters and reports, might think the preserver was in case of shipwreck and imagine him wearing it from Gravesend to Sydney although it was an idea that had come to him on one of his inland visits when, fording the Kerikeri after rains, he had come close to losing his hold of Selim's pommel. He felt again how it was to be strung out in the water like a filament of weed, one shoe borne away with the current, Selim swimming, golden, hot-breathed, wide nostrils raised high, unseen hooves churning dangerous beneath them, his whole self concentrated in the hand that clung to his saddle, his right hand, rubbed red in the water's cold and in that instant more dear to life than his heart. It was the oddest thing, he supposed, to feel so content at sea and unable to swim. Yes, he preferred to take his cabin from London and would have done so had Miss Selina not threatened to come to the docks with Orange Deb to see him off and she a bold enough pullet to be as good as her word. Indeed, at Gravesend pier, when he first caught sight of Miss Bloomfield, monstrously tall but taller yet in a feathered black beaver hat, the vandyke ruff that frothed at her chin so exhausting the ambition of her cambric day dress that its hem stopped well short of her ankle, *behold, the whirlwind of the Lord goeth forth with fury: it shall fall with pain upon the head of the wicked*, he had thought himself undone.

His sister's sturdy gaze met his a moment. Her eyes, brown like his, had a honeyed constellation visible at their centre in certain lights. Perfectly cast, she had no need for eyeglasses. Although shorter than him, slighter too, of course, and alto-gether more womanish, he knew her for his reflection. He felt easier having her to hand. With her beside him, like the silver backing of a mirror that gave him back to himself, the stren-uous business of living, of life itself, fell away. He wouldn't return to England, that was both his intention and his inclination. What they were exactly he could not have said, but other possibilities, their incoherent shapes pressing at him, took sustenance in the space warmed between him and Sarah. Now, she organised the ladies below and Yate allowed himself a turn about the deck. Seen full on, he was tall and broad across the shoulder yet he lived in his body with such consideration that he appeared smaller, almost delicate. He seemed like a man returned home from a long journey, much changed or in disguise: he assumed a familiarity with everyone and everything, paddling at the piglets through the rails of their enclosure and casting looks of tenderness at every passing face, while he himself, unrecognised, excited nothing more than a warm curiosity. Here were four men bringing three pigs on board, very ticklish after being cranked off the side. Their shirt sleeves rolled past the elbow, their breeches tucked into top boots (one man though in bare feet with his trousers rolled), they escorted the pigs to their sty, paying no heed to their near-human screams. The first pig had one man at each ear, its front legs lifted off the deck by means of those handles, its back legs wheeling and sliding; the next pig was dragged with less ceremony by a back leg and the last carried over the shoulder like a baby. Yate stood behind the sty to watch the men work. The fellow who was dragging his pig backward by the leg had his free arm flung wide for balance and through the open front of his shirt Yate could see the line where his weathered skin gave out to creamy pink. He had brown hair, coarse like a dog's, that curled in the damp, and a frank stare.

Yule be eaten her 'fore too long, said the man, making a grab at the pig's other back leg and steering it as a wheel-barrow into the enclosure.

No doubt. The man had an honest look to him – the pared-back transparency that comes from labour and can't be had from books – and the veins stood out becomingly on the back of his hands.

You kin feed her up an over the line she kin feed you.

Yate wanted to say something to him but the only thing that came to him as he stood was Godspeed and he the one sailing.

Praps them sheep are more to your taste, said the man. A couple of sheep carcasses were being winched high into the standing rigging over the forecastle, where they hung, like the two thieves, one on either side of the best part of an ox. They were standing close enough to each other that Yate could see the pale creases at the corners of the other man's eyes.

Go well, said Yate and went forward, looking into the galley as he passed. There was nothing there but an oversize cauldron of water creaking over the flame and a painted statue of the Virgin, her plaster face sputtering under the light of three candles. At the forecastle Yate watched two men hauling boxes into the rigging, a slight, smudge-eyed boy with a pink yawn neat as a cat's on the tag end of the rope. He made so little difference, the boy, that he was sworn off by the second mate and sent aloft, his ears red with the men's toasting, his gear so new it still had the creases.

Yate had stood for so long on the forecastle looking up at the ox, splay-ribbed, swinging by the neck like Mathusalah Spalding at the Old Bailey, that his own neck had taken a sympathetic crick. Seeing him standing there, so angular and unlikely, head cranked to the sky like some river bird, and thinking also to curb, at least for the duration of the voyage, his lively dislike of anything parsonish, the ship's doctor picked his way to the forecastle over the ropes and luggage, past the hen coop near to bursting and a clump of newly boarded steerage passengers, as disgruntled and wet as the poultry.

Doctor Fowles, said the doctor.

Mr Yate, said Yate. The two men nodded amiably, inclining their upper bodies toward each other as a further politeness. The doctor found Yate quite a physiognomic study, a long face that was still in the live way of water, hair drawn back over a high, intelligent forehead, skin lightly pocked across the cheeks and, behind his round eyeglasses, a spirited, welcoming glance, a sharp nose yet full, almost womanly lips. Yate's diagnostic glance was more to the point: consumptive.

You've sailed before?

Many times, said Yate. This is my second voyage to New Zealand.

And I think you've sailed previous with our captain?

Nearly ten years ago now. He was no captain then but an able seaman. Known to us all as Johnny.

Johnny, said the doctor, Johnny Aitken, and the two men laughed out a companionable moment. A couple of miles up the river a steamer from London hoved to and seemed, from the movement on deck that could be made out at that distance, to be preparing its passengers for disembarkation. The doctor and the missionary went after, the one to see whether he could better make out the scene, the other to take possession of his cabin. Yate looked one last time into the rigging but the boy was idling up there, in no hurry to return to the squeal and stink of the deck. As so often on board, Yate considered there was much to admire and that everything was tricked out to his satisfaction.

From the top, his head reeling with the air and tiredness, the boy watched the missionary go, his dark form picking a path between the water barrels. A long night and little sleep. He had signed his articles at St Katherine's Docks half a week past, Samuel Hall, shipping for the first time as a boy but known more familiarly in the forecastle as a greenhand or a lubberly farmer. From the first, Mr Cat had taken a strict air with him on account of his never having been to

sea before nor seeming to have much knack for it, but the
sternness sat with the second mate so awkwardly, was cush-
ioned on every side with a compassion even more
awkward, that he was like two mates, one vicious, one
kindly, and each very much ill at ease with the other.

How the ship's husband ever signed you on, there's no
telling, Mr Cat would say. He might have thought he were
running a Sunday school. Then just as if he were thinking
of running such a school himself, he would add, You're a
sound boy – it'll turn out well for you. Or, passing Hall on
the deck where he was set to picking old rope to oakum for
the carpenter's caulking bucket, Thinking of your mother,
boy? and before Hall could blink away the water that
prickled in his eyes, I own she's thinking of you.

These first experiences of contrariness would ever be
Hall's sensation of being at sea, later to be refined by other
oppositions such as being at the one time nauseous and
hungry, or thinking, while he sailed homeward up the river,
only of his next outbound passage. He learned to take a
quick comfort in his cow-tongued second mate, smooth
one way and rough the other, seeking out his proximity in
the surreptitious ways available to him. The first time aloft,
his feet cramping in the slings and his heart beating so hard
it could be seen through his shirt, the only trick he could
turn to make his arms yield their purchase on the main
yard was to look across the spar and draw courage from
the second mate's easy footing in the earring. Weighing the
anchor, when Mr Cat called the Heighs, the most heartfelt
Hos were always sung by Hall. So it happened that Mr
Cat's black look did not often fall on Hall but that Hall's
eyes were already fastened on him.

At eight bells the previous night, when the men began
retiring to the forecastle, Hall hung to the back since he had
learned that by ship's custom the men do not go below

singly when they can take it two and three at once and
several times he had been crumpled against the hatchway
while behind his back one watch tumbled above and
another below, all the breath knocked from him and bruises
raised on his tendernesses. He never felt more a boy than in
the bilge-stinking forecastle where the lamp's wick danced
green and pink with the foulness of the air and the men
sported without restraint.

Think you the cappen with a cabin to youself?

Ruther be ashore. Sleepin like a cow with a cunt at my
arse.

Halfway down the steep ladder, his legs already enjoying
the warmish fug of the forecastle, he was hailed by Mr Cat.

Hall, you can stand anchor watch tonight. Keep a bright
lookout else you'll wish yourself back in the nursery. It's a
safe anchor, son, and will be good practice besides. The
second mate went abaft to the quarterdeck to keep a sharp
eye on a couple of Gravesend wherries being rowed about
just shy of the ship, waiting their moment, he supposed, to
slip beneath the bows and assist to shore any seamen requiring safe passage for themselves and their advanced wages.
Assuming himself the object of Mr Cat's ceaseless scrutiny,
while also taking that gentleman as his own, Hall felt the
enormity of his responsibility no more than if he had been
asked to captain the vessel and walked his watch out, fore
and aft, the full length of the ship, taking care to look over
the taffrail and the bow on each circuit. The wind blew the
rain in under the brim of his hat, the waves hammered the
planking and Hall kept his watch, his new rig, bought that
day from the slop seller, soaked through and sticking dank
to his skin. Shortly before midnight, the wind grew louder
yet and the deck began to kick unpredictably under his feet
as the vessel turned in the tide to crab the waves.

Mr Cat, called the boy, lover-like outside the second
mate's cabin. Mr Cat.

Does she begin to swing? The second mate had gone to

bed with his clothes on and had his door open before he had finished pulling on his boots.

Ay, sir, she slews round.

Call the pilot, said Mr Cat, hurrying forward to raise the men, and, again over his shoulder in more sympathy, Call the pilot.

The ship riding smartly to anchor once more and a new watchman to take his place, Hall followed the men below. The two Lascars taken on from Gravesend that day had worked up an intricate argument about which another man, not knowing the material details, was yet prepared to make one and then another ruling so long as each time he was provided with a swallow of the crank they had also brought off with them. A fellow called Staines, an older man with his cheeks grizzled grey, watched all from his hammock as if he had been at a cock baiting. Earlier, he had made a rough suggestion that Hall take the berth next to his. A Finnish sailor had steered Hall to the hammock furthest from Staines's, tight in the corner, beneath a leak as it turned out though the boy didn't discover that till later. Now the Finn, his left eye true to the horizon, his right smoked over and webbed with white, took up his book and began to mouth his silent way down the page. A ginger-hackled giant, he read intently, the book held close to his one good eye, its pages fluttering between his great hands as if it were some simple thing he had the luck to capture. While the men shook the water from their hair and tamped their pipes, got under their blankets and covered their eyes with their arm some of them, others begging into a game of bones; while they scratched and swore, gruffled and farted; while they told their stories and scotched those of their fellows, Hall strung up his wet duck trousers like a flag and laid himself out for sleep.

The hatch banged open.

All hands to deck. Hall's dreams were dark and oily as a slick of river water midstream and he came up from them with difficulty. The men were on their feet, some already squeezing through the hatchway, others bare-arsed, hopping with one leg in their trousers. Across the way, one of the Lascars, legs hung over his hammock, held his head in his pink-palmed hands. Hall sat up with a wild stare and for a long moment did not know where he was. Even dressed and above, he felt he may as well have been sleepwalking for all the sense of reality offered him by the confusion on deck. He could not understand the orders rapidly given by first the pilot and then Mr Cat but had the horrible knack of standing in the way of those who did so that several times as they lay aloft or forward in the execution of their tasks he was rudely shoved and once knocked to the wet deck. At first he tagged after the men to show willing but, seeing he was most often a hindrance, he removed himself to the waist where he stood clear of so much as a bitt or a belaying pin and fixed his eye on the second mate as on the noonday sun. Although Hall did not know it, a nearby collier had lost its mooring and drifted hard against a brig, the force of the impact rolling her watchman out from beneath the longboat where he had been sleeping just in time to raise the alarm as the bentinck boom, running clear between her main- and foremasts, made off with half her rigging. Now, the collier was drifting dangerously on the *Prince Regent* while the pilot and Mr Cat laboured to escape m\ishap by weighing anchor and backing and filling her sails. For near on an hour and as if he still dreamed, Hall stood upright in the wind and the pelts of rain, as wooden and shining as the figurehead of the golden lamb he had much admired on the London Docks.

The new day came in like a carnival. All was bustle and commotion as a fleet of light craft worked from shore to ship and back again, loading further livestock and luggage. The wind furred the water white and grey and the sunlight, like the salt spray, fell undiscriminating on every surface.

Captain's ashore now, said Launcelot Busby. He was knocking together wooden braces as a hutch for some hares that Mr Yate had secured cheap at the last moment and, bent to his task, spoke through a mouthful of nails. He come on the steamer this morning and is in town now giving the passengers their muster. He spoke without looking at Hall, who obliged him by listening without much seeming to. Hall was tired in a way that was half pleasant. Since he had been signed on at the Docks, he had lost his customary sense of how the world was held together and was piecing it up again for himself, little by little. His happiest moment as a sailor had been two days after signing up when, as the tug was hauling the *Prince Regent* from St Katherine's Docks, the ship swung round into the river and he caught sight of his mother, standing unexpectedly outside a ship's chandler on Fountain Stairs, his two younger brothers alongside, waving her handkerchief at him as he went to sea. He leaped to the mizzen ratlines then and snatching from his head his tarpaulin hat, still so new it squeaked in his hand, he waved it at that dear white spot now almost lost in the distance till his heart ached near as much as his arm and he was half relieved to be knocked from his ropes by the careless descent of a sailor who, far from offering his apology or picking him from the deck, had cursed him for a soldier, a curse he was still some weeks from understanding as the most contemptuous to be had at sea.

The capting, what's he like?

Well, he's a man, like any another, said the carpenter.

Has he got his self a beard?

No, he's got no beard. The older man stepped heavy on

the last word as if the absence of a beard signified much for the captain's character. But he's a man and a fair one. Not ten years ago he was a sailor before the mast like you; now he's master of the ship.

Busby had been in better days himself the master of a whaler and ridden out his youth and health in the fields off the Cape de Verdes and Japan. With a few drinks in him, he liked to tell how he had been towed near halfway round the world in the boiling backwash of a harpooned sperm whale; how he kept a wife in Akkeshi and another in Nantucket but slept best at sea; how he had been shipwrecked off the Cape and made shore on a teatray with his own beard for a sail. He owned the things he had not seen were not worth the looking. The men called him Blubbersby, although not to his face, for he had a spouter's quick temper and had bloodied his fists many times in some inn or other over a supposed slight to what it still pleased him to call his profession. Still there was not much of the tryworks about him now as he watched Hall fall in with a couple of the men, under orders from the mate to winch supplies of preserved fish over the main yard, no more than a boy really, fresh from his mother's careful nursing. That boy has no more sense than a bag of hares, Busby thought, shaking the yellow-eyed animals down into their cage, and is unlikely to make a happier sailing.

No significant weight on the end of a rope and cursed out by Mr Cat in front of the missionary, Hall was sent aloft to drop a line and block over the yard and lash the cases of fish under the top as they were hauled up from the deck. Over the creak of the rigging and the whewt of an occasional gull, he could hear in imperfect snatches – *cheerily ho, cheerily ho* – the song of the men as they pulled the rope together. His nostrils filling with the punkish smell steaming off the furled sails, he secured the crates under the maintop, the tip of his tongue caught between his teeth as he parcelled each one off with the square knot Mr Cat had taught him. Although only at the head of the mainmast with still the maintopmast, the main topgallant mast and the main royal mast rising impossibly over his head, the deck lay beneath him in the shape of a shoe, cast off and flung down. His own shadow lay unseen on the water's wind-combed surface. He saw the missionary turn and walk, birdlike, the passage left him between the water casks that remained lashed on deck in two long rows, each one looking to Hall no bigger than the bung that sealed them shut. He could make out the backs of the sheep being packed into the longboat as tight as weevils in a biscuit. Some men were loading boxes into the hold, throwing them one to the other along the deck and down the hatch, although Hall reckoned the ship was already full as an egg with the hogsheads of stout and rum, the barrels of flour and the casks of gunpowder, the ploughshare moulds and iron wheels, all kindful things they had taken on board while still in the docks. Off to the lee side, there were some further passengers coming aboard, one of them he guessed to be the captain, from the eagerness with which the man, unchallenged, took the quarterdeck, and just behind them, crossing paths with a supply boat now pulling hard away from the ship, another boatload making for the side. From the maintop, the world lay split open for Hall like a book of fancies. Ever since he came on board the *Prince Regent*, he had been breathing in this dreamish sensation as if sleeping and waking were the same game. His hair clouted about his face, his breath snatched direct from his lung before it ever came to his mouth, Hall saw a steamer from London lay off passengers some two miles from the ship and head back down the river like a toy boat while, barely needing to turn his head, he could make out a barque round the North Foreland and enter the roads in full sail. Above him, high aloft on the *Regent*'s fore topgallant mast was a man, perhaps it was Edwards, hard to say at this distance and with the sun behind, to whom Hall himself must appear a tiny dreamed figure, some dollhouse creature impelled by such forces as could only be guessed. A giddying sense of his infinitesimal worth overtook Hall then, not the sense that he was valued at nothing but the realisation that the world would be some incalculable fraction worse off, would be diminished minutely but all the same diminished, if he were not of it.

The figures that from the ship could barely be made out were the remaining missionaries, the Taylors and their four children, accompanied from London by Mr Taylor's cousin, George, and their friends, Mr Fox and Mr Negus. The wind was so high and the water so much agitated that it was with some difficulty that the passengers were transferred to the small cockle boat that drew alongside. Mr Taylor went over first and, as the boat tipped unsteadily beneath him, was handed Arthur, then Basil, Laura clung to her mother a little before coming off, the baby barely a weight in its crocheted blanket and finally Mrs Caroline Taylor, eyes reddened from weeping and too distracted even to mind the wind belling her skirt to show her stocking. After a week of farewells – the worst, surely, poor nurse – Mrs Taylor felt at last, as the boat shoved off, as if she were truly breaking the dear connection with her native country. She looked about for some last scene to treasure during the unimaginable nights to follow but could fix on nothing familiar at Gravesend. Everything had been strange to her since October, since Richard resigned his curacy at Coveney. The very next evening the comet had come again, its long tail clearly visible but its portent ambiguous. Now her own children, hunched at the front of the cockle boat, seemed unfamiliar to her, their faces pinched and strange as if something else looked out through their eyes. And the baby – Mrs Taylor gave a rough cry and half started to her feet – the baby, she had left her on the steamer. Divining her fright, Mr Taylor held up the infant for her to see. He had her bundled inside his great-coat to keep her from the spray and the occasional wave shipped by the boat. Almost entirely obscured in a travelling shawl and a large white cap, Mrs Taylor saw at once that her baby too had grown strange, resembling in miniature nothing more than the palely shrouded greegree man of West Africa whose illustration she had recently seen in the Missionary Papers.

Alongside the ship, a round, chair-like structure cut out of a barrel was lowered for Mrs Taylor who was hoisted aboard, her legs covered with the Union Jack. After the buck and roll of the cockle boat, there was scarcely any motion apparent on the deck of the *Prince Regent* but Mrs Taylor continued unsteady. By the time Taylor had boarded with the children, the baby's mouth hinged open in a violent scream, the ship's doctor had made his introduction and had Mrs Taylor on his arm. Handing the baby to his temporary care, Taylor shepherded his family to their cabins. As he followed to the cuddy, Doctor Fowles jogged his charge in the crook of his arm but her thin, angry screams persisted. He changed his grip and jiggled her in the other arm; he held her face down and patted small circles on her back; he turned her about and peeled back sufficient of her cap to allow a view of her face. In the cuddy's half-light, he saw that she was as yet too young to carry her character on her face. Her skin was damson, eyes crimped so tightly shut that even her lashes were gone from view, her chin and nose negligible: she was, in truth, not much more than a mouth and that pinkly split and roaring.

Come, come, said the doctor, and when that did not quiet her, Come, come. After what seemed a long while but was in fact no longer than it takes a man to lay off his coat, shout at his children and persuade his wife out of her wet clothes, Taylor came to the cuddy to relieve the doctor of his strident charge. He handed her back with mixed feeling: his first case and he could not in any conscience consider her cured.

Doctor Fowles considered that he had managed his cabin admirably. He returned to it frequently during the day to assure himself of its orderliness. Seven foot square and every inch bent to some practical purpose, it had been much described in a letter to his wife that the doctor had sent ashore with his cousin, already now disembarked for home. It had not seemed so lovely twelve hours previous but the doctor was experienced enough to know that many things are tolerable by day which cannot be borne at night. He had been the first passenger to board. Save the crew, there had been no one else about but the custom house officer and the pilot. Hard put to imagine a grimmer pair of toby jugs, the one full as crabbed and crotchety as the other, and with no society but his young cousin, Doctor Fowles had sat in the cuddy, his face jumping ginger and orange before the open stove, until he fancied the small lamp there burned low as his hopes. Yowling without, the wind sucked and growled within as well, making such easy passage through the window frame that the doctor, his face close to blistering in the stove's heat, felt his shoulders seize and his back take up the chill until he could imagine himself no worse off had he been aloft, bent over the main topgallant yard with the rigging men. He coughed and, from habit, held a handkerchief to his lips. Now bent against, now blown before the wind, had the pilot on one of his inscrutable passages between the quarterdeck and the forecastle cared to glance into the cuddy, had he cared then to tot up his estimation of the ship's doctor, he might have reported a narrow man with fair, freckled skin, handsome enough in this light, hair curling to his collar: a consumptive whose uncertain health made his age hard to reckon. Had the pilot paused to consider the noble bumps of the head now inclined toward the stove, the arch of the nose and the roof-shaped eyebrow, he might have concurred with the doctor's own assessment before the looking glass: a man of religious sentiment but scientific principle, a man whose frequent failings were the best signature of his being modern. Nothing could be less likely, however, since the pilot did not so much as pause nor turn his head, having no curiosity let alone fellow-feeling for anyone not at home on the water, by which he meant really the river (and by 'the river' meant only the Thames), although, congress or commerce necessitating, he would count a seaman among those who deserved his interest and attention. Born on the river, as he liked to tell, the pilot had no patience for landsmen, most especially when they went to sea, taking a ship for their parlour and their promenade. Wrapped more tightly in his prejudices than even his dun-coloured pea-jacket, he would sooner have sat to dinner with a waterman still damp from handspiking a body from the river's greasy stew than traded a story or so much as a nod with the doctor.

Earlier, the doctor had spent a pleasant hour with the first mate, Mr Bennett, standing him a peg of brandy and being stood one in turn. A gentleman of alluring person and captivating manners, the first mate was yet salty enough to make the doctor, still no further down the Thames than Gravesend, feel as if he had already put to sea. With Mr Bennett now on shore with his sweetheart, giving his legs and who knows what else the last stretch they might enjoy for some time, there was nothing for it but bed, the reliable refuge of the unhappy.

Come, Davey, said the doctor to his cousin. It blows a mean puff.

They stood and shook out their legs together, the one so recently a boy that he had not yet lost the habit of friskiness and expended his excess spirits in ponyish movement. The doctor placed a hand on his shoulder a moment, whether to quiet him or draw off a little of that vitality for himself could not be said for certain. He closed the stove door and took up the lamp.

The captain's cabin, he said, waving the lamp to one side as an indication. The rest of the poop houses those missionaries I told you are headed for New Zealand. We sinners must sleep below.

You'll make a sailor yet with your poops and your belows. His cousin followed him downstairs, shambling up against him when he paused to make out the door to his cabin, the foremost on the starboard side.

No later than ten o'clock – Doctor Fowles had an idea taken from some novel or other, that time on board ship was reckoned in glasses or was it bells? but knowing no more than that he kept for the moment to his pocket watch – no later than ten o'clock, he and his cousin turned in to his single berth.

No sooner was the doctor's cousin in bed, undressed to his shirt tails, clothes hanging on one of the numerous hooks with which the doctor, on the advice of more travelled friends, had that afternoon equipped his cabin, than he was asleep. Slower to bed and, once there, kept awake long hours by the novelty of his situation, the doctor was barely able to maintain his berth: the youthful sprawl of his cousin crowded him to the edge of his ticking while each roll of the vessel, threatening to take from him even that much comfort, near pitched him to the floor. In modest imitation of the winds above that whined through the cordage, his cousin snored lightly and Doctor Fowles, strung between that soft whistle and the squeal of the chain cable, felt very much alone. He thought of his wife – *his wife!* – and his children; he thought of all those, sleeping now or perhaps awake, whom he could not expect to see inside this twelvemonth, if again. A melancholy came on him then, a humour he was accustomed to regard if not quite as a friend then as a familiar: *my great bear*, he called it to himself, the muzzled immensity of the thing recalling to him that animal he had once seen standing upright, front paws chained to a ceiling beam in a house off Whitechapel Road. On deck, the sailors' voices.

Does she begin to swing?

Ay, she slews round.

Call the pilot. Call the pilot.

From his miserable bed, the doctor heard the pilot's grumbling instruction as he made the ship ride properly to anchor against the changing of the tide. The ship's head righted and the pilot returned to his couch, all was again silent but for the high-tempered wind and the slow step of the night watch. Such was Doctor Fowles's first night on board.

Now, though, with fresh travellers arriving on each boat and a patch of sunlight rocking on the far wall of his cabin, the doctor was in better humour. As his berth was longer than his bedding, he had set up a study at its foot, only a travelling desk and some few books but he referred to it as his study just as he now called his medicine chest his dispensary and his row of hooks his dressing room. He sat at his desk, cross-legged as any opium smoker, to make some notes in his diary about the passengers but was soon forced above again for fresh material. All the missionaries were tight in their cabins, no doubt giving thanks for their safe passage, but several boats alongside were disgorging such persons that the doctor felt the cast of a pantomime could hardly make use of a more colourful swag of characters.

The Parkers were still milling about uncertainly. There seemed to be some dispute over the fare from Gravesend and, on this account, the boatman was withholding the last piece of their luggage, a sorry-looking sack of what might have been mess supplies. One minute, Mr Parker seemed inclined to let the sack go and consider himself still up on the bargain; the next, he bunched his hands into fists of commendable size and swore at the boatman sufficient to lift the varnish off the bulwarks. Far from being compromised by her husband's indelicacies, Mrs Parker chipped in with her own curses when she remembered and, while her husband limited himself to the boatman's person, she allowed herself a more liberal range over his entire family, not sparing his ancestors and any future line he might engender. The doctor wondered if Mrs Parker was not in her altitudes. Certainly she was more unsteady on her feet than the roll of the ship's deck warranted and kept such a firm grip on her grimy baby, swinging it so incautiously that she might have mistaken it for a bottle. Her four remaining children seemed like twenty as they poured here and there, widdy-widdy-way, twisting their noses into every corner, no more discountenanced at being bitten by one of the pigs whose tail they were intent on straightening than being shouted off the quarterdeck by Mr Bennett.

Mr Gordon, a young Scottish gentleman now boarding with a cage of nineteen canaries who each, as might be expected, had its own name but seemed to the doctor now and throughout the voyage a mess of indistinguishable feather, had blanched, the natural colour of his cheek drawn over with a greenish touch. Waxy as a rind of cheese, he fussed distractedly over his birds, entirely unable to enjoy the sallies of an extravagantly dressed gentleman alongside, supervising the loading of his considerable effects. Not seasickness but proximity to the Parkers had caused his upset as was proved by his quick recovery when the first mate ordered a couple of his men to bundle the family below. The doctor, himself a little cowed by the Parkers but not letting on as much even to himself, came forward to make his customary introduction.

Doctor Fowles.

Mr Gordon.

Doctor Fowles.

Mr Armistead. This last, an attorney going out to make his fortune or at least give his English debts the slip, seemed not to have the least consciousness of the spectacle he presented and stood before them as if he were dressed in nothing more eye-pulling than Gordon's pertersham overcoat. Armistead wore a light blue coat unbuttoned over a scarlet waistcoat with a Hussar point, a pair of skin-coloured inexpressibles that were next to invisible and may as well have been gloves for the closeness of the fit they afforded, button boots in kid with pointed toes, and the whole tog-out finished off with yards of gold chain. Several times, the doctor ran his eye up and down in order to memorise the detail of the man but finding when he had the glass butterfly brooch he had forgotten the rhinoceros cane or that he could not seem to hold in his head at once the frothy insinuation of the shirt frill and the white neckcloth worn robber-baron-style, he wished he could fetch his diary up and take his notes on deck. The doctor's was not the only eye held by Armistead's appearance: the men who ferried his boxes, the first and second mates putting their heads together on the quarterdeck, young Patrick Kelly going out to meet his father, everyone stared and stared again. Even four-year-old John Bedgood, the cartwright's son, who looked to the doctor an unhealthy little brat, his legs put on three-cornered triangular and indescribably queer, stood in front of Armistead as before a cathedral and, mouth agape, looked his fill. Captain Button and his wife, accustomed as they were to seeing to their own comforts before giving anyone else their consideration, paused long enough in their chivvying and chiding of the steward's boys to take in Armistead's display. Little Master Button frankly stared although his sister, Miss Button – recognised at once by the doctor as a beauty in the Fanny Kemble style, her milky brow and curious dipping gait distracting him momentarily from Armistead's ruby and gold shirt buttons – was too cultivated to gape at a man to whom she had not been introduced but yet she managed, in going first before and then behind her mama, to slide her eyes over him several times as if he were so much unremarkable scenery. If Armistead was aware of the stir he created, he gave no observable sign. As he turned to the rail to oversee the lifting of his boxes and back again to count them piled on deck, the doctor thought he most resembled a stage coquette whose idea of acting was to give her wardrobe the very best airing possible.

By late afternoon, all the passengers, cabin and steerage, had been drawn to their berths as water down the scuppers. Mary Ford had a bed to herself and, not on that account alone, thought herself grand. Thirty-eight years previous, she had been transported to the colony on charges of theft, though if truth be, it were cadgin more like, a pair a stockins that were but a piece a rubbage anyhow, not worth the seven years they'd done her for, nothin like. Married now and a woman of property, she could still feel smashed up and frightened thinking on it.

It's water, girl, she said to herself, not quite understanding the expression but drawing her usual comfort from it. She meant that she need not worry herself with it, it was of little consequence, although, in her experience, considerable now, that was hardly the nature of water. She wore her fat like a consolation and a safety. Nobody could touch her.

Head to the footboard so she could keep an eye on her companions, she eased herself down on her bunk. She thought on the farm she'd had with Mr Everett at Nepean Road and the foal that time, still wet and nearly pink in the light of the evening, his frisk-hoofed jig to the fenceline, knees like knots in the slenderness of his legs, sniffing on every side, soused on the world though he knew only such a bit of it. She thought on her husbands; she had buried them both.

It's water, girl, she said again. To Mary Ford's left, the little Parkers swung and whopped it up as their parents, the only ones of the whole assembly not bothered to unpack and bustle about, sat up at the long mess table that divided the two rows of bunks and had themselves a drink.

Your health, m'pretty, said Mr Parker, without looking up from his mug.

And here's to you, my wap-eyed angel, Mrs Parker returned, a salute received as cordially as it was given. Beyond the table where the Parkers sat, it grew too dim to make out the arrangements but every now and then one of the Pedrano family or one of the Bedgoods stepped out into a greasy spray of light bearing away a bonnet or some home foodstuffs, once a Bible, as they settled themselves into their narrow quarters. The single men, Patrick Kelly and James Lyne, had been bunked together behind a makeshift wooden partition and were getting acquainted in the tight turn under the deck. To Mary Ford's right were the Davidsons above, Mrs Eylard below with her daughter. She called herself Missus any rate and good luck to her, though if any Mister Eylard was waiting at Sydneytown for the pair a them, Mary Ford would whistle *Rule Britannia* out her arse.

Above, Yate had settled himself and his sister into their cabins before venturing along the passageway. His companions were accommodating themselves with such difficulty they might have thought themselves no worse off in steerage. No matter how he ordered them arranged, Armistead could not stow all his chests and cases in his cabin and, resigned to having some stored in the hold, had them all open at the one time and shifted items from this one to that and back again according to some system, if system there was, known to himself alone. Mrs Button had again an unhappy sensation of the voyage, seeing her husband apply himself to the near-military operation of securing their family's two cabins. When what little furniture they had with them was caged or lashed in place, she hardly liked to take her eye off their chest of drawers, even her dressing case and work box, as if they were so many wild animals she full expected to rush her at their first opportunity, hearts bent on injury. After much scraping of shins on packing crates; much calling for the steward and his calling, in turn, for his two sorry boys; after the allocation and reallocation of clothes to coat-hooks and children to bedding, the upending of boxes to find some item always lodged in the last; after comfortings and recriminations, a cross word trailing its own apology; after makeshift dinners and teas, an order of sorts had been asserted and Mr Taylor ventured at last to suggest to his wife that all was ship-shape.

Night came as it must and one by one the lamps were put out. The vessel's unfamiliar pitch rocked dreams loose from strange, unplumbable places. Little Alfred Button was a sailor with his shirt open across his man's chest while in the bunk below Miss Button dreamed her dear Mr Whitlock dead, his face creamy as in life but weeping blood, two crimson tears. Across the passage, the doctor took the liberty of dreaming of Miss Button. He dreamed her just as he had seen her, her swan-like step and lustrous skin so exactly replicated from life that in the morning he counted it a wasted opportunity. Somewhere beneath his berth but rolled to the same rhythm in her own, Mary Ford lay on her back, her chins wobbling against her bosoms, and dreamed she was drowning a beautiful death, descending like a carved figurehead to the sea floor, her life streaming from her nostrils in bubbled ropes of pearly light. In Mrs Eylard's dream, all her teeth were loosening and jumbling from her jaw so that she squeezed her daughter hard enough to make her call out, the cry lodging in the sleeping ear of Mr Pedrano who made an economy of it in his own dream, where it was the shouted call of a stranger who hailed him from the other side of a street in his home town. He was walking at his leisure along a familiar street when his name was called – *Lewis, Lewis* – but the street turned to a stream, then a river's gush, and how was he to cross over? There were rickety bridges and spars floating downstream, spinning in weirs before being taken under, and his children out of sight and almost certainly in danger before he woke glad only to be alongside his wife in the dark pitch and swell of the close cabin. Miss Baker dreamed of a whipped syllabub she once had described to her. Taylor's baby, Parker's baby, Bedgood's baby all dreamed the same dream, the only dream they had ever dreamed, some pink shapes, some pinker, as can be seen through eyelids closed against the sun. They dreamed their pink shapes and twitched their limbs as, on deck, the hares jerked theirs in sleep. Yate dreamed his father was ill and that it fell to him to make hundreds of tiny incisions on every surface of his skin that opened up beneath his knife like so many buttonholes. Hall dreamed that Staines tipped a light to his face and was not sure that he dreamed since the gold and yellow of his sleeping was the lick and leap of the lantern. The goats dreamed their goatish dreams; everyone slept and their dreams bound them one to another until morning.

The first Sabbath on board and the ship rode at anchor off the Kentish coast. Yate took the service. His congregation looked to him a little pettish as if they had not yet cast off the ways of land. Perhaps leading them in a familiar hymn would restore them to themselves. Yate caught his sister's eye and steadied himself there a moment. Doctor Fowles found it rather provoking to be settling into sea life and all the while remain anchored to English soil: Margate, Broadstairs and Ramsgate in plain and picturesque view off the starboard side. On Friday afternoon, the wind having moderated sufficiently, the captain had ordered a steamer to tow the ship down the river past the Nore lights but Saturday morning the men had been late in calling the estuary pilot and the ship could not be got around South Foreland before the turning of the tide. It was not until Saturday night that the *Prince Regent* had finally stolen around the foreland, coming to anchor off Deal a little past midnight where it had remained since, it being impossible to take the channel in the westerly wind. The doctor was reading Cooper's *The Red Rover* and, a little smitten with Tarry Bob and his hearty marine ways, was impatient to go to sea. Miss Button and Mrs Taylor were as sick off Deal as they could have been taking the Horn and the only two cabin passengers who did not attend service in the cuddy. With the optimism of the voyage fresh upon him, Yate expounded a chapter of Isiah: *though your sins be as scarlet, they shall be as white as snow; though they be red like crimson, they shall be as wool.* As he spoke, he had in mind the twenty-two bare-faced sheep in the longboat, pasture traded for grassy seas, their long, thin legs as black as their faces.

During the service, the cook prepared the ducks for the cabin dinner. He sat on the deck, resting his back against the wall of the galley, a pile of loose-necked birds at his feet.

Charlie and Sadler, the steward's boys, stood unhappily by.

Come, *mo pitit ye*, they got no mo' bite in em, said the cook, grinning like a dog, his teeth white in his face. He liked the boys, even without knowing them. They reminded him of boys at home. Children were like that somehow, he knew, as if they could be children anywhere. The men here, the women too, never put him in mind of those at home. It was as if the whiteness calcified on them somehow after so many years and they could only be the one thing. He liked the steward well enough but the man was hard on his boys, a rough tongue and a rougher hand, and their passage would be easier if they were handy in the galley. Sadler hunkered down and took up a duck. It was still warm and felt, he imagined, like a luxurious glove. He stroked it once, twice, and looked up at Charlie to show it was not so bad but Charlie stayed standing, first on one leg, then the other.

You don't mind petten them when they're alive, said Charlie in the reasonable way he used on himself, and you don't mind eaten them when they're dead, but still he stayed standing. The cook sliced open one of the birds, a yellowish daub bubbling along the knife's blade as it split apart the private meaty world Charlie was afraid of. Easing his fingers into the slit, he grubbed out the grain-bulged crop and a bloodied glisten of organs. He handed the cleaned duck over to Sadler, yellow varnished eye still shining roundly in the sleek head feathers, and started on another.

Now, take em and trow em in the duck pon, *garson*, said the cook, pointing over his shoulder with his knife at the large pot boiling on the galley stove. An you, take this – the bucket of shining entrails – and feed em fishes. When Sadler returned, his face ruddy from the steam, the half-dozen ducks by the feet in two hot handfuls, the cook showed him how to pluck the birds.

Pull em fedders *tèl kòm sa-la*. Sadler sat alongside, his feet reaching just past the cook's knees. They worked away companionably, their hands warmed by the feathers. Sadler was quick, the cook saw that at once, his fingers small and fast. He bit his bottom lip as he worked and, between birds, he wiped his hands on his trouser legs like a grown man.

See this, Charlie? the cook said. Your fren here's a smart boy. Charlie thought the ducks better with their feathers gone and if only, he thought, they didn't have heads neither. Just then, two skua gulls came coasting high on a wind current, their pinions stretched to the furthest extent, wing tip to wing tip. With his lap full of damp feathers, the cook looked skyward, head tilted so far back that his mouth hung open. You didn't usually see them off Kent, he knew that much. The rust-coloured gulls banked low, wings whaling as they braked in the air over the poop and slashed their claws across each other's cheeks and throat.

Koman to lèm sa astè! A damn bad business. But it was Charlie and Sadler's turn to be fearless. They laughed like boys and, each taking up one of the featherless ducks, danced it about and pecked the one at the other while the gulls swept away to starboard. Birds were one of the signs that could be sent. Lizards another. And the way the pig fell on slaughtering would tell where the next wind would blow from. You had to read em right, mind, but the cook had an eye for the birds and a bad feeling about these two.

Se en lavètisman. Stop your fooling. *Kèkchoj ap ale arive.* The cook took up the ducks and retreated to the galley fire to singe off their pin-feathers. He could see trouble coming like some mighty wave, black and glassy, already rolling from a distant coast.

Mary Ford brought the Taylor children on deck. She hadn't a way with children and would have been the first to admit as much. She treated them like valuable animals, fed them, curried them, kept a weather eye on their gums and excrements and so far they flourished. When it was perceived, the day after the Taylors boarded, that the servant girl they had engaged for the voyage had given them the slip, taking herself and her luggage from the vessel, Mr Yate had taken matters in hand and interviewed Mary Ford for the post, five shillings a week, payable weekly, and, after some wheedling, a pudding from the cuddy table every Sunday dinner. Already Mrs Taylor could not have done without her although, often enough, she did not know how she did with her, the fat old woman grated at her sensibilities so. In the tight confines of the Taylor's cabins, Mary Ford could seem to her lodged like a ship in a bottle. The longer she bustled about, fussing at the children with the baby caught to her apron-front like her next meal, the smaller the cabin grew. She drew her breath in vast rattling mouthfuls, the very air insufficient for her, and her skirts made an insect-like rasping as she forced her way between the furniture, along pathways grown newly diminutive. With the old nurse in attendance, Mrs Taylor inevitably took to her bed and lay there, one arm across her tear-scraped eyes, oppressed by her coarseness, her voice, even in kind inquiry, pitched to raise gooseflesh. She had a proprietary hand for the children and Mrs Taylor was never more grateful than when she heard them all leave the cabin.

Arthur led the way with an eldest child's sense of precedence; Basil came next, still in his skirts, a year short of Arthur and ever in awe of his greater talents and capacities; Laura piloted by Mary Ford's speckled hand resting pastry warm at her shoulder and the baby slung like a horseshoe over the old nurse's free arm, pop-eyes fixed intently on the comings and goings of her gaitered half-boots. Yate saw Mary Ford take her place on the poop with every signal of enjoyment, as happy to be becalmed off Deal as anywhere else she could think of.

I see you have your charges well under control, Mary, said Yate, giving his index finger to the baby to examine.

I has them under control, sir, or they has me; I wouldn't like to call the difference, said Mary Ford with happy complacence. The baby transferred Yate's finger to her mouth where she mashed it between her gums and the untested edge of her first teeth, one curl standing up on her skull like the last feathers of a duck's tail.

Mind how you go, bub. Mary Ford gave the baby a reproving shake and gave herself up to her view of Deal. The boys had ventured off the poop and were down at the goat pen, absorbed in some game, Basil looking over his shoulder now and then to check their nurse remained in sight.

Say I'm the captain.

Who can I be?

I'm getting to that. Say I'm the captain. Arthur looked around, eyes half-lidded in thought. And say you're the third mate. We'll count the animals. It's called taking the 'ventory. Basil pursed his lips as his brother spoke. His breath fluttered at his throat. He was considering.

Say, he said, because that was the best word; say I don't want to be fird mate? Say I want to be first mate?

First mate doesn't take the 'ventory. It's the third mate's job.

What do I do? Eyes slitted to their fringe of lashes to exclude all the world that wasn't Arthur.

You count all these animals. And you say: ay ay sir. Basil laughed with his hands on his knees, a row of dimples across his knuckles.

Ay, ay, ay!

Not like that. You say: ay ay, sir.

Ay ay, sir.

How many goats, Mr May? Arthur held the fronts of his waistcoat and rocked back on his heels as he had seen Captain Aitken do. He had almost decided to be a captain, if he couldn't be a sailor.

How many goats, Mr May? Basil looked from Arthur to the goats. They smelled terrible but he pretended not to care. There were two small goats with shaggy brown wool and pricked white ears that swung round at the boys and away, with white stripes running down their faces and little tan beards shaking wetly under their chins as they chewed, and yellow eyes, cold and yellow, and white tails pointing out behind. And there was a big goat, brown and black, with a meaner face but the same yellow eyes, one of them weepy, and a pair of horns tipping back over his shoulder and his wool hanging in long hanks over his legs with his hooves shining black beneath.

Free? said Basil.

No, you say: three goats, sir.

Free goats, sir.

Very good, said Arthur but not in his own voice. And how many pigs, Mr May? Basil knelt beside the pen to count but there were too many and the little ones rolled over and showed the white down where their legs joined their bellies before he could count to the end – fifteen, fourteen, twenty – and some of them he counted twice and had to start over, more than once. Arthur grew tired of waiting and shouted a few orders – Let go the anchor! Climb up the topsills! – to keep his interest up.

Twenty ten, sir.

Very good, said the unruffled Arthur, making a few stiff-legged turns of the deck. And how many geese, Mr May?

Yate leaned against the starboard bulwark and watched the boys, their tawny heads bent to each other and the circle of their game while a whole imagined ship pressed against their shoulders. Boys had that knack, he knew, that facility for bending the world to their pleasure. They were young and the blood ran in them hotly, their boyishness coming off them as rankly as the stench from the goats. Although it was their own completeness they most admired, they were as yet unshaped, still being made up, their final form only glimpsed as potential like a body half-carved from a marble block or like the early sketches Mr Whichelo had made for Yate's own portrait, painted in miniature on ivory, in which he could see his sister's face more readily than his own. He nodded across the boys' bright heads to Mary Ford, still sitting on the poop, Laura and the baby now too at her feet. A boat was pulling alongside and Yate made out the heavily bearded face of Captain Brash, the ship's husband, sitting in the stern. What he could be wanting with the ship Yate could not figure, nor could Captain Aitken, he guessed, seeing the alacrity with which that man came above. The captains withdrew below and Yate studied the two men who remained in the dinghy, the boatman pushing off the side of the *Prince Regent* with his oar when a swell threatened to bring them too close. The one looked a solid, steady fellow but the other drew his look, a handsome, aristocratic head that would have looked well on a coin and a bleached blue eye that Yate felt would see right through him if ever it ventured to pick him out from the view. The captains coming up again, the two men were hailed on ship – *Mr Morris, Mr Denison* – and they took their place on the lee side of the quarterdeck where they shuffled awkwardly with Mr Bennett and Mr Cat in a hop-footed quadrille. Yate reckoned his man was Mr Denison and reckoned further that Mr Denison could take the lengthier examination, which he made at his leisure from the poop with Mary Ford at his side, unmoved. He thought he saw a grace in the man and beneath that, a restrained energy as when a dog, nose to the scent, is held back by his master's command.

Who might you think those gentlemen are, Mary?

Ah, they'll be gennlemen of some stripe, sir, you can be sure on it.

It was left to Yate to take his news from the doctor whom he found below a half-hour later, packed into Armistead's cabin with Mr Bennett and Mr Cat, the four of them very long-faced. Dr Fowles told in tones of injury how Captain Brash was here with orders for the two officers to quit ship for what reason no one could tell, although it seemed there had been some words exchanged between Mr Cat and the river pilot and the whole business was put down to the latter's malice. The four had taken a fancy for each other, entering into handsome plans to pass away the voyage, so that Yate was unable to discover anything of the new men who were universally held to be common-looking fellows such that no one could associate with. The doctor organised a short note expressing sorrow at the officers' departure and it was signed by all the cabin though by none so lightly as Yate. That evening after tea, taking the moon on the forecastle with the men during the last dogwatch, he overheard a further intelligence from Staines, the grizzled able seaman with a well-tended gut and a pair of legs as bowed as croquet hoops.

Mr May has landed with his bottom in the butter. He might set up at the captin's table all he likes but he hasn't got his hand out a the tar bucket, said Staines with a rare constraint. He found himself in an awkward place, Staines.

Not used to a cabin passenger taking his place on the fore-castle as easy as you please, a Bible waver no less, one of two headed for New Zealand, and feeling all the same that he had no right, he decked his rage out as civility, tamping his pipe hard with his flattened thumbnail. The other men lay about in their usual attitudes but, until Yate took his leave, wary as jackrabbits in snow. So, Mr May was to be elevated to the captain's table, thought Yate as he made his way back to the poop. Which meant he was promoted. But only to second mate since he would still be expected to get tar under his nails, working the rigging with his men. The new officers then were first and third mates and there was no doubt in Yate's mind as to which of the two would be sitting up to dine with the cabin until he shared his deduc-tions with the doctor who, stroking his mournful guitar on the poop like a Spanish troubadour, told him Mr Denison was without question to be the third mate although how Captain Brash had passed over the very able Deck, an excellent sailor and a friend, apparently, of Taylor's family, no one could tell.

The new officers must have brought a favourable wind on board with them, or so the cook thought, since no sooner had Mr Bennett and Mr Cat taken their places in the Deal boat and the men sung out Let go the painter, let go the painter, than a gentle air filled the sails and the *Prince Regent* weighed anchor, together with twenty-five other vessels of various sizes and destinations which had been likewise held off Deal, waiting a break in the weather. The sun broke through and enamelled the smooth surface of the water yellow and green. The day had turned itself out beau-tifully and everyone came up on deck, even Mrs Taylor, to note this fact for themselves and to feed their spirits on the picturesque scene as the fleet of tacking vessels crossed and recrossed each other, the smack of the sail and the moan of the spars travelling clean across the water. The ship leaped forward in the water like a horse on homecoming and made good speed to the next headland opposite Dover where every sail hung suddenly limp and it was only by constant tacking back and forth that she could keep her own and prevent herself being shifted back to Deal. All the delightful day the eyeful of boats sawed backwards and forwards across each other's foam, spangling white in the sun. There was much chatter on deck and witless remark, much coming and going and thoughts of old England, as again and again the ship stood out across the straits toward France till the white cliffs sunk in perspective and now stood in so close as to be almost under their chalky shadow.

Hall's fingers were bent like a canary's claws on its perch and were so painful on straightening that he had ceased trying two hours previous. Ever since Mr Cat had been taken off the ship, he had been put to work at the weather main braces until the skin of his palms had grown pulpy under the rough burn of the rope. Between England and France they flew, back and forth, topsy-tivy, the air thick with shouts and the heavy breathing of the men, until he could not keep it in his head what coast was what but all the while he seen Mr Cat brung off of the ship, sayen none but looken for him with those stab-blackly, love-sorely eyes. Mr Cat would not be coming back, he dint think. At first, Hall thought it was some off-ship errand the second mate was traditionally required to do, some ship business he didn't know about, but as the day wore on like a bruise and Mr May took up all Mr Cat's offices, he came to realise he would not be coming back. He didn't know how Mr Cat's departure made him feel. It was like a black-edged letter someone would read to him later. Most of the morning and the whole afternoon had been all-hands work and his head smacked with the relay of shouts and answers.

Mainsail haul! That was the captain on the quarterdeck shouting to the new first mate.

Mainsail haul! The first mate answered from the fore-castle and Mr May called it across from his station at the lee main and fore braces.

Mainsail haul, sir! Edwards bent his back to the task, Hall wedged between him and ham-faced William Piggott.

Let go and haul!

Let go, sir! All gone, sir! On and on they sailed, back and forth between France and England, making no ground but losing none neither, the after yards swinging round overhead each time with much dismal creaking. Hall's palms were dabby with blood, the run of the rope as it was let go carrying his blistered skin away with it, and his fingers were bent exactly to the rope's circumference, whether it was in his grasp or not.

'Vast bracing! Haul off all! He never once hauled but with all his strength and when he put his hand to the rope the fit was so perfect, so painful and perfect, it was as if it remembered him, not the other way about.

Helm's a-lee! If he cried it were only once, his few tears unremarked on his salt-spraided cheeks, because his poor hands were so badly crampled and because he didn't know what would come of him, Mr Cat having gone.

A very gay tea was that night had in the cuddy. The head of the table was empty as Captain Aitken remained on the quarterdeck and since the new mate, Mr Morris, was also occupied with some business on the forecastle, Yate supposed that Mr May was too shy to take up his position at Alfred Button's elbow, considering one last tinpot supper from the galley would suit him fine. Everyone else sat up at their places in high spirits, their faces ruddled with the wind and sun they had taken during the day, and seemed inclined to linger even after the steward's two boys had cleared the table. Gordon was drawing out Captain Button on his military career, like a great boy who could not wait to run away and wear a scarlet jacket. Late of His Majesty's 46th Regiment, now on half-pay and bound for New South Wales, Captain Button was a dour and private man, hard and round as his name suggested, and reluctant with a story. He sat helpless, as if Gordon had him on the end of his fork. Though Yate had tried more than once, Captain Button could not readily be imagined upright in his stirrups, sword raised, in pursuit of a Burmese cavalryman. He had wet lips in a yeasty face and was no more dashing than a grocer. Mrs Button sat as always at the captain's left hand with her daughter alongside her but with the captain's chair empty and quite enlivened by the events of the day, she turned and addressed herself more generally to the table.

Of Indian adventures, said Mrs Button, much can be told but my husband must relate to you the story of the man-eating tiger. All eyes, none keener than those of the Taylor boys, fell for a moment on the doughy Button.

Some years ago now, Mrs Button continued, I was accompanying my husband and his regiment on a march in the upper part of India. They had to pass through a thin, that is to say, a narrow chasm in the mountain. On one side of the road there were thick woods – Arthur Taylor enjoyed a spiderish sensation in his stomach – and on the other the ground fell away entirely, a precipice.

Mrs Button had a lively face and she counted her figure elegant still. She was accustomed to society, to the hurly-burly of regimental life, and experienced her transportation to New South Wales most painfully. Her shoulders gleamed blue and white as a seagull's breast and the few ringlets free at her nape suggested a wild beauty to which she could still lay claim in her own person and that of her daughter beside her, looking like her younger self and blushing, in a manner the doctor judged becoming, at her mother's forwardness in claiming the attention of the table.

A tiger was said to have made his home at this pass. Wasn't that the case, Captain Button?

It was, my dear.

And over the months, he had carried off sixteen people in his soft jaw. He would spring from the woods on great padded paws, his black eyes burned back as if to the bone, and seize someone from the travelling party before carrying them straight over the edge of the precipice, out of sight.

Having been born in Ceylon, Mrs Button had a very natural way with herself and accompanied her story with much gestural interpretation, her girlish fingers weighed down with a woman's rings as they made an efficient sketch of the ravine, the close, dark wood, the jaw of the tiger, her gigot sleeves suggesting all the while the slim bare arms they held from view.

Sixteen people. Am I right, Captain Button?

You are, my dear. While her mother blazed in the oxygen of their attention, the doctor found his eye straying to the decorous Miss Button, whom he could have wished had less of an English education.

It is the custom in Indian marches for the ladies to be carried by the men at shoulder-height in a covered palanquin. All at once, there was a rude cry, Tiger, Tiger, and my palanquin was dropped to the ground. Mrs Button remembered the fearfulness of that fall, one corner hitting the ground first and tumbling her from her seat with all her cushions and writing implements falling about her. Perhaps that was why, she thought to herself, assailed on every side by plumpy down-filled missiles, she always imagined the tiger as having a soft jaw. For truly she felt as if she knew him. It was as if they had faced each other off on that abandoned road. She had scrambled to regain her seat, push her skirts down, check her hair with one fluttering hand although she realised the foolishness of such composure before a tiger, a man-eating tiger who would swallow her, coughing down her puckered crepe together with her white flesh. There had been a mad, upholstered moment as she sat, hands folded in her lap, her fist of a heart pummelling her throat and the blood bleating in her ears. Beyond the brocaded curtain of the palanquin was silence, unnatural and profound. She imagined the carrion breath of the tiger, attributing to him the unkind yellowed smile of Lieutenant Campbell taking his leave for Calcutta. When she could stand the solitary half-light of the palanquin no longer, she opened the curtains and stepped down on the road, crushed gravel with a glimmer of quartz. She turned in every direction, her head bobbling like the needle of a compass, her dress slippers shuffling up a drift of slow dust. She was as alone in the world as ever she had been. A picture occurred to her then, not one she might have anticipated, nothing to do with the green pleasures of her plantation childhood, nothing to do with her husband nor even her baby daughter, but a picture of herself seen from above, the whole empty world stretched out on either side as she turned and turned in the dust, head tilted back, skewered on the slack-jawed scream spooling without end from her throat like a scarlet ribbon.

She lay in that palanquin, Captain Button said into the silence, screeching like an Indian parrot 'til the bearers came back double-quick. He was making an effort to be hearty, rubbing his palms on his thighs, keeping a nervous watch on his silent wife. Mrs Button took her daughter by the hand and, as the gentlemen got to their feet, excused herself prettily and left the table. Mary Ford came in to usher Arthur and Basil Taylor to bed. She made a number of thick-waisted bows and dips that might have been intended for a courtesy as she made her way about the table. Dr Fowles followed her from the cuddy.

Do tigers eat ladies? he heard the smaller boy ask.

They perfer little boys.

The moon shone bright on the deck and the doctor's chest swelled in painful emotion. The lights of Dover shone like glow-worms, he thought, like glowing glow-worms on, on a mossy bank. Shakespeare's cliff stood pale in the distant perspective, its silent grandeur nearly moving him to tears. He fetched his guitar from his berth and, face hollowed silver in the moonlight, sang a lowing song of his own composition which later that night he would tran-scribe into his journal for his wife and, always just beyond her, posterity, but which for the moment had no destination more ambitious than the shell-like translucency of Miss Button's ear.

> *The night winds sigh, the breakers swell*
> *And shrieks the wild sea view*
> *Adieu! Adieu! My native shore*
> *Fades o'er the waters blue.*

He had almost sorted out a second verse in his head, the difficulty of making a rhyme with *nymph* the only compli-cation, when Yate came up on the poop with some muddleheaded idea that the third mate was to be first mate that needed setting right, after which Dr Fowles could never remember the lines to his satisfaction.

A fair wind had come up that night and for the next two days the *Prince Regent* had been getting down the channel bonnily, as Captain Aitken put it, out of sight of land for the first time which made everyone feel they had put to sea at last, until a dead calm set in Sunday and held them off Cape Ushant, making no way. Taylor led the prayers in the cuddy and, having set the substantial bookend of Mary Ford at one end of his family, he took his sermon from Ephesians, drawing glinty-eyed on the verse that ran *Servants, be obedient to them that are your masters.* If

Yate thought this a dubious means of impressing upon Mary Ford her spiritual and worldly duties, she was thinking on something else altogether, the fruit pudding she would be owed off this very table come dinner. *Children, obey your parents in the Lord.* The captain did not like to give the passengers too much knowledge regarding the business of the ship else they would all consider themselves the match of the master. As it was, most of the gentlemen hung off the bulwarks twice a day to take the water temperature for their journal entries and were ever plaguing his men for the name of such-and-such a sail or the difference between a brace and a halyard in order to give their letters home some nautical relish. Still, after Sunday's service, he gave notice to the cuddy at dinner that the ship was now in the chops of the channel and if a fair wind came on they should begin to go famously southward on their journey. This news was taken with the figs and almonds brought in by Mungo, the steward, and chewed over with interest by all excepting Mrs Taylor, who had indulged an antipathy to the sea since childhood and, long convinced she would not make the voyage alive, was as indifferent to its getting along as to its foundering off the English coast.

The other vessels that had started off from Deal with the *Prince Regent* had made various speeds and those several remaining in view were strung out whitely in front and behind like, like a pearl necklace, thought Miss Button as she sat in the cuddy after dinner, her swan neck curved over her letter-writing. They put her mother in mind of ladies taking the floor at a regimental ball, rustling out their foulards according to the rank of their husbands or the seniority of their service. Above, walking the poop deck on the arm of Mr Armistead's frock-coat, Mrs Button allowed herself a sigh.

Madam, you tire? that gentleman inquired with a gallant downwards consideration of her figure. Given the small turn of the poop and the near motionlessness of the deck, it was hardly possible that she could be tired, yet a weariness had its teeth in her. She allowed herself to be led to a corner seat, young Mr Armistead tucking himself up alongside her, his long lavender legs crossed at the knee, his polished cut steel shoe-buckle taking the late afternoon sun as he dandled his foot back and forth. A bank of fluffed cloud sailed high above looking for all the world like the ships below with every canvas out, their studdingsails and skysails hung to catch the least cat's paw of wind. Master Alfred Button was hanging shy of the two Taylor boys, following them about the deck at a small distance but making no further claim on them. He lay on his back on the planking when they lay on theirs and the three of them stared up at the sky cupped overhead, pale and blue.

It's a lion, see? said Alfred, pointing up at the cloud. He winkled his way over on his shoulderblades and buttocks to lie alongside Basil. That's his back legs and that's his big beard.

Do lions have beards? Basil was not sure. Goats had beards but Basil could not think what a lion looked like.

They do, said Alfred, pushing his chin at the sky.

They have manes, said Arthur. It's like a beard that grows all the way around. Basil lay in between the two older boys, rolling his happy head one way and then the other. He still couldn't see the back leg and then it was gone, the leg and the lion both, stretched out in a muscular length that looked like a snake to Mrs Button from the poop when she hung her head back, blinking against her tears in the watery winterish light but before she had decided whether to show her serpent to Mr Armistead it had coiled up and smoothed itself out into a cat that grew denser and larger by the minute until one of the Lascars, darning his trousers on the forecastle, saw a panther, a snow panther, ears tucked against the sleekness of its skull and its tail hidden from view. In the middle of his gentlemanly inquiry as to why she and her family were travelling to Sydney, Mrs Button stood, drawing Mr Armistead quickly to his feet.

You've heard that the doctor is travelling for his health, no doubt? Let's say we're travelling for the health of our daughter, said Mrs Button and took her leave. Over her bent and urgent head, the cloud broke in two, one half taking on the shape of nothing much, perhaps the head of a wild pig with a tusk and feathery hair, the other growing so long and thin it seemed to Yate – who was taking his leisure in the sun on the bowsprit – like Waianiwaniwa, the waterfall some two miles from the mission station, and to Hall – setting the fore royal studdingsail with his head almost in the sky – like a tree with a foam of branchtops. Mrs Button hurried to the cuddy where her daughter was still busy with her writing materials.

Who do you write to, Sophie? It would hardly be proper for Mr Whitlock to receive your correspondence.

I write only to his mother, mama. She will tell him news of me. Sophie delivered herself of this so guilelessly, her face turned up to the light like a saucer of milk, that Mrs Button was nearly tempted to some ugliness to show her daughter that the world was not the nosegay she thought. The necessary control cost her much and her face jerked under a run of contrary emotions.

Are you quite well, mama? called Miss Button as her mother fled the cuddy.

Monday night raised a storm. It came on to blow late in the evening and continued boisterous for several days. The steerage passengers had the worst of it. Secured below in the full dark, they were crammed first against the head of their beds, then pitched against the foot, as all around them their cans, teapots, plates and cooking utensils

clattered and fell. Cold-cocked by a free-swinging jar of
plum preserve she had suspended from the bunk above,
Mary Ford did not sit up again even when a loose water
puncheon that had been rolling back and forth with a
curious gobbling sound across the rough planking smashed
open against the corner of the Bedgood's berth which splin-
tered away and brought the upper bunk down on the lower,
spilling little John Bedgood and two of the Pedrano
children loose on the sodden floor and coming close to
crushing the baby between its parents. Mrs Eylard
exhausted herself in screams and moaned softly until
morning and the opening of the hatches. The Parkers slept
the night through, Mr because he was himself a sailor and
not afeared of a squall, Mrs because she was used to worse.

Tuesday night, Yate woke to the violent rolls of the ship
and an odd bleating as if the sheep had been tipped from
the long boat and, in their distress, had made their way into
the cabin. He got up and felt around in the dark for his
trousers. Next door, Miss Bloomfield had convinced first
herself and next her young companion, Miss Baker, that
they were sinking. She sat up in bed, her greasy hair turned
up in curl papers beneath her muslin nightcap, and howled
until Miss Baker was as persuaded as she that their lives
had only minutes left to run, and those few perilously wet
and cold. Yate slipped his bare feet into his shoes and
opened his door a cautious gap lest the sharp-hoofed sheep
might think to take their final sanctuary in his cabin. All
was silent. He stood a minute in the passage, one arm
braced against the wall, listening to the boom and crump
of the water. Though Miss Baker would rather have met her
end in bed and thought she could even bear being shipped
to the fishes if she were still tucked beneath her travelling
rug, she recalled that she was to be a missionary and
throwing back her covers knelt beside her friend's bed,

taking a firm hold of the footboard to prevent herself being flung across the cabin.

O Lord, said Miss Baker. She had a child's voice still and in her cold and fright a tremor ran through it. O Lord, we are not worthy. Miss Baker had been surprised that her friend did not join her in prayer but how much more surprised she was when that woman pushed aside her bedding, her long shanks flailing, threw a wrap around herself and left the room altogether, calling back over her shoulder, almost angrily it seemed, that there was no time for such nonsense. Hearing her friend raise the alarm in the passage and thinking any moment a dark wall of water might take her as she knelt beside the bed, Miss Sophia had trouble remembering the next words of her prayer. By the time she hurried out, the entire cabin had been roused. Mr Yate and his sister were restraining Miss Bloomfield, one on either side, Miss Yate chafing Miss Bloomfield's wrist in a brisk fashion. The Taylors had risen also from their sleepless bed, he wild-haired like some Old Testament prophet and on hand to catch his wife fainting dead away at the sight of Mr Gordon coming above from his cabin as wet as if he had risen from the deeps. The sea had breached three panes of his stern window, Gordon said, and quite swum him out of bed. His hands shook and his lantern threw a watery light on the small company. Miss Bloomfield, having perceived not only her error but the impropriety of appearing before gentlemen in her nightwear, had removed her nightcap only to suffer the worse indignity of being seen in her curl papers and, chastened, was shepherded back to bed by Miss Yate while Mr Yate retired below with Gordon to fit his deadlights.

Aside from his midnight excursion, Yate passed a better night than most since he was accustomed to sleep at sea in a sailor's hammock, rocking in the dark air of his cabin while his bed pitched empty beneath him. The cuddy was unattended when he came in around nine for his breakfast although he saw the doctor, wrapped in a thick pilot coat, clinging to the companion ladder to survey the wild waste of water. Yate joined him on the poop and the two men stood together, knuckles white on the railing. The doctor said something but his words were as the wind that screamed in the rigging and beat the water to a froth. Something about the desolate scene moved the doctor to wonder. He felt himself newly small before the might of God, a speck of insignificance.

This God, he said in cadences he fancied liturgical, who rides upon the thunder and whose step is in the deep, is our God and in Him do I put my trust, but it seemed as if the missionary had not heard him. He envied Yate his daily rapture and, clinging still to the poop railing, held himself open to the sublime force of the sea. Although Yate had seen more than one storm at sea, it was impossible not to be moved by the sight, the grey water running mountains high against a grey mountainous sky and the ship itself no more than a feather before the wind. Two other vessels were still in sight and, like the *Prince Regent*, ran wherever they could with all their sail close reefed. The nearer of the two ships, a large three-master, was bucking like a horse unused to the saddle, showing now her topgallant yards, now her copper-bottomed keel, her forward parts throwing a lather of spume. Captain Aitken had the maintopsail double reefed and the ship had the look of a thoroughbred, thought Yate, buckled up and harnessed for competition. Now her head was reined high at an angle of some forty-five degrees, or so it seemed, giving only a giddying view over the prow of the ashen sky, and in a moment down she went again, as in a steeplechase, looking to pitch headfirst into the whirlpool opening like a sinuous eye before her, an avalanche of water toppling from above into the same abyss.

Useless to speak to each other, though they stood but some two feet apart, Yate and Fowles retired below. As he passed his sister's cabin, the pitch of the ship swung her door back on its hinges and in the moment before it eased itself shut once more, Yate glimpsed the most curious pictorial arrangement, worthy of Cruikshank's pencil. There was dear Sarah, foot to stockinged foot upon the bed with Mrs Taylor, the picture of nausea. Miss Bloomfield lay on the floor, clinging by her hands and feet to the legs of the sofa as a sloth upon a maple branch. A little more decorously, Miss Baker sat on the sofa, a pup on a chimneypot, her face eaten up with green and yellow melancholy, and next to her, Mrs Bedgood, like patience on a monument, nursing her infant and holding her little boy between her feet that he might not roll under the washstand. Each minute the ship lurched, the very walls of the cabin creaking as when a protesting nail is pulled from its wood, and all would change: Mrs Taylor would faint away, Miss Baker cry and Mrs Bedgood try to assist her to a better spirit. Although his heart went out to Sarah who looked so very sorrowful, her eyes closed and a light sweat beading her forehead, Yate hesitated a moment longer in the passage, biting back a fit of mirth at the unexpected panorama. It seemed so like many a ladies' parlour scene but grotesquely altered by some satiric hand. Holding the door fast to prevent his accidental discovery, he told himself there was not a trace of amusement in others' misfortune but the lightest thought of Miss Bloomfield swinging lankily from the sofa leg or Johnny Bedgood juggled from foot to foot as if his mother were in training for a country fair threatened any composure he could scrape together. With an expression at least as strange as any of those that turned toward him at the opening of the door, Yate entered the cabin and going from one to the other pressed on each lady some reviving biscuit from his sister's store, assisted them all to their various berths and sat with Sarah through the long lurching afternoon.

Whether it was the proportion of Sarah's cabin, more squared off than his own, or the spray-filtered light that drifted from her window almost wetly, taking the edge off everything before he secured her deadlights and wrapped them both in murk, Yate was reminded of his own bedroom at Waimate to which he was returning. The bedroom, his adjoining study also, had not been finished when he had left two years previous although, as if by force of memory, he imagined it complete. In London he had received a letter from Henry Waru who said he had fixed the finishings to the doors and laid in the mantelpiece and the grate. A compact room with flat-planed kauri walls, his bedroom took the misted morning sun in winter. It was his habit to lie in bed beneath the window with the curtains open a minute or two before rising, one of his boys fetching a washbasin of shivering water, the globular landscape blurred oyster and green behind the glass. Pinching his eye-glasses to his nose, the view beyond his window was reeled to his eye, quarter a mile and then quarter a mile farther the other two mission houses rising from their acreage of haze and in between, standing short-legged in skeins of mist, a draggle of philosophical sheep. Nothing like home but he thought Sarah would feel for it as he did. She had slept a half-hour and woke hungry and weak to take his crumbled biscuit like a baby bird, gaping and dishevelled.

All week the storm continued unflagging. The days darkened and the sun, obscured entire behind black banks of cloud, cast its pewterish light on everything, without much alleviating effect. The sea and sky pressed heavy against each other, catching the ship between in an inter-minable grey fold. Hall had been wet to the skin for days and learned for himself the truth of the Finn's claim that no sailor ever caught cold from salt water. He had no water-proof and however he duddled himself up, a half-hour on deck and his whole skin would run claggy with the rain and sea spray. His hands were cumbly-cold and painful chapped. When he could, he kept them tucked into the warmth of his armpits. His hands had been a subject of interest in the forecastle three nights previous. After the day of beating off and on between England and France, every man of the starboard watch had seen Hall try to turn into his hammock, his hands next to useless like two broken plates of meat. Overmars, a Dutchman of so few words that Hall had only ever heard his Ay ay, sir, had lifted him bodily, one massive arm behind Hall's head, the other beneath his knees, and laid him down to sleep.

Thank you, said Hall in a low tone intended for Overmars alone, thank you, sir, but the Dutchman, even as he pulled the boy's bedding over his shoulders, kept his eye on Staines who was up on his usual elbow and attending everything from his hammock. Before falling into that bright hectic sleep he had grown accustomed to in the forecastle, Hall heard Staines's grubbling voice.

He oughter piss on his hands if he don't plan on been a milkmaid. They're in sore need a toughnin up. Sailor's ways or more rough usage, Hall could not be sure but he had tried it since a few times in secret and thought perhaps his hands seemed a little easier.

One night mid-week he had been called up from his watch below with Piggott to furl the fore topgallant sail. The two of them had furled it earlier but in the fingering wind it had come undone and now it thrashed in the buntlines, a pale apparition, threatening to jerk away the yard altogether. Mr Morris seemed to find them an amusing prospect, the pair of them on deck for the larboard watch.

Lay aloft there, said the mate as Hall and Piggott scrabbled for their footing on the pitched deck, staring about uncertainly in the dark wet as if the forecastle hatch had opened on to some strange country they could only guess at. Lay aloft and hand that fore topgallant sail. Hall started out after Piggott, following the soles of his feet up the rigging. The ship was riding at such a tilt that the climb might have been easier than usual had it not been for the terrible wind pressing them hard against the ratlines which sang an unearthly tune beneath their numbed fingers. Hall's progress to the yard was slow. The ship's masts were angled low over the water and Hall saw, with disbelieving eyes, that the low end of the yard was only a few body lengths clear of the tallest waves rearing out of the darkness, their obscene height marked by a ruff of luminous white suds at their head. As he bucked back and forth, one foot slipping from the yard and only his insensible arms saving him from the drop, the nausea that had been with him these last stormy days churned his guts and rose in his throat, a yellowish burn. He turned his head like a cothy calf and the vamment spilled from him in heaves as water from a pump. Piggott and Hall lay across the yard, perhaps closer than was efficient but feeling very much like each other's only comfort, and hauled and beat at the wet sail. Hall had lost all feeling in his fingers and at one moment was so buffeted by the wind and knocked about by the end of the sail whipping loose that he felt as if he might have been himself some light piece of canvas, a royal or a skysail, hung out to the wind and let blow. He saw for the first time how it would take next to nothing, a half-second of relaxation, a happy blankness, to be swept from the yard and this slippery world. It warmed him, this unexpected knowing, like a friendly word or a full belly. He hoarded it to himself and clung the tighter, grappling the last wet slaps of the sail into his arms. He thought how Piggott would go down alone to the mate first and then to the men in the forecastle. No point trying to put about in this weather but all would be grim, the saltiest of them turning over in their hearts some small remembrance of him, although when he actually went below, the yellow curdle drying in his hair, Staines said only, Someone's been shittin' through their teeth. His mother would weep for certain and recall him always as her bravest and best. His few effects, auctioned off to the men, would be worn around the world in all the places he would never see. Hall turned his face into the wind for the sight of healthsome William Piggott, fisting the last length of sail. With the stiff canvas furled to their satisfaction, they frapped it in place for double measure with some extra turns of rope and made their descent, slow and careful.

For the duration of the storm, there was not much to be seen of the passengers on deck. The steerage passengers stayed below hatches, many groaning in the half-light of their berths as the ship lurched from wave to wave. Mary Ford took her breakfast below, black tea in half cups but, at the first clear opportunity, surfaced from her hatchway like a breaching grampus and slithered aft across the teetering deck to roll and snort in the comfort of the Taylors' cabins. Wednesday being pudding day, Mr Bedgood, feeling that much better than his wife, took delivery of the allowance of currants and suet and charged himself with making pudding for the whole steerage. In the finish, it proved the entire meal since, on a sudden toss of the ship, the tub of fresh boiled beef sent down for dinner was upended at the top of the companionway before it even made the table. The doctor was called for Mr Pedrano's wife, who had taken nothing but tea since the storm blew up and now, lying on her back with her hands clasped tidy at her waist like the carved woman on a mausoleum, was refusing so much as that. He didn't look too fresh himself, Mr Pedrano thought, with his candle-wax face and caved cheek and a cough like the devil with a rattle, but he was pleased to see the doctor take his seat at the side of the bed, one hand warm on his wife's own, and spoon into her open mouth a little rum diluted with lemon juice. The stench in steerage was gut-turning, the ventilation always imperfect, but with the hatches closed for days on end the air grew clotted and pestilent. The doctor was pleased to regain the deck, awe-somely tilted and wet as it was, and doubly pleased to make the cuddy and a game of cribbage with Armistead.

Mungo had arranged for Busby to lash the chairs to the floor and erect temporary posts between them to assist the cabin in keeping their places at meals. It was not his proper name, Mungo, but the doctor had christened him such and there was a tight enough fit between the polished man and the name that it stuck until Sydney where he cast it like an old skin, hawking his farewell over the taffrail as the ship weighed anchor for Newcastle. For most of the storm, as the ship was beaten north off her course, she lay almost on her beams, all level surfaces sloped to such a degree that it was impossible to walk without laying hold of some fixture. The weather side of the ship rode so high, the lee so low, that those seated on one side of the cabin table had two feet advantage over those who took their places on the other. Yate was much employed in settling the ladies and near wore out his elbow ferrying them from cabin to cuddy and back against the anxious pitch of the floor. At Friday breakfast, as he braced himself in the cuddy doorway, an arm around his sister's waist to prevent her rolling back into the passage, he could not help but note Armistead and Doctor Fowles close to grappling over Miss Button while her mother, steadying herself high in the opposite doorway, looked on with a curious, half-masted smile. The two men were very often at odds in their mutual assistance of Miss Button. So keen were they to lay hold of her themselves and so reluctant to pass her on to the other's care, they might have mistaken her for one of the carpenter's temporary supports. With one arm caught fast by the doctor and her other secured in Armistead's, that bewitching little person could do nothing but tip her tiny steps this way and that with every lurch of the ship like a spanker caught between contrary winds while Miss Bloomfield, whose natural level seemed always to be the floor, rolled backwards and forwards at their feet, branding herself variously on the hot edges of the stove but not raising a flicker of chivalrous concern in either man. Pretending always to defer to the other and yet never giving up the trim arm that would release Miss Button to the competition, the doctor and Armistead manipulated the bewildered girl to her place, receiving their share of her stammered thanks with much cordial head-nodding over a job well done. When everyone had taken their places, the Taylor children wedged in to their seats by Mary Ford before she retired with the baby to put things to rights in their cabin, the steward began ferrying in the breakfast things, bunting one of his boys before him with his cruel boot. He was a practised man, the steward, and, even when the ship dropped or lurched, he absorbed its effect in the lithe motions of his body, without dropping so much as a piece of toast. The passengers were not so accomplished and it was but minutes before Mrs Taylor, at table only on sufferance, filled her husband's pocket with a pint cup of coffee filtered through his lap. The children screamed for Mary Ford, holding hard to the tablecloth while their plates and cups made the grand tour of the table. The doctor had spread a finger of bread with anchovy paste from his private store and was baking it on the stove prior to offering it, medicinally, to Miss Button when a dreadful wave hit the ship broadside and he, being high on the weather side, was flung from his chair headlong over the stove to land, ribs bruised, toast ruined, in the opposite corner.

Steady, my dear, said Yate to the skittish Miss Baker coming away from breakfast. The captain seldom making

the table these past few days, the passengers had taken Yate
for their constant referee in matters maritime. We shall
have nothing worse than this, he said, although the voyage
was to prove him wrong.

By Saturday morning the storm had subsided entirely
although what wind the ship had was still blowing against
her from the southeast. Driven off course for a week, by the
time the storm passed, the *Prince Regent* was not so far
south as she had been when she first cleared the channel.
No one who has not gone to sea, who has not waited out
day after long day for a fair wind, could guess at the elation
attendant on a change in the weather that enables the ship
to go forward on her way. So it was that when Yate heard
Mr May come below at four on Sunday morning after his
middle watch to call up Mr Morris with the joyful intelligence that the wind had changed for fair these two hours
past, he gave up his first prayer of the day with a light
heart. *I will love thee, O Lord, my strength*, prayed Yate,
strung up in the darkness of his cabin, *my buckler, and the
horn of my salvation*. Breakfast was taken by all at nine
with the comfortable satisfaction that the ship had been
seven hours sailing its proper course. The doctor went
below to steerage and ordered everyone above where,
shortly, from the poop, they could be seen taking the deck,
weak and uncertain as day-old kittens. Around midday,
Sail-Ho! was given and a little after, with all the passengers
clumped to the bulwarks, Captain Aitken spoke to the *Rio*
packet, homeward bound. A pretty little ship, thought
Yate, her masts and spars so delicate and her look altogether so rakish as she passed under the stern. Her sails
white in the sunlight and pooched to the breeze, she tossed
on the waves, easy as a seagull. The captain made his
signals as to the ship's name and destination and Miss
Button, biting her bottom lip in a way that made the doctor

bite his own, hoped the *Rio* would make her report in London since it seemed to her so very improbable that she should be able to send a single letter home till she reached Sydney. She had always thought that at sea there would be frequent opportunity of sending letters but saw now the practical difficulties of two ships under sail sending out a boat to each other. Perhaps the *Rio*'s report would be posted in London and Mr Whitlock would hear of it. She would have liked to ask the captain the likelihood of this but dared not for fear of upsetting her mama. Mr Whitlock had been led to expect a letter frequently and, alarmed at not hearing, would fancy a thousand dangers, thought Miss Button, or worse than that, a crease dented her brow, will think me inconstant. Yate led the service for the cabin passengers in the cuddy before dinner but knew he had been more prayerful standing and watching the *Rio* slide past in a glaze of white and was worshipful again, later that night, as some large ship, likely bound for Liverpool or Bristol by her steering so far north, swept along all sails set, at too much of a distance to be hailed, her shadowy shapes just made out in the silence and darkness of night.

7 *March, 1836*

Latitude 46.5n, Longitude 12w

Monday, the weather came up rough. The water took on a leaden complexion and ranks of unnumbered waves, their heads lathered white, measured out the distance to the grey horizon. Although the ship rolled hard in the heavy sea, her bow breached often by a violent wash of foam, the winds continued favourable and she regularly made eight knots an hour. From her cabin, Mrs Taylor felt each lurch and fall of the vessel in her own person as if she were some finely calibrated nautical instrument. She lay in bed, a rug over her legs, one hand to her Bible. Though she usually found ease there, she had not been able to read or even pray. The crowdedness of the cabin together with the pitching of the ship made kneeling so impossible that she and her husband had grown accustomed to offer up their prayers standing side by side like winter cattle at a corn crib. She could not bear to be on deck where she might see the waves, intolerably high and careless, and from her bed shrank inside her skin each time the ship took water. Since childhood, she had been frightened of the sea. Early in the voyage, she had regarded the sea as she regarded the devil, a brutish force that felt out a man to find his weakest point and took a satisfaction in running him to his ruin. Yet scarce three weeks later, she had learned the miserable lesson that the sea was not so much against Christian endeavour as indifferent to it. Whether or not this ship and its cargo of ambition was on the high seas or safe in dock or, thought Mrs Taylor losing herself in the luxury of situations other than her current one, not yet built, my husband but a boy of

Arthur's age, his life before him like an unread book, these same grey waves or others just like them would mount up at the self-same place and break open their watery masses in much this manner. If it had seemed to her at first that the sea opposed their passage, batting them between Dover and the French coast, much as a cat murders a mouse little by little for its own entertainment, then that was nothing more than the human folly of one too ready to reckon the world through her own importance. Having long thought the sea her froth-headed enemy, she realised now it had no feeling for her whatsoever nor her dear family and might overturn their ship and float them all to a sodden grave without being itself changed by so much as one pennyworth. There was a comfort in having the sea as her enemy for it provided a rasp-edged certainty against which she had honed her faith but now she lay on her bed, as if at the high-tide mark, eyes closed, one hand washed up on the bleached bone of her Bible.

Mrs Taylor allowed herself to be persuaded to the cuddy table at midday and of all the company was least surprised when a tremendous sea breached the vessel and, falling through the skylight, broke over the lunch dishes with a receding hiss. The table's centrepiece, a haggard chicken, its skeleton clearly visible through the webbing of its skin, made like a rare fish and swam the length of the board before roosting in the lap of the doctor who, noting how attractively Miss Button fainted away amid the ruins of her luncheon, had instead to deal with the less picturesque prospect of Miss Bloomfield and Miss Baker in twin hysterics. Mrs Taylor stood, shaking two spoons and a mustard pot from her skirts, and made her unsteady way back to her cabin. If she were going to be drowned, and really she had no higher expectation of the voyage, she would like to be able to hear herself scream. Dr Fowles was having one of his low moments. He stared into his lap with an almost medical attentiveness for certainly the bedraggled boiled chicken put him more in mind of an anatomy primer than a meal. As a young man apprenticed to a surgeon apothecary, the doctor had attended the family of a fellow named Anderson who went about the county with a miserable bald-withered horse and ramshackle caravan exhibiting various wonders at the fairs that lay in his road. Anderson went through a large number of animals in his line of business – rattlesnakes, monkeys, marmots, even a bear – and the arrangement was that in death his menagerie passed to the young apprentice for anatomical study and dissection. With the scrawny chicken dampening the folds of his trousers, the doctor remembered well how he had hung almost hungrily over those fairground specimens, pinning back their hides to his table the better to uncover with his scalpel the lungs or the chambers of the secret heart, where now a carcass intended for dinner only made his gorge rise.

Captain Button marshalled his family and drove them from the cuddy in tight formation as if they were parade ponies. The remaining ladies, some of them with their hair down and dripping, were escorted by Yate to their various cabins, limp or resisting as was their character. Like a couple of Anderson's monkeys that the doctor had been just now recollecting, Charlie and Sadler hopped about the abandoned table, raking up the scattered cutlery while keeping the seats of their breeches clear of Mungo's talented boot. They did not seem to notice that the doctor had the lunch fowl in his lap or, if they noticed, they thought it his privilege. It was Dr Fowles's own assessment that he had grown obsessed with food. He wrote of little else in his journal and, with Armistead and Gordon for his drinking companions, liked to review meals famously enjoyed on shore. Only the night previous, he had dreamed very satisfactorily of fresh bread and creamed butter, spread thick enough to take a crenulated toothmark, but awake and seated to breakfast he was like a ghost who could take no mortal sustenance. If he could eat hard biscuit and meat there was plenty of excellent quality yet, by his own prescription, he was to take meat no more than once a day and the biscuit was so hard he could not entice it down without butter and theirs – here the doctor winked out tears of frustration – so horribly rancid before they ever left Gravesend that none but an Eskimo could touch it. For the last three mornings his breakfast had passed untouched and, except for a cup of tea and some shortbread from his personal cache, he had taken nothing until four o'clock. The case of shortbread had been sent to him by a friend for the voyage and he had thought it a kindness rather than a necessity. Now, he considered it only a small exaggeration to say the biscuits had saved him from starvation and he retired to his cabin like a rat to its hole to eat them in secret, rationing himself to no more than five per meal.

Heaven grant they last until we get some soft bread, thought the doctor, pushing his tongue into the corners of his mouth for any crumbs. Yesterday's dinner had appeared promising, a meat pie and some boiled rice, but the piecrust was flavoured with the infernal butter and he could not take the curry that was to accompany the rice. He had quite fallen out with the captain over it and now he suffered not only his narrow cramping stomach but the dark brow of that man from the head of the table as he contemplated the doctor like the approach of so much squally weather. Being unable to manage the curry, the doctor called for some moist sugar and was much humiliated before the delicate Miss Button when the captain stopped Mungo in his errand saying there was no provision for sugar at dinner time. This was a smasher, no doubt about it. His cheeks hot with shame, the doctor said that if the captain were to be such a stickler for the handbook perhaps he might allow them the fresh bread promised daily by the owners but yet to be seen in the cuddy or could see his way to varying their interminable meat with fish once in a while. Captain Aitken, quick to anger, a choleric temperament the doctor took for Scottish, clenched his fist around his fork, his face purpling with rage.

There is no bread while the weather continues rough, he said, shoving his chair clear of the table. And if you want fish, you're free to fetch it. It is lashed under the maintop. Dr Fowles said nothing but bent his heated face over his plate, picking through the rice on his plate with a desultory fork. The belly is an unbred beast, caring not for the sensitivities of others. Nothing could deaden its coarse demands: the doctor felt everything – his manners, his education, his feelings for the ladies – all lost to the rude insistence of his stomach. The rice was of the commonest kind, quite musty, and could not be eaten without some qualification. Setting his jaw to the head of the table, he tried it with a little sherry but it would not do, nothing would do, and excusing himself, he rushed from the room, the crescent moon of Miss Button's lovely face casting a salve on his heatedness as he passed. Below, with his five pieces of shortbread, he cheered himself by imagining his revenge on the blackguard owners who deserved no better than to be hog-tied to a keg of their ham-oil butter until they had eaten it between them.

That night, the doctor's cabin shipped enough water that he woke to sodden pillows, his nightcap so wet he could wring the moisture from it. The forecastle had also sprung its usual leak but where Dr Fowles could move his bedding toward the foot of his overlong bed to avoid the dribbling from the timbers overhead, no such trick was available to Hall whose hammock hung beneath such a steady trittle of water that howsoever he twisted himself, his limbs fashioning themselves after the various knots he had been taught since boarding, he only succeeded in soaking himself in new places. Hall was also enduring that sailor's disgrace: seasickness. He thought he had his sea legs but it was only the weather letting up for a few days. On deck or below, his world was washed with the mustard tints of nausea until he swore he would rather die than be as sick.

You'll come through, boy, said Thomas Lamb, larboard watch, when he came across Hall hanging off the lee side bulwarks, his boiled rice and biscuit long heaved up, gagging salt water through his mouth and nose. Tell you, Samivel, all the best sailors take sick at first.

Hall never knew whether Lamb said something or whether the cook had seen him rush swobfull from the forecastle, his last wretched meal spattering to the deck with each step as he made for the ship's side, but that night the cook approached the forecastle after the evening meal with some liquid preparation in a handleless cup.

Pou vomisman, said the cook. Hall gave a nervous start. He turned his face away from the cup but not before its flowery perfume recollected for him his mother's front door, the smell of sunshine on earth tamped flat and, only the next morning when the cook dosed him again did the memory fasten itself to him correctly, the strong mozy smell of geraniums. Sitting up with the men after a day's work, Hall did not care to be singled out for babyish attentions. He had been listening goggle-eyed to their jawing of sailors lost at sea. Swept off the yard in a gale, struck by lightning and scringed to the quarter iron of a royal yard, mashed to a pummace by a rollick of brandy barrels got loose in the hold, it seemed there were more dead at sea than live. Hall edged closer to the forecastle hatch's square of lamplight. His back turned against the darkling sky, he felt the icebox breath of dead men along the nubbled curve of his spine, the smoke rising blue from the men's pipes like sea wraiths. Staines had a story of a ship's boy, not much olderen you, his eye suckering to Hall's in the failing light like a ground-gudgeon to a river bed, kilt on his first sailing. This boy –

according to Staines, chambling the stem of his pipe – fell
an unlucky star from the fore topgallant yard and before
the carpenter could spade him into his coffin he had first to
chisel his feet out of the deck, his legs driven in to the
ankles. Black and quite substantial but with a ghost's easy
glide, the cook appeared at Hall's side.

Pou vomisman. Hall's skin came over goose-pimplish
and he turned his face from the cup and Staines's lighthouse eye.

You sick *a tou manman*, said the cook in his moleskin
voice, his teeth like bones in the dark fall of his face. He
pinched the boy's nostrils shut with an expert hand, fun-
nelling his mouth at the sky, until Hall was forced to take
a breath and the sorzle was poured into him in one guttering swallow. He coughed hard enough to make his eyes
water and jumped to his feet but already the cook had
gone, taking his scented cup with him. That night and
many nights after, Hall did not go below after his watch but
slept in the galley on some sacking before the hearth. He
kept his food down and dreamed well, his face bruckled
with soot when the cook waked him just before seven bells
for his medicine and, oftentimes, a honeyed biscuit he
called *janikek*.

The next day was squally but the wind fair. Rolling heavy
in the water, the ship made good way. Mr and Mrs Taylor
gathered an hour in Yate's cabin with his sister to
commence their study of the New Zealand language. There
had been some slight hedging talk of whether to include
Miss Bloomfield and Miss Baker but it had been settled,
without too much being said, that they were not adequate
to the task.

Everything is not for everyone. Mr Taylor had the trick of
making his opinions sound aphoristic in his own mouth.
With his long, narrow jaw and his upper lip nibbled back

over his gums, he looked a pious sheep. His wife sat alongside, a book of translated scriptural selections open on her
lap, the tightly printed page quite a discouragement to
her ambition to master the New Zealand tongue. Like her
husband, she had read closely Yate's *An Account of New
Zealand and of the Church Missionary Society's Mission in
the Northern Island*. She had read closely and wept. As keen
as anyone that the heathens should be loosed from Satan's
bonds, she feared the word of the Lord would be insufficient
armour against the New Zealanders, ignorant and cruel,
who mounted the severed heads of their enemies on the
roofs of their houses like weathervanes. Now she looked at
the first passage in her book, a translation of Genesis apparently, and felt perhaps she was like Miss Baker and Miss
Bloomfield, not made strong enough. Every second letter
seemed to be *K* and, although Mr Yate was saying in his
careful way, see, it is a mellifluous tongue not unlike Italian
(which she did not know either), her first attempts at silent
pronunciation reminded her of the doctor's cough, rattling
and hard-edged, sour with death. Her breast aching
suddenly for her infant, she remembered the house at
Coveney, her little parlour and the scrubbed kitchen table
that took the afternoon sun. She preferred Yate's descriptions in his book of the birds of New Zealand: the tui or
parson bird that mimics the calls of all the other birds; the
rare, turkey-sized kiwi; even the tiny piripiri with its eggs no
larger than a pea. These names sounded in her mouth like
eerie bird calls. Often, she returned to the feathered comfort
of these passages and never put aside the book to sleep
without reading again the lines *Nothing can possibly exceed
the exquisiteness of a morning concert as performed in the
ample woods of these islands*, which soothed her exceedingly. Consoled by her privately but stoutly held conviction
that she would not make the voyage alive, Mrs Taylor still
cried at night when she thought of her children motherless
in a barbarous country.

Yate stood, uncertain, not sure how best to proceed. He was not clear in his mind whether ladies had any facility for language learning and he did not want to deplete them. The voyage would be tiring enough. He saw Mrs Taylor immediately open her copy of the New Zealand missal to mouth a few lines to herself before suddenly rocking back on her chair as the ship rolled, a pinched unhappiness tightening her features. Whether this indicated a propensity or an inability for language was the question. Perhaps he could talk it over in private with Sarah who, even now, had taken Mrs Taylor's hand in her own, exercising that womanly sympathy he knew could pass beneficially from one lady to another through the skin. At Waimate, certainly, the native girls attended afternoon school where Mrs Clarke taught reading, writing, arithmetic, catechisms and sewing, and did tolerably well in the annual examinations. He frowned a moment longer at Mrs Taylor, now taking his sister into her wavering confidences, before turning to her husband.

Mr Taylor, let us begin with you. Taylor sat beside his wife, black and thin as a stovepipe. His knuckles showing white, he held his book shut with some force as if it contained something he did not care to loose on his world.

You say the New Zealanders have a distinct name for every tree and plant in their land, said Taylor. Some six or seven hundred. (When he could get it from his wife, he had been rereading Yate's *Account of New Zealand*.) But the thing that strikes me is while they have a name for every passion, every vice, every bad feeling of the human breast, they have none for any of the virtues which Christianity teaches us. Yate nodded, waiting, for this too was his own observation, published as such in his book directly after the passage describing how the natives had correctly named, down to the tiniest moss or lichen, each of the three hundred plant specimens collected by Baron Hügel.

No word for hope, said Taylor in his pulpi[...]
for gratitude. Nor charity.

Quite, said Yate. Although we've successfully in[...]
some dozen or so words of this sort into the New Zea[...]
language by our translations. He gestured at the book
Taylor held tight, thinking this a good opportunity to begin
the lesson.

But what I was thinking, said Taylor wheedlingly, was
that we have here an instance of what man is by nature,
what he is able to attain without revelation. Think but of
pagan Greece or Rome. Yate put his obliging mind to the
task but found he had not much idea of the Greeks or the
Romans. He thought of Paul, flogged and imprisoned by
the Romans for curing a young girl of her possession. He
thought of Edward Parry Hongi, a natural scholar who had
taken his alphabet in less than two hours, his berry mouth
pursed over his slate.

Are you very unhappy, Caroline? Sarah asked so quiet it
was almost as if she had not spoken. Mrs Taylor's hand lay
unmoving under her own but tears welled up in her eyes.

It's nothing, said Mrs Taylor, the tears sliding down her
cheeks with shameful ease. I have trouble sleeping, that is
all. And lie awake all night thinking fearsome thoughts of
the ship sinking. Or exploding. And now there are the
bugs. I cannot pray.

Sarah thought Caroline had said bugs. Bugs? What
could she mean by it? Mrs Taylor swallowed a sob. The
nights were worst. It was next to impossible to keep her
place in bed, the pitch of the ship causing her and Richard
to fall, often painfully, one upon the other. Only without
thinking about it was sleep any longer possible. The bed
gaped open like a trap each evening as she sat up a little
longer, eyes smarting in tiredness, a book held careless in
the lantern's wobble of light. Everything sounded louder

n the dark, the continual creaking of the ship and the rattling
of cups and cans, the unhappy cries of the children. Braced
against the wall of the cabin, Richard's sleeping bulk bearing
down on her with the ship's roll, she wished red-eyed for
morning when she would rise from her bed more harassed
than she had retired to it the night before. Her unhappy
hand flipped like a fish in Sarah's competent grip. The days
were truly wearisome. She, and poor Laura too, had
already taken several serious falls. It was impossible to
have a meal in peace, either in the cuddy or their cabin, the
plates and cups being shaken from their hands and only
last night the water was upset, the baby's food spilt across
the room. Appetite itself was wanting and the ship poorly
victualled. The butter so horrible no one thinks of using it
though Mungo presents it at every meal. No fresh bread
though it was stipulated we should never be without. And
Arthur and I bitten to pieces by the hard-backed black
bugs we hear ticking in the dark when the lamp is put out.
Even the decencies of life are quite fallen away. No opportunity to wash properly since coming on board or continue
religious duties in their regular order. The ship leaks nearly
two feet a day and the ship's company quite inadequate to
the size of the vessel – what would become of us were any
to fall sick and the pumps to choke? Or then again, the
vessel carries several tons of gunpowder in the hold with a
very large quantity of rum and muriatic acid. Should a
barrel get stoved, which it easily might, there are ninety-
nine chances in a hundred the spirit might take fire and the
ship and all it contains inevitably be blown up. Mrs Taylor
wept silently, her face turned from the men.

Did you say bugs? Yate heard his sister ask, tentative,
and turning, saw Mrs Taylor in a most unhappy way.

Ah, my dear, said her husband, venturing to squeeze her
shoulders with a loving arm though it made her weep the
more. She was his life and health but he could wish her
more suited to the sea.

I trust, he said, choosing his way with care, I trust I can say the Lord's name be praised. If we were to be punished for our sins according to our deserving even our present lot is infinitely better than we deserve. Richard was so good it pained her. Her weakness stood out against his straightforward faith like a sail on the horizon. Before he could speak of Jesus our pilot who will not suffer to make shipwreck of our souls, Mrs Taylor was on her feet, smiling a watery apology and freeing her hand from Sarah's warm double clasp.

Please excuse me, she said. I'll leave you to your lesson. She removed herself from the cabin, followed, after a minute's hesitation, by Sarah. Yate and Taylor looked at each other with some awkwardness.

It strikes me, said Taylor returning to his theme with the persistence of a terrier, that the New Zealanders might be likened to the highly civilised inhabitants of pagan Greece and Rome. He paused to see if Yate was with him. Their languages too, celebrated and beautiful, had no words to express those Christian graces revealed unto men by the Son of God. Mrs Taylor hurried along the passageway, one hand to her breast, the other at the lurching wall for balance, calling for the carpenter. Sadler, or was it Charlie, poked his head around the cuddy door and was dispatched immediately for Busby.

Immediately, called Mrs Taylor at his back, more shrill than commanding.

Mouth grim stitched shut, Mary Ford sat in the best chair in the Taylors' cabin, plumped high on her indignation. Accustomed to see Mrs Taylor layin about half the time like the luckless, legless beggar she had seen down the Docks on his trolley-cart, Mary Ford eyed her off as she bustled about near to raise the dust, the baby yawpin in her mother's arms. It had given her quite a turn to bring the children down and

see the ship's carpenter sawin into the Taylors' marriage bed
as if he had somethin against it personal. The saw spanged
and yelped in the slatting, the wood dust rising thick in the
air, and Mrs Taylor looked as happy as Mary Ford had ever
seen her. She had lifted the baby right from her and, giving
her two skinny lengths of canvas got from the sailmaker,
set her to work sewing up the divided mattress. Mrs Taylor
knelt down and run the shears through it herself, the heavy-
headed baby close to tumbling backward from her arm.
With a dimple of disapproval deepening in one cheek, Mary
Ford ran a neat looping line of her running stitches through
the yellowed canvas. She thought it bad luck to the hilt to
saw in half a marriage bed and wanted no part of it. She had
enjoyed a marriage bed in her time and thought she would
still rather roll between the sheets with a husband, even such
a one as Mr Taylor, long and forbidding as a column of
arithmetic. The weight of the half-mattress almost pulling
her from her seat, she thought of the Parkers' double berth,
a feeling coming over her then near as queer as the one she
had got when she came down to the Taylors' cabin to find
Busby straddling their bed in his boots, his saw chewing it
from footboard to headboard.

Impossible to say that Mary Ford was fond of the Parkers
but it would be nothin short of a lie if she didn't allow that
she had a bit of a soft heart for them, bad language aside.
Mr Parker was a portly man – she noted this with a fat
woman's eye for corpulence. His legs were stout, his gut
considerable, why, even his fingers were plump as sassages.
There was nothing but admiration in her when she said to
herself, and not for the first time, it's like he's bin drawn
with a great big pincil. Even his Malmsey nose, red and
redder yet after a tipple with Mrs Parker, seemed to her a
sign of his having been generously made. As she sewed and
bit off her thread, she kept an eye on the Taylor boys, Arthur
hangin so close over the men's work, Basil as always right
behind, she feared an unhappy leg or arm might be sawn off

and hammered back on before their soap bubble of a
mother took any mind. Two laws there were for fat men
that Mr Parker didn't seem to put much store by – not laws
ezackly, expectations more like. The first was that a fat man
should have thin legs. The number of portly gentlemen that
she had seen quite let down by the skinny shanks they
thought to make a feature of would not bear counting. But,
as has been marked and will suffer remarking, Mr Parker
had stout legs, two of them, ringed with creases all the way
down like a chubby baby's. The second was that a fat man
should take himself a fat wife. But here's Mrs Parker,
narrower than a piece of string though not half so tidy. To
see the Parkers side by side at the steerage table of an
evening pouring the same amount of grog down their
throats was to witness something close to a miracle of
nature, the capacity of the one identical to the capacity
of the other despite the discrepancy in their exterior
dimensions.

The Parkers' berth was alongside Mary Ford's and they
took their pleasure there as elsewhere, full-throated and
unapologetic. She often lay awake waiting for them to
come to bed, her hand between her own generous thighs
marking time. Not every night for certain, but if not,
reliably every second one, the Parkers' bunk creaked and
moaned like a ship on a reef and Mary Ford, eyes tiring
against the close black air, would smell their wafted warm
sourness as the dark bedding rose and fell. Mr Parker
lowed, calling in the dark as if he had lost himself, and Mrs
Parker sung out, her voice low and lower, and sometimes,
slap of flesh on flesh, Mary Ford bit her own pillow, her
body whittled down again to girlishness and twisted, hard
and silver, in her sheets. The two wordless voices cathe-
draled up, up into the blackness until they seemed no
longer human, the one spiralling about the other like the
light worming between the lays of a rope. Then a shivering
expectant silence as when, during land clearing, a great tree

is about to fall. Two nights previous, into that breach the white mothiness of Mrs Eylard's nervous face had fluttered at the other side of Mary Ford's bed.

God save us, Mrs Ford. What was that noise?

The Parkers is having a dream. Mary Ford's voice sounded rough in her own ear. She had been dreaming with them, breathless and beautiful, and now she sat, sewing the Taylors' mattress in two while Mr Busby, with a couple of the ship's men, braced the broken bed to the wall in two pieces, one hung over the other like the bunks in steerage, Mr Taylor standing in the doorway, a long dark exclamation point, his mouth as round as his eyes.

The weather quieted the day after the doctor's birthday. He had attained thirty-one, the captain pledging a bumper at dinner as there were to be no hard feelings between them. The sky's pale tent pitched high overhead, the air had the trembling clarity of water. Poor sailors always, the sheep stretched their necks in the longboat and were soothed by the loamy smell of land: Cape Finisterre, the southern point of the Bay of Biscay, slipping past unremarked, just out of sight, on the larboard side. Hanging every sail, the ship dripped with light and under a steady wind was headed for Madeira, full south at nine knots an hour. Near every passenger took to the decks and, mistaking the ship's robustness for their own, felt much improved by the voyage. Each warm day was followed by one yet warmer. The cabin gentlemen renewed their scientific interest in the atmosphere and, after much measurement in shade and sun and even the drawing up of charts in certain journals, were in cordial agreement that over the last three days the mercury had climbed to sixty-one degrees, a fact as good as evident to those without thermometers in these same gentlemen's shedding of pilot coats, mufflers and shawls as the days wore on. One morning as Yate was at the taffrails, sun on

his back, watching the white foam driven many feet beneath
the wave by the rudder's agitation, bubbles caught like seeds
of air in a windowpane, he saw Armistead at some little
distance trailing his thermometer in the water by means of
a stout string, the doctor standing by to crane his head at the
instrument's reading the instant it was hauled aboard. As
everybody in the cuddy knew, the doctor had broken his
own thermometer some days previous and was now
dependent on Gordon for the use of his, which he could not
venture to throw into the sea. Still, wanting to keep his
record complete, he had persuaded Armistead that marine
heat was, scientifically speaking, as interesting as atmos-
pheric and the two men accordingly took their satisfaction
each midday. Yate himself did not much care to know the
temperature. It was enough for him that he no longer slept
with his coat and travelling cloak spread across his bedding
and he guessed that in a very few days he would throw aside
his blanket and counterpane to sleep beneath nothing more
than a sheet. He had made this voyage before and knew
how it unfolded. Half a week the other side of the equator
and the thermometer fever would have almost entirely
passed. There would be other diversions: fishing for albatross, say, or the festivities at the passing of the London
meridian.

After five days of making good headway, the ship was
becalmed all Saturday, her canvas hanging slack from every
yard. Barely a swell broke the varnished surface of the sea
and the *Prince Regent* which had so recently been described
in letters and journal entries as a racehorse, a lightning bolt,
even – the reckless Miss Button – Cupid's arrow, now
wallowed low in the water as a winged mallard. On deck at
sunrise, the dawn light pinking a passage across the still
water, Yate thought to make his morning prayer from the
roof of the chicken coop. *From the west, men will fear the*

name of the Lord. Praying was, for Yate, the opposite of sermonising. Where the preacher reached out to his congregation with all the cunning of his tongue, licking their leveret souls to soft-boned shape, the prayerful man was alone, making of himself a poem. A prayer could be something of a dream, a furred fall into patterns unthought waking. An effective man in the pulpit, at prayer Yate was his own glittering lure. He talked himself down the familiar lines of his breviary as down the rungs of a ladder, until he stood in some unfamiliar place, bleak and blasted. Sulphurous in his nakedness, bereft of hope, always he was surprised that another line, another and another, could split open his dusty husk, his new skin verdant in the blood of sacrifice. *And from the rising of the sun, they will revere his glory.*

Some scuffling of bare feet on board, a shouted laugh, disturbed Yate as he sat back on his heels, the unspoiled day before him. Their feet slipslither, polished white with soap suds, Charlie and Sadler were trampling some clothes clean on the deck before the forecastle. Gripping the other's shoulders, they laughed tight into each other's faces. Somehow part of his prayer in a way he had yet to reckon, Yate watched their foolery, his heart full and tremulous. Came Mr Denison in a pair of canvas breeches such as the men wear when they bathe off the side. Elegant, easy, burning white. He took one of the foaming undershirts from beneath the boys' feet and rubbed himself all over with it, his hair standing up in white points, his chest already white now whiter, his long thighs and calves rubbed pink. The boys fetched buckets, their running like falling, hair over their eyes, bright gobbets of water plashing as they went. Lustrous coins dropped bronze and gold from Mr Denison turning and turning on the soapy deck, the boys running breathless to fetch more water, laughing, while the world spun under its plummy morning sky. *For he will come like a pent-up flood that the breath of the Lord drives along.*

Without the breeze's cool relief and the sense of purpose effected by the ship's making swiftly for her destination, the delight of the previous days palled as passengers, steerage and cabin both, idled the day away on the stretch of painted ocean. The air itself was heavy and many a leg and corseted belly was speckled scarlet with prickly heat. By the captain's order, an awning was spread over the poop deck and the ladies sat beneath it. Breathing. And fanning themselves. Beneath the dead sails, Yate alone stood long hours in the full sun and thought on all he knew. Nothing's known until it's lodged in the body, burrowed tick-like beneath the skin, sure as any memory. Nor anything lost that takes the shape of prayer, the gap between words. Yate had the pieces of a patterned saucer broken in the cabin's last squally meal and let them slip, one by one, off the side of the ship into the still water, over and over turning, crackled blue glaze, white underside, many fathoms twirling through the transparent deep before being lost to sight. He thought of the statues that had distracted him during his audience with the king at Brighton Pavilion, their unholy forms made in God's image, and Mr Denison's porcelain whiteness that he now carried with him, heavy at his neck as the errant sailor's albatross.

A dead rustle, a creak shrill as a curlew's cry, the sails swalloped full, bagged empty, filled again and a fine breeze coming up from nowhere ruffled the sea, driving the ship forward on her way before the fall of night. Yate retired to the close comfort of his sister's cabin where she read to him an hour, orange motes rising and falling behind the lids of his closed eyes. Sarah's reading voice was measured, steadily talking him down to sleep as the lead line is dropped by the boatswain hand over hand till it bunts the sea floor. He lay on her sofa, jacket and shoes off, half-entertaining a chain of curious unconnected thoughts that

on waking, the slap of water and the ship near silent, Sarah
fitting a shawl across his shoulder, he could give no sensible
shape. He tipped into deep sleep then, restorative, dreamless, and woke at two bells, his sister's breath slubbing the
darkness. On deck, he carried his shoes in his hand and
went forward in his stockinged feet. The wind continued
warm and favourable and the ship was getting on fast. They
might have made the Trades early. One of the men was
sleeping in a shadow thrown between water barrels, curled
like a cat in a coil of rope, only pulling his cap brim close
over his eyes as Yate passed, one foot squeaking light in his
damp stocking at every other step. Two others of the watch
were leaning on the lee bulwarks as easy as at the races and
eyed him as he went.

Fair night, Mr Yate, said one. Piggott, was it? A brawny
fellow anyway with a broad meatish face.

Couldn't ask better, said Yate. Which was a sudden truth.
He didn't stop but went forward, tall and shining as a
candle. The night sea, usually a dim stretch of nothing, an
occasional whitecap striking enough light to be seen, was
alive with phosphorescence, the waters radiant, soft
tumbles of starry steel light falling away from the ship's
planking on either side. Yate lay along the bowsprit and
watched the ship's prow pleat the water back on itself,
throwing a million sparks. It was the Sabbath, their fourth
afloat.

Before dinner, Yate led the prayers and gave a short address
in the cuddy. Some steerage passengers, the Bedgoods and
Mr and Mrs Davidson, attended the service, dressed in
their best and looking as serious as could be wished. The
text for the day was Proverbs 3. *Wisdom is more precious
than rubies: and all the things thou canst desire are not to
be compared unto her*. Little Mrs Davidson, dark and
creased as a preserved fig, nodded her head as if she had

always suspected as much. At dinner, Yate asked the captain if the ship was already in the trade winds but the man would not be drawn.

Trade winds or not, he said, mopping at his mouth with a napkin, she's a sweet breeze. The doctor pulled a sympathetic face at Yate and, dinner over, came around the table to tell him of the troop of porpoises that had swum beside the ship that morning. From his cabin, Yate had heard the indistinct call of the lookout, the clamour on deck, but after a second's ear-cocked suspension, he and Sarah had remained below, reading to each other in turn from the Scriptures. His sister's favourite book was Job.

You should like them all equally, said Yate. There is not one to favour, although he himself preferred Isaiah. Sarah looked at him close, the book open before her on the table, always that giddying fall into eyes so like his own.

I like them all exceedingly. Only I like Job best. They were at the plague of boils. Since morning, Yate had been sticking to his sister as close as a pilot fish. He had woken with as fresh a sense of the health of his body as a man who had come through a fever. Yet his heart felt poured full and he hardly knew how he was to get through the day without its slopping over.

The doctor was standing, hands tight behind his back, head and shoulders pecking forwards and back at Yate to give some sense of the porpoises' astonishing motion as they dived off the top of one wave to the next. Though his extraordinary movement recalled a porpoise not at all, Yate thought his clamp-lipped grin went some way to sketching that good-humoured fish. In return, Yate told Doctor Fowles of his sighting of the phosphorescence and was much gratified by the doctor's keen interest. The doctor resolved to collect a bucketful of the animals and examine what species they belonged to.

If I am zoologist enough, he said to Yate, although nothing was plainer than that he thought he was. The weather being so mild at last and the evenings so idle, the doctor had suggested to Armistead and Gordon that they should get together a lecture series, each gentleman addressing the others on a topic of interest after tea. Those two being most agreeable, he now obtained Yate's approval.

Not necessarily a religious topic, said the doctor, licking his teeth in politeness. With two missionaries in the cabin, he feared being sermonised.

The lectures began a few nights later, Captain Button as the eldest of the company, addressing the cabin after the ladies had retired.

Seniores priores, Dr Fowles had said when drawing up the schedule. Captain Button's topic was, unsurprisingly, a military one. He detailed the changes a man must pass through from a recruit to his being finished as a soldier of the line. As he spoke, Yate thought in a parallel fashion of the transformations wrought in a native boy who becomes a Christian or is, as they themselves have it, christified. After all, both the soldier and the Christian attain their status through repetitive training: the one in drill, the other in catechisms. The main difference seemed to him that whereas, according to Button, the soldier is made when the man becomes a machine, submitting his body with all its instincts for self-preservation to the discipline of another, the Christian, however pious and holy, never conquers his evil heart entirely but must call for Jesus Christ's forgiveness over and over. Yate saw he had caught the attention of Dr Fowles and wondered if he had betrayed his inattentiveness. He smiled across at the doctor, nodding to show his appreciation of the Captain's presentation which seemed anyway to have drawn to a close, the conversation becoming more general and turning to Button's participation some years ago in the invasion of Burma. Yate had heard from his sister that

Captain Button had distinguished himself in the Anglo–
Burmese war – she had got it no doubt direct from Mrs
Button – but he had never seemed a convincing regimental hero. Too doughy and heavy in the seat. Captain
Button was shaking his sorrowful head over his brandy
and recounting the British losses. Outrageous shipping
costs, whole regiments killed by dysentery without ever
seeing the enemy, the war debt never honoured after the
British withdrew.

Damned Burmese, said Captain Button. Several gentlemen sneaked their eyes at Taylor and Yate to see how they
weathered a manly curse. Those monkeys knew we didn't
dare return. Captain Button's eyes glittered with the recollection or the brandy. He had only landed with his regiment
when ordered 150 miles up the coast to quell an insurrec-
tion, a task that occupied as many months as were expected
days to accomplish. Still, he had missed the worst of the
war and taken an immense booty besides, his share
amounting to £600 sterling.

No wise man predicts the fortunes of war, said Mr
Taylor. He did not enjoy Captain Button's language but
enjoyed still less the manner in which the other bluff gentlemen looked to himself and Mr Yate. Daily on the
increase was his feeling that the gentlemen did not count
him among their number, parcelling him off as a man of
religion with the ladies and children. A clergyman was yet
a man of the world and might be as stout and adventure-
some as any.

The following morning at breakfast Yate saw that Taylor
was strung up on some excitement. He stirred his tea distractedly for long minutes, tipping winks toward the foot
of the table where the doctor sat but would say nothing
when questioned, preferring to look knowing, one long
finger laid alongside his nose. When Taylor and Fowles left

the cuddy together, Yate went on deck and took his usual position in the sun, on top of the hen coop. Again, a beautiful day. For the whole week the sails had hardly required handling, the wind blowing always from the same quarter. Just south of the Canaries, the ship was making good speed and took the breeze so smooth that Hall stood his first trick at the wheel, the force of the wind and the wave thrumming through his skinny arms. At breakfast, Dr Fowles had recorded sixty-nine degrees. Now Yate saw him standing in the waist in conference with Taylor whose agitation could be made out across the distance. So far on the voyage, Taylor had kept to the cuddy and the poop and looked ill at ease on the deck among the men. Scrubbing out a pot with a handful of sand at the galley doorway, the cook kept his head turned at him as though he were a mad dog that any moment might want throwing overboard. Taylor seemed the world's only ornament. The cook watched him close, the captain from the quarterdeck, the entire cabin turned out on the poop and even the men, lounging off-duty on the forecastle, lifted their heads from their scrimshandery. Near every eye was on him standing amidships in his shirtsleeves. He spoke once more to Dr Fowles, turned and, as the smirking doctor hung back, Yate saw at once Taylor's goal as if through the man's own eyes: his swashbuckling descent from the maintop with a wooden case of preserved fish.

From the moment he climbed into the main shrouds, Taylor ever only looked up to the maintop, beneath which the boxes of fish were lashed. He had heard – actually from his wife although how she came by it he didn't know – that a giddy fearfulness was the chief problem for a man aloft for the first time. Awake in the night, tucked narrowly into his half of what had been their bed, he had resolved not to look down, even on his descent, and hoped this precaution enough for, he did not need his wife's reminder, he had a weakness for heights that made him nervous even of his top bunk. Yate watched the slow ascent, Taylor's resolute face tipped up at the lashed boxes, just as every face on deck was tipped up at him. When Taylor was no farther than halfway up, Captain Aitken gave his men their call.

Spreadeagle, men.

Ay ay, sir! One man, three men, four sprang to the rigging and, with showy leap and clamber, made quick work of the distance between themselves and Taylor, still climbing steadily, his only view the boxes of fish and his own white hands, first one, then the other, appearing and disappearing on the hairy ropes. Taylor did not know – it seemed his wife had not known it either – that by sea custom sailors are entitled to exact a penalty from any passenger straying into their aerial world for the first time. From below, Yate gave Taylor five more seconds before he was taken by the men when suddenly someone with the look of Mr Denison, blond and limber, eeled headfirst from the maintop and claimed Taylor for himself. Mr Denison was so much on Yate's mind this past week that his falling, angelic, from the bellied whiteness of the sails seemed at first another apparition. Thinking the movement of the shrouds was the doctor coming behind him as they had arranged, Taylor was as surprised as Yate when the third mate dropped from the maintop with a savage cry and fastened him by the wrists to the rigging. His arms stretched apart as far as they could be, Taylor's face was suddenly flat to the ropes, the deck a distant dizzy spin beneath him. Rough hands seized his legs and, parting them to their limit, bound them also to the rigging. The instant Taylor took his eye from the boxes of fish, they ceased to exist for him and he hung in the wind, a senseless sack. It was quite some minutes before he understood the men's demands. Mr Denison retired some little distance, leaning back in the shrouds, one easy foot kicked up behind him as if he idled in a gentlemen's club, a pose Taylor thought insolent when he recollected it later. He could not see the rest of the men although the one called Staines spoke threateningly of some eagle that for a wild moment Taylor thought might fly down as to Prometheus and gouge out his liver.

Spreadeagle, sir, said Staines again, pressing so close and disrespectful that Taylor felt the scratch of his chin's growth on his own ear. You hangs here, sir, till you stands us grog all round.

Dinner was a quiet affair. Taylor stayed in his cabin nursing his pride and his right foot, the instep painfully chafed by one of the men's ropes. After dinner – in truth, before dinner also – Captain Button was in the habit of herding his family about himself and retiring to his cabin. In recent days, however, Mrs Button was often seen to leave the cabin again after no more than a half-hour seclusion and seek out diverting amusements in the cuddy or, weather permitting, on the poop. She never retired with the missionary ladies to Miss Yate's cabin, considering herself a little above their society, or perhaps it was, for the self-same reason, that she was never invited. Her eye rolling a little wild and close to bloodshot, her nose reddened, she looked often enough as though she could do with some distraction, but if her colour ran high the agitation only suited her. Or so Armistead considered. For all his youth, he knew himself as a man of the world, a man moreover with time on his hands and a business eye for a shapely turned profit. Although he had been accustomed to take a glass or two of porter with Fowles and Gordon at this time of day, he found himself more often of late making leisured laps of the ship, his thoughtful tread and downcast gaze calculated to prevent any amiable approach from, say, ghastly Miss Bloomfield who was often seen to stride the

poop after dinner in a manner richly suggestive of diges-
tion. Coming upon Mrs Button then, laid up in some
out-of-the-way corner, a book or some light needlework
flying in her hand like a signal flag, it was the most natural
thing in the world to salute her, to accept her offer of a seat,
make a little facetious conversation: in short, to gull her
with his gentlemanly civilities. On his approach, Mrs
Button would look up with such a grateful countenance
and lay aside her occupations so keenly that he hardly considered her fair game. On account of his highly developed
sense of sport, he was almost gratified to see one afternoon
that great dangler, Gordon, sitting alongside Mrs Button in
an empty corner of the cuddy, like a boy in his father's
boots.

You must read it to me, said Mrs Button.

I have only got out the first line, said Gordon, flushing to
the roots of his red hair. Like the captain, Gordon was a
Scotsman but what would be considered a deficiency in any
other man was in him a positive attribute for he was the
dullest water-coloured character imaginable and if it were
not for his being Scottish, thought Armistead, and keeping
nineteen wretched canaries, he would hardly be noticed at
all.

Mr Gordon has been writing some poetry, said Mrs
Button. The sly young dog, thought Armistead. The ladies
like a bit of poetry, a little sentiment with their lovemaking.
The doctor was forever taking up his guitar and warbling
something of his own devising about nymphs who sported
at the crest of the brine but who looked, for all that, so like
Miss Button they might have been sisters. Armistead stayed
on his feet, ignoring Mrs Button's offer of a seat, since he
felt he needed the advantage. He was not much for poetry
himself although – the recollection warmed him even now
– he had enjoyed an unexpected measure of success with
Miss Archer and *the light music of her nimble toes/patting*
against the sorrel as she goes.

Let's have it, said Armistead as if he were a fighting man. Gordon picked up his much scored-through manuscript and cleared his throat in a nervous cough. He bobbed his head like a chicken swallowing dry grain and slid his eyes around the cuddy, seeming to linger very much on the door leading out to the passage.

So soon, said Gordon. So soon as the rosy-fingered morning shone once more. It is not finished yet, you see.

The rosy-fingered morning, said Mrs Button. She rested her head on her shoulder, as if she could only support so much pleasure. The rosy-fingered morning. Mr Gordon, I think you are a poet, sir. But just when Armistead thought he had some work ahead of him – and a ship the one place where his sorrel line must arrive a little false – Gordon was bowing and blushing his way from his chair, taking his awkward leave of Mrs Button as if they did not much care for women in Scotland.

Please, take a seat, Mr Armistead, said Mrs Button in her voice of lovely desperation.

I thought we might rather take the air. Though Armistead would not sit in a chair warmed by Gordon's fundament yet he did not object to profiting by another man's labour. However rosy Gordon's fingers, thought Armistead, he could never hope to come in for more than the dog's portion of Mrs Button, a lick and a sniff at best. Offering his arm to the lady, who felt to him almost boneless, quite filleted with poetic satisfaction, he walked her on the poop for a sweltering quarter-hour and then, when she begged to be let sit, for ten minutes more.

And it's windy weather boys, stormy weather boys
When the wind blows we're all together boys.

Five bells and the men were holystoning the deck: John Clerk and Sam Hall, Pirkka the Finn, Will Piggott, Staines and Edwards. Yate could not see Mr Denison anywhere. Neither grey nor the palest blue, the sky was as yet pure light, the day barely pegged out beneath its lucent canopy. The men knelt shoulder to shoulder in a ready row, the planking at their knees sprinkled with sand and water, scrubbing the wood blond with rough blocks of freestone. Their shirtsleeves rolled, their trousers cuffed, the men's faces shone pink and damp with the exertion and the tropical heat, already clotting the morning air. Forward and back they rocked, scouring the deck in energetic pushes. All the while, they called and answered in unison, keeping their time. The men shoved forward in their row, arms extended full length, backs dipped as a cat stretches its spine; together, they sat back on their haunches, freestone blocks pulled toward their knees. Staines tipped his head back and, not missing a stroke, called the next lines, his voice a little pumicey as if rubbed through with sand.

Up jumps the shark with his five rows of teeth
Sayin you eat the dough boys an I'll eat the beef.

Forward, back, forward, back: the men called the chorus.

And it's windy weather boys, stormy weather boys
When the wind blows we're all together boys.

Yate had walked a circuit of the deck but still no sight of
the third mate. The ship was off St Antonio, the most
northwesterly of the Cape de Verd islands – some distance
off for the water ran wide in every direction and there had
been no shout of land. His back to the sea, elbows resting
on the bulwarks, Yate looked up into the puff-bluster world
of the sails as though his eye could pierce their cover to
lodge in Mr Denison, long and loose-legged, keeping his
watch at the masthead. The scrape and grate of the men's
freestone gnawed Yate's ear but still he stood his watch, his
eye flicking quick to any new movement overhead that
might reveal a man descending, bright of hair and tooth.
William Piggott shook his head so the sweat flung clear of
his eyes and sung out:

Up jumps the mackerel all blue and grey
Gives the capstan a turn – anchor aweigh.

A fresh hand of sand, a lick more water.

And it's windy weather boys, stormy weather boys
When the wind blows we're all together boys.

Some dark figure against the mainsail but it was nothing
more than the shadowy bunt of a coil of rope dropped from
above and hauled aloft again by some unseen hand. Yate
thought once more of Mr Denison about whom he knew
almost nothing. He wondered after the spiritual health of
his soul. Hall's shirt stuck to his back. His stomach, too
empty even to grumble, cramped in hunger. He was not
unhappy, scrubbing down the deck with the men at the end
of his watch. Deeper than the slightness of his chest suggested, his voice could be made out from the others at the

chorus, his provincial tongue making the lines his own. It was a harder stretch for him to cover the same distance with his freestone but he worked equal ground as the other men; none could say he dint. In this heat, he still favoured sleeping in the galley. Though the squally weather had passed over, the forecastle was sweltersome enough to suffocate a man. He would have slept on the deck if the captain had not warned him of it, on account of the heavy dew off the coast of Africa and the fever too. It was his turn to call the chanty but the lines about the herring and the lobster had been taken three times already.

> *Up jumps a mermaid with a tail for her legs*
> *Sayen work's all done boys, get yourselfs to bed.*

He had heard Mr Cat sing this out one time at the capstan or something very like but now Staines was squinken at him like it warnt proper, laughen with his mouth open enough to show the black pegs at the back and given eavelong looks at the missionary.

> *And it's windy weather boys, stormy weather boys*
> *When the wind blows we're all together boys.*

The men were getting to their feet slow, hands to the ache in thigh or back, leaving the two boys, Clerk and Hall, to throw water across their work and swab it down dry. Watching Hall cross the deck with his bucket, one hip thrown wide like a girl's, Yate only knew he had missed Mr Denison tumble from the ratlines when he heard him knock three times at the forecastle scuttle and call up the other watch.

All larboard watch, ahoy! Seven bells. Do you hear me, you dead men?

The weather being so calm and unchanging, the ship rolling on her way smooth and steady as a bird dog, both watches took breakfast together at seven bells. Not yet their time on deck, the larboard men stood yawning a minute on the forecastle and rearranging themselves inside their trousers, before the two Lascars, arms about each other's shoulders, went to have their kids filled at the galley. They had narrow wrists that recollected for the cook the bones of small birds, and bruised thumbprints under their eyes. Their names on the ship's articles were Bai and Prasad but they were known, universally and changeably, as Madras and Bombay.

Sweet morning, *ès-pa*? The cook ladled his skilly into first one wooden tub and then the other. From habit, each man stood a moment longer, as if he thought there might be the chance of more.

Get on there, Bombey. It was Staines, come with the Finn to collect breakfast for his watch. An odd pair, the cook thought. The one stocky and bandy-legged with sharp stoat eyes, the other tall, one good eye always dreaming to some far horizon, white as fishbelly where he wasn't weathered red.

Sweet morning, *ès-pa*? Their tubs filled to the same mark with the steaming oatmeal and bran, the two men continued to stand.

No mo'. The cook showed the men his shining teeth and the bottom of the pot, scraped clean.

Got any biscuit for us? The jut of his belly taking the weight of his kid, Staines polished his eye at the cook. Like you gives the boy?

No mo'. He stood in the galley doorway and watched the two men walk forward. Something about the short man reminded him of who? Heavy as a cow but without the cow's good spirit. Watching Staines close as he hefted himself onto the forecastle, the man's neck and chest so thickly articulated he had to pivot from the waist to turn his head, the cook remembered of a sudden the snake with his dusty belly and split leathery strip of tongue.

The flying fish came when Hall was drying his swab, keen to get on the forecastle with his breakfast pan on his lap. He had heard them described, enough to recognise them at once, yet they were nothing like he expected. There were so many of them first off and they came so very close to flying. Standing at the starboard bulwarks, his mouth hanging open, Hall saw maybe one hundred fish, their queer bodies upright on the water's surface, tails thrashing for balance, spread their huge fins and spring into the air like a flock of birds, making some fifty yards before dropping back into a wave combing off the ship's prow. And another twenty or thirty rising on their tails, their blunt heads adrip with water, and skirring into the air on their blue wings. When they took flight, there was the sound of parchment on parchment. He had seen a pair of porpoises some days ago and the phosphorous that shines like half-crowns in the dark water, but these flying fish were the thing.

Further down the railing, Yate stood like some impossible saint, the sky behind him filled with the whirring of airborne fish, his eye gone out like a baited line to Mr Denison, fetching his coffee in a tin cup from the galley.

Good morning, Mr Yate. He had the content, chalky face of a man at the end of his morning watch and, Yate saw, a way of being courteous that was not yet deferential. You know you're in the tropics, sir, when the fish make like birds. Yate could not quite catch at his meaning but stared a minute longer into his eye, paler blue than the noonday sky. He turned to see what Mr Denison looked at. Ah, the flying fish were here. Their launch into the air and the papery scrape of their outstretched fins in the wind seemed a sign of some proportion. Yate thought Mr Denison must have seen the sight a hundred times but still he set his intelligent face to the scene, the burnt nut smell of his coffee rising in the heat of the morning. One fish, larger than the others, leapt into the sky and, tail dropped forward, its entire body arched tight, swooped high above the water, its long glide arrested by the ship's rough railing and a clumsy tumble to deck at Hall's feet.

Something like a herring but with a big black eye, the broken fish flailed at the deck, held to the spot by one large fin sticking, thin and wet, to the planking. Hall thought to take the animal in his hands and release it as he did the smaller field birds caught at home in his pigeon snares but, hesitating a moment, wary of the barbed fins, he sat back on his heels while the shimmering blues of the fish bled down to grey. He had his back to the forecastle so the men could not see his business, one cautious fingertip just denting the slick flank, when there was a shout from the poop deck and the doctor running toward him.

My fish, said the doctor, while still at a little distance. That's my fish. One hand behind its gills, the other at its tail, he lifted it from the deck and, admiring its curiosities, caught his breath on the slow walk back to the cuddy where he instructed the steward to cook it for him. When Yate caught up with him, he was sitting alone at his early breakfast.

Had you seen a flying fish before?

Never, said the doctor, wiping some grease from his mouth with an emphatic finger.

And what do you make of it?

Delicious. Dr Fowles paused a moment. Very like trout. Only shorter and drier. Yate glanced at the doctor's plate in some surprise.

At this rate, said the doctor, eager to get back to his fish before it cooled completely, we shall eat well for the next week or so.

After his breakfast, the doctor sat on the poop, quite distracted. He had been disappointed to learn, both for the advance of scientific learning and the prospect of future fish meals, that the advent of a flying fish on the deck of a ship was a very rare occurrence. Yate himself had never seen such a thing although this was his third voyage through the tropics.

Are you sure? The doctor had looked at the sad mouthful of fish caught on the tines of his fork. Not only Yate himself but Mr Denison, the third mate, had never seen such a thing either.

Nor heard of such from his father, an old master in the British Navy, said Yate, which was not strictly true for although Mr Denison had spoken most charmingly of his parent, he had not mentioned him in connection with flying fish. Still, if he was no longer speaking to Mr Denison, there was undoubtedly a pleasure in speaking of him.

Nor, continued Yate unblushing, from any of his four brothers, all likewise at sea. The doctor sat sorrowful on the poop and knew himself for the sort of man that gratified his body's appetite before that of his mind. He wished he had drawn a likeness of the fish or at least taken the measure of its proportions. This afternoon, he resolved, he would detail in his journal those few facts he had observed before handing the fish over to Mungo: the squarish cut of the head, for instance, or that the seeming wings were nothing more than enlarged thoracic fins.

An unsociable hour but here was Armistead walking the poop with Mrs Button on his arm. The doctor supposed such topsy-turviness might be put down as yet another effect of the tropics, it being so warm later in the day as to make such exercise unthinkable. He had measured seventy-eight degrees the previous night in his cabin though the window and door were open and he slept now without any coverings, not even a sheet. Indeed, the cabin passengers all went nearly naked, some of the gentlemen having cast off their stockings. Armistead had made no such concession, he saw, and was putting himself about in his usual style, the wrist ruffles of his shirt visible at the cuff of his morning coat as he walked Mrs Button back and forth through the wake of his eau de Portugal.

Good morning, Dr Fowles.

Good morning, Mrs Button. The doctor tilted his head at Armistead.

I was saying this moment to Mr Armistead how health-some I find our walks. Mrs Button took a firmer grip of the parsley kerseymere of Armistead's upper arm.

And Miss Button too is well, I trust?

She is well, said Mrs Button, as if someone had said she were not. Armistead had reached the end of the poop and, turning, pointed Mrs Button in the opposite direction. She looked at the doctor over her shoulder.

I wish you'd call on her this morning.

Is she not well then? The doctor had several times imagined Miss Button or Missy, as he called her to himself, quite unwell, near death in fact, restored to life by his hands and bound to him ever after by indissoluble ties of gratitude and affection. In these daydreams Miss Button suffered prettily some gentle disease, opening her eyes for the first time in days to see him, grave and diminished, weeping at her bedside. The doctor himself was frequently younger by ten years or so, the same age he was when he took his wife. Now, he was heartened to find he was not self-serving enough to wish for the actual prospect of her illness.

She's not herself. Mrs Button had been turned at the far end of the poop deck and was walking again toward the doctor. Please say you will call after breakfast.

At eleven, said the doctor. After breakfast, he was to call on Mr Taylor who had at last agreed that he could examine his injured foot. He had blamed the doctor for his being spreadeagled by the men last week, suspecting him of alerting the captain to his progress aloft. All offers of medical assistance had been refused until this morning when the doctor came upon him bathing Basil in a tub of salt water on deck and observed his foot dangerously swollen and raw. In this weather, the doctor would need time to bathe himself before calling on Miss Button.

Half after ten, the doctor washed in his cabin, stripped to the waist, before buttoning himself back into his freshest clothes. He brushed his hair and sleeked his whiskers. He furrowed beneath his nails with his trephine pick. His medicine chest included a miniature mirror for the purpose of examining the interior of the mouth and he used this now to inspect himself in very small sections. His eye looked well, he thought. Bright with a clean shining white. He fingered a hot red pimple forming at the base of his neck and twitched his collar over it. Perhaps a poultice this evening for half an hour to prevent its becoming pustular. Everything turned putrid so quickly at this latitude. Taylor's foot was much worse than he could have imagined. The rope had worn a runnel in the soft flesh of his instep and the edges of the wound were not healed but puffy and leaking a clear fluid. Their cabin was quite dismal: Mrs Taylor lying unwell in the bottom bunk and Taylor himself in an armchair, his foot raised on a packing case. It was Taylor's birthday. Thirty-one: the same age as the doctor.

The Lord alone knows how short or long our appointed time on earth may be, said Taylor on the doctor's congratulations. No need to tell the doctor that birthdays carried the sulphurous stink of death. Some weeks previous, on the occasion of his own, he had recorded in his journal the hope that on his next birthday he would be pushing for home, health restored. Had he stayed in England much longer he should not have lived beyond thirty-one, he was certain of it.

It is high time, said Taylor on a wincing breath, as the

doctor packed his foot with a vinegar bandage, to put away
the things of youth and live as a man.

The doctor presented himself at the Buttons' cabin five
minutes after eleven. He had sat on his bed and three times
counted out those five minutes before they elapsed. Captain
Button opened the door himself.

Yes?

Mrs Button requested that I call on Miss Button.

Yes. Captain Button waved the doctor into the cabin. It
was the mirror image of Armistead's, directly opposite on
the starboard side, with a bunk braced against one wall
and the rest of the room got up as a parlour. The small
window was quite overwhelmed by a fall of brocade
drapes and the doctor stood a moment before he could
make out the lay of the furniture in the dimmed light. He
skirted the aggressive turned leg of a serpentine sofa and
squeezed himself between a deep-buttoned chaise and a
mahogany pedestal sideboard, the glossy surface of which
gave off in rippled reflection the portrait of Captain Button
in his regimental colours hanging above.

Dr Fowles. Captain Button announced the doctor and
ushered him toward the door of the connecting cabin. An
oak elbow-chair stood sentry beside the doorway and
Captain Button sat at it, toying with the pair of carved
dolphins that supported the armrests, his back to the
feminine rustling of the aft cabin.

The second cabin was smaller but better lit, an animal pelt
of some kind covering what little of the floor was not taken
up by the Buttons' bed. Dark and glossy, a fur of some
length. The doctor frowned at the floor covering, trying to
identify its origin. Too thick and shining for a donkey, he
guessed. Perhaps a panther from the regiment's time in India.
It was an unwholesome thing to feel beneath one's shoe.
Slippery and almost live. Propped on a bank of pillows, Miss

Button lay under a silk throw on her parents' bed, one slender finger still caught between the pages of her book.

Mrs Button, said the doctor and, with a little bow, Miss Button. As if he called unexpectedly, Mrs Button hurried about the restricted space of the cabin, turning up the lamp, patting her hair with the back of her hand, tweaking her daughter's finger from her book. His nose filled with floral scents he could only imagine emanated from Miss Button, the doctor made his careful way toward a curlicued rosewood chair beside the bed, his shoe slithering a little on the animal skin. He wondered about the propriety of standing his medical bag on the bed and, in his hesitation, Mrs Button eased herself behind him and into his chair.

Take a seat, please, said Mrs Button over the rustle of her skirts. The doctor looked about the cabin but there was no other chair to be seen. A washstand, a dressing table, Lord help me, a lady's underskirts on a peg. The doctor turned away at once. In the first cabin he thought he remembered several chairs around a card table and had almost resolved to return to Captain Button and request the use of one when Mrs Button patted the quilt with her ringed hand.

You must sit on the bed, Doctor Fowles, said Mrs Button. We're shamefully unprovided. Please don't embarrass us any further on this account. Miss Button lay as before, her book now turned up on the counterpane. In his awkwardness, the doctor read its upside-down title. *The Ruins of Tivoli*. A novel. It was not how the doctor thought Miss Button might have occupied herself. He hardly knew what to think but set himself on the bed with care, his feet not quite reaching the floor, medical bag across his gingerish lap.

On a voyage such as this, we must all live as best we can. Mrs Button clapped with pleasure and showed her lovely neck. From the far cabin, the doctor heard Captain Button's chair creak beneath him.

Although he was too polite to look at his watch, the doctor
thought it must be nearing midday. Mrs Button had talked
a great deal but none of it had any bearing on his patient
who lay behind him, every so often the slight movement of
her leg beneath the throw giving him a most uncommon
sensation. In speaking of the situation they were bound for
in New South Wales, Mrs Button had grown quite morose.

Whatever will become of us, she said now with a gay
laugh but the doctor thought her disappointment more
truthful. After the giddy romp of regimental life, New
South Wales could not seem much to a woman such as Mrs
Button. Buried alive in the back woods of Argyle at her
husband's say-so, no neighbour within four miles, she
would be without her usual amusements and pleasures. The
doctor was at a loss to know how she would employ
herself. Missy would do better, he thought, though she
seemed no less unhappy than her mother at the prospect of
New South Wales. She had youth on her side, a natural
buoyancy of spirits and a pleasing interest in her papa's
welfare.

And what of Miss Button's health? said the doctor, not
quite daring to turn to her himself.

Ah, said her mother. It's nothing particular. I said to the
Captain she could use a tonic. Miss Button looked well,
flourishing he would have said. Her cheek was flushed certainly but there was nothing remarkable about that. She
had her mother's complexion. The doctor took her hand in
his own, warm and the nails a healthy pink. He felt for her
pulse, fancying it quickened to his touch.

Are you sleeping? And eating? Miss Button nodded at
each question, the ringlets at either side of her face nodding
longer. He could not bring himself to ask after her bowels,
not even her stomach. The skin on her wrist was so soft and
white, a blue vein forking beneath the surface, that the
doctor laid her hand aside with reluctance. There was
nothing wrong with her, he felt sure. On the voyage she had

perhaps lost her usual vigour. He opened his bag and removed a wooden stethoscope.

Nothing to take fright at, said the doctor, screwing the two tubes together. A little like the telescope Captain Aitken uses, do you see? I can listen to your heart with this.

My heart, thought Miss Button, knowing that organ to be the seat of her mother's unhappiness. My heart. She felt something lighten inside her chest as she imagined her heart's secrets leaking into Dr Fowles's ear through his wooden tube. The doctor inserted a small cedar and brass cone in one end of the stethoscope and drew aside a corner of Miss Button's silk throw. She was naked beneath. Or only in her chemise. The doctor started up, a hot flush rising to his cheeks. Anxious not to discountenance his patient, he bent his stethoscope to her neck, turning aside his snail eyes with their gross trail of slime. Mrs Button smiled direct in his face, so close he could feel her breath on his skin.

I'll leave you for the moment. Hearing nothing but his own blood bumping frantic in his ear, the doctor took fright when Mrs Button stood and smoothed her skirts.

Madam? said the doctor. It's a routine procedure, I assure you. But she was gone. It was most improper. The doctor drew up the silk throw and pleated it about Miss Button's dimpled chin. Expecting any moment Captain Button, regimental sword drawn, he sat in the chair. He unscrewed and screwed his stethoscope. Miss Button was happy to watch him. She had not been happy for some time, she realised. He mashed the toe of his shoe into the fur rug.

Bear, he said. Bear. Miss Button did not understand the doctor but she felt no alarm. None at all. She found him a most interesting man. He slipped on all fours to the floor and rubbed his cheek on her mother's rug.

Now the bear is an amusing animal, said the doctor, and Miss Button was convinced of it at once.

When the doctor had taken his leave, she lay back on her pillows and listened to his voice murmuring in the forward cabin, her mother's darting about and alighting now and then in the emphatic way she favoured. The doctor had told her the most scintillating story, that was the only word for it. When he was training for a doctor he had met a man, Mr Anderson, who exhibited wonders at county fairs. Once, the doctor had come across him at home off Whitechapel Road with a live bear chained by its front paws to a ceiling beam, in the act of shaving it from head to foot.

You wouldn't have recognised it, said the doctor. No naturalist could have told it for a bear. The beast had such an extraordinary appearance when the operation was complete, its skin smooth as a man's but mottled like dark soap. This poor creature was installed in a sort of sentry box so narrow that it was obliged to stand on its hind legs and, dressed in a mob cap and a woman's finery – here, the doctor had blushed again, remembering the chemise – was towed about the countryside as a pig-faced lady. A pig-faced lady. The very idea gave Miss Button a creeping thrill. She did not know anyone who had been to a fair. When the pig-faced lady became known to everyone, Mr Anderson had dressed the bear in a sort of frock-coat with scarlet trimmings and a fur cap, and toured it across England and Scotland for a further two years as an Ethiopian savage. The doctor had a lovely voice that seemed any moment would tip into laughter. A breathiness too but that was no doubt the consumption. Miss Button could hear him still, talking to her parents in the forward cabin, although she could not make out what he said.

Overheated and excitable, he was saying. Not suitable reading for a girl her age. Then, at the door, taking his leave, the handle of his medical bag in both hands for courage, I will call on her again one morning soon.

The doctor continued in high spirits for the rest of the week. The ship went west of the Cape de Verd islands, a day and a night's sailing. Always a cautious man, the Captain feared a calm that often detained ships taking the shorter eastern passage. The evening lectures had been called off due to the heat, to be resumed when the thermometer sunk to seventy degrees. Some excellent papers had been given, the doctor noting important findings in his journal. After Captain Button, Mr Yate addressed the company on the probable manner in which New Zealand and the southern lands had become peopled, the conclusion of the evening's investigations being that the Islanders have one common origin and were probably Malays from the islands in the Indian Ocean. Mr Armistead gave a narrative of a personal inspection of the coal mines at Whitehaven but the doctor was not aware that he brought forward anything not generally well known and that would not apply to any mine one cared to name. The doctor gave a brief introduction to the study of Zoology which he thought improving but could not properly comment on himself. Mr Taylor gave an excellent description of the sub-sections of a Roman road he had the good fortune to examine near Whittlesea on the estate of a Mr Liddle. Mr Gordon spoke of his native Scotland but as all he had to say might be found in a guidebook the doctor only noted that it was possible to get up Ben Lomond without a guide thus saving oneself the expense and the burden of a trouble-some companion. With the lecture series suspended, the period after tea before the ladies retired to their cabins around nine, was the most delightful of the day, cool and frequently amusing. By his own calculation, the ship would cross the equator by the end of the month and the doctor teased and joked with the young ladies about the line, how it lay across the ocean for miles in either direction and that Mother Carey's chickens and other sea fowl come to lay their eggs upon it. Miss Button laughed behind her hand but would not believe him. The doctor had not seen her look so well. Her eyes shone even in the dark of the night poop deck.

And I suppose we'll see a pig-faced lady sitting on the line with her legs crossed, sir? said Miss Button, which many thought in monstrous taste and not at all like her. Miss Bloomfield and Miss Baker were half-persuaded of the line's existence, especially when Captain Aitken told them there was sometimes a little difficulty in getting a ship over it and that if his men could not heave her across with their handspikes he must fire a gun to summon a pilot on board.

The doctor's calculations were not far wrong. On the last day of March, the captain announced after his noonday observation that, the wind continuing fair, they could expect to cross the line that night, half an hour this side of midnight. As evening drew down, the doctor glued a thread of cotton across the glass of his telescope and called out that the line was finally in sight. One after the other, Arthur Taylor and Alfred Button stood on a wooden case to see and, afterward, stood soberly together and talked of the line and the Southern Cross and icebergs, things that made them feel almost grown and at the same time small as insects. Miss Baker and Miss Bloomfield looked and told each other many times afterward how the line had looked.

Like a dark rope, said Miss Bloomfield.

Exactly like a dark rope, said Miss Baker. Mrs Button asked Dr Fowles to show her daughter.

She doesn't believe in it, you know. Mrs Button arched an eyebrow and showed her two neat dog teeth in a becoming smile.

She's as clever as her mama then, said Armistead, gallant as ever but with a look not altogether friendly. Like many of the other passengers, sitting up to see themselves across the line as if it were the new year, Miss Button was in her evening best. Her shoulders bare and gleaming, the doctor thought she rivalled the moon. Not unwilling, her black satin slippers scuffing quick across the deck, she approached the telescope. His back to Mrs Button's inquisitive gaze – Armistead's surveillance split between that lady and her daughter – the doctor guided Miss Button's eye to the telescope's cold metal ring. At first, she saw nothing, her own lashes pressed too close to the glass but, drawing back a fraction, a magnified world burst in at her, a distant wave rearing close, its tumbled crest catching the last of the light. And some dark twist now visible on the water's surface.

Exactly like a dark rope, she heard Miss Baker say again. The doctor caught hold of her hand and, pretending to make some mechanical adjustment or other, stretched it toward the lens. She remembered the touch of his flat, rough fingers. Her arm was only just long enough for her to keep her eye to the glass and see the obscene pink nubbins of her fingers appear at the other end. The doctor directed her fingertips lightly over the lens, across some small ridge or seam in the glass. He did it again. And again. Until she understood that the line she saw was some device of his making fixed to the end of the telescope. She took her eye from the metal ring and her fingers from the doctor's, both movements a dropping back into ordinariness, the scale and size of a life she already had by heart.

When the ship had pushed forward into true darkness, the sails crackling white overhead, Dr Fowles was prevailed upon to take up his guitar. Resisting at first, Armistead had sent Alfred and Arthur below to fetch it up. The doctor sat and stroked the strings but did not feel like singing. The guitar was a warm weight on his thigh. He was stitched into the kind of happy thoughtfulness he feared a human voice might coarsen. Across from him sat Mrs Button, some story she told climbing and falling in the moon's metal light, the end of her shawl tucked about her daughter. Armistead paced the deck in front of the ladies, a brandy glass in one hand, the other dancing out in some gesture that drew down laughter all around. The doctor felt rocked in some quiet understanding between himself and Miss Button that he did not quite fathom. There had been too much brandy but even regret could get no purchase on him tonight. A rude trumpet sounded and from the forecastle the men's rutting roar. The sailors were welcoming Neptune aboard. Captain Aitken had warned the gentlemen to keep the ladies to the poop and some coins in their pockets if they ventured past the waist themselves.

The men work better if I allow them their sport, he said. The doctor had five shilling pieces in his pocket and thought to look in on the festivities with Armistead once the ladies retired for the night.

On the forecastle, the men were as pickled as Lord Nelson brought home from Trafalgar in his barrel of brandy. At one end of an empty hen coop sat Edwards, sawing out a tune on his fiddle; at the other Lamb with his flute, his deck-stained feet kicking up in a jig while he played. In a half-barrel lashed makeshift to the foremast some ten foot above the deck, Yate stood alongside Mr Denison, his narrow face bent to the mummery below. That morning, Mr Denison had come to Yate's cabin and, standing in his doorway on one diffident leg, invited him to observe the men's celebrations.

As my guest, Mr Denison had said. Yate accepted at once, his curiosity about the ceremonies of sea life a small part of his interest in men's lives everywhere and the eventual possibility of their being brought to God. Edwards and Lamb put their heads together over the coop and set to, more lively. In a giddy circle, bedmates Patrick Kelly and James Lyne whirled, one hand at each other's waist, the other flung overhead on the curve of an arm, Kelly making some fancy work with his feet and, two beats slow, Lyne following suit. The men clapped out the time and drummed their heels on the deck, those that were sitting. Parker danced in just his trousers, his arms twisting slow above his head, his belly swagged over his belt, breasts shaking with each step, until his wife snorted porter out her nose, the only woman present.

A rough shout from the men at the far end of the forecastle, the flute played on three lonely notes. Neptune and his queen appeared in view, dragged on a gun carriage, waving to their subjects on either side.

Here comes the old man himself, said Mr Denison. With a swab suspended from his chin for a beard and two mops as his wig, Neptune took up his position beside a large bath that the men had been filling all afternoon. From the pallor of his skin and the way he was content to let the strands of mop fall across one eye, Yate picked him for the Finn. His wife was less easy to tell, done up in Miss Bloomfield's cap which was certainly not come by in any honest manner. At the sight of the third mate strung up on the mast, Neptune nodded his head and raised his trident to him. It was just as Yate had expected: Mr Denison commanded the respect of his men. He noted the easy way in which his companion returned the courtesy: a shouted laugh and a flourish of his bottle. Mr Denison had provided the two of them with a supply of port wine, a bottle of which he raised to his lips from time to time, his Adam's apple shuddering the length of his throat. Yate had taken only a few sips, out of politeness and a desire to participate, but already knew himself intoxicated by the gleaming nearness of the man.

Behind Neptune came his attendants: a barber, a parson, a bear and his keeper. The bear was the cook togged out in the skin of a sheep the cabin had enjoyed one dinner, still in sight of England. Yate considered the bear unsuccessful. With his black face and the wool curling white, he looked

more a sheep than anything, and his keeper – one of the
Lascars – put Yate in mind of a monkey he had seen
brought ashore once at the Bay of Islands. He didn't get a
proper look at the barber with his tar pot since his eye went
first to the parson and shied away at once in a heated confusion. The men were laughing, one of them wiping his
eyes with the back of his hand, and lifting their blown faces
to look at him where he stood trapped in his barrel at the
foremast. With his wet hair combed back from his forehead
as Yate wore his, a sailor's canvas coat tarred up to look
like his dark suit jacket and a scrap of cotton as a neckcloth
worn in the mailcoach style favoured by Yate, the parson
bent to the men as he passed, his asides mercifully carried
from Yate's hearing on the rough waves of laughter they
effected. Yate was not able to look at Mr Denison although,
several times, he felt his elbow at his ribs. It was Deck he
saw at last, Dick Deck, the man Dr Fowles thought should
have been promoted to officer on the departure of Mr
Bennett and Mr Cat. He was quite disguised beneath round
eyeglasses of twisted wire. Mr Denison waved his bottle
again in salute. Finding it close on empty, he drained it and
lofted it over the gunwales into the sea.

You must excuse them, Mr Yate, he said, on seeing his
guest's discomfort. They're a rough lot but good. Mr
Denison looked at him plain, as one man to another, and
Yate felt himself cleansed in the pale blue of his regard.
Though it might have seemed blasphemous, he knew, it recollected for him the eye of God against which no device is
protection.

A lusty shout bloomed purple and red from the deck,
unwrapping its weighted petals about Yate, who turned
from Mr Denison to look over the barrel edge as if upon
another world. Neptune had a large book open and read
from it the name James Lyne.

James Lyne, repeated the parson and James Lyne,
shouted the men, until it seemed the very wind in the sails

had it. Lyne was fetched up by the parson and sat on a board across the bath with a blindfold across his eyes. He looked a small boy suddenly and straight sober.

Have you ever crossed the line before?

I haven't, sir. James Lyne tilted his blindfolded face this way and that for a chip of light, fear screwing his mouth down at the corners.

What will you give to lighten your punishment?

I didn't know – I hadn't thought. Listen – he cocked his head like a blind man whose ear must stand for his eye – would you like a bottle of porter?

A bottle of porter? Can't you do better than that? The barber made a great business of stirring the vile contents of his bucket, the filth from the bottom of the pigsty made liquid with the addition of tar.

Two bottles of porter, said James Lyne in a quiet voice.

Done, said Neptune. To one side, Patrick Kelly was already being prepared by the parson. The barber stepped up – Yate recognised Staines from his barrel-hooped legs – and slapped each of James Lyne's cheeks with a paintbrush daubed in the mess from his bucket, scraped it off so keenly with a well-notched rusty iron he carried as a razor that he fetched blood from his chin, and tipped the young man backwards by the heels into the bath where Lyne was ducked a couple of times by the bear and the bearkeeper. By the time Lyne had pulled away his blindfold and blown the water from his nose, touched his chin with cautious fingers, his friend Kelly was already on the board, pledging three bottles of porter in a cockier voice than he himself had managed.

Samuel Parker, said Neptune, consulting his book once more.

Samuel Parker, said the parson. Parker was fallen across his wife's lap but roused to his own name and was up, clamouring.

Samuel Parker, he shouted. He's here. Who wants him?
He shuffled forward like a boxer, fumbling his own feet and
catching himself before he fell. The men roared at the night
sky.

Samuel Parker, shouted some. Others, Who wants him?
Have you ever visited Neptune's domain before?

Have I? Parker was enjoying himself, playing to his wife
as ever. I've crossed the line that many times Neptune's
dizzy looking at me.

Travel safe, friend. James Lyne was feeling better with
Kelly beside him again, two blooded boys, their clothes
drying on their backs and a lick of gin prinkling the sweat
out of them. Mr Bedgood was called and scraped something terrible for refusing to give over any coin where old
Mr Davidson paid up five shillings and a bottle of brandy
and got off without any tar or even water. Yate was also in
better spirits since he had decided Deck's performance was
something of a tribute to him.

I'm pleased you thought to invite me. He was anxious
that Mr Denison not think him ungrateful. His mug was
unaccountably empty and, if he moved his head too quick,
the hot sounds of the deck below smeared together as
coloured lights.

Next time, I'll be your guest at a festival of your South Sea
Islanders. Mr Denison looked unchanged, his face alert, his
eye steady as if he stood his turn at the helm. What it might
be to sail true under that hand, Yate wondered before some
baying below drew his eye down incautiously and he felt his
head reel, the world tip and spin on the foremast's axle.

The cry was up for Samuel Hall and John Clerk, then,
John Clerk being brought to the bath, for Samuel Hall alone.

Samuel Hall, said Neptune, one finger to his book.

Samuel Hall, said the parson, going all about the men on
deck and even looking through the forecastle, but nothing.
Samuel Hall. Samuel Hall. Yate's head rung with the calling
of that name. No one called louder than Staines, his barber's

brush flicking gouts of muck among the men, some of whom grumbled when he was not looking their way.

Hall, shouted Staines in his gravelly voice. He had got himself up on rumfustian – rum and gunpowder, a pirate's drink – and though he might any moment fall dead to the deck until morning, he was ridden for now by a drunkard's single purpose. Some of the men looked out Hall beneath their own feet and behind the man next to them. They called on Lamb and Edwards for another round of music. On fresh intelligence, the parson went to search the galley. At every footfall, Staines looked so keen over his shoulder that poor Clerk, who had nothing at all to give, got off light with not much more than a dab of tar and a touch of the razor before being given, heels over head, to the bear.

Patrick Kelly and James Lyne stared about the circle of men's faces, mottled with drink and the puckered moonlight coming off the sail. They had no idea which sailor was Hall.

He's the one not here, said Kelly.

Easy to say, said Lyne, though it had taken Kelly some calculation. They went to look for him together because they had crossed the line together. They were men now. Lyne, who was simple and kind, had not forgotten how fearful he had been on the board, eyes covered, or how cowed, with the blood dribbling on his chin, but from this side he remembered it as a benediction of sorts, the rough blessing that men can bring down for each other. Kelly was singing and poking about the ropes as if looking were more his thing than finding. Lyne stood in the waist, thought on where he would hide, then straight to the chicken coop, crouching, and stared between the slats at Hall's wide eye. Later, when he thought over all that had happened, and even later yet when he was off the ship, a grown man with land his own, he remembered that silent eye. It had seemed an animal's eye, dumb but trusting in that way some beasts can call out a man's mercy. He had looked into it a stretched minute. Then he shouted for Kelly.

I've found him, called Lyne, and not unkindly.

The chickens were unsettled and trampled each other in their haste to put some distance between them and the new intruders but Hall came easily, slid out of the coop by the armpits. His clothes, even his skin where exposed at the knees and neck, were crusted with effluvium from the bottom of the henhouse and some downy white feathers through his hair made him look, thought Lyne, fresh hatched. He could not look at either of them but stared at his own feet as he was walked forward to the forecastle. The men had heard Lyne's shout and were got up again in rowdiness. Staines ran here and there on his beggary legs, forward to agitate the men, back to check that Hall was still being brought up. He was in such a state of savagery when Hall saw him, his shiny face a melt of sweat, that the boy shrank back fearful and was only glad for the parson's blindfold. With his eyes bound tight and his hands tied behind his back, Hall was processed about the deck, Staines leading the way in some elemental dance, Kelly and Lyne assisting on either side since no one told them not to. A length of rope had been tied to the base of the foremast and stretched tight at Staines's instruction who danced over it, Lyne and Kelly stepping across unthinking and with gentle hands picking up their charge who stumbled and fell heavy to the deck. There was a mewling whimper when they bent to right the boy.

It will be better when it's over, said Lyne, hot in Hall's ear. He had grown to like the young sailor.

They walked on, the fiddle lowing, the men banging the deck and shouting Samuel Hall, Samuel Hall, as if the two words had yet to give up their magic. The rope was somehow before them again and Hall was down, then up, spitting a scrap of tooth, a little blood welling from a splintery graze on one cheek. Lyne and Kelly looked at each other and could not walk Hall any more. He was taken from them by the parson, who held Staines off with one stiff arm, and put on the board over the bath. Yate could see the bear had one black paw to Neptune's shoulder for his attention.

They're rough on the boy, he said. It was an evident fact but hung in the air like a question. Mr Denison bit his lip, watching.

Have you ever crossed the line before? But for Staines, who still shouted and rampled, his breath coming short and hard, the forecastle was silent. The men watched the boy on the board, as still and quiet as if they sat at a Sunday service on the quarterdeck, bothered by the half-thoughts that tumbled and bumped inside their heads like summer blowflies. Their hearts went out to the boy but they would as soon have torn him to pieces and not known the difference.

Have you ever crossed the line before? A shake of the head, the smallest movement that might have been a shiver.

What'll you give to lighten your punishment? Hall sat absorbed in the dark world of his own body where there was no future, only past. He had lost half a tooth and his tongue went now to the rough siding that remained, the unfamiliar gap.

What can you give, Sam? Still Hall said nothing for he had nothing. He was a ship's boy and had the clothes on his back, a hat and a jacket in his kit. He had a whale tooth the cook had given him and a silver button. Everyone knew what he had. He had nothing.

Neptune conferred with the bear a minute but Staines had the captain's speaking trumpet somehow – the men showed their wolf teeth when they saw that instrument of the quarterdeck on the forecastle – and jammed it tight in Hall's mouth.

Speak out, said Staines in his rough voice. What ull you give?

My whale's tooth, said Hall or would have but Staines tipped a bucket of bilge-water down the trumpet at his first word and held him by his twisted shirtfront so he could not fall away as he coughed up his lung.

He's drowning, said Yate to Mr Denison. Then louder to the men, I will give one pound for the boy to cross the line safe.

Done, said Neptune.

Not done, crowed Staines. Men, come, let's ask our guest down to join us. He turned up his great face, whiskered white at the chops, to Yate and addressed him direct. You're sittin' aloft with your poop-deck face on but come down, come down. Stand as parson for the boy if you're so keen on him.

Stay, said Mr Denison, staring down on Staines but Yate already had his leg swung over the barrel's side. He had broken the tapu of the natives preparing a new net at Rangihoua and would not be frightened by an English sailor. Besides, two mugs of port wine burned in his belly and, unable to look on Mr Denison at such close quarters, he would make the man look at him.

The deck was a different place when not seen from above, alive and laid out to no pattern. His human height no protection, Yate elevated himself in speech and took the forecastle for a pulpit. *Examine yourselves, whether you are in the faith; prove your own selves*.

Men, said Yate, examine yourselves.

Zamine yournself, said Staines raising a laugh.

Look into your hearts and see the canker there, the rotten pulpy spot you hide from your fellows. Think of the worst thing you have ever done, the secret thing, the thing you would undo if only you could. Think of it. The men shuffled uneasily together like cattle before a storm. Unwilling, they thought. They were one man and slept together with their heads all pointing in the same direction. Of their singularness, the gauzy privacies that held them apart, they did not like to be reminded.

Think of your most evil deed. Are you thinking of it?
Each man touched his secret scab, shifty-faced.

I have done worse, said Yate. A collective breath went up
from the men like a prayer. He had thought to tell how he
lived in the shadow of the Cross, corrupt as he was, but
there was no need. The men were broken already. Staines
had fallen to the planking, his head rolling like a thirty-two
pound ball in the mess from his upturned bucket. Yate
could not bring himself to look at Mr Denison in their
crow's nest so looked instead at Hall, who sat unmoving
over the bath like Justice in her blindfold. One eye pushed
shut by his swollen cheek, Hall waited, swallowing the
metallic blood from his broken tooth. Yate dipped his
finger in the tar, drew a line on Hall's forehead. He took
the boy's scuffed feet in his hands, the hard whorled skin
on the soles, the dirt under the nails, and tipped him back
into the arms of the cook who made off with him at once,
dry and held tight to his chest, his dark brow pulled low,
the most like a bear Yate had seen him.

Dr Fowles and Armistead made the forecastle at last. The
party on the poop had run long, the ladies retiring late, later
it seemed than the men who were all below already or
sleeping where they fell, their cheeks seamed in the morning
by the roundings of the rope. Like ghosts of themselves, the
chickens had got out of the coop and were roosting where
they could. Armistead would not handle them but the
doctor made his rounds, swinging them by their scaled feet,
their beaks open in fright at the dark and the ship upside
down. He was standing like that, his hands lost in the feathered lightness of white wings, when he saw the cook come
by in sheep's clothing, one of the young sailors fainted away
in his arms. They passed without a word, leaving the doctor
to watch the man's spraddled footprints dry on the deck.

Every bee was dead. Their striped bodies lay lustreless at the bottom of the glass hive, the delicate joinery of their hinged legs still discernible, their once-glistening wings bent and broken. It was an unhappy sight. Yate had often imagined the bees' whiffling homeward flight, their legs saddled with pollen from the flowers around Waimate. He would perhaps be riding home from a neighbouring village with a couple of his boys, the bees streaming overhead, copper and black in the last light of the day, the late summer air riotous with their honeyed life. He could have wept. It was a sin of pride, he knew, but he had wanted to be remembered as the man who brought bees to New Zealand. In 1814, the Reverend Samuel Marsden had brought a stallion and two mares to the Bay of Islands along with a small herd of breeding cattle, the gift of the Governor of New South Wales. Yate's own horse, Selim, came from that bloodline. As the Reverend's guest when he first arrived in New South Wales, Yate heard the story of the horses being landed on Christmas Eve and the New Zealanders' amazement when he had ridden one of the beasts the length of the beach opposite Rangihoua. More than a dozen years later, the old man still took an energetic pride in that livestock.

They hadn't seen anything bigger than a pig, do you see? Marsden said, his bibulous countenance presiding over the Saturday dinner at the Parramatta parsonage. Yate was a little unnerved by his host. Marsden's face was florid, although he professed to find water the most refreshing liquor, and his neckcloth was tied like a tourniquet.

When the cattle barged among them, they scattered like hogs on ice. Marsden's family had heard the story before although the youngest daughter, Martha, laughed into her pocket handkerchief at the thought of a hog on ice, drawing Yate's wink, his own smile hidden behind his napkin. There was to be dancing after dinner. Martha had told him so. The floor covering had been taken up in the drawing room and, Mrs Robert Campbell on the piano, Yate danced – awkward and trip-footed – with each of the Marsden girls, passing his partner on to Mr Campbell or Mr Palmer at the conclusion of each set: Miss Elizabeth Marsden, spinsterish and named for her mother; Miss Mary Marsden, a waft of violet dusting powder; Miss Martha Marsden slim as a boy with a warm, muscled hand. Her right side afflicted by a paralytic stroke, Mrs Marsden took her seat against the wall, her brick-faced husband standing alongside, his foot tapping out his impatience. Marsden had Yate by the elbow the instant the dancing was done.

I sent the Poll Suffolk bull out from England myself, he said, before Yate had caught his breath, the twank of the piano and scuff of feet still hanging in the air. And persuaded the officers of the 73rd Regiment to sell me their thoroughbred cow.

If a barrel-chested bull could stand as emblem for the ruddy magistrate and principal chaplain then Yate had supposed a bee might be his own modest monument. A doubly appropriate symbol since to his mind the diligent bee also described the industriousness of the New Zealanders. Unlike the Islanders, whose laziness had been widely lamented in missionary reports, the natives of New Zealand didn't shy away from hard work. Yate had written as much in his book. He supposed it was due to the climate where nothing grew unhusbanded. Nine months in the year, the New Zealanders were employed in their grounds, tending and cultivating, harvesting and planting. There was no

effeminacy about them. Graceful in the extreme, any one of
them might be put in evening dress and, tattoos aside, stand
unremarked in a gentleman's club in London. So Yate's
thoughts took wing, tumbling over one thing, alighting
on another, Miss Martha Marsden, prick-eared Selim, the
kumara grounds, returning at last to the hive, as the evening
bee.

Hunkered on his heels, Yate saw his skull of a face reflected
long and white in the glass of the hive. His desiccated
fancies lay among the bees, a two-inch drift of deadness
that once had quickened with insect expectation. He saw he
was a proud man that needed humbling. He counted
himself as God's servant – all his work, His work – but
under that guise was guilty of promoting his own earthly
satisfaction. Better to be forthrightly bad – to drink and
take the Lord's name as a curse, to covet another man's
belongings, to give up prayer – than to smuggle evil in your
heart disguised as piety.

I am a prideful man, Yate said to himself but even the
remonstration carried with it something of a boast. He
knew he was prey to a persistent conceit that needed
grubbing out yet his self-admiration was so bound to his
Christian labours that at times it was difficult to tell the
one from the other. It wasn't possible for him to know, for
example, whether he served foremost his vanity or God
when, against instructions from the parent committee, he
solicited subscriptions for the church at Waimate, all dona-
tions to be labelled *Mr Yate's Church*. Or whether, as a
young man having finished his apprenticeship as a grocer,
his travelling to London to train as a missionary was the
result of a divine calling or the desire not to be his father
and grow old in the mean limits of Shropshire. Even now,
he sensed in himself an arrogant gratification in posing the
problem, in putting it first this way, then that, as if his sal-

vation could be secured through argument and sophistry. Evil seizes the heart and blasts it as the mummified apple hangs on its branch through winter.

The glass hive for which Yate had held such high hope seemed to him now an admonishment, a reminder of his susceptibility to the sin of pride, the promise of its vitreous architecture come to nothing in the smudge of dead bees. For a moment, he was shamed, deeply shamed, and thought to drop the elaborate folly overboard and be done with it. It would be invisible in the clear sea, sinking unseen, end over end, its seams forced by rills of water, the bees in flight one last time on unfamiliar currents.

Let it stand as a lesson to me, he thought, relaxing the muscles that had clenched with the imagined effort of heaving the apparatus from the deck. Many things were lessons to him. One more or less could make little difference. At times the world itself seemed laid out for his instruction and improvement and he, making his way, failing but penitent. The hive was too complicated a figure for a sermon, although the mummified apple was good. He could use that.

Dr Fowles had been very taken by the hive, its scientific camber and its sheer glassiness. One evening before the gentlemen retired from the cuddy, he had asked Yate whether there was suitable sustenance for bees in New Zealand.

There are plenty of castor oil plants about.

And are their flowers known to be fit for the feeding of bees? It was a question Yate had not considered. He had believed, as Dr Watts had written, that the bee *Gathers honey all the day/ From every opening flower*. The doctor was inclined to think his colleague more poetic than scientific on the question of bees and they had enjoyed a very amiable conversation on the subject. Perhaps, thought

Yate, Mr Marsden might permit me to take a small number of his Brazilian honey-bees for propagation purposes. It would be a suitable atonement to be the agent whereby that man introduced yet another species to New Zealand. He shook his head over the striated corpses. His heart had been set on the English bee.

Undoubtedly, it had been too hot for the bees. Mr Taylor told him the temperature had reached eighty-eight degrees in his family's cabin these last nights. Though he kept the hive in shade as much as possible and wrapped in wet sacking for the hottest part of the day, the bees had been overwhelmed by the pervasive heat. The rest of the livestock was doing little better. All the hares but one were dead. Most of them had weakened little by little in their cage and one poor unfortunate had leapt overboard and swum in sight for several minutes. Yate had never before seen a hare swim. He was unsure whether this was a natural skill or a desperate undertaking. Low in the water like a dog the hare had made its way, its white-mittened paws wheeling in front, ears cast back on its shoulders, the wet knuckle of its head a freakish sight on the crest of a wave. It had struck out from the ship and made some thirty yards before it was seen no more, sunk or pulled by fishes beneath the water's surface. The one remaining hare turned its back on Yate. He had thought to keep them caged at Waimate until they littered and could be released into the bush to breed at large. One hare was not much use to him. He would ask the steward to put it in a pie for tea.

Dr Fowles had taken three dozen of the poultry under his particular protection. He kept their water bins filled, had been chopping a little garlic through their corn and feeding them the scraps from the cabin table that the steward's boys were accustomed to scrape overboard. The sickly birds he transferred to what he called the hospital from which the cook could make his selection. No eggs had been laid during the voyage except for one that the cook called a cock's egg, misshapen and full of blood. It was as if the ark had been captained by Job, not Noah. Pestilence or perhaps a pining for land had diminished the animals' number in plague proportion. Only the pigs and the goats proved sound at sea. Yate could hear the surviving sheep panting in the longboat, their rasping breath a considerable distraction in the hot still of the morning.

The ship had been becalmed the last two days, what little wind there was dying away to nothing. An uncommon thunder of rain drilled the decks for a half-hour and then the breeze, slight and inconstant, fell off entirely, leaving the ship to put her bow this way and that as she turned listless in the water. Already, the sea was littered all round with the ship's floating rubbish, a skim of ash from the galley fire and lumps of human ordure that jiggled in shameful view, nibbled by fish in the poppling water. The sails hung slack and the sun pressed heavy as a coin on a dead man's eye. Not a breath discomposed the water's surface. The heat below nearly insupportable, the passengers were all on deck, the cabin class beneath the poop awning, steerage wherever they could take their relief.

Shark alongside! Mr Denison gave the call and everyone, even the captain, was moved to look. Any novelty is a welcome amusement on a ship but when the vessel is held back for hours, days, and lies inert on a lifeless sea, then all on board contract her sluggishness and feel themselves becalmed in endless day. One hand and foot to the shrouds, Mr Denison swung lazy back and forth, amusement enough for Yate as he waited until the crowd at the stern thinned. He was a handsome man – graceful, with a marine eye – and Yate thought he would pick him for a seaman even if they met on shore.

There were five sharks, close below the rudder, deep but

the water so transparent that their size and number, the
very shape of their eyes, were easily made out. Marled grey,
the sharks were not more than three foot in length.

They are young sharks, surely? Mrs Button's question
was directed at the captain but she had contrived to stand
so close behind Mr Armistead at the taffrails that he felt at
his back the firm pressure of what he thought might be her
breast. Or her elbow, he said to himself, though he did not
believe it. Ears aflame, the front of his trousers bunted out
like a full mainsail, he made himself think cooling thoughts.
The principles of long division. Captain Button, war hero,
at the rail not three yards away.

Yes, quite young, said the captain. But with a full com-
plement of teeth. Mrs Button showed the captain hers. He
enjoyed Mrs Button exceedingly and would have had her
kind on every voyage if it had been in his power. However
dispiriting the circumstances, she had a talent for pulling
together a society about her.

Swimming around and between the sharks quite unmo-
lested were some small fish about the size of perch but
striped black and white around the body. The doctor had
never seen them before although he had read of such and
their companionate relation to the shark.

Why do the sharks not eat the little fish? It was Mrs
Button again. Armistead could feel her no longer but even
her voice fell on him as a warm weight. He did not permit
himself to turn but kept his eye on the sharks, circling grim-
mouthed beneath the rudder.

Those little fish are pilot fish. The captain was at his best
explaining things to a woman. A man other men could find
abrasive, he was universally liked by women.

They guide the shark to its prey and are allowed the
pickings. Mrs Button watched a minute longer before
returning to the poop deck, her attendants – Captain
Aitken, Mr Armistead, even her husband, and the two
Taylor boys with her son, Alfred – following in her wake.

The sharks swam slow and sparing of motion, tails beating from side to side, the muscular movement rippling up their bodies to their pointed heads, while the pilot fish passed under and over, quick darts of fearless light.

The doctor did not think the fish led the sharks to food, a supposition soon confirmed when Mr Denison ordered the cabin boys to throw over the side some chunks of salt beef which were mouthed down by the sharks without any assistance on the part of their pilots. Perhaps they live on the excrement of the shark, he thought, turning over the happy problem in his mind. Or are hatched in the shark's intestines as the gadfly is in the horse. The doctor had bathed that morning in his trousers and shirtsleeves in a tub of rainwater collected on deck and felt fresher for it. He was getting about in what he thought of as his sailor's suit – no stockings or shoes, thin linen trousers, a shirt open at the throat with a black Barcelona tied in a loose knot and, when on deck, a broad straw hat. The heat was little bother to him, his cough greatly improved. He would have liked to study the pilot fish a little longer but he had a round of patients to visit: Mrs Davidson was reported ill, Mrs Taylor had fainted several times in the heat and become quite feeble, Miss Bloomfield had a tooth that needed his attention and Mrs Button had asked him to call on Miss Button after dinner if he had the time.

Yate was a little giddy from the sun and the effort of looking up at Mr Denison against the bright sky.

Have you fished for shark before? Mr Denison came down from the shrouds, one hand to Yate's shoulder as he jumped to the deck. Yate had not previously been much interested in shipboard fishing although it seemed a commendable pastime now. Mr Denison squatted to some tackle on the deck, a stout line thicker than a man's finger, a chain and swivel and two hooks, a foot and a half in length.

We'll have one of them on board before the captain shoots the sun, said Mr Denison, the hooks an insinuating weight in his hands. He was something like the sun, the third mate, and couldn't be looked at directly. Yate took up one of the pieces of salt beef, harder than he'd expected, like a piece of cured leather, and worked it onto the hook that Mr Denison held. Against the ironmongery and Mr Denison's square, weathered hands, his own seemed insubstantial, as girlish as his sister's. He shivered and the hair on his arms stood widdershins as he thought how his hand would look pierced through with the shark hook.

A goose on your grave, said Mr Denison. And when Yate looked blank: That's what my mother says for a warm shiver. He stood, smiling, a hook in each hand, checking the balance of the line. Yate had a feeling, a not quite godly feeling, that he had lived this moment before. He couldn't place it but it felt familiar all the same. The queer stillness, the same thick glaze of light, the figure of a man before him on the verge of some inconsequential action. He couldn't go any further, couldn't say what might happen next or when the sense of repetition might fall away but it seemed he had lived this before. Mr Denison, tall at the ship's stern, was spliced to the present moment. The length of rope coiled easy in one hand, he whirled the two hooks in a tight circle above his head, paying out some slack as the weight of the meat swung them wide, and then let them go, shining like harpoons, arcing across the sky to fall to the water some twenty feet distant. He put the line in Yate's hand and looped it once about the stern-post.

Now you're fishing, he said.

With the line in his hand, Yate was transformed. Mr Denison leaned on the rail, his crinkle-eyed face to Yate who kept a close watch on the rope, the dark length rising from the water, spangled with brilliant drops, as the ship lifted in the imperceptible swell. He knew he was watched from the poop deck and even from the spanker-boom, where half-a-dozen men sat aloft, eager for amusement. The sun on his head, the weight of the hooks and meat on the end of the rope and, more than that, the live weight of the water, Yate felt himself concentrated in a prayerful way. He dared a look at Mr Denison, damp curls and cheek pinked in the heat, and just beyond him Arthur Taylor and Alfred Button, come off the poop to dangle overboard a string and a bent penny-nail, sweet-talked from Busby.

My papa had a man come to his house, said Alfred Button, since Arthur was holding the string and not letting him have even the end of it. He had a fish to sell that was so big it had a shoe in its stomach when he caught it. Arthur could see over the rail but not close enough to the ship where his nail dangled with its ball of bread. He looked at Alfred consideringly.

Was it a whale? he said but Alfred had gone to fetch a crate. They stood on it and shared the string, pulling it and watching the bread jerk in the water.

I used to fish like that with my brother, said Mr Denison. Off the bridge with a mealybug for bait. He had a reeling way of talking, the words running through him easily. Yate liked to think of him as a scab-kneed village boy.

My mother used not to give us bread because we ate it before we got near the river. Tiddlers was all we caught. Enough to feed the cat. Yate pulled the rope in until it was wet in his hand, the hooks dangling their temptation just shy of the sharks' nosing grey passage. One shark broke from the others and, white belly to the sky, passed beneath the bait, bumping it, mouth open but not getting a purchase. The tremor passed up the line to Yate's hands and arms as the shark turned wide, eye visible once more, a flicker of pilot fish at his tail. Yate had the foolish thought that the shark had felt his soft-skinned weight and animal presence at the end of the line. He looked to Mr Denison.

Buttons, the cat, said Mr Denison. Yes, he was Buttons. He gave a shouting laugh and elbowed Alfred nearly off his crate, joking or not Yate couldn't tell. We'd put them on a string, any sprats we caught, and swim them, you know, across the yard or the kitchen if we could get away with it and him pouncing and pretending not to care and pouncing again. The shark looped back, a little quicker in the water, took the salt beef in his teeth and ran the line out.

Mr Denison, said Yate, the men whooping on the spanker-boom. He wanted to hand the line back but Denison only let the slack run through his hand as it spooled up from the coil at their feet.

You're doing fine, he said. Give him a pull. Yate pulled and felt the rope burn across his palm.

If he won't check, said Mr Denison, let him play. You're doing fine, and for a moment adjusting the line he rested the top of his head against Yate's ear. A tang of sweat, a ropy mildewed smell, and something else Yate could not place so that his heart ran out with the line, singing off the stern-post, run through and mad with tenderness.

Arthur Taylor and Alfred Button stared pop-eyed into the sea, their own string forgotten in their fingers. They could not see the shark at this distance but the rope gigged and shuddered which was nearly as good.

Almost out of rope, said Mr Denison, dropping another restraining loop around the stern-post. Let's try and stop him at the count of three. Yate had almost forgotten there was a fish on the line so much did it feel as if some incandescence was uncoiling from his chest and springing, sharp and bright, through the water.

One, two, three. They both leaned back on the rope, Yate skinning his knuckles on the taffrail, Mr Denison, head back, laughing at the sky. The line slowed, ran again, slowed and slackened.

Bring him in, said Mr Denison and Yate hauled on his own, arm over arm, until the slight grey form could be seen, head jerking from side to side like a dog with a rat. His arms ached but he asked for no help. Mr Denison coiling the wet rope on the deck as it came up, pulled until the shark was just off the stern, beating the water white with his tail. Untroubled, the other sharks continued their leisurely circuits beneath the rudder. Arthur Taylor and Alfred Button were whispering to each other.

He's bigger than Basil, said Arthur.

He's got blood in his mouth. They would remember this forever. The shark was heavy and heavier again out of the water, a trickle of black blood, clagged as treacle, running down its belly from its mouth. It thrashed and belted the ship, then the line was light in Yate's hand and the shark had fallen away, bait gone, the hook swinging empty.

A good fight, said Mr Denison, seeing Yate's face stretch in anguish. The shark flipped its tail in the sun and swam away slow, the water about his head furzy with blood.

Shar-ark! It was Edwards from the spanker-boom. A big one, sir. Off to starboard, coming quick. Mr Denison rebaited one hook, checked the other, and threw them out in a whirling curve that barely hit the water before being taken and run out, the rope screaming on the stern-post, a blue wisp of smoke coming off the wood. The men were down at once, Edwards, Piggott, the Finn, even young Hall with a hatful of water to throw on the line where it burned.

Tally on, men, called Mr Denison, and they caught hold of the rope's end, bracing their feet against the sides, and pulled until the veins stood out in their foreheads. The captain sent a few more men aft, Bombay and Madras, bare-chested and unaccountably in skirts that Mr Taylor hardly thought proper before the ladies, Thomas Lamb and, last and slow, the cook, wiping his head with a rag and muttering. Soon the shark was in sight, sawing up the water this side and that. Armistead made it out at twice, three times the length of the first.

He's twenty feet if he's an inch, said the captain although it was closer to six. Mrs Button gave a delightful scream for which he forgave himself the exaggeration. The men had thrown up a block and were hauling hard. A smile for Sarah and a secret display of his rope-razed hand, Yate was back on the poop when the monster was lifted. The shark got his jaws around the railing, taking a piece of the timber with him to the deck where he floundered, the men jumping shy of his clacking teeth, until, like a woodcut dragon slayer, Mr Denison finished him with a boat-hook through the gills. It was only Alfred and Arthur that saw the first smaller shark attacked by his fellows, mouthing the blood that clouded his head, then taking gobbets from him until the water smoked red and he was dead, the ravaged capsule of his belly seen last, sinking from sight. The bread pellet was gone from their nail when they brought it up.

I reckon a shark took it. Arthur looked crafty at Alfred.

They ate him up, said Alfred. Like cannonballs.

That night, after the ladies and missionaries retired, Fowles, Armistead and Gordon convened on the poop over a bottle of brandy. The ship still making no way, it was yet too warm and close to go below. Armistead told of the landing of the shark, which adventure the doctor was sorry to have missed. Mrs Button was still very excitable when he had called on her daughter after lunch.

The biggest the captain's ever seen, she said. Quite a man-eater. Even Captain Button was uncharacteristically animated by the event, caroming off the sideboard in his crowded cabin as he showed the doctor how the shark had thrashed the deck before being subdued.

Papa, said Miss Button, covering her ears with her pretty hands. She had grown quite bold where Dr Fowles was concerned. Her right elbow was a little stiff – her mother worked it professionally for the doctor while Miss Button moued and ground her comely teeth. Some furuncle on the joint, he imagined. There was no real treatment for it. Either it would heal by itself or it would worsen, rising to the surface where he could treat it by lancing. Still, since no doctor is ever given credit for an ailment that mends itself, he prescribed a barley-water tonic to be taken morning and night.

Dr Fowles was more concerned with Mrs Davidson. She had taken to her bed with headache and fever, and her husband said he had never seen her took so bad. Hot and dry to touch, she complained of weariness.

That bone-tired, said Mrs Davidson. Never known the like. The doctor feared typhus, so dreaded in ships, but said nothing of that, hoping it was no worse than a diary fever that would pass off tomorrow. The very air in steerage was moist and unhealthy, a miasmic atmosphere that could run a contagion through the ship in twenty-four hours. Dr Fowles turned Mrs Davidson's hands over in his own and peered at her face in the dim light but there was no sign of any red spotting. He would have liked to make a full examination but felt inhibited by the presence of the older man.

Has your wife any smuts coming up on her skin anywhere? said the doctor. On her legs or back? Or stomach?

I'm sure I wouldn't know, Doctor, said Mr Davidson. He had taken some obscure offence. The doctor administered some antimonial wine with a rhubarb cathartic and promised to call tomorrow, early.

Now he poured himself a further medicinal measure of brandy and put up his feet, enjoying still the sensation of bare legs. Armistead was describing the contents of the shark's stomach, mostly salt beef it seemed.

I'd like a look at that cadaver, said the doctor, giving his brandy glass an idle swirl.

You'll be lucky then, said Armistead. The sailors ate him for dinner and they look hungry enough to have boiled down the bones. These days the doctor noticed Armistead did not miss a chance to needle him.

They might have given you a slice, said Armistead, if you hadn't been below helping yourself to a piece of Miss Button. He slapped his thigh and gave a yelping laugh. Gordon and I've been waiting all day to hear whether you got a finger in that buttonhole. Hearing his name, Gordon sat up with a gormless smile. He had been hanging his head back, star-gazing. The two men looked at him, their eyes wet and shiny with liquor. Dr Fowles had cause again to regret that if their conversation grew more lively and wide-ranging after the ladies retired for the night, it never gained in delicacy.

I called on the Buttons after dinner, he said with some stiffness. You will be pleased to know that Miss Button's is a slight complaint.

Seeing this would barely hold them, he threw them Miss Bloomfield instead. The qualifications of that young woman often furnished them with a subject of amusing conversation. Of enormous height, coarsely dressed and with slovenly if not dirty hair, Miss Bloomfield had yet another peculiarity, better unmentioned, which the three men had frequently discussed to their mutual hilarity. Her very name was a joke among them and Gordon gave a bark of anticipation. The doctor had been called by Miss Bloomfield that morning to see whether he could stop a decayed tooth for her as he had recently for Miss Yate.

She had such a quantity of hung beef about her teeth, said the doctor, I told her to close her mouth, the tooth could not be stopped. He could have extracted the tooth, of course. It could have been got at easily enough with a tooth key but he had thought – he still thought – there was some justice in her suffering for her filthiness.

Be glad you were only required to look in her mouth, said Armistead. I'll bet her cunny's as ripe. He and Gordon fell against each other, glasses aclink, near crying with

laughter. The more the doctor saw of men the more grateful
he felt for women. He was persuaded that without them
men were little better than swine.

And on the subject of ladies and their crinkum-
crankums, said Armistead, this morning at the taffrails Mrs
Button rubbed me so keen I swear she brought herself off
on the back of my breeches. Gordon looked slow-witted at
Armistead, his mouth open, a fat drop of saliva falling from
his upper to his lower jaw on a silvery string. He did not
understand the joke although he had a fair idea what was
meant by crinkum-crankum. Even the word was funny. The
doctor looked disapproving so Armistead laughed alone.

It seems I must remind you that Mrs Button is a married
woman, said the doctor. And a mother.

I apologise, said Armistead with false contrition. I meant
only to ask your opinion. As a medical man. He knitted his
fingers across his chest. How long do you think she will
stay in heat? Dr Fowles retired to his cabin without saying
goodnight. He would not stand for Miss Button's mother
being used this way. As he went down the companion
ladder, he heard glass breaking and Armistead shout, You
rosy-fingered baboon, a laugh bubbling at the back of his
nose.

The weather was unchanged the following morning. Still
no alleviating breeze, the sky hung overhead scalded and
clanging as a saucepan lid. The men worked silent, heads
bowed, scraping rust from the chain cables and mending
the chafing gear. After breakfast, Dr Fowles hurried to call
on Mrs Davidson. He had slept an anxious night on her
account and hesitated to go below for fear of what he might
find. Most of the steerage passengers were having a
washday, their clothes soaped on deck, rinsed in a rain
barrel and hung from every rope that could be spared. On
her hands and knees, Mrs Eylard was working hard a pile

of gay shirts and trousers that the doctor recognised as Armistead's, her daughter soaping the cuffs and collars.

Hot work, Mrs Eylard, said the doctor.

It's not as bad as that. Mrs Eylard creased her face against the light. She had the underfed look of his chickens.

I have my daughter for assistance, she said, and the gentleman gives us more than a pound of soap which is a good allowance.

How did Mrs Davidson pass the night? The doctor ran a finger inside his neckcloth.

She was bad yesterday but I think – here Mrs Eylard ducked her head at the temerity of giving a doctor her opinion – she is coming on tolerable.

Happy news, said the doctor, and hid his relief in ruffling the hair of Mrs Eylard's daughter although it looked a little lousy.

Below, the doctor strained his eyes in the clobbery light of steerage. Old Davidson was keeping his bedwatch, his head bent in tiredness or prayer. The air was as hot as the previous day and, if possible, more fetid.

Doctor, said Mr Davidson, getting to his feet when he perceived him in the lick of light beneath the hatch. We're over the worst. I would've come and told you myself only I didn't like to leave my wife. Mrs Davidson did look much improved and, though still hot, her tongue and gums were moist.

She must take a full glass of sugared water every hour, he said to Mr Davidson. And this afternoon you must help her on deck. She will need shade but the fresh air and light will be good as any tonic.

Thank you, Doctor, said Mrs Davidson. She had a genteel voice and, unwashed and on her pillow, a kind of refinement. Slippery with happiness, the doctor emerged into the life of the deck. The foredeck was festive with laundry hung like bunting off every line and shroud. Even the bowspirit flew a pair of trousers. A breath of wind from the southeast, not enough to crinkle the water, twitched a shirtsleeve and died away. Every head lifted, even the goats in their pen stared up with golden eyes, as the sails creaked and filled, sagged again. So the morning passed, the gentle wind sometimes moving the ship enough to give steerage then stalling and fading, the bow turning in the water like a man who has lost his way. As the *Prince Regent* made further south, the frivolous puffs came closer and closer together until the ship was making three or four knots an hour under a wind that grew stronger by the day.

The ship making good headway again and the weather warm, every day seemed a high day. It was in this spirit that one afternoon Mrs Button visited Mr Armistead in his cabin, unannounced. Walking the poop before breakfast he had pressed into her hand his card, which she read later in privacy. *Call on me in my cabin at three*, his signature as ornate as his shirtfrill. Mrs Button smarted under this impertinence all morning until in the stifling hour after dinner she stole to Mr Armistead's starboard cabin as if this had been her only intention. She did not knock but scraped the door soft with her fingernails and, hearing nothing within, let herself in. Armistead was sitting in an armchair with a book open on his knee. Bored beyond belief by the book, borrowed from the doctor who claimed it had kept him burning his lamp late for a week, and already anxious that he had been so foolhardy as to commit himself to paper and, potentially, Captain Button's wrath, he thought he felt a little queasy. Looking up, he was not able to pretend immersion in some deep occupation, which later he regretted. Indeed, as the door opened he had started in his chair as if he feared a violence. Mrs Button leaned back on the door most attractively, her hands pressed either side to the woodwork, breathing hard through her mouth, her eye going piteously to his.

Armistead collected himself at once and went to Mrs Button. He kissed her, one smooth hand behind her putting the latch to the door, his lips polite at her cheek and then more confidently to her mouth, her teeth like gritted pearl under his tongue which shrank from the hot metallic taste of her own. His cheek was prickly, unshaved since morning. Her husband never came to her without shaving close but then he thought it a similar courtesy to drag her about the world on half-pay and settle her in some rustic backwater, hemmed in by convicts and Indians. Mrs Button arched her back and pressed her legs against Mr Armistead's. Such a feeling of fierceness came over her that she thought again she was not made for a woman. Her teeth at his neck, Armistead felt the slack of material where her legs parted. A wash of scornful desire stiffened him in his trousers. He kissed her arm to the elbow and paddled the bodice of her dress: it seemed she stopped at nothing. Gordon and Fowles would not believe it. Drawing Mrs Button with him, Armistead stepped backwards across his carpet until the armchair nudged the back of his knees. He ferreted a finger beneath a promising piece of lace that ran between her breasts to her ribboned waist, looking for a button or a hook and eye. Perhaps it fastened at the back? Nearing his crisis, a ring of blood crowded the edges of his vision. He tugged a little at the sleeve to see if he might ease out her shoulder but it was not possible without tearing a seam.

Her hands at his chest, Mrs Button pushed him back into the chair and as quickly opened the falls of his trousers. His manly cock stood upright and Armistead gazed on it with the usual pride. The two of them had not spoken to each other, their rough breathing and the squeak of her corset some kind of mute communion. Mrs Button thought of her husband, her dear indulgent husband, only yards away, sleeping in his armchair in the fug of their cabin, his surveyor's maps spread open on the table. From their black-inked notations she could not tell what sort of place the underside of the world might be but feared New South Wales was most substantial in the mapping. A scratchy sort of place and empty. That was the thing that troubled her most: a vast spread of a country inhabited only by ambitions of a topographical character. Hers were of a different order, she supposed, although she counted them ambitions still. Now she rolled Mr Armistead's shirt tails over his belly, a line of fur ascending to his navel, and raised her skirts as far as her knees – those creamy bare knees, when everything was lost to him Armistead would remember their exquisite dimples – before his sap was drawn down and he was seized by convulsion.

A number of things happened next that were, at best, surprising. Mrs Button sighed in a coarse way that suggested impatience, however unlikely that seemed. Her skirts dropped once more, she went on her knees before him and took him in her mouth. Armistead gave a yelp and thought himself unmanned. He didn't dare struggle for fear of injury but begged to be released.

Please, Mrs Button, he whispered. Please.

She stood nearly at once, head to one side, looking down on him, and just as he was feeling easeful she raised her skirts to their fullest extent and, bare, straddled his trousered thigh. She had hair like a man, an auburn cloud of it at the fork of her legs. He looked again, yes, a dark fleece against her plump whiteness, before his disbelieving face was pulled to her and he could see nothing but the coloured pressure of her shoulder on his eyeball. She rutted forward and back on his leg for some long minutes, his head knocked carelessly at times on the back of the chair. And rested, breath coming hard. As she straightened her skirts, one hand to her hair, he saw she had left a strange curdy paste on his trousers.

Good day, John. The door closed quiet behind her and he did not know her Christian name. Armistead was not sure how he felt. He would have liked to lie in a darkened room. His ears sung from the knocks his head had taken and he cupped a protective hand about his member, now shrunken and inglorious. He had never been so successful with a lady although he counted it a strange sort of success. His trousers were ruined for he could hardly give them to Mrs Eylard to launder.

There was no one about on the poop, only Mr Taylor and Mr Yate, the two missionaries bound for New Zealand. Although she liked the idea of the clergy, Mrs Button was not comfortable with them. They were not quite men, she supposed, though Mr Taylor sat at his sketchbook as easy as any gentleman. He was taking a likeness of Mr Yate, his hand true to that man's pale stretch of a face. Captain Aitken was at the waist, talking with a couple of the men from steerage. Mrs Button leaned on the railing and waited. She smelled the wind and knew however trapped she felt on board the ship she would remember it soon as a freedom. The captain came to her as she had hoped he would, grumbling and shaking his head but turning his troubles to her amusement. It seemed a petition had been drawn up and a delegation sent to ask him to evict the Parkers from steerage.

The Parkers? Mrs Button had not paid close enough attention to steerage to know them from the rest. The fat old sailor and his skinny wife, apparently. Five children too, one still a baby.

Bad language, said the captain. Mrs Eylard has taken a turn on the strength of it. The captain thought Mrs Button worldly enough and enjoyed her laughter, her eyes closed as she tipped back her head. Still, he did not tell her the entire complaint, that the Parkers were extremely filthy in their persons, the wife using their dishes for certain other purposes at night. Mrs Button could not imagine where else on the ship seven passengers might be stowed.

I thought perhaps they could bunk down with Miss Bloomfield and Miss Baker, said the captain, his voice low to avoid offending the missionary men. Mrs Button laughed again, silently this time, with her eyes closed, which the captain thought the one good thing to have come from the affair. I'll remove them to the third mate's cabin in the forecastle for half a week and cut off their grog, he said in a more sober way. Mr Denison can sleep with Mr May or on deck as he likes while the weather holds. He went aft to effect the order, nodding crisply to Mr Taylor and Mr Yate on his way.

Taylor's foot was still troublesome, although better than it had been. He sat beneath the poop awning, Mr Yate before him. No one in the cuddy was at all seriously inclined. He feared their levity had a prejudicial effect. Here was Mrs Button, back on the poop deck with Miss Button, the mother more frivolous than the daughter, both indifferent to the danger of their immortal souls as far as he could tell. Every day he rejoiced to find Mr Yate and his sister more and more to his mind. Taylor had written this in his journal. He trusted they should always be brethren though he was Christian enough to admit to himself that he had not always imagined his relations with Mr Yate would be so congenial. A grocer's apprentice, as Spencer Wigg told it, Mr Yate had no formal education except for what he took in his year at the Church Missionary Society's Islington school and might be expected to resent him, a learned man who had taken his Masters from Cambridge. If Mr Yate harboured any discontent, there was no sign. Under his tuition in the New Zealand language, Taylor had already made a grammar and started on a dictionary and translations of the gospel of St John. Mr Yate was sensible too of his colleagues' more delicate requirements. With the weather so hot, he was kind enough to invite Caroline, poorly and irritable, to bathe in his side gallery which he filled with water for the occasion. Now the two men sat close, as Taylor sketched. He did not flatter himself on his ability yet he thought the portrait tolerable. It caught at the long white hank of Yate's face without seeming to caricature it. Taylor was telling Mr Yate about his troubling conversation with Pat Kelly, an Irish lad in steerage going to join his father at Sydney. A good boy, conscientious in his prayer and his observance of the fasts, yet he believed the word of his priest over the word of God, a situation that had Taylor near despair. The poor lad was praying to St Peter and Mary but not to the great Saviour himself, saying Jesus cannot refuse any petition if it is brought to him by his mother. He was worse than a savage since they might yet be saved.

Isn't it quite wonderful, said Taylor to Yate, what power the Roman priesthood has over the minds of the people. Yate nodded. With the effort of keeping his head still for Taylor's pencil, his thoughts had ranged far from him and there was a moment of vacancy before he felt housed in his body again. The Roman priesthood. Marsden had early been of the opinion that, if allowed their popery, the Irish convicts would rise up in rebellion and the colony be lost. It hadn't happened, of course.

There are yet no Catholic priests in New Zealand, he said, Mr Taylor seeming to need the reassurance. But Taylor was already elsewhere, almost laughing at a faith so obstinate as to skirt reason. He had argued with Kelly about Genesis. Taylor said death was Adam's harvest for eating the fruit forbidden to him by God but Kelly insisted that Eve was the one visited with God's curse.

And he demonstrated his case – here Mr Taylor broke off with a wheezy laugh – by saying that women have a larger swelling in their necks than men. Taylor held his sketch paper flat to his knee and laughed until tears came to his eyes. He hoped he was not such a stick as to pass up on a good joke. Perhaps the women of Ireland are subject to the goitre.

The following day, Sunday service was held for the first time on the quarterdeck, all the men who could be spared from ship's work in attendance. The bell rang for prayer and most of the steerage passengers went aft, the Parkers excluded. Doctor Fowles was quite relieved not to see them. Yesterday, when they had been turned out of their bunks, Mr Parker went quietly, dead drunk, but Mrs Parker, surely no less affected, had clung to the railing and screamed the most shocking imprecations at the men until nightfall. The ladies had been unable to sit on the poop as was their usual custom but had taken their tea in the cuddy and retired early. This morning, pretending to take fits, Mrs Parker had sent for the doctor but refused the strong dose he mixed for her. She was a fright, Mrs Parker. A seamy neck with the dirt standing in the creases, thin, her infant sucking the nourishment straight out of her. Even the sailors did not look as rough as they sat in their cleanest clothes on the hen coops at the back of the congregation, the cabin passengers at the front on the cuddy chairs, and steerage in between on stools and crates.

On a crate for preference, an eye to Taylor's baby who sank low and lower in her mother's heedless arms like a flag being taken down at sunset, Mary Ford sat up in her Sunday best. She had wet-combed Arthur and Basil's hair and put Laura's up in ribbons. Mrs Taylor was sickening in the heat but the children continued well, the boys brown as savages and twice as hungry. She had learned from Charlie, one of the steward's boys, that there was to be a fruit tart in the cabin this afternoon, plum he thought, and she sat like a patient cat, all moist tongue and anticipation. In front

of her sat Mr Bedgood side by side with Mr Pedrano, the
back of his shirt collar darkening with sweat. They still had
a coxy look to them, even at prayer, on account of having
the Parkers removed from steerage. Not for long, Mary
Ford supposed. Without their grog, they'd be sorry fast.
She had seen it comin, a course. Mr Bedgood had said to
Mr Pedrano that it weren't decent and Mr Pedrano had
said to Mr Bedgood that it were not for himself but the
ladies. It weren't so much the swearin and drinkin but Mr
Parker goin to his wife night arter night they couldn't stand.
She thought she knew Christian piety when she seen it. And
she thought she knew blue balls. Now Mr Bedgood was
giving his responses, making out each word with care like
he was biting off taffy. Mary Ford rolled her eyes, prodi-
gious. No doubt he thought the Lord would take special
heed of his voice among the crowd. She made herself think
on the plum tart. The Bible and prayer book were set on a
barrel covered by the Union Jack and, Mr Taylor having led
the prayers, Mr Yate was set to preach on the resurrection.

There is something solemn in divine service at sea, Yate
thought. Every sail set to catch the freshening breeze,
nothing overhead but the wide blue heaven. And on a ship
everyone feels so sorely the precariousness of life that on
shore slips through them, careless, day by day. Then the
congregation on board ship is much varied: the captain
with his neat beard, compelled for this half-hour to know
he is not the supreme master of his vessel; his smallest cabin
boy, nail-bitten and thoughtful; the virtuous women from
the cabin and the brawling sailor with tattooed letters
picked out on his knuckles. All these bow their heads
together, their distinction of rank lost for the duration of
the service. So too in New Zealand, at Paihia say, where the
natives assemble alongside the mission families from the
station and those European residents of the bay as are

disposed to attend church. It was not always so, of course. When the station at Kerikeri was first established, the natives living in the settlement would start up at the sound of the Sabbath bell and take themselves off rowing or fishing. If they came into the chapel at all, they would be dressed in some fantastic style – a jacket worn wrong way about, the sleeves of an old gown drawn on as stockings – or nearly naked. Nor were they shy of calling out if something in the sermon was not pleasing to them, That's a lie, that man lies! Now it was the greatest punishment to prevent a native from attending church, they had grown so fond of it. At the ringing of the bell, or in the outlying villages the striking of a musket barrel with a stone, they thronged in their improbable clothes or rubbed down with red ochre and shark oil. A lucky few carried copies of the hymnals printed up for them, the rest making do with whatever they could lay their hands to, a shipping almanac, a broken-backed novel, even a sheet of newspaper stitched into a booklet and written over with the liturgy in lamp black or powdered charcoal. At times he wondered if the New Zealanders were not more religious than those Europeans who came to chapel from habit or for the society. He recognised as his own their struggle to believe, the devilish backsliding, the midnight sweats. They came at matters of doctrine sideways but Yate knew it for a sign of their sincerity. George disputing they were all from one father since his skin and Mr Yate's were different colours; Piripi weeping outside his study door because he didn't understand why some virgins were wise, others foolish. Yate thought of the chapel at Waimate, its sonorous bell clappering across the wild landscape, the brass clamour making his rooms ring. He never tired of hearing it. Mrs Clarke had made a flag for the chapel with a cross and a cunning dove carrying in its beak an olive branch and the words *Rongo Pai*. Now he stood on the quarterdeck, a barrel for his pulpit, the word of the Lord running through him as lightning blasts the kauri high on the spur. He spoke of the life after this one, the life everlasting. *For in the resurrection they neither marry, nor are given in marriage, but are as the angels of God in heaven.* Mr Denison sat at the back, high on the railing, attentive, his whole spirit seeming to Yate to lean out across the heads of the men and the passengers to catch at the words fresh minted from his lips. In his white shirt and white duck trousers Mr Denison seemed already an angel, raised over the heads of the others, benevolent and watchful.

It only looks like a cloud to me. Gordon thought the doctor might have taken him for a cock-shy. Armistead and he were always exercising their wit on him. He would not have his leg pulled. Only, if it were not a cloud, he would have made a monkey of himself without the doctor's assistance. Taking his sights along the doctor's finger, Gordon glowered at the horizon, at a small grey-blue cloud that hung at the edges of seeing, at one moment seeming perhaps a little solid and hard-edged, the next, a vaporous trick of the light.

It seems more of a cloud, said Gordon, his face sulky with the effort of not looking a fool.

Mercy's sake, Gordon, said the doctor. Have you been at sea so long you've forgotten the look of land? It seemed the doctor was laughing at him anyway. He had come up from dinner when the figs and almonds were served, helping the doctor with some scraps from the table for the fowls. Having refreshed their water, the two men leaned in a companionable fashion on the trusses of hay fastened to the bulwarks surrounding the poop, their eyes unfocused in the acreage of sky and sea. And then all this business of land. The doctor went to consult the man at the wheel. Gordon looked again to the horizon. The cloud did not seem to be at all dispersing or changing its form. Perhaps it was land, the first they had seen in forty-four days. Gordon wondered if he had the courage to steal the doctor's prize and give the shout but still he stood, uncertain.

Dick Deck, friend of the Taylors, was standing his trick at the helm. He grinned pleasant enough at the doctor on his approach and allowed that it might be land but he couldn't say for sure at this distance. That was enough for the doctor.

If ever I saw land in my life, that's it, he said, and, tipping his head back, called Land! Land! in the ululating style of the sailors. In a few minutes the poop was crowded, every telescope on board in requisition. The captain confirmed his sighting which made the doctor preen a little. A ship full of experienced men and he the first to discover the Isle of Trinidad or rather, as it turned out, some islands about twenty-five miles distant: Martin Vas Rocks. The doctor made sketches in his journal until a storm coming on hid them from view. He did not think them picturesque but of scientific interest, possibly volcanic. Gordon would not listen. He affected to find the prospect of land very dull indeed.

More of a rock, all things considered, said Gordon and studied instead one of the shipboard cats that, like him, had other matters on his mind. Five cats had the run of the ship and grew fat and glossy on the rats from the hold. Mice, the captain represented them as to the ladies but he never sailed without his ratters. This one lay on her side, pink-padded feet clustered close, and licked her brindled flank, slow, eyes slit shut, now and then nipping her teeth at a flea or a knot in her fur. She pointed her back leg straight to the sky and rasped her tongue beneath her tail. Then on her back, the abundant spiky fur of her belly on display, she sleeked a front paw and ran it over the back of her head, her ear flattening and pricking back up as it passed. Gordon found the operation most soothing. When thick drops of rain spattered the poop, he went below to his canaries with a lighter heart. Really, it was more accurate to say that he and the doctor had sighted land together.

Not even the storm in the night lowered the spirits of the cabin passengers. The next morning, the wind having died away again, they assembled early on the poop and watched Martin Vas Rocks bearing due west. The ship made good speed, continuing south, and the sight of land, even if only barren rocky outcrops, was heartening. The thermometer had dipped as low as seventy-eight degrees but was now back to a steady eighty-three. Mr Taylor was sketching the rocks with the aid of a telescope, cross-hatching them with care, one eye screwed half shut with the business of making out their detail. He was not very good at water so the sea appeared insensible on his page, the waves more even and orderly than ever they were in life. His impression of a water spout seen near the rocks the previous night was more commendable, the thin column of water ascending to the clouds. A number of the passengers had testified to its authenticity. Caroline had been resting below and had not seen it but said she almost felt she had, so fine his sketch. The captain had told Taylor he did not expect to see land again before reaching New Holland and, taking his eye from the telescope, he made the news general. All looked again at the rocks that were to sustain them until their destination, lying at this angle like two great black whales, nose to nose.

Mrs Button sat close under the shadow of her husband and was very attentive to Miss Button, no doubt on account of her having not been well. Armistead's agitation was not lost on the doctor. He flickered from starboard to larboard like a pilot fish that had lost its shark. Captain Button was unusually expansive. He told some story that grew most in the telling about sworn enemies – two regimental wives, one of whom was the daughter of the notorious Captain Bligh – which ended with one lady saying, My dear, I believe I take rank of you, the other sniffing the air and replying, Rank enough. Dr Fowles did not think Captain Button had done his story justice but Mrs Button, laughing like a silver fall of cutlery, fussed at her daughter with one hand and reached out the other to Armistead, saying very prettily, Come, Mr Armistead, won't you laugh with us? Armistead's eye was shy of Mrs Button's, yet neither could he turn away. The doctor saw him hang uncertain, his forehead pleated, the colour jumping in his cheek, and thought better of him. No doubt the young man was regretting the coarse use he had made of Mrs Button in conversation with himself and Gordon not so many nights hence.

Mid-week, the breakfast conversation turned to mermaids and the probability of such things existing. Dr Fowles had just come into the cuddy after seeing Captain Button, taken suddenly ill with a violent pain to his left side that threatened to require lancing or bleeding, although the doctor hoped neither. Tired as he was from all the doctoring he had been called to do in the last few days – James Lyne had taken a bowel complaint and Mrs Bedgood lay in bed with an inflammatory disorder – he was much amused by the considered opinions of his companions. The ladies were disposed in favour of mermaids but Gordon, smelling a trick, could not say one way or the other. Mr Yate spread his hands wide in a shrug as if to say there were more wonders in this world than he felt able to pronounce on. Much appealed to as an expert, Captain Aitken would not venture a decided opinion either but said the men believed in such beings. He knew for a fact that they were always sighted on rocks as a harbinger of shipwreck.

They sing, said the Captain, forgetting for the moment that he was not certain of their existence. In sweet, unearthly voices that ride men to their death.

I'd like to hear them, said Mrs Button. Armistead scowled into his coffee. Would she had a fish's tail instead of that furred cleft she's bewitched me with.

I think it's possible, he said, his lips thin with spite, to imagine a woman that is half fish, but not a man.

A poser, sir, said the doctor. How is the race to be propagated? Miss Button looked down the table at the doctor's teasing face. She wished she had her father's pain that he might call on her again. Of course, she still wrote to Mr Whitlock every day. Recently, all her news was of Dr Fowles and she wondered that Mr Whitlock might not find her as congenial as he once professed.

The doctor saw he had attracted the ire of Mr Taylor, who smelled fogs a day before they rolled in and could always give a learned and unsatisfactory explanation for every thing.

I cannot settle the question of their propagation, said Taylor pursily, but I can vouch for their existence. It seemed he had once seen a real mermaid at a fair, purchased afterward by a public museum for a high price. It was said to come off the Island of Formos, bought by a ship's captain from some Chinese fishermen. The argument seemed settled in his favour and he relaxed into smiles and nods.

Would you say the beast had the look of a monkey as far as the waist, Mr Taylor? asked the doctor.

Quite monkeyish.

And below the waist something of a codfish?

Yes, Taylor said, giving the word a slow stretch. A cod would do it.

And I'm guessing you saw this marvel exhibited about Norwich some twelve years ago?

Closer to ten years, I'd make it, said Taylor, the unhappy centre of a ring of expectant faces. Did you perhaps see the mermaid yourself?

See her? said the doctor, more exultant than when he had first sighted land. I manufactured her. Alone of all the cuddy able to make sense of the doctor's boast, Miss Button gazed upon the doctor's mermaid-making hands. Of course. The pig-faced lady. She saw that it would be connected somehow to the doctor's friend who exhibited wonders from town to town. And so it proved for the doctor was recounting his adventures with Mr Anderson: how that man had exhibited his own son as a dwarf, a boy of four years kitted out in false whiskers and touted as thirty-five years of age with three brothers no larger than himself, his mother only twenty-two inches high and his father the mayor of Antwerp and a great friend of the King of Holland.

That poor boy, the doctor laughed, his hands flat to the table and taking his weight. When people tired of the dwarf, I experimented in dying his skin with lunar caustic. It had taken many trials but finally the doctor had mixed the perfect solution, not so robust as to remove the boy's skin yet strong enough to produce a blackness that did not fade for months, and he was taken the rounds again, exhibited as the piebald child of a white man and a black woman. Captain Aitken enjoyed a joke. Even Armistead had unwound sufficient to smile a little at Mrs Button. He felt easier with her husband confined to his cabin. Miss Button hugged the story of the pig-faced lady to herself, glad the doctor had not shared it with the company. The breakfast table was more lively than any dinner setting they had yet enjoyed. Lurking at its edges, Charlie and Sadler laughed so well at the dwarf boy they upset a jug of milk and hung about for the end of the story, not wanting Mungo to learn of their accident. Mr Taylor alone was unhappy, his wife a little anxious on his account. He remembered well the black-and-white boy. Half and half, he had been billed. Taylor had stood at his enclosure a long while, thinking there would be no safety in the world for such a sad character, the sins of the boy's father written in his flesh for all to see.

And the mermaid? said Armistead, cutting his eyes at Mrs Button. I suppose you'll tell us you sawed the poor boy in half and sewed him into a fish tail. Gordon thought that unlikely. Mr Taylor had already said that the top half had looked like a monkey.

The thing was half cod, said the doctor, half monkey. Sewn together, stuffed and varnished with enough skill to fool the most intelligent members of the public. Here the doctor gestured at Mr Taylor but the man was not to be mollified. He was nursing his hurt and if he could be tricked then at least he would not be tricked of that. The doctor wondered if Anderson was still in business. He had never been without a monkey in his troupe and since they did not live past six years, consumption the usual cause of death, a number of their corpses had come the doctor's way. They were quite like humans in their internal organisation. He went below to record his triumph in his journal.

Quite unchristian, said Taylor, when the doctor was out of earshot. And not at all remorseful.

Thursday the ship was becalmed, Friday, Saturday. Too close for sleeping in his cabin, Yate walked the deck in the deep of the night as was his habit. Five bells. He knew most of the men by name now and would talk to them a little, his voice furring the dark, softening their hearts for their own salvation. Not easily won, the men liked him in spite of themselves. He had a way of going among them inconsequentially, like a blackbird that stalks the lawn, and pausing, as if distracted in the execution of some more compelling task, to crook his brazen spectacled eye at one man or another, there was some tame wildness to him that each man hoped to husband to himself a moment. Then, he didn't come the preacher with them. His hesitancies and the sense he gave of being in the middle of something else made even Staines feel it worth his while to draw something from the man, a few words, a slow-focused smile, as he passed in the dark of night. Tonight though, there was no work going forward and the men were sleeping where they could, one man watchful at the wheel while the ship idled on a stilled sea. As Yate passed the galley, the roaring stillness of

the world cupped to his ear like a shell, he heard a whick-
ering that he knew at once. He put his face to the crack of
the door and made out a pair of eyes in the felted dark: one
was Hall's, split wide and staring up at the slow groan of
the hinges; the other the cook's, maundering back in his
head, indifferent to the interruption. No one in sight over
his shoulder, Yate opened the door further, the room
washed in tricksy moonlight, to stand stock still, his senses
netted together and quivering like a bird dog on the point.
Hall wriggled out from beneath the cook's weight and,
hauling up his trousers, flew at the door and was gone from
sight.

    The ship lay utterly still, the sails slack on the yards. The
cook's feathery breathing, the crick of the boards as he
came to Yate, one large hand fastening his trouser fronts, a
look so deep it was like drinking. Taller than Yate, the cook
stood before him, looking down on his face. The space
between the men was the measure of a breath. Yate
stretched out a hand, his skin impossibly white as if all
light must cleave to it, to feel the fine greased leather folds
of the cook's neck. Still the man stood, wordless, a dark
plinth. There was never anything to be said and yet it was
most like learning a new language, carried forward on
nothing but trust. Yate would not say that two men ever
understood each other complete with their imperfect
bodies. A slow palm down the cook's shirt front, he felt still
the twill when he removed his hand. He unbuttoned the
falls of his own trousers and stood, breathless and
unbreathing. The cook crouched in front of him, one hand
at his leg where it trembled at the knee, the other pushing
the door shut and Yate was lost in blackness, remembering
the soft jaw of Mrs Button's tiger. His hands in the cook's
crimped hair, he rocked back and forward as in a lazy
homecoming saddle, his thoughts winging about his head
like insects kicked up from the damp evening grass.

Just before he left London, walking late at the Horse
Guards Parade where men sometimes meet, Yate had fallen
to talking with a young man, George Webster, a footman
for a gentleman at Grosvenor Square. Mr Webster was not
handsome, his eyes crowded close at the bridge of his nose,
but he was amiable and willing. He let Yate stand him a
drink at a room he knew in the Bull public house in Bulleen
Court, the Strand. Mr Webster was apparently no stranger
at the Bull's private room and was greeted warmly by its
inhabitants: three soldiers, a printer's apprentice, and two
womanish men – Orange Deb and Miss Selina. Powdered
cheeks and painted lips, Miss Selina flagged her handkerchief at Yate and wished to be introduced.

Miss Selina, said George Webster, who had unaccountably taken Orange Deb's hand in his own and was even
kissing it from time to time, Mr Williams, since that was the
name Yate had given him. Miss Selina was well made and
could have passed for a woman, Yate thought, but for her
height and the directness of her stare. He had no wish to be
taken to the watch house and began making his farewells.

He is a nervous fellow, said Mr Webster, settling Orange
Deb across his knee. For a missionary that goes next week
on the *Prince Regent* to save the savages.

Savages, said Miss Selina with a judder of delight. Can't
you leave off them? All the men are already too well-
mannered. She had Yate by his wrist and led the laughing.
Yate wished Mr Webster good night and at his back heard
Miss Selina call, When do you sail? Orange Deb and I will
come to the docks and wave you away. One of the soldiers
with hair like a blacking brush was watching Yate close and
left with him saying, I am going your way, although he could
not have known which way that was. Yate feared a robbery
but in a lane off Charles St the soldier let himself be kissed,
his lips chapped and cold but his tongue an unexpected sour
warmth. He drew out his yard, half-hard and already
leaking, and hefted it a moment on his palm like a coster-

monger with his thumb on the scales. Yate unbuttoned and rubbed himself against the soldier in the cradle of his hands, as he had learned from Pehi.

You can call me sweetling, if you like, said the soldier in a rough voice Yate remembered long after. He caught the soldier by the red shoulder of his coat as his own knees buckled and he spurted his stuff ammoniac between his fingers. Without discharging, the soldier packed himself away, still weeping and no stiffer than before. He accepted a shilling and turned back the way they had come.

Yate palpated the rills and ridges of the cook's skull beneath his napped hair.

Sweetling, he groaned as his seed leaped from him. He would have slumped to the bench but the cook bent him over smart and, like some honey-tongued demon who could only discharge as incubus what he had absorbed as succubus, gave to him the same caudle he had been giving the boy. When he was finished, Yate kept his face pressed to the bench, the resinous smell of the tree still in the wood, the grain a rough comfort against his cheek. He was unnaturally light with the cook's weight off him and would have floated content in the dark of the galley but for the soft determination of the hands that were stroking his head and back, getting him to his feet, chucking him beneath the chin, patting him back into his clothes, shaking him down and steering him for the moonlit deck. At the door, Yate turned to speak but had nothing to say.

He left behind him the galley's dark hollow as if it were another country, the cook's luminous teeth his last view of the shore, and made his way across the silvered deck, past the sleeping men laid out in threes and twos according to no pattern he knew and despite the captain's warnings about the danger of sleeping in the direct light of the moon. He could not see Hall anywhere though he looked in the usual places. There was a ruckus from the farmyard. Mr Parker was celebrating his return to steerage with a couple of bottles of porter and, not wanting to disturb his companions below, straddled the roof ridge of the pig pen, a bottle in either hand, and sang to raise the dead. His wife sat on the deck, her share of the night's merriment already consumed by the look of her. Her hair was wilder than usual, gobbed and tangled at the back where a goat had chewed it through the railings of its enclosure. She had not liked the look of him, the yellow-eyed munter, and had given him the devil of a smack, though he continued to stare at her unblinking, chewing his own beard for want of anything better.

> *Up jumps Sally with her twat in a twitch*
> *Sayin give me a man that can scratch my itch.*

Mr Parker's voice was like a dog on broken glass. After he sang he poured a liberal dose direct into his mouth and ruttled the roof slats of the pigsty with his heels. Mrs Parker sang the chorus, eyes closed, her head slack.

> *And it's windy weather boys, stormy weather boys*
> *When the wind blows we're all together boys.*

Her singing voice was unexpectedly sweet and full, drawing from Yate some bruised emotion he didn't have the name for. She sang the shanty slow, almost churchy, at half-speed. Yate looked at her shin-bones showing white in her bare legs, her dirty neck bent beneath the blossoming weight of her voice. Mr Denison was beside him of a sudden and the two men looked a moment at each other.

Good evening, Mr Yate. It's late for a concert. Yate shied his eyes away and back. He was so drained of his vital liquors that for once he could look at the man direct. In the moonlight, Mr Denison's hair was struck like silver coin.

He smelled newly wakened and Yate looked at him more easily than he had for days.

I've been walking the deck, said Yate, which was not quite true. And thinking.

Ah, thinking, said Denison. That's not always easy on a ship. He was serious now, his bottom lip pushed forward as if he thought he might be laughed at.

Mr Parker saw he had something more of an audience, the third mate and one of the preachers, the horse-faced one travelling with his sister. He had worked out another verse but it was too spicy for present company. Clinking his bottles to mark time, he tried for another, sitting atop the pigs, swarmed by rhyme, *disgrace, face, arse, waste, chase, wed, legs, bed*. His wife woke with a sad smile and, thinking she had missed her cue, went again through her chorus. Mr Parker wet his throat and waited.

> *Up jumps Hannah with her two wooden legs*
> *Sayin another pair a stumps, I can make meself a bed.*

He threw his arms wide as if to take his applause on the chest and bowed deep in every direction.

Come down, Sammy, said Mrs Parker, her ordinary voice no clue to her singing one. Before you do yerself a damage. Yate had not yet thrown the feeling the cook had given him, a trammelled lightness in the loins and head as if he walked in a dream, daytime people appearing before him in portentous guises, Mrs Parker drunk on her angel's voice, Mr Denison a messenger sent to save him.

I have been thinking too, said Denison. Of what he could not have said or would not but it seemed to him his thoughtfulness all turned on Mr Yate these days. If he weren't such a sailor he might have thought he were being called for a missionary.

Are you a religious man? said Yate. Mr Denison did not immediately answer the question which hung between them, pale and waxing, like a second moon. He tilted his head one way and then another, considering.

I am, said Denison. I like to think I am. He hid his eye from Mr Yate a minute, looking up the mainmast that scratched the night sky. Such a calm as this might signify a storm but he saw no sign, every star pricked out and no smell of water in the air.

If you are still wakeful, Mr Denison's voice went careful like a man feeling his way in the dark, we might continue our conversation in my cabin. The two of them walked forward in silence, their progression seeming to each something of a ceremony.

Mr Parker let them pass from sight and waited a courteous minute to be sure they were out of earshot.

> Up jumps Lizzy with a cunt so tight
> Once you were in, you were in for the night.

He laughed out loud, the only man alive on the ship it seemed. Over the edge of the sty he looked to see how Mrs Parker had taken the joke but she were resting her eyes again, propped out of reach of the goat. He tipped the bottle to his mouth but it were empty. Dry. He would have liked to be blazing drunk for now and wake the next morning in a tangle with his wife, a dumb headache already taking the edge off the day. Mr Parker chucked the empty bottle over the side. It fell to the water with a smack and sank a little, glugging again. He held the remaining bottle up to the light, its level hard to make out through the thick brown glass. Less than half left. Maybe less than a third. Something about the new horizon of his liquor made Mr Parker lose his balance as he set himself true to the tilt of the porter. The first he knew of it was the sliding of his seat trousers over the roof and the lightness of one leg as his foot kicked up at the night stars. He roared as he fell but hit the planking silent, a arker woke – *and it's windy weather boys* – her husband's dark shadow passing over her like a bat.

Sammy, Sammy. She poured his name into his ear smooth as a poisoner but he did not stir. His neck had a rough twist in it she did not like the look of, his head hanging limp to his shoulder. He still had a hold of the bottle, not a drop spilled. She squeaked it from his hand, took a hard drain of it and went in search of the doctor.

Mr Denison's cabin was small but neatly kept, despite so recently having housed the Parkers, an open window to starboard, cambric curtains pulled aside, a writing desk, a wooden chest with the initials E. H. D. carved in the lid over a tidy anchor, a square-tucked bed. Yate took the writing desk and Mr Denison sat cross-legged at the foot of the bed. Between them on the floor was an elaborately knotted rope rug that Yate guessed was of Mr Denison's making.

It is, said Mr Denison, pushing at it with a shy foot. He had started learning fancy work at sixteen years when an ordinary seaman on a ship to Calcutta. His older brother had taught him a basic turk's head that he had done in reverse and traded for a diamond knot.

That's how you get a new knot at sea, said Mr Denison. Teach a knot to learn a knot. The diamond knot had taken some work but when he had it off he traded it for a star knot. He was an able seaman by then, sailing for Swan River and Singapore.

Not everyone takes to it. I doubt the captain can do much more than a standard manrope and most of the men are but wall-and-crown sailors.

There was more craft in the mat than Yate had thought. He tried to follow a strand with his eye as it dipped under and over, turned back on itself, but he lost it in a giddy thicket of lines, himself drawn into the pattern.

What's this one called? Yate said. The flowery one.

That is the star knot I mentioned, said Denison, made awkward by his correction. The hardest knot he had learned was a Japanese one, kazari-moosh. He had been learning it from an English sailor who had worked on a Japanese whaler but only had the first bit when the man deserted at Port Royal. It was four-and-a-half years before he found anyone else who knew it and then it went by a different name, the music knot. They spoke together like this, of ordinary things that grew precious in the alchemy of their conversation. Once as a boy, Yate had been walking on a marsh when an immense flock of ducks had flailed up into the air beside him, the sky thickened with the sound of their beating wings long after they had wheeled from sight. The recollection came to him complete although he had not thought of it in years: the clean, almost citrus smell of the grasses as he stepped on them, his boyish breath fogging the air, the squeezing call of a duck overhead. The charged air in the cabin and the same happy apprehension brought it back to him, as if he alone had witnessed something remarkable. He would tell it to Mr Denison when they understood each other better. For now Yate told of the shells he had collected in New Zealand for the British Museum, ten of them new to science as far as he could judge. He had named one for himself, the *Venus Yatei*, which had seemed an allowable vanity given the inconsequence of the shell, so plain it had been overlooked even by avid Monsieur Quoy of the *Astrolabe*. He would like to name a shell for Mr Denison. So they talked until eight bells and the changing of the watch.

Yate slept four sound hours, joining his sister in her cabin before breakfast. The ship made no progress and only rolled a little in its place as the sea swelled in from the northeast. He was in the habit of telling Sarah everything about Mr Dension as he learned it.

His initials appear to be E. H. said Yate. They were carved on his sea-chest though I suppose it might not be his own.

E. H., said Sarah. Didn't you ask him, William? But it had not been the night for that sort of confidence and Yate had made no inquiry.

I think he will be an Edward, said his sister. Doesn't he seem an Edward to you, William?

Sarah, said Yate in remonstration but enjoyed his own small sense of shock. His mind skittered clear of any possible Christian name, the initials themselves seeming sufficient intimacy.

Yes, I think he'll be an Edward, said Sarah, laughing. And we'll call him Ned.

Ned, said Yate but could not attach the name to Mr Denison with his yellow hair and his bare toes long and proportioned like fingers.

You don't think he could be Egbert, William? Sarah was teasing him. I suppose we could like him just the same.

Ebenezer, said Yate snorting and starting back as if he gave himself a turn. Ezekiel. They hooted and blew and dried their eyes for breakfast.

There was bread served at the cuddy table, still warm when sliced and smelling of beer. Three loaves had been made by the cook that morning and the cabin sat to them as to a banquet. The butter being intolerably rotten the bread was taken dry, Mrs Button affected enough to dip it in her coffee. Mr Taylor was thoroughly sick of the Button family and their troublesome ways. Only yesterday he had counted thirteen glasses of water taken down to their cabin, much more than required by the rest of the party. At half past nine, when the last loaf looked like being eaten and Dr

Fowles had still not appeared, Miss Button organised the steward to take two slices to his cabin. The doctor was lying poorly and low-spirited in his bed though later he claimed to have been cured just by the sight of the bread, one slice having clearly taken the mark of Sadler's dirty thumb.

Bread, Sadler? The doctor leaned up on an elbow and stared at the steward's boy, getting his tray around the door with difficulty.

Sent by Miss Button with her complymints. It was his and Charlie's joke that the doctor was gone on Miss Button and Sadler was pleased to see the doctor pinking in confusion.

Even his teeth was blushing, he would later say to Charlie. With the cabin to himself again, the doctor sat up to his breakfast and thought he had never eaten such good bread. Sweet as cake, a soft crumb and dependable crust. Its being sent by Miss Button only made it the more toothsome.

The doctor had passed a terrible night. Mrs Parker had somehow got into his cabin around three, snivelling and swigging from a bottle, so that at first he thought he dreamed. Some trouble with her husband. She hardly looked at him but stood like a child, wiping her nose with the back of her hand and talking to herself about the pigs.

Snapped his neck like a twig, he thought he heard her say. There was no doubt Mr Parker was a violent man but whose neck he had broken the doctor could not make out, his wife next to insensible.

Well, get out, said the doctor, frightened to rudeness. Get out, woman, and let me dress. She was still waiting outside his door like some devoted dog a quarter-hour later, bottle cast aside, the doctor presumed empty.

He's a good man, she said, her breath a scorching stink in the doctor's face. She turned and led off, looking back to see she was followed. It was Mr Parker himself who lay on the deck, his neck at a frightening cant but his breath smogging the mirror the doctor held to his mouth.

If he's gorn I'll not have yer stealin his bones. Mrs Parker hung back from the body as if she were frightened of her husband at last, her voice making the distance like a cat-o'-nine-tails. He'll be buried as a sailor over the side.

He's not dead, Mrs Parker, said the doctor, testy, which brought her on at a run, gulping on her tears and grabbling her husband's hand to her bosom. Though the doctor thought he might be by morning with that split in his head. He called three of the men to carry Mr Parker below to his bunk, Mrs Parker refusing to give up his hand and bearing it along as the portion that fell properly to herself. The doctor had hardly got back to bed and was not yet asleep when one of the men knocked at his door to say Mr Davidson had taken sick. Whether it was his disturbed sleep or the morbific air of steerage the doctor could not say but, on returning to bed, he had turned quite sick and faint and could not get up to breakfast.

Quite restored by his two pieces of bread and the sympathies of Miss Button, the doctor rose and dressed. Both his slices had been wedgily taken from the loaf, considerably thicker at one end than the other in the style of someone unused to handling a knife. He wondered whether Missy had sliced his bread herself. He thought it possible but not likely. That was the problem with being a scientific man, thought the doctor as he turned up his sheets. You ruled against your own pleasures too readily. After he had returned from bleeding Mr Davidson, he had dreamed the strangest thing, a dream of skeletons cavorting in a grave-yard dance. He called it dreaming but knew he had not been properly asleep, only dawdling at the limits of consciousness. There would be some rational explanation, he was sure. Probably it was his mind exercising its displeasure at Mr Davidson's astonishing boniness. Intending to cup the man at the base of the spine, the doctor had been dismayed by his patient's fleshlessness and it was several attempts before a cup would adhere. Or else it was his anxious fear that there would be death on board. Either way, the dream stayed with him and even continued to elaborate itself until the doctor resolved he would write it up as an eerie tale for the philosophical improvement of Miss Button, whose literary tastes ran in that direction. He had not felt more enlivened in days. There would be enough creaking tombs and moonlit frights to keep Miss Button interested but instead of the usual gullible young lady with her passion for ruins and an inexplicable compulsion to explore them by night the doctor proposed for his hero a medical man, not unlike himself, who would educate the reader with ruminations on the nature of life and death, the existence of the soul.

The doctor sat immediately to his journal, his jaw unshaven, hair unkempt. If he could get the first sentence down, the rest would come easily enough, like cows following each other home for milking, but the first line was more difficult than he had imagined. For one thing, however he signalled his doctor's virtues, the man seemed a prig. *Dr Thomas Wartle*, he wrote, pleased to have got the name in without having to introduce the man, *was honest and kind and an excellent doctor as well, respected by all who knew him*. It was not what he had hoped. Perhaps Wartle was not a solid enough name. He drew a line through the sentence and began again. *Dr Thomas Bartle, a kind man and an excellent doctor, kept a fearsome secret he could tell no man that chilled his blood*. That was more the sort of thing but when he thought how much it would take to get his flat-footed Dr Bartle from his circle of admirers to the midnight graveyard with the hair standing in terror on the back of his neck, the doctor despaired. He would have liked the piece finished and Missy tucked into some dim alcove while he read to her, the guttering lamp waggling their tall shadows together on the wall. The leaden Dr Bartle was the problem, his merits weighing on the story like a drag anchor. He crossed out his sentence and chewed the end of his pen. *It was the time of night when the graves gape wide that Dr Thomas Bartle (kind, honest and a medical man of some excellence) pushed open the little wicker gate leading to the church-yard*. The doctor read his sentence and liked it better and better. He lay back to think of his second sentence, nearly swallowing his pen when there was a rough knock at the door. Sadler again, smirking in the most familiar way.

It's only Basil Taylor, said Sadler. Mrs Ford thinks he has the ringworm.

Mary Ford was as accurate as ever in her pronouncement though Mr Taylor was so mortified he would not believe it unless he heard it from the doctor direct. He still had not forgiven him the business with the mermaid and now here he was having to consign his children's health to the hands of a fairground charlatan.

It is ringworm, certainly, said the doctor. Mary Ford pressed her lips together but took no satisfaction in being right. The poor lamb had a flaky rash on his back, the rings standing out red and raw, and many damp, crusted scabs she could feel beneath his hair. If she'd been at home, she would have fixed him a draught of yellow root and that would a been the end of it but the doctor was prescribing some soap and a tarry ointment. Feeling himself the centre of such undesirable attention, Basil's bottom lip took up a tremble and his eyes wetted with tears so that Mary Ford took him in her skirts and petted him a little.

Is it possible the other children may take the worm from Basil? said Mr Taylor.

Probable. Very probable, said the doctor. And I am afraid you and your wife and Mrs Ford too. Mr Taylor covered his eyes with his hand and even Mrs Taylor roused herself to a piteous moan. The whole family might be diseased, thought Taylor, like a curse of goats. Basil and Arthur were always playing down at the animal pens although he had spoken to Mary Ford about it. Undoubtedly that was where they had taken the ringworm. Unless Mary herself had brought it into their cabin from steerage. The children were a great trial to him. Whether the change in food or their close quarters he did not know but they seemed to him more peevish and fretful than ever they were before. And his own foot so far from healed. Since Mr Taylor sat so convenient with his head in his hands, the doctor sidled near.

It's an unpleasant business, Mr Taylor, said the doctor. But if I just might– He ran his fingers through the other man's hair and beneath his collar.

Dr Fowles returned to his cabin with more urgent a step than he had quit it. All the while he was with the Taylors, he had been thinking Dr Bartle's thoughts, some of them fine enough to only want transcribing. He would have Dr Bartle wondering handsomely about the form that spirits take. Do they keep the same form as when they walked the world embodied or do they assume the stature of maturity, removed alike from the weakness of infancy and old age? This was a question that interested the doctor exceedingly. Also, does the soul immediately quit the body at the moment of death or, as some ancient and modern philosophers suppose, linger about its dull remains, haunting the grave where lies the mortal instrument of its past pleasures? The doctor returned to his journal at once and had Dr Bartle make short work of the path from the church gate to the churchyard while he pondered the question of the after-life from a materialist perspective. He thought it sound but feared Missy might judge Dr Bartle's half-page speculations as lacking in sensation. Some dramatic business was needed. The skeletons should be got on with. He did not plan a lengthy piece or else he would be writing when they docked at New South Wales. *The bell strikes twelve.* The doctor was literary enough to know the value of a plain sentence in its proper place. *By heaven, said Dr Bartle, it is that time of night that churchyards yawn and if it be true that such things are, now is the time for conviction.* The thing he liked about Bartle was his willingness to follow rational processes of deduction even in supernatural matters. It was clear he was a handsome fellow. He had not given Bartle his description yet but he would have dark hair and pinked cheeks, fat whiskers and a confident laugh. *Dr Bartle's attention was attracted toward an immense square tombstone that he fancied had moved. With his dark hair and rosy cheeks, he dropped behind an upright stone to convince himself of the fact. Dr Bartle was not deceived.* The doctor was undecided as to whether it was more effective to have the skeleton lift his monstrous slab and emerge as easily as a man from a hatchway or to show something of a struggle, the bones of the hand and arm seen first, the smooth back of the skull and finally the horrible countenance as the heavy stone was pushed aside. Dr Fowles rolled up his sleeves and went to work, stopping only when he heard the bell for service on the quarterdeck.

After dinner, Yate lay in the netting along the bowsprit, no wind yet, the ship still idle, but a heavy sky overhead, purpling at the horizon. He put his face to each quarter of the compass but, though he thought the temperature had dropped a little, there was no trace of a breeze. It had been Mr Taylor's turn to preach and he spoke from the gospel of St John, the same verses he had recently translated to the New Zealand language. *In the beginning was the Word, and the Word was with God, and the Word was God.* Mr Taylor's foot was still troubling him and he stood on one awkward leg behind the flag-draped barrel. *All things were made by him; and without him was not any thing made that was made*. The congregation was restless, made petulant by the motionlessness of the vessel, day following day and still she held her place as if anchored on that wide expanse of sea. Yate endured the calm better than most. He often thought his relation to the voyage different than that of his companions. Not a one of them had travelled to New South Wales or New Zealand before. For them, the voyage was a long departure; for him, an arrival. Where they could barely guess at what they would face in the new country, everything dear and familiar falling away at their backs, he knew just how the coastline would look from Pinchgut Island and, again, off the Bay of Islands, how the Society's schooner would anchor, a small boat lowered for the rowing ashore. Without closing his eyes, he could recall every detail of the Clarke house to which he would return, this time with Sarah; the Waimate dogs barking at his heels; his tidy wooden rooms and the pear tree in the dooryard, taller than he had last seen it and bare at this time of year.

His first landfall had been at Paihia in the new year of 1828. He arrived in the *Herald* from Port Jackson. *In the beginning*, Mr Taylor had preached and always, for Yate, that moment when the ship's boat nudged sand and he stepped overboard – the water thigh deep, not as warm as expected, the picket-fenced missionary houses white beneath the dark humped hills on the western side of the harbour, the sea washing almost to their doors – he counted as his beginning. Not his being taken by the grocer, Mr Wynyard, as a boy apprentice, not his travelling to London to train for a missionary, not even his being ordained deacon seemed more of a beginning than his first standing on a New Zealand beach, trousers wet to his skin, shoes in one hand, being introduced to Mr Williams's wife and children. The Reverend Mr Williams had already been on board the *Herald* to welcome Yate personally and inquire after Mrs Yate, disappointed to learn there was no such party. All the natives of the place came down on the beach to stare at the new arrival and trade with the ship's men, those of the settlement in European clothes, the others splendid in their patterned skin. The following day he preached in the open air, the chapel at Paihia not yet plastered or shingled. He spoke from the First Epistle of John: *God is love; and he that dwelleth in love dwelleth in God, and God in him.* Monday the committee met and his destination was fixed for Kerikeri. That was his beginning, his new birth. He was twenty-five years of age.

On the poop deck, an infrequent sight when Yate came aft. The Button family, Captain and Mrs, Miss and Master, all sitting out before tea. Alfred Button had fallen down the companionway and, though at first the doctor suspected a broken thigh, had taken nothing worse than bruising to his back. Yate saw the accident had recalled for Mrs Button her maternal sentiments. She pressed her son's head to her cheek, looking sorrowful at her husband who sat curved over his wife and boy like a bent candle, saying, My little dragoon, my hero, and other military endearments. The doctor hovered still, Miss Button turning from him to her brother with equal affection. On the deck beneath the poop, Charlie and Sadler were talking over their troubles.

Call this coming to sea, said Charlie. He had a bruise wealing up over his eye and a bitter taste at the back of his mouth. Mungo had given him a drubbing for the spilling of the milk jug earlier that week.

Mungo says you toldem it was me upset the milk, said Charlie. He did not know that it was true. If he'd had the chance, he would have said it was Sadler and slipped the loveless hands of the steward. The milk was spilled Wednesday and here it was Sunday and Mungo needing someone to beat on.

That's a lie, said Sadler, thinking he could not hit Charlie but might have to take a punch or two himself. That's a blasted lie. The lump over Charlie's eye was already shining blue and would be black before morning. Perhaps they could get something for it from the cook.

Boys! Boys! It was the doctor, peering at them from the poop. That's no way to speak to each other. He cast a glance behind him and lowered his voice. Particularly when Mrs Button and Miss Button are taking the air and hearing every word. The doctor's head withdrew.

Miss Button, said Sadler, whispering, and got a wincing smile from Charlie. But here was the doctor coming off the poop toward them so they hung their heads and shuffled their feet.

Instead of saying, That's a lie, said the doctor, looking severe but speaking gentle, you should say, I believe you are mistaken.

It's very wrong of us, said Charlie, wagging his eye at Sadler. But then, you know sir, we ain't gentlemen. The doctor laughed and took him by the chin to examine his eye.

Next time Mungo has a go at one of you, he said, pitch into him together.

My oath, we will, said Charlie, brave in the sun on the deck and feeling the doctor's finger kind on his bruise.

That one with the knock to his eye, said Hall. Coming up alongside Yate, he spoke as if they were resuming some conversation. He was the one from the galley last night though Yate had to look hard to see the resemblance. There was no fright to him now and nothing of shame. He had an open face and a smooth chin but his arms had muscled and his skin taken the weather since he came on board two months ago. Halfway to a man.

That one with the shiner, said Hall. Once we get to Sydney and the passengers are leaved off, he's to go before the mast.

Is he? said Yate. He felt his ears take up a heat as he remembered how he had taken the boy's place last night, the vinegary weight of the cook and the three loaves of bread this morning like a wedding breakfast.

One cabin boy will do for then, see? Up close, Hall had an easiness to him and plumbed his world with a trusting certainty. I tell him the food's cruel as cruel. But he don't know what it is to be up the topgallant, reefin in a gale, and wants to be a sailor. He shook his head and looked Yate direct in the eye.

You'll have to look out for him, said Yate. None of the ship's brutalities seemed to have come off on the boy and, for one moment taken out of time, Yate imagined what it might be like to be entrusted to his childish care. Hall nodded, serious and slow, as if Charlie's well-being were really in his dispensation.

He says he can take rough usage on the return home, said Hall. He's not plannin to sail again.

And you? said Yate. Will you stop at home too?

Oh, no, sir, said Hall, queerly sympathetic. I'm a sailor. They stood a minute longer at the railing, watching the dark clouds mass high at the horizon.

Them's raindogs, said Hall. And still conversational, Louie says your bees are dead.

Louie? said Yate.

Mr Ferule, then. Hall was smiling some private pleasure. The cook, he said.

Ah.

Did you lose em all, then?

That evening a sudden squall set in while the cabin sat to tea on the poop. The ship rocked forward from her setting when the wind hit and the flying jib boom was carried off from the end of the bowsprit, the sail rent full length. A mass of rain fell, obliging the cabin passengers to pack into the cuddy for the first time in many weeks. Truly, the doctor had forgotten how tightly they were confined. He looked out the window. The dingy oil lamps were lighted and threw their dull gleam in lines on the streaming deck. In tarred jackets, the men were hauling new canvas. The children screamed as they had in previous storms and pulled the tablecloth as the ship yawed.

At the end of his morning watch, the ship going southeast under a fresh breeze at six knots an hour, Hall was on the topmast with a bucket of grease, skimmed by the cook from his pots of boiling meat. Under orders to slush the mainmast from the royal masthead down, he was making quick work of it, coming down fast, since the further from the deck the more the mast swayed and, on an empty stomach, the swottling smell of the fat nauseated him. Starboard, a large piece of mast floated by, rolling in the swell a moment and showing its barnacled sides, then lost to view in the green pitch of the sea. The bucket hooked over his elbow and swarmed tight to the mast, Hall looked squinny-eyed until he made it out again, one thick end riding high on a wave. It gave him a feeling of falling to see the height of a mast stretched out in the water, rigged with barnacles, travelling still. Even allowing for the distance, it seemed at least as thick through the middle as the one he clung to, belike from some ship wrecked on her way or laid on her beams in a storm so that her men had to chop down the mast to save her turning turtle.

When Hall told Louie after breakfast, the cook sucked his teeth slow and ran his fingers through his hair.

Hou wa, he said. That's bad luck. Hall had known it without being told, his heart clabbering in his chest and his feet suddenly anxious for the deck when he saw the mast roll in the water like a dead man. Louie busied himself at nothing while Hall told the story in full, how he had seen the mast from the corner of his eye, how he searched for it again and saw it rearing up on a wave. It was a thick one, he reckoned, and covered all about with mossy barnacles.

The bad luck mightn't be for you, said Louie, though no one else had seen it, Hall was sure. All the same, carry your whale tooth with you *tou-l-tan*. After the business crossing the line, Hall had sewn his whale tooth into a pocket in his hammock but he fetched it out when his watch went below and stitched it inside his shirt. It was a heavy piece, pulling his shirt front down, but a comfort all the same.

That night, after six bells, Mr May called out for someone to lay out and loose the jib. The wind had come up and the ship was canting through the white caps at eight knots an hour. Hall had been taking the day most careful, the dead roll of the ship mast foremost in his thoughts, his whale tooth hanging a blunt protection across his heart. He had only gone aloft twice more, once to furl the royals and once to loose them, both times as slow and cautious as if it were his first stint off the deck. When Mr May called, he was the closest to hand and, though he hesitated, no man came forward.

Lay out, boy, called the second mate again so there was no help for it. Hall jumped between the knightheads and went out on the bowsprit, an underweight boy, his arms hardening with the ship's work, not yet his full height. The wind was on the starboard quarter, the ship rolling heavy at times. Inching forward, Hall got out on the weather side of the jib-boom, his feet sliding fearful on the foot-ropes, both arms thrown about the spar. It was a world of wind and water. The jib-boom bucked up and down as he climbed along its length, the sottering sea a thrash of white and grey beneath him. He looked back along the length of the boom, back across the bowsprit to where a man was standing at the bows, waiting to hoist the halyards. A raw and rafty drift of mist obscured the man from his sight but he clung a moment more, shaking the spray from his eyes, and it was Staines, bow-legged and butter-toothed, like a familiar in a dream. Hall turned his head to his task and pushed on the last few feet, holding so tight to the boom's girth that the whale tooth ranched his chest. He was casting off the gasket, his fingers slippery with salt water, when the ship gave a tremendous roll to windward and the whole weight of the furled sail slipped from the boom, knocking him backwards into the absent clutch of the air.

With empty arms, Hall fell. Dropping beneath the blasted eye of the sky, he looked direct into Staines' pulky face, strangely close across that distance, split and anguished as if he himself were falling, his hands going out like claws to Hall who only fell and fell. The martingale stay caught him across the hips and turned him so that the sea was beneath his feet once more, his hand flung high behind him, catching providentially, as he would always later say, at the stay and near jerking his arm from his shoulder. He got his other hand up to the rope and hung there, a wordless prayer, twenty feet over the water. Unable to get a leg up over the stay, Hall went hand over burning hand the length of the rope until he got his knees to the spritsail yard and Staines, white as nip, came out along the jib guys to help him back on board. It doesn't do to take misadventure too serious at sea. This much Hall knew and would have made light of it but he could not speak a word. The incident had passed unnoticed, Mr May and the men going about their business, unknowing. Staines pressed his urgent face at Hall.

I seen you, he said, in that hot rasp of his. I seen you fall. Hall went forward on his lamb's legs, a whale-tooth bruise welling on his chest that would have shipped water had he fallen and floated in the chambers of the sea.

A new moon, the third since sailing from Gravesend, appeared in the night sky at the start of the week. Some of the cabin passengers took to sitting on the poop deck for hours in the evening to contemplate the heavens, lightly wrapped for it was still just balmy enough. They lolled back where they sat, pressed in their places by the dark scoop of sky, tumultuous with stars. Some of the gentlemen lay on the deck; Mr Taylor had been heard to snore. On Thursday, after tea, the usual company assembled: Mrs and Miss Button, Armistead, Taylor, Gordon and Dr Fowles. The ladies twittered to their seats, Mrs Button throating a cry of pleasure beneath the heaving constellations, and then, after a little self-absorbed meandering, the gentlemen took up their places as if determined by an implacable planetary pull: Armistead in some oblique relation to Mrs Button, the doctor in slow orbit of her daughter. Armistead always hoped that Taylor would fall asleep as he sometimes did and that Gordon, well, he was such a useless appendage it little mattered if he remained or not.

The doctor thought he had never seen the atmosphere more transparent, as if the eye outstripped itself and made out the stars with a telescope's capacity for detail. The sky itself was a curious brown, the richness of its colour heightened by the jellyish clarity of the air, the young moon burning alongside a large planet. Looking now at the night sky, now into the starry eyes of Miss Button, Dr Fowles was taken by a reliable giddiness and laid himself out on the planking, soulful and scientific, at some discreet distance from the ladies. Armistead was twitting Mrs Button with some witticism or other, Mr Taylor making his usual exclamations as to the beauty, the wonder, the sublimity, and their voices washed across the doctor like phosphorescence. He felt he was drowning in light. If he turned his head a little on the deck, Dr Fowles could see Missy's little foot and even her well-covered ankle in her sandal. He did not think it wrong exactly but did not look often. Once, Miss Button had tied her sandal in front of him. She knew her own attractions.

Do you see that planet? his voice a reassurance to himself, going out to the world, solid as a grappling hook. But the ladies could not see and called out Where, where? in their agreeable voices, Miss Button anxious to see for she had never seen a planet and felt the insufficiency.

Close to the edge of the moon, said the doctor. And near as bright as the moon itself. He pointed to show the place but his own finger against the star-spankled sky was at once so undiscriminating and puny that he withdrew it.

I see it, said Miss Button, her head thrown back on her provocative neck, and again, looking at the doctor, I see it. Mrs Button caught her daughter's hand between her own.

I see it, too, she said, though she had her eye fixed on Dr Fowles.

It's only the evening star, said Armistead to the neat curl of Mrs Button's ear. He was finding the doctor more than a little tiresome, calling on the Buttons half the morning, paddling his great hands over Miss Button in her undress and now ready to lecture them all on the night sky. Mrs Button had been strangely distant since their tryst in his cabin, warm but unforthcoming, always in the company of her husband or daughter. At first he had not cared, relieved only that there was to be no awkward scene, but more recently he wished for a further visit and poured out his hopes nightly on his mattress. He could not rid himself of the qualm that he had not acquitted himself as well as he might and thought if he only had another chance at her he would enjoy Mrs Button to his hilt.

Known as the evening star to some, said the doctor, that's the planet Venus.

Venus, said Mrs Button, kissing her daughter's hand so pointedly that Armistead twitched in his trousers and even the doctor was not unmoved. The goddess of love.

Taylor thought the conversation had taken an unsuitable

turn. He did not want to embarrass Mrs Button, naturally, and thought only to put their commerce on a sounder footing.

Here, he said, half-sitting up and unsure as to what he might say, only to see Mr Yate and Mr Denison had joined them, standing silent at the top of the companion ladder. Taylor thought it quite conceivable that Mr Yate had heard everything and would take him for a fellow of very light character, lying on his back while ladies spoke of love. Mr Denison's hair flared white under the moonlit sails.

Star-gazing? he said. It was horrible. There was a companionable murmur from the others on the poop, Miss Button forgetting herself sufficient to say Planet-gazing, I call it, with a plump look in the doctor's direction. Mr Taylor scrabbled his hands through his hair.

Here, he said but the two men were gone, making their way forward, the night still drawing down.

Mr Denison had come for Yate at his cabin and proposed they look at the stars.

It's a rare night for it, he said, hanging in the doorway, his blond hair darkly flattened from his cap, and Yate laid aside his pen. The poop was crowded as a marketplace and he was glad for Mr Denison's suggestion that there was better watching to be had from the cross-trees. It was the last dogwatch and most of the men were sitting idle on the forecastle as they came up. The cook was teaching Hall some scrimshaw work, Yate noticed, their heads almost touching over the five inches of bone. Not teaching him exactly, though Yate never knew. He was honouring Hall's escape from drowning by etching the scene on his whale tooth with a jackknife. It would take him many nights to complete, the incisions only dyed with tobacco juice and standing out from the polished white as the *Prince Regent* passed the Isle of St Paul, late May, but since Hall would not be parted from the tooth, not even for a half-hour, he worked on it beside the boy, scratching in the ship in full sail, the seas curdled about her bows, the tiny Hall adangle from the martingale stay, the whole lot bordered with checks and crosses. For as long as Louie worked the tooth, on the forecastle or in the leaping candlelight of the galley as the days ticked down to evening like a cooling saucepan, his thick, burned-knuckle thumb smoothing off the tiny curlicues of enamel, Hall told the story of his fall, over and over, until it yielded no new detail and the cook remembered it as fully as if it had happened to him.

Yate climbed after Mr Denison up the foremast, losing his head a moment at the foretop when he saw the deck incompletely and a long way down through the huff of the sail. They reached the oaken cross-trees at the topmast head. The new moon hung in the sky like a soup spoon and the ship sailed smooth, her canvas hardly shifting for the constancy of the breeze.

All well, Mr Yate, said Mr Denison, half a question, half a laughing promise. Yate had never been so high before. Though he had been aloft in the mission schooner, only to the maintop and she a much smaller vessel. He would have climbed to the skysail if Mr Denison had invited him. And might have climbed further still, making a ladder of the stars in the thin air of his friendship with Mr Denison. They stood either side, one arm each about the mast, looking out through the neat slices of the topgallant shrouds at the sea tufted with froth here and there. By some trick of the wind, the voices from the poop rose a moment to the topgallant sail: Mrs Button's laugh and the doctor, Forgive me, ladies, it is only a manner of speech.

The cabin passengers seem quite frisky, said Mr Denison from his side of the mast. I'm not sure Captain Button knows how much life there is in his ladies.

The doctor is like a calf taken from his mother, said Yate. All eyes and tongue. It was the tropics. He had seen it before. When we take the Cape, he and Mrs Button will remember they are married.

And then, I think, said Mr Denison, the movement of the ship encourages amativeness. The word had a snub-nosed weight to it that was almost shocking. Amativeness. Yate turned it over in his head. It went some way toward explaining the rush of blood he felt on looking at Mr Denison or even thinking of him. He was a young man in whose heart a work of grace was visible. Yet Yate did not think it could be so simply put down to the ship for hadn't he had a similar sensation in his tent with Edward Parry Hongi, the dark square of ground pitching and yawing, and, beyond the loft of canvas, the soft-lipped sound of Selim grazing in the night?

Of all his boys, Edward had been his best travelling companion. He took the place of Cosmo Gordon Pahau. Edward had a mild character, nearly shy, and a sharp intelligence that fed on everything. After Cosmo's daughter was born and he was taken up by his domestic duties, Edward became Yate's right hand. He was married but as yet had no children. The first night, travelling overland to Whangaruru, Yate had retired after prayers with his boys. He wasn't asleep when Edward came to him, his silhouette a moment in the tent flap, then the sound of his undressing, the neat folding of his clothes.

Mr Yate.

Yes, Edward? Outside, horse snort and the call of a night bird. Edward lay himself down beside Yate, sliding under the covers when he raised them on his arm. In the dark, he was more darkness. Hardly a weight, quick breath, the smell of crushed fern in his hair, buttocks cold to the touch but quickly warmed. He let Yate feel his piece, soon standing against his stomach, and handled Yate with fresh outdoor fingers. Yate straddled the boy's thighs, the blankets pulled high on his shoulders, the air chilling their stomachs. He sleeked his own yard and then lay on the boy, rubbing until the tent was fugged with their panting breath.

Mr Yate, said Edward at his crisis, his voice quieter than ever. I am going. He slept against Yate, back to belly, and in the morning knew what to do without being shown.

Do all *pakeha* do these things?

While they are single men.

Who taught you to do it?

My father, said Yate although in truth he had learned it with Pehi and George soon after coming to Paihia.

Edward Parry Hongi. Leaving his wife at home, he travelled with Yate all around the Bay of Islands and twice to New South Wales. Yate gave him a pipe and six figs of tobacco, a Bible, a red jacket, two blankets and a locket but he would as easily have had nothing. Not like Toataua who never unbuttoned his trousers for less than a pound of tobacco or Samuel Kohe only ever coming to his room on the pretence of looking again at the picture of Sarah who he planned to take for his wife.

The sky was true black at last and liberal with stars. Leaning forward a little at the mast, Yate could see Mr Denison's high brow and sharp nose but since that was sufficient movement to cause Mr Denison to look at him, he leaned back and watched from behind without being noted. He knew it was fanciful but he thought about being wrecked at sea and making land somewhere with Mr Denison. Just the two of them and Sarah.

Could you ever be happy not at sea, Mr Denison? said Yate, his voice small and uncompassed in the great welter of sky. The mast stood between them and neither looked in the other's face.

I've been to sea so long, said Denison, it is a hard question to answer. There were things on shore he missed, for certain. Rain on the roof, say, or walking home late, the windows darkened all about and a sinewy feeling in his heart as if he could walk forever, some sound coming lonely a mile away, a dog's bark or a turn of piano music. Did Mr Yate know the thing? Certainly he did. The sail creaked on its yard. There was a coarse lift of laughter from the poop, Armistead's yelping bark and the insistent snicker of Gordon.

It seems the ladies have retired for the night, Mr Denison, said Yate. Mr Denison swung round on the mast, one foot between Yate's own.

Call me Edwin, he said.

William, said Yate and they descended through the sails to the deck, their names fresh on them as new paint.

The next morning the doctor made his rounds: Mrs Taylor had a violent headache and her husband's foot needed further attention. Mr Taylor could take no weight on his foot and the wound seemed no smaller than last time, the tendons almost laid bare. The doctor sniffed at the afflicted foot but was not too alarmed by its smell. He judged the ankle and the lower leg sound. An application of caustic, he thought, a harsh but reliable treatment. Sailing as surgeon to Hobart Town, a friend of his had a patient whose foot had blackened on the voyage, requiring three amputations in all, the last cut over the knee. Dr Fowles shrank inside his skin at the thought of needing his catlin knife and swabbed the cavity with thoroughness, though Mr Taylor called out, Lord help me, and struggled in his chair. Patrick Kelly was taken ill with a bilious attack but the rest of the steerage passengers seemed to have eaten better. As always, the doctor kept Miss Button for last. She was complaining of a painful tumour, no bigger than a nut, forming just beneath the ear. He slipped into his own cabin to wash his hands before calling on her. Her colour was perhaps a little high but, really, the doctor thought her hearty enough. He palpated the extraordinary curve of her neck but could hardly feel the obstruction, little more than a pimple. Her skin was so shimmeringly white his own hands seemed foreign to him, brown and swarthy. Mrs Button stood by, affecting not to watch.

It's only a small imperfection, he said, pimple seeming too gross a word.

But she's not well, Doctor, said Mrs Button, though he thought it was she who seemed red-eyed and unrested. She's been weeping all night and unable to sleep. Perhaps she needs a full examination? Miss Button sighed under his hand most persuasively.

No, no, said the doctor. I'll make her up a cooling lotion. And tonight I'll come by and administer an opiate. That sounded more promising to Mrs Button. She imagined the doctor handling her stuporous daughter, luminous in her nightclothes. There was something not quite manly about him. He was attentive and chivalrous but it never amounted to anything. She supposed it was the consumption that sapped his strength.

Now that the ship was getting on, the doctor had lost all interest in his gothic story. After seeing Miss Button, he read it over in the hope that he might present it to her that evening but it seemed listless and flat, beyond resuscitation. That sort of literature needed a becalming, he suspected, for the writing and reading both. He had quite forgotten what improvement he thought to secure in Miss Button through the figure of Dr Bartle but the man was a fool, clutching at gravestones and capering with skeletal remains. It was not just Dr Bartle. He knew himself for a fool and spent a sad afternoon reading poetry in his cabin. His linen jacket exchanged for his Scotch plaid loose coat, still he shivered a little. That morning, Armistead's thermometer had registered seventy-two degrees, the weather cooler than it had been. The evening lectures were to resume when the temperature sank to seventy degrees and the doctor wondered he had heard nothing about it. They had become altogether too indolent, amusing themselves on the moonlit poop with unprofitable banter. A stricter organisation was needed as when the gentlemen had gathered together to give each other the benefit of their learning, but the doctor feared it would not come off a second time. Already Captain Button spent most of his day secluded in his cabins, Mr Taylor was an invalid, and Armistead and Gordon were not of a serious bent. He would have liked to hear more from Mr Yate but he was too busy proselytising among the men, fishing for the soul of the third mate.

The first of the cape pigeons were sighted Saturday, sporting in the air above the ship. Pretty birds, white with black spots, they were a welcome diversion. Mr Taylor and Dr Fowles made sketches of them from the poop, the doctor noting more than once that their chief peculiarity lay in their possessing only one external nostril. Since the ladies had out their journals and letter-writing materials for the occasion, this fact was transcribed many times for the edification of family and friends. Miss Button found she could no longer write to Mr Whitlock as she once had. The prettiness of her previous letters reproached her and though she headed each page with a dogged *Dear Mister Whitlock*, her sentences were laid down with chaperoned primness. *Dear Mister Whitlock, The Cape Pigeon is a spotted bird about the size of a large pigeon. It is web-footed and has one peculiarity I never before observed in possessing but a single nostril.* She sighed and looked over at the doctor, his curls now grown over his collar, just as he looked up at her. He was sketching his cape pigeon in the detailed style of Thomas Bewick although he saw that Mr Taylor was

allowing himself to be artistic, his flock of indistinct birds
flung against the skysail, a gay pennant streaming from the
top of the mast. Last night, after dosing Miss Button with
opiate and, at her mother's insistence, sitting with her until
she fell into open-mouthed sleep, Dr Fowles had returned
to his cabin and tried to quiet himself for bed by reading a
little of Bewick's *History of British Birds*. The little egret
with its plump white breast and curved neck had reminded
him of Miss Button and, although he knew it for a folly, he
had studied it for some minutes with an unscientific
interest. Now she sat before him, bending her milky neck
his way.

Soon we shall see our first albatross, said Dr Fowles. Mr
Morris, the first mate, had told him that in these latitudes
albatross were reliably sighted a few days after the cape
pigeons.

An albatross, said Miss Button. She was not exactly sure
what it was. One of those water leviathans, she was sure,
that she had thought would spout about the ship but of
which there had been no sign.

I shall catch one and preserve it for you as a souvenir.
Not a whale then, thought Miss Button, and was left with
the word alone. Albatross.

Yate was lying on the sofa in his cabin, preparing his papers
for the Sunday service. It was Mr Taylor's turn to preach
but since his foot made it impossible for him to stand for
any length of time he had asked Mr Yate to take his place.
His papers all about him, he had nearly settled on a scriptural passage when there was a knock at the door and Mr
Denison was standing there, Edwin, his hair like a torch in
the dark passage.

Edwin, he said, the name still a taste in his mouth. Come
in.

I thought you might like to see the cape pigeons, said

Denison but he closed the door behind him and took a chair alongside the sofa.

My sermon for tomorrow, said Yate, waving a clutch of papers.

I'll not bother you. Denison sat over on one buttock, straightening the opposite leg to fish a length of plaited twine from his pocket. He worked at it, smoothing it flat now and then on his thigh, the fine lines passing quick through his fingers. It was the easiest thing to work beside him. Yate fixed on the Psalms: *Weeping may endure for a night, but joy cometh in the morning*. Scoring out a word here, writing in his margins there, he read over his pages, rocked in his cabin and a new sense of ease. Now and then, he looked at Edwin, a long forelock curtaining his eyes, his mouth held straight in concentration over his fancywork. From the sofa, he could smell him, a familiar scent but one he had not identified until that moment. Not at all the briny smell of a seaman but an earthy nose of humus turned up by the plough, full noon and the birds wheedling after the horse. Bent to his pages, Yate felt now and again the hot stripe of Edwin's glance and felt picked out and polished in that moment as when once in a cathedral, the sun making the window overhead, of all the grey parishioners he alone had been tinctured purple and red.

Finished with his papers, Yate rustled them together and slipped them beneath the sofa. He lay back on the arm of the sofa, one hand beneath his cheek as he had used to put himself to sleep when a child. Edwin brought out the boy in him, that was one way of putting it. Not his innocence exactly although that hung about him as bright and unmistakable as the halos of the saints in the Society's tracts for children. More the newness, the spanking unexpectedness he brought to the world simply by being in it. Yate looked at him, the third mate of the *Prince Regent*, a miracle in the shape of a man. Edwin paused in his work, ducked a look at him and went on pulling the slender strings one over the other, straightening them with his nail each time he made a row. They talked of nothing in particular. Edwin had an old aunt from Kidderminster that had been a missionary to India. Yate did not recognise her name but Kidderminster was not much more than ten miles from Bridgnorth where he was born. He had been apprenticed there seven years to a grocer.

Figs, said Edwin with a grin since that was what they had called the grocer's boy at home.

Oh yes, figs, said Yate. And prunes. And loaf sugar in the paper wrapper. Hams and herrings, though what he most remembered of Mr Wynyard's was the windowless bedroom he had been given under the stairs and the damp smell of mice in the flour middlings. Mrs Wynyard was as short as a child with a soft, whiskery upper lip and a watery nose. She took him with her to hear visiting preachers when they came through town and gave him a sugar mouse for Christmas.

On Yate's invitation, Edwin went with him to Sarah's cabin for prayers. He had a cautious voice for praying, like a curl of smoke that separates as it drifts upward, his fair head bent between theirs.

More and more cape pigeons flew about the ship, riding the gusts that came off the sails and, now and then, diving into the sea, wings parcelled back, a tidy thrust of foam as they hit the water. In the afternoon they were joined by larger birds fashioned like gulls but the colour of well-baked coffee grounds. Nellys, the men called them. On Sunday, the doctor saw his first albatross. He was idling on the poop, biting back the impatience that always took him Sundays when he could put his hand to nothing. The breeze was strong, the water tossed up at the bows and a long braided track of froth in the vessel's wake as far as the eye could carry, but Captain Aitken, of the opinion that ten knots an hour was as much as the *Prince Regent* would safely take, had ordered some canvas taken in. Dr Fowles thought him too cautious and said as much.

Slow and steady wins the race, said the captain, turning on an angry heel and making for the quarterdeck. He could put a man in irons for less but must keep society with his cabin passengers. Slow and steady. The doctor rolled his eyes. There was only one tortoise that ever beat a hare. He would have to break his shins a few times before he was converted to the captain's doctrine. Cheerless, he watched the royal and topgallant sails being clewed up when, in a gap of unexpected sky as a canvas was hauled, came an immense bird, biblically white, that glided on the air long minutes without moving its wings. An albatross. One wing dipped, it rolled a ranging circle above the masts, close enough that the doctor could see the notched ruffle of its pinions. Still he did not give the call but turned his own tight circle on the poop, one hand shading his eyes, all pettishness fallen away in the white rush of the bird overhead. Nothing to be done for it today but there would be some sport tomorrow. The doctor went forward to the forecastle to stake three shillings on whoever first landed him an albatross.

Monday, the ship was all day catching seabirds. Any sailor not on his watch had a line and hook overboard for the doctor's three shillings. Half a dozen nellys had been hauled in, hand over hand, and one albatross hooked by Busby but got away on a broken line. Pat Kelly and James Lyne, Alfred Button and Arthur Taylor, Mr Parker were all morning throwing their baits over. Even the doctor had a line out for a half-hour but he was too excitable for fishing and gave it up to one of the men so he might hurry from man to man, wherever it looked as if a catch might be made.

Cheerily, cheerily, he said to one grey-jowled sailor who had an albatross hovering in the air over his bait of skinny

pork afloat on a few corks some fifty feet off the ship.
That's it, sir. Staines swiped him a look but, unmindful,
the doctor was off to check on Kelly and Lyne, who had
raised a cheer, only it was another nelly, hooked through
the wing and beating up into the sky, the water dripping
back the length of line until, in a flail of feathers, it fell
free. The problem was the length of the line, the doctor
saw after an hour. A short distance from the ship, the bob
of the bait in the water attracted a squall of cape pigeons
not large enough to swallow the hook, which chattered
and pitched together, drawing down the larger birds.
Once on the water, however, the albatross was a clumsy
beast, unable to keep pace with the ship so that the line
must be paid out fast to keep the bait within its reach. His
own line had been quite inadequate, he realised. Mr
Parker had length enough and the sailor with his jaw
grizzled by a day's growth who was paying out the log
line.

In the cuddy, Miss Button sat with her mother, head swiv-
elled to the window through which the doctor could be
seen hurrying about, his coat flung out behind. Mrs Button
thought it most unbecoming in a medical man, consorting
with the men over a carrion-eating seabird. She had fetched
her daughter earlier from the poop on the pretext of
inclement weather.

I see, Mr Armistead, she said, wetting her lip a little, that
you have not been tempted to the hunt. Nearly mad with
his priapic itch, Armistead smiled uncertain. If there were
hidden freights of meaning in her sentence, they could not
be got by his fossicking.

I have temptation enough, was all he allowed himself,
setting himself against the spectacle of the doctor. He
wondered that Mrs Button no longer sought him out alone
but was always trailing her daughter, moonish for Fowles.

A half-hour in his cabin was all he asked, a quarter-hour even. He bit back a moan, remembering how she had lifted her skirts for him, her knees dimpled and shapely. Mrs Button saw Mr Armistead's eyes smoke over. No doubt it was a more difficult business to hook an albatross.

Mr Armistead, I was hoping you might talk to my daughter of New South Wales. Mrs Button rested her hand on the table so close alongside his that he felt its warmth. She's curious about her destination, naturally, and has long exhausted our store of knowledge. Armistead looked at Miss Button, an unregarded book open in her lap, alert to the window's square framing of the deck.

Well, he said, pushing his palm flat to the wood to snatch a moment's contact with Mrs Button's hand. Well.

Let us exchange places, Mrs Button was saying, that we may both listen to you with advantage. An awkward tilting against the table, a fluster of perfumed skirts and he was sitting in the tropical warmth of Mrs Button's seat, still indented by her haunches, the promise of her leg pressed hot against his beneath the table and Miss Button's face turned on the other side toward him, a polite blankness.

As I understand it, said Armistead in a dull voice, all his vitality sunk beneath his trouser buttons, New South Wales is a place of opportunity and adventure.

An albatross was caught and brought on deck before midday. Armistead had addressed the ladies on the climate and flora of New South Wales, its commercial and agricultural possibilities, and was making a delicate beginning on the convict problem when the doctor's call went up. He felt as if a thousand ants were walking on his back. Mrs Button had not left off rubbing her leg against his and once or twice had even teased him above the knee with her bold hand. If it had not been for her daughter sitting at his side, remarking in her musical voice Is it so? and My goodness, he would have pressed himself on her there in the cuddy, devil take the man who said he wouldn't. Here were the missionaries up from their New Zealand lessons and even Captain Aitken going on deck and Miss Button on her feet, thanking him for his kindness but impatient to be quit of him. He stood in some discomfort and followed the ladies onto the bright public of the deck. The doctor was paying out Mr Parker, his voice ringing like the coins. Armistead looked for the albatross. He had expected something like an eagle but here it was, an immense stupidity, wings partially spread but unable to rise, waddling the deck, its feet turned against each other, its call reminiscent of the bark of a dog disturbed at its bone. Soon it tired and squatted in a corner, an overgrown fowl, balefully watching the company. The men tied its bill and would have run a needle through its skull but the doctor, keen to preserve his specimen, finished it off with prussic acid.

After dinner, when most of the cabin passengers had retired below – Armistead in his cabin, door open an hour or two, unvisited – the doctor dissected the albatross on the deck. He had brought a chair from the cuddy for Miss Button who sat upright, most conscious of the honour and her being the only lady present, Mrs Parker excepted. The doctor had removed his coat and rolled his shirtsleeves to the elbow. Charlie and Sadler stretched the bird flat on the deck for Dr Fowles to take its measurements: eleven feet from wing-tip to wing-tip. Miss Button sat with the doctor's coat across her knees for warmth. She had rather a sombre feeling on seeing the albatross pressed to the deck in just the attitude she had observed in the morning sky. Dr Fowles was running his hands over the bird, explaining to his audience the mechanisms of the wing which seemed hugely complicated. He smiled up at her, his fingers entirely lost in feathers.

An oddity of the albatross, said the doctor, is that he has no stomach. He had fetched up his case of instruments which glinted beside him like a jewellery box.

No stomach, said old Mr Davidson in a foxy voice. He thought the doctor might be playing a joke for the young lady.

He et down that skinny pork orright, said Mr Parker. His wife nodded and jutted her chin as if she would fight someone on it. The doctor sliced low on the bird's belly, the scalpel easy in his hand as a pen. Miss Button's ears contracted at the light crunch of the blade on feathers and she pinched her hands beneath the cover of the doctor's coat. There would be blood, she was certain. She had not thought of that before.

Just a small incision for I'm preserving this skin for a friend. Another smile for Miss Button as he rummaged inside the albatross. No, the albatross doesn't have a stomach. The doctor was on his knees, his head twisted back to address his audience. His food goes straight from the gullet and gizzard to his smaller intestines.

Well, said Mr Parker. A gullet, as if he already knew as much.

Fancy word for a stomach is all, said his wife. They did not impress easy. The blood was coming now, staining the feathers and pooling across the deck. It was not so bad, thought Miss Button, if you did not look at the whole bird. She wrapped her feet about the legs of her chair to keep her seat. His hands bloodied to the wrist, the doctor drew out a livid coil of something and a pouch of membrane.

It's astonishing to see what is stowed in the gullet, said the doctor, going in again with his scalpel. A great quantity of oily stuff, slow and dark and glossy, ran out on the planking. Miss Button saw the young Irish boy from steerage pinch his nose and press his face into his friend's shoulder before she smelled its rankness herself. So offensive it filled her mouth with water. She looked away, her own entrails making a violent claim on her consciousness.

The remains of fish certainly, said the doctor, lying a fish head on the deck, its eye socket shining empty at Miss

Button, who pitched on her chair like a boy at the skysail yard. The doctor foraged a moment longer. A medusoid invertebrate. Otherwise known as a jellyfish. Even human – he bobbed his apology at Miss Button – excrement.

I seen him swaller that one, said Staines, happening by, a wink tipped at the doctor but Miss Button was falling from her chair or her chair was falling, she couldn't have said, a weird throttling sound in the back of her mouth, the hem of her skirts dragged through the butcher's shambles as she ran for the cuddy, every eye fixed to her and the doctor following her two steps with his baffled face and murderous hands.

Her head swaddled in a damp towel, Miss Button lay on her parents' bed.

There, said her mother whenever she ventured to speak. There, there. The room was darkened and now and then the uneasy face of Alfred Button hung a moment in the doorway before being hurried off by the ringed hand of his mother. Captain Button shifted restless in his chair. Best left to her mother. She had given them quite a start, bursting in with her gory skirts and her shoes so foul they couldn't be let stand in the cabin, no sense to be had from her, wringing the doctor's coat. Mrs Button sat at her daughter's bedside, stroking her temple.

I do not think the doctor a suitable companion, my dear, she said, her voice pitched so low her daughter did not raise her eyelids, the insinuation swirling inside her head as if it had no external source.

But mama, said Miss Button without opening her eyes, almost cherishing her derangement. He doesn't mean–

There, there. He has shown you no consideration. The firm cool hand across the forehead and a lavenderish smell. And then, a married man. Mrs Button dipped her voice still further as if she named some perverse order of criminality. Married. At first the word meant nothing to Miss

Button. She lay as before, her head weighted with the towel, eyes closed against an imagined light, its sense dripping down to her little by little. A married man. Dr Fowles was a married man. He had let her make an attachment and all the while was married elsewhere. With his bears and his pig-faced ladies. She saw him again, kneeling on the deck, one hand grubbing unmentionables from the dead albatross, leering up at her while every man in steerage laughed and exercised his elbow on his fellow's ribs. And for this she had nearly cast off her dear Mr Whitlock whose face she could still draw from memory though it no longer quickened anything in her. The doctor married and Mr Whitlock like some unhappy effigy of himself, she was once more without prospects. Miss Button cried and slept through tea.

The following day, the twenty-sixth of April, the ship having passed the London meridian in the night, the steward promised a better dinner than usual. After breakfast, the cook selected two animals from the croodle of young pigs in the sty and slit their throats at the forecastle head, the men watching to see where their heads pointed since that marked the direction of the pig's breeze that would follow.

An easterly, said Mr May with displeasure as the first pig tottered about, her front hooves clicking unsteady against each other. The cook stood back, patient, the first pig not yet down and the second gouting and making its last leap. They went out together, their heads nuzzled close in the scuppers, snouts to the larboard quarter which no one could complain about. Dinner was a high occasion, the pork singed and roasted, boiled beef and veal with soup preserved from England and every time the captain raised his glass, pledges made to dear friends left at home. The Taylors were tearily sentimental, Miss Bloomfield talkative.

Mr Yate was on his feet, his cheeks pinked, running a plate of pork on deck to Mr Denison. Only the doctor was in poor spirits, his face long as a pull of taffy. That cursed albatross. Miss Button would not meet his eye though she continued merry enough at her end of the table. She sported with Armistead, who the doctor saw had taken Gordon's seat so he could attend to her more closely, and seldom so much as glanced his way to see the unkind effect she was having, the stammering conversation he made with Miss Yate and Miss Baker, his tongue quite withered at the root.

While Miss Button favoured him no longer, her father took him for his best mark and sat turned in his chair, one eye cocked at him across the ruins of the meal. Captain Button had called on the doctor in his cabin before breakfast.

Captain, said the doctor, his voice warm but his door half-shut behind him against his cabin's disarray. How is Miss Button this morning? He had thought it wise not to call on her the previous evening, preferring to let her parents settle her. Button blew horselike through his nose, balling a familiar piece of Scotch plaid between his hands.

Your coat, sir, said the captain, making it seem a most shameful object. The doctor had not completed his toilet and stood to his disadvantage in stocking feet.

Is everything well? he said, lamed by its clearly not being so. Perhaps Missy had taken a fit and he so neglectful as not to have called. I'll call on Miss Button after breakfast. Captain Button was enduring some internal struggle.

If you know what's good for you, he said, cheeks red with restraint and his voice louder and louder as if they were on two ships passing each other, You'll stay clear of her till we dock. He mashed the coat against the doctor's chest, Dr Fowles's high exhalation a surprise to both men, and walked back to his cabins with a dueller's measured step.

The whole day Miss Button avoided the doctor, her opalescent shoulder turned against him so steadfastly he took it for a form of attention. He could not settle in his cabin, his plaid coat hanging from a peg, unfinished business. With a lacklustre heart, he turned over his specimens. His dried Portugesese man of war, only a tint of its mazarine blue remaining; a sea slug, pickled in a jar; the feathered skin of the albatross that had brought bad luck, after all. It seemed his coat had not been much cared for, webbed with creases that even a damp cloth did not get out. He went frequently on deck in his light linen jacket, hoping for a private interview with Miss Button. Early evening, he heard her in the passage outside his cabin, purporting to call for Alfred. He hurried out at once, a specimen jar sloshing against his chest.

Miss Button, he said, quiet and careful, mindful of her father's proximity. Forgive me. He did not know his crime but was no less contrite for that. Her head went up like an animal startled, nose to the wind.

I don't believe, he said but could no longer feel his way with her. Miss Button stared at his hands, clasped about the jar, her upper lip travelling back over her teeth as if she were about to sneeze. A gastropod mollusc, said the doctor, offering it to her unobstructed sight. All its colour leached into the preserving fluid, obscenely white, its tiny, sawn-off face mouthing the glass. Commonly known as the sea slug. Quite a good specimen. This last less confidently given. He had imagined a quite different communication passing between them. Mrs Button came from her cabin.

Sophie, she said, and with one tender backward glance at the doctor, led her daughter away.

All week an albatross flew with the ship. The doctor marked it as the same bird by its having a great many feathers out of its right wing. All day it flew, and all night. Having trouble sleeping, the doctor was often on deck to free himself of troubled thought, standing at the taffrails shaking his head as a dog throws water. Something pacifying in that glimmer of white wing, the soundless passage of the great bird. Despite Mr Coleridge's famous verse, the men seemed not to have any superstition regarding the albatross, although at night, the ship pressing through the oblivious waters, the doctor felt his primitive heart unclasp when he sighted the white circle of the bird about the masts. On the third night when the albatross still flew with the ship, the doctor calculated that as the vessel made four hundred and fifty knots in that time and the bird went three times the distance of the ship, since it kept her speed yet looped immense circles about her, it could not have flown less than thirteen or fourteen hundred miles in three days. And still, to every appearance, as fresh as when it was first sighted. The doctor noted this in his journal but would have liked to tell it to someone living. Miss Button was no longer his interlocutor nor Armistead who had become her companion, taking on her injury as if it were his own and speaking now to the doctor only in tones of sore disappointment. And Gordon not much in the way of company. He thought of his wife.

The doctor passed his dispirited days in the cuddy. He read a book on archery and made some notes on the history of the sport. An antique and healthful practice, a truly national sport, he regretted its passing. Archery provides superlative exercise, he wrote in his sprawling hand. It opens and expands the chest, strengthening the arms and shoulders, which in females is very necessary and by that sex neglected. He sketched a lady drawing her bow, in bonnet and skirts of a sporting length, a pointily bearded attendant at her side with a quiver of arrows and an emaciated sleek of a hunting dog. A further merit of archery is that it suffers no one to endure alterations of heat and cold as in such violent games as cricket or battledore. Also at the cuddy table was Miss Yate, undertaking her correspondence and stealing her eyes at his illustration. It hadn't escaped her notice these last days that the gentlemen were ill at ease, as disarranged as roosting hens with a fox in the yard. The toy of Mrs Button, Mr Armistead endured some persistent pain and the doctor too had suffered a hurt, probably at the hands of her daughter, that he didn't understand but probed his wound over and over as if the cause might yet be known from the effect. Sarah had an acute sympathy for men, their habit of falling for the myth of their own robustness. Not having to trouble with anything else, women were more adept at managing social engagements. From behind their teapots and sandwich tables, they managed affairs to their advantage without seeming to. Poor men, who could hardly speak to each other except of material things, breeding cattle, the weather, the revolution in France, what chance did they stand against the sophistry of women, the handful of meanings plaited together and floated on a single sentence or their wordless vocabularies of downcast eyes and tossed curls? William was not like a man in this regard but then he was her brother, his general likeness to other men obscured in the welter of particularities she had of him. She was still developing her theories of society and thought they might be furthered through reference to the doctor's journal, but he was only distracting himself with sketches.

I hadn't thought of a lady archer, said Miss Yate, seeing herself observed.

But, yes, said Dr Fowles. It's not considered masculine. Madam Bola, an opera dancer, said that until she was taught the longbow she didn't know the most graceful attitudes. Miss Yate did not know much of the opera but was open to the possibility.

An opera dancer, she said for she had thought it was more about singing. She so resembled Mr Yate the doctor would have liked to make a study of the entire family. The afternoon passed pleasantly in her company, the doctor copying into his journal several useful receipts she told him for lemon sponge, rice blancmange and a stuffing for birds. Like the doctor, she was hungry for arrival.

2 May, 1836

Latitude 37s, Longitude 16.25e

The ship breasted the Cape Tuesday evening. Romancing Mrs Button, Captain Aitken claimed that in this vicinity the winds were so strong he would be obliged to call two of his men aft to hold his hat on his head. There was no sign of the captain's winds, the sea continuing so calm and tranquil that the general remark from those that knew was that conditions had never been seen so promising in that latitude. Taylor took it for a sign of God's smoothing the path for his labourers. He thought often of the gales they were spared to save himself dwelling on what would otherwise seem his afflictions. His foot continued bad, making him a prisoner of his cabin, and he had taken a violent cold that next seized on the children who, dirty-nosed and drooling, were still far from well, even the baby sickly. Though the weather was fine enough, Mary Ford could not be prevailed upon to take the children on deck and was so often in their cabins she reminded Taylor of a story he had heard of a cow falling through a small hatchway into steerage and, being too broad to remove, left there for the remainder of the voyage to Melbourne. Taylor struggled with ungodliness. He supposed it was to be expected. His fellow passengers were not as agreeable as he could have wished. Captain Button and his wife, priding themselves on being a better cut than the rest of the company, were selfish in every action. Even the doctor, who might have been looked to for a better example, he considered mean and irreligious. It pained him terribly to find fault with one of his own company but Miss Bloomfield was a weak body, filthy in her person and disgusting in her manner. Being compelled to keep such close society, he and his wife could not help noticing the peculiarities of others.

I daresay they have noted ours, he said to himself, keeping his foot clear of Mary Ford as she shipped her ponderous bulk from the main cabin to the children's.

There once was a king, Taylor heard Mary Ford say, had three sons. Taylor did not approve of her devilsome storytelling though it quieted the children's mewing. They quite adored her and sometimes called out for her in the night, their voices fierce and directionless in the dark. She settled herself at the foot of Laura's bunk, the slats complaining under her weight, and the two boys climbed down to join their sister. Laura in the middle, all three got themselves beneath the covers, with eyes so round and sickbed hair Mary Ford could have swallowed them. She'd no children of her own, not for dint a trying, and had only left off caring these last years, the lives she might a birthed dead entirely, no longer pulling at her skirts with their webbed baby fingers wherever she went.

There once was a king had three sons. Basil could not listen to Mary Ford's stories if he could not see her. Once he lay in his own bunk with her voice coming up at him and cried until Arthur had called him a baby.

Is it the one with the robber's donkey? he asked now, looking into the soft collapse of her face.

That doesn't have a king in it, said Arthur, who was hardly frightened at all.

Each son was clever. Once she started a story, Mary Ford did not stop until it was finished. Each son was brave and the king did not know how to choose which one should be king after he was dead.

The oldest one, said Arthur. The oldest one is always king. Basil leaned forward to stare at him, his forehead taken up in creases, and then back at Mary Ford. Arthur was the oldest and he was next oldest. Laura was a girl like the baby.

So he called them all to him and told them whoever brought him the most beautiful little dog at the end of a year would be king.

A dog, said Laura, wriggling between her brothers. Mary Ford nodded at the rightness of it, her chins multiplying against her chest. She had learned the story from her grandmother who she couldn't recollect otherwise, a drifting night-time voice.

The youngest son travelled to a forest where he found a lovely palace made of every sort of finery with cat servants and cat minstrels and a table set for two. This was the thing of her grandmother's stories that Mary Ford sucked at like a sugared almond. For all their lovelessness, robbers tied into sacks and drowned with a spit of cats and oysterish eyes put out with red-hot sticks, virtue already had a home and a journey was just a way of finding it. The Taylor children breathed open-mouthed when the youngest son was joined at the table by the most beautiful white cat he did ever see with a purring voice and a delicate locket on her little paw.

What's a locket? said Basil.

It's for ladies, said Arthur. Laura's eyes were shutting, the lids nearly closed, a slick of white showing like a crescent moon.

The youngest son passed his year most pleasant, hunting and watching plays –

Were they all cats? said Basil.

– until one day the white cat came to him and said he must return home. The youngest son had no dog to give his father but the white cat gave him an acorn. Inside the acorn was the smallest dog in the world. Her grandmother had a bit where she did the youngest son holding the acorn to his ear and the dog barking his titty-totty *bow-wow* but Mary

Ford didn't do the voices so her youngest son just rode home with the dog in his pocket.

The eldest brother had a dog no bigger than a shoe, said Mary Ford, and the middle brother had a dog that could stand on the palm of his hand but the youngest brother opened his acorn and there on a white cushion stood a dog so small it could easily have passed through a ring.

The youngest brother, said Basil sneakingly but Arthur paid no mind. He had seen how the story was going.

Taylor shifted bad-temperedly in his chair, his foot's tenderness preventing him moving beyond the reach of Mary Ford's voice. The ridiculousness of it. A dog so small it fitted in an acorn. He twisted where he sat, his leg cramped with keeping his foot still, and a hot swell of pain rode him out. The rest of the day he remained in his cabin, making distracted notes for his New Zealand grammar, and missed the sighting of the whale. Dr Fowles had seen it. Close to the side of the ship, no further than a quarter-mile. At first just the grey fin, its sharp point standing some three-and-a-half feet from the wave. Then the slow surge of its body, the water running off the olive-grey hide in ropy rivulets, its twisted lips wrought about with so many wrinkles that they reminded the doctor of a cabled hawser. A herring whale or fin-back. The men hallooed from aloft and all on deck crowded to the taffrails but the doctor felt the whale had surfaced alongside for him alone. His consolations these days were zoological.

The doctor clung to the poop rail, leaning out like a figurehead, trying to look into the eye of the whale, one sentient animal to another. But the eye proved such an absurd crinkle, its miniscule orb deep-buttoned in the whale's immense head, that the doctor wondered it could see at all. The ship slid southeast, or the whale nor'west, hard to tell with no third point to anchor the perspective.

At a distance of perhaps a half-mile the whale breached, its single plume of aerated water climbing tall, a silver poplar of water, upright a moment, the next tumbling down to nothing among the unremarkable waves. Doctor Fowles kept his face turned to the scene and thought he felt the spray on his cheeks, warm yet from the lung of the whale.

She blows, shouted Busby for he had a spouter's blood and could not help himself. Crimped by the same swage of excitation, the doctor hurried down to the carpenter's side.

A fin-back, said the doctor on his approach.

No good putting the boats after that one, said Busby though his heart started in his chest as if any moment he would give the order to clear away. She's too fast, the fin-back, and always on her own.

A warm-blooded fish, the whale, said the doctor.

Now the sperm whale, she's a different story altogether, a swimming larder of spermaceti.

And distinguished from its fellow fish by having a pair of lungs. And a spiracle, of course.

I been among a herd of them, slapping the water to curds with their massive tail flukes, the air raining red with their spouted blood and that full of upside-down longboats, they might've been umbrellas.

Before the day's last light drained the sky, Dr Fowles visited Gordon with a bottle of brandy. He lay on Gordon's bed, the sea coming within a foot of the open window as the ship's stern dipped behind on each swell, Gordon at his desk working on the preserved head of a cape pigeon.

A solid specimen, said the doctor, refilling their glasses.

She's a pretty one, said Gordon with complacence. The doctor would have liked a stern cabin. Perhaps he could secure one for his return passage. Now, bolstered on a pillow, his glass loose in his hand, he looked down upon the

wave, swelling so near at times, the brine effervescent to his
nose, he might have run his hand through it. The rudder
worked the water to a milky ferment, globules of quicksil-
ver running like a spawn of tadpoles deep in the purplish
green. Keeping the head and feet, Dr Fowles had thrown
the skin of his albatross overboard yesterday. It had been
stinking for several days. The quantity of grease in the skin
makes the albatross a difficult subject for preservation and
the gunpowder and rum he had used were clearly not
sufficient. He might have stripped it back again and rubbed
it down with alum but the easier thing was to pitch it away,
the wretched hide floating in a slick of iridescence until it
went from sight. It's not difficult work to prepare the head
of a bird for mounting, Dr Fowles thought. Little more
required than to clean out the cranial cavity and neaten the
line of decapitation. After all, the structural support is
already in place in the form of the skull. Yet Gordon was
making heavy weather of it, his cheeks puffed out in
brandied concentration.

What do you plan doing with it, Gordon? said the
doctor.

Oh, you know. A memento. For some reason the doctor
couldn't hit on, Gordon had introduced a padding between
the skull and skin of his pigeon, a handful of oakum at his
elbow that he forced into place with a crochet hook. There
were very few places at which a cape pigeon would suffer
upholstering and the doctor thought Gordon's specimen
quite disfigured, its face curiously pouched, its feathers the
worse for being overhandled.

On his third brandy, the doctor was feeling melancholic,
poetic, almost happy. Miss Button had not addressed a
word to him in over a week and, first to his regret, then
relief, the doctor found her indifference promoted his. As
if they had never been loosed from her, his thoughts went

back to his wife. Married eleven years, the more the doctor saw of life, the more he prized her.

How ardently I loved her in my youth, thought the doctor, the brandy fumes tearing his eye. And now with what steadfast affection. Even for his health, he wouldn't wish to be young again, making his way like Gordon with his weak chin and his aviary, or heartstruck by the twaddlesome goings-on of the likes of Miss Button.

We don't see much of Armistead these days, do we? said Gordon.

We might not see much of him, said the doctor, but we see sufficient. He lay back laughing and Gordon laughed too in a minor key, sure for once he was not the joke. There was a tapping at the door which opened to Armistead, a little abashed to see Dr Fowles, but showing as a token of friendship a bottle of his own.

You old devil. Gordon laughed the more, Armistead's unexpected appearance seeming to him to clinch the humour of the situation. We were just this minute talking of you. The doctor measured the interval of time it took Gordon to recollect the nature of their exchange by the colour that mounted his cheek and the alacrity with which he bent again to his cape pigeon, now gawping spherical as a puffer fish but admitting a little more oakum behind its draggled cheeks.

I must've known it, said Armistead, pulling uncertain at his ear but, as he did not inquire, Gordon gave himself up once more to the brandy's warmth and kicked out a chair for his friend.

Evening, Armistead, said the doctor for the sake of friendship.

Evening, evening, said Armistead, taking his place with a slippery look. I couldn't wish better than gentlemen's company at the end of the day. He topped Gordon's glass, filled his own and waggled his bottle at the doctor.

Nothing for me, said Doctor Fowles. I'm for bed. He had

taken more than enough brandy and then, however peaceable he felt about Miss Button, he did not think he had to
bear the spectacle of her most recent beau in rut.

Thursday evening, the weather continuing fine, everyone
who was able strolled the decks after tea. The sun just
setting behind the ship, the air took on that pearlish
quality that precedes true night. An albatross still flew
with the ship, high over the foremast and at sufficient
height to catch the last of the sun's light direct, the illumi-
nation of its white underside and neatly stowed feet a
compelling sight from the twilight deck. The eastern sky
was the darkest blue, one shade off black, the western
quarter the fading orange of the last coals in the grate.
Taylor was on the poop, his foot on a stool, engaging Mr
Yate in matters of religious philosophy. He had been much
exercised of recent days with the question of the heathen.

Can any of them be saved? he said.

A good many are saved already, said Yate, and it's my
hope that very many more might be saved in time. He
thought of the letter Wahanga had sent him at Waimate,
acknowledging his evil nature and requesting baptism. *As
the wind digs up the waves of the sea, so the devil digs up
sin in my heart*. Such a home-made conceit but how well it
called to mind the Prince of Darkness, his cloven heel to a
digging stick, working over the New Zealanders' hearts as
if they were his own kumara grounds. Wahanga's letter was
one of those published at the back of his book and he
wondered that Mr Taylor was not more familiar with their
record of native baptism.

But I was thinking of those heathen we have no contact
with, said Taylor, those who have never heard of the
Saviour and who must live out their lives never knowing
the world to come.

Ah, said Yate. It was not an uninteresting question. Are

men to be damned for never hearing the Christian word?
He feared they were.

I'm not speaking of evil men, said Taylor. Not those who
disrespect the missionaries' message, spurning the Sabbath
and, Taylor lowered his voice, giving up their wives for for-
nication on the ships in harbour. He didn't care to offend
the ladies Button who sat either side of Mr Armistead
calling on him for a song, *The Battle and the Breeze*
perhaps or *Life on the Ocean Wave*. Although truly both
of them seemed to him quite resilient to offence, perceiving
none, hence taking none.

Not those men, not those men, said Taylor, shaking his
head clear of the violent pictures that formed unbidden.
There was a tuning of fiddle strings from the forecastle, a
sawing note refined and loosed to the night.

It's a good question, Mr Taylor, said Yate. I've thought
on it often and conclude that the unbelieving man –
however good, honest, true – who never learns of his sin or
Jesus, his redeemer, must lie down at last, a maggot's meal.
Taylor knew Mr Yate was right and was only pricked more
by the desire to preach God's word.

A ball, said Miss Button, her face near feverish.

Mr Armistead, said her mother, her voice like a rush of
water clearing an obstruction, you must ask the captain to
give us a dance one of these evenings.

Dr Fowles came on the poop in time to hear this last. He
bent his waistcoat to the ladies in an ironic bow and sat
half-turned from them, the last seam of marmalade light
running the sky at the western horizon. He did not think
there would be a dance, the atmosphere cooling so fast that
in a few days they would be again swaddled for winter. Mrs
Button was feeling her daughter's arms in a manner that
might have been wanton had it not been maternal.

You're cold, Sophie, said Mrs Button. Perhaps Mr
Armistead would be kind enough to walk you a little?
Armistead sat a moment longer, a lady on each side, like a

capital turkey being taken home for Christmas dinner, before starting to his feet.

Miss Button? he said, offering his elbow. They walked the poop, a not unhandsome couple the doctor supposed, Miss Button in her swathe of shawl, the pat-a-tak pat-a-tak of Armistead's heels louder than their murmured conversation. Mrs Button sat neat as one of the ratting cats, licking her lip, her eyes whipped to and from. Remarkable that he hadn't detected it before but Miss Button's dipping step, which the doctor had always considered rather subtle and fine, suggested she had one leg a little shorter than the other. The fiddle again, rallentando, the last long note getting up an answering bleat from the goat pen and a rack of laughter from the men. And he wouldn't need much pushing to see her swanlike neck and breast for the disfigurement it was.

The fiddle started in on some wrenching tune, the slim, metallic notes of a flute sidling up and around. There was something particularly tender about music heard at night, Yate thought. He remembered Edwin telling him of walking home late, obscurely stirred by the sound of a far piano. Perhaps it was only that the eye being less assiduous after dark, the ear becomes more sensitive an organ. However it was, even the sailor's rough fiddle and flute were able to carve a space of refuge for him out of the tottering wall of night. Having little to do after four bells, the men had assembled on the forecastle to dance, Edwards on the fiddle, Lamb, the flute. The doctor thought the peculiar steps used in the dance highly characteristic of the sailor. The heels mostly kicking, the toes carrying the beat, elbows raised, hands above the head, the whole action was effortful and made for healthy exercise. Miss Button was only amused by the men's antics, laughing into Armistead's shoulder. Captain Aitken came up on deck, drawn by the music.

What do they celebrate, Captain? said Mrs Button. A birthday, not a wedding, I think.

Nothing in particular, said the captain. They're just passing the time. He took his seat alongside Mrs Button, hoping to do the same.

Mr Taylor, said the doctor, approaching the missionary men. How is your foot? Yate stood to offer the doctor his seat.

No better yet, said Mr Taylor.

Not healing across?

Larger, if anything. And weeping these last few days.

A clear substance? As he descended from the poop and went forward, Yate heard the doctor say, Smelling more like bread or like cheese, would you say?

On the forecastle, the men were dancing, the one called Staines light on his feet and precise despite the slummock of his gut thrown wide as he turned. The air was bright with music and the men's heat. Yate dawdled amidships at the shadowy foot of the mast, the sails soughing overhead, the wood beneath his hand feeling so live it might have sprouted leaf, green and furled. He stood there a minute, the still centre of the men's clapping and the stamp and slide of their feet, the whirl of their bodies as Staines, red-faced, flung himself down, the two Lascars circling each other on their stilty dark legs, the air above their heads eloquent with the tracery of their pale fingernails, pink and shy as shellfish. His head tilted as if to catch some quiet word, all the available light seemingly clustered to his face, Edwin sat on an upturned crate, long legs crossed at the ankles, one knee bouncing on the other, keeping the fiddle's time. Sweet mercy. The sight of him. Yate walked forward across the forecastle's ragged circle of light, not stopping again or looking back but feeling the drag of his glance at his shoulder. He made for the companion ladder and went below to Edwin's cabin where he lit the lantern, eased as always by the room's neatness, everything squared off and

in its place. The music skirled into the cabin behind him
like the wash of a wave scouring out the bow before it
could find its way down the scuppers. No dancer, Yate
turned in a circle, his froggish heart croaking as the men's
feet scuffed at the planking over his head, the doorway's
dark promise revolving past, not yet, not yet, not yet.
Edwin came as he hoped he might, as he knew he must,
hesitant and smiling as when he called at Yate's door, his
arms looped at the lintel. He ducked his head into the cabin
and said nothing. Yate went to him like a bride. He kissed
him on the mouth with the door open, the loamy scent of
his breath reminding Yate of long-shadowed afternoons as
the season shortened to winter, lips warm and dry, the clink
of a tooth on tooth, and kissed him with the door shut.

   Muffled by the door, the music could still be heard in
snatched passages between the banging of the men's feet on
the cabin ceiling. *Let him kiss me with the kisses of his
mouth for love is better than wine*. The ship's rolling
motion, always more pronounced toward the bows, and
now a new unsteadiness. It brought to mind a fleece being
spun into wool but whether that was the stretching and
bobbing or the being made over into some new substance,
Yate couldn't have said. An extraordinary sensation and
unanticipated. He put his hands to Edwin's chest, half to
support himself, half to prevent his getting out from under
his kisses. A vein banged blue at the base of Edwin's throat
and he put his mouth to its fat flutter. He thought suddenly
of Selim's neck, warm to the touch, the hair soft one way,
stiff the other, and opened his eyes to the marvellous pallor
of Edwin's skin, too close for focus, a blur of soft-grained
light. With his every sense caught up with Edwin, with the
man at last beneath his hand and not unwilling, Yate felt
the loss of him, their arrival at Sydney already a departure,
the indifferent ship continuing for Newcastle and India
without him.

   Edwin had his eyes closed, their movement visible under

the thin skin of his eyelids, his mouth open, breathing heav
Yate set to kissing him again, taking into his own mouth h.
body's hot breath, until he felt the graze of Edwin's cock-
stand through the doubled fold of their trousers. There was
a break in the music from the forecastle and then a new tune
wreathed itself about the cabin, slower than the last, the flute
flinging high its hollow bright notes, the fiddle following.
Yate unbuttoned Edwin and fumbled a moment with his
shirt-tails. His thighs long and whorled with blond hair.
Blanched stalk, like a tuber forced in the dark. The sack with
its pucker of darker skin that fell to one side when Yate
hefted its pursy slithering weight on his tongue. Edwin said
something then, the possibility of human speech sounding a
raw surprise in Yate's ear. *William* he thought it might have
been or *Will you*, the thrill of either such that he couldn't
choose between them. He let down his own trousers and
took Edwin in his mouth, the collar of skin rolled back, the
tip the colour of weak tea. *Will you, William?* Edwin's voice
breathy, Yate came off almost at once, kissing and sucking as
if he might draw further speech from him. There was a salt
slipperiness under his tongue and Edwin's seed came down
quick, the first spasm in his mouth, the sour taste of old coin,
the second caught in his shirt-tail. Smiling and easy, himself
already, Edwin sank down the wall, his shirt still rucked,
took Yate's hands in his own, kissed each solemn palm and
bent his fingers over the place his lips had touched.

William, he said, and it was a baptism. They stood
together, smoothing their damp shirts against their bellies
and buttoning their trousers. We can probably catch the last
round. Edwin cocked his head at the ceiling where the slow
scrape of the men's feet could still be heard and ran his hand
over the brushed back wing of Yate's hair.

Yate hung his head back and watched the sails on the
foremast bellied with wind off the larboard quarter,

hardly shifting on their yards. Knees drawn up, he sat
beside Denison on the forecastle, close enough to feel his
warmth through the stretch of his trousers. A clear night
sky with its skinkle of stars and every so often the white
sweep of the albatross over the royals, the last bird to
keep with the ship. Yate felt some kinship with the bird he
thought not quite holy, some pure and lofting sentiment
thrashing feathery in his chest that might spring from his
throat in front of the men and beat into the air to circle
the ship, one eye bent to the deck and Edwin's daily
doings. To a shout from the men, the cook took the centre
of the circle, solid and dark as whinstone. Piggott and the
boatswain, who had been reeling about, sat down with
good grace. Keeping his tune, Edwards made his bowing
shorter to match the cook's handclap which the men took
up directly.

Juba this and juba that, sang out Edwards.

Juba killed a yellow cat, the cook replied. He grinned
and rolled his eyes white in his head. The step was one Yate
had not seen before. Not like the sailors' heel-and-toe, the
cook's bare feet patted careful at the deck as if he were
setting it in place. He clapped his hands and, to the same
beat, slapped one hand, then the other, against his thighs.
Clapping again, one hand to his knee, still the careful
patting-down feet, other hand to other knee, a double clap,
right hand to left thigh, left hand to right thigh, some
whistling from the men, clap, clap.

Juba this and juba that, called the men.

Juba wore a fancy hat. Feet slapping harder, tamping the
deck, white teeth, white eyes, both knees slapped together,
both thighs, clap, clap, faster now, double time, puffs of dust
rising from his breeches. Yate could hear Lamb's breathiness
in the flute seeming now almost human, the notes from the
fiddle falling like a hammer. He looked sideways at Edwin
without shyness and in the wild din, the dervish of clapping,
the deck vibrating so that they hardly knew whether they

tapped their feet or not, they smiled at each other and looked away together.

Juba that and juba this.

Juba stole himself a kiss. From somewhere, the cook had a pannikin of water that he set on his fusky, crinkled head. He clapped his hands together and slapped his thighs and knees, faster, faster, without spilling any water.

Juba that and juba this.

Juba played a game of whist. Clap clap, clap clap. Head steady, the cook slapped himself down, thigh, knee, knee, thigh, his great ashen feet pedalling the deck. The men were drumming their fists on the planking as fast as they could, with no ear to the timing. Panting and laughing, Lamb laid his flute in his lap; Edwards could saw no faster and was outstripped. Abruptly, the cook stopped. He stood a moment, chest heaving, and threw the pannikin high with a toss of his head, the water spilling from it in the air, keeping its wobbly shape, falling, a few drops straying wide, the whole spattering to the deck, the container landing last with a tinny roll. Some of the men went below to their hammocks, others filled their pipes and set their shoulders to the night. Yate squeezed Edwin's hand. He walked aft to his cabin, the albatross keeping its white vigil overhead.

At the close of the middle watch, Yate did not quite wake but drifted in the shallows of his sleeping, turning in the eddies of the noise on deck: the helmsman relieved at the wheel giving the course in a loud voice, twice a man calling some indistinct name or order and the ruttle of feet the length of the ship. A footfall outside, the officers changing watch, the familiar squeak of his own door. Yate half sat in his hammock, twisting to see over his shoulder. It was Edwin, his eyes bruised with tiredness but laughing, his length in his hand, its slim white flank like some deep-sea

fish that never sees the light. By the time Yate was up, his
legs caught in his nightshirt, a little kick required to
dismount from the hammock, Edwin was leaning back on
the closed door, kicking his shoes off, the toe of one working
the heel of the other, his jacket open, unbuttoning his shirt
with one fumbling hand. The salt crust of the night was still
in his hair when Yate pressed his lips against his forehead,
holding his head between his hands, his fingers stroking the
bald knuckles of bone behind his ears. As if skinning a hare,
he removed Edwin's jacket with three strong pulls and
fumbled his shirt buttons through the buttonholes. Edwin
kept a hand on himself, giving an abstracted, loose-fingered
pump when he remembered, smiling his lazy smile, a stream
of talk coming from him that neither of them heeded: send
me away if you like, it's getting colder out there, I knew I
wouldn't sleep, you don't mind? His face was a rubbing in
pink and gold. Naked, he reminded Yate of the time the ship
was becalmed and he had washed on deck with the
steward's boys. Though this time there was the feel of him
like a rare wood.

The albatross had quit the ship in the night. Dr Fowles and
Mr Armistead made a gentlemen's bet as to the date of
their arrival, the doctor wagering they would touch land in
the second week of June. For several breakfasts, every passenger in the cabin discussed the bet and whom they
thought best stood to win. Captain Aitken would not
venture a date.

We'll arrive when we arrive, he said. And not a day
sooner. He directed this last philosophically to Mrs Button,
at her customary place on his left hand.

True enough, Captain, said Mrs Button and they smiled
at each other. Armistead was so tired he hardly fretted over
the exchange. Aitken was too much a dodderer to try
anything, probably. He'd been able to keep him at a cordial

distance previously but now that he had Miss Button to manage as well Armistead found himself stretched a little thin. Fowles too might need warning off. He seemed recovered these last few days but the captain was the less predictable quantity with his run of the ship and his undisguised admiration of Mrs Button. Armistead spent his farmdog days trying to herd Miss Button and her mother to himself and run them from place to place, all the while avoiding the attention of Captain Button. He had thought they could not arrive any sooner than July but perhaps that was just wishfulness on his side.

Surely June, said Mr Taylor to Mr Yate at breakfast, Saturday.

Surely, said Yate but he found there was no urgency in him. When he had first sailed out in 1827, he had been on the *Sovereign*, transporting some eighty female convicts to Hobart Town. The women had not been as bad as their reputations but still he had been impatient to make the shore. Captain McKellar and the ship's surgeon allowed him to preach between the decks. Strange to address himself to a female congregation. Tricked out as ladies, they sat rough-faced, grinning as if they knew some joke but wouldn't tell. His voice sounded like the buzzing of a fly. In a letter to the Church Missionary Society secretaries, he wrote that he was of passing influence only, as a morning cloud or an early dew, but he had not felt as picturesque, stopped under the low deck, his nose stuffed with the close heat of the women.

Perhaps I can come with you when you go among the men this afternoon, said Taylor. He noted that each day Mr Yate went forward, a familiar sight now, his black, crooked length bent to speak with a knot of men as they worked or even going below to the forecastle. He was a practical man, Mr Yate. Little use in chafing with impatience to get to the New Zealanders when there were doubtless on this very ship men that needed saving.

If you can accommodate my poor leg, that is, said
Taylor, fussing with his foot.

Before tea, when Mr Taylor was in his cabin preparing his
sermon for the following day, Yate sat on one of the empty
chicken coops to watch the last of the men's work going
forward for the day. The cold was settling in. Several of the
men parcelling the running rigging had their collars turned
up or were in their canvas jackets already. Charlie was
mucking out a pot on the deck outside the galley, his bare
arms and feet splotched pink. He rubbed the muscle in his
thigh as if feeling livestock at the market and squinched an
eye at Yate.

Sunday tomorrow, sir, he said. Hadn't you be getting
your sermonising together?

It's Mr Taylor's turn, said Yate. They were far enough
distant that they must call to each other. The boy nodded,
his head up a minute longer as if he would say more.

Hall tells me you'll go before the mast after Sydney.

I plan to. He threw another handful of sand into the pot.
Sir, remembering.

A good life, the sailor's, said Yate not knowing quite
what he meant but wanting some luck for Charlie. He went
over and looked in his pot, the dried skin of the men's
oatmeal soup. No doubt that the boy ate better off the
cabin leavings. The pickings from the roast carcasses when
there were any, fruit pudding even, raisins and nuts if he
and Sadler cleared the table before Mungo. But he'd be a
sailor and work twice as hard on biscuits and old horse. His
skin was still a boy's, even unscrubbed there was a fresh-
ness to it. The babyish scale of his feet and hands. There's
no telling what it might take to turn a boy a man. For all
his wanting to be a sailor, Yate hadn't seen Charlie much
with the men. Talking to Hall sometimes, two old coves,
but mostly shy of the forecastle, preferring to spend his

time with Sadler, even putting the jape on the Taylor boys
when Mary Ford minded them on deck.

You done with that pan, *garson*? The cook put his head
round the galley door.

A minute, Mr Ferule. Charlie winked up at Yate or
perhaps only blinked, one eye hidden beneath a hank of
hair, and knuckled at the pot till it rang like a tin bell.

The galley was thick with mutton fog, the steam boiling off
a fatty pot, making halos of the candle stumps that burned
on a low shelf before the statue of the Virgin. His back to
the door, singing *Peggy does you love me now*, the cook
was flensing green off a piece of pork.

Mr Ferule? Silence and the slight hunch of the rabbit
that pauses in the open field on the chance it has not been
seen, ready to bolt at the least sign.

Mr Yate. He did not think the cook had spoken to him
before. Sweet and deep as a dip of molasses. His skin
polished in the heat and the hair on his chest furzily sprouting. He looked at Yate, long and level.

Haven't seen you in the galley a while. He turned back
to his meat.

Nor any of your bread in the cuddy. The cook's smile
started behind his eyes and burned a slow fuse to his teeth.

Will you take a drink? he said, wiping his hands on his
trousers.

Just a drop. The cook turned his piece of mutton with a
potstick which, shaken dry, he used to prise up a board
beside the stove. He drew out a slim bottle and poured a
cloudy measure into two glasses.

Finished, said Charlie, clanging in with the wet pot to
stand, dripping, off the end of the table, the men companionable as two draught pieces. Are you getting up a party?

Go 'long, *garson*, and the boy went, looking to tell
Sadler.

Your health, said Yate. The cook accepted the salute with a nod and swallowed his glass off in one gulp.

Piten de koken. He shook his head at the empty glass, wiping his mouth with the back of his hand.

Piten de koken, said Yate, which made the cook shake his head some more and laugh, a wheezy squeeze of the bellows. Yate tipped his head back and was gagging beneath the pungent draught. One eye streaming, he coughed up half a mouthful of whatever it was, not gin, something the cook had fermented himself. He retched piteous into the crook of his arm, wiping his nose, his eyes closed against his sleeve, hearing the bottle's thick-glassed clink as the cook poured himself a second measure, his free hand patting Yate between the shoulder blades. He lay a moment, half folded across the table, the air passing bulky in his throat's rawness, pacified by the queer thought that he was a cabin boy, only yet half made, petted by the cook and called *garson*.

It's a bit rough yet, I'd say. Yate could hear the smile in the cook's voice and sat up, mopping his eyes. Over the gallop of the boiling water, Mr Yate, Mr Yate, came Mr Taylor. The cook clicked his glass against Yate's empty one, drained it and was standing by the stove again when Mr Taylor, glancing into the galley but not expecting to find his quarry there, wheeled gimpily and came to the door.

Good afternoon, gentlemen. Taylor was all nervous teeth. He stared at the popish altar, candles, a nigger-faced Virgin Mary with one black foot on the serpent's head, a saucer of food scraps, was it?

Good day, said Yate but Mr Ferule had pulled back into the blackness of his body, shuffling and smiling, silent as the missionaries left the galley.

Were you drinking, Mr Yate? Mr Taylor leaned heavily on Yate's near shoulder as he walked, throwing out bright looks in each direction as if he had already arrived at New

Zealand and was not content to let the smallest character of this strange country escape him.

We were talking, said Yate in a manner that invited nothing further.

Of what? said Mr Taylor, insensible. Yate did not know what to do with him. The cook's drink, curling warm in his belly, charged him with benevolence but the men would not attend to him. They kept their heads to their work and, if they did look up at his approach, they cast their eyes away smirkingly. He had noticed this before. One missionary could be a man but two missionaries were always missionaries. He steered for the poop but Mr Taylor stopped, his hand cast off from Yate's shoulder, wobbling and looking back to the forecastle where the men were beginning to assemble for the last dogwatch.

Let's talk with the sailors, he said, taking the weight on his bad foot in his excitement and sucking his breath through his teeth. I can tell them of the sermon I've prepared.

They'll hear it better tomorrow, said Yate but already they were further forward than the galley. Edwin came down to meet them, handsome in a light blue jacket Yate had not seen before that made his eyes the bluer.

Mr Yate, I looked for you this afternoon. He did not seem as gay as he could sometimes look aloft or even below in the half-light, but eager and ordinary in a way that was touching. Can you come to my berth?

I'm with Mr Taylor, said Yate, awkward with unhappiness.

And I'm with Deck, said Edwin. We could play a round of cards, if we fancied.

I am a friend of Deck, said Taylor, sensing some difficulty and imagining it his. Or rather a friend of his father. An excellent Cambridge druggist.

Dick Deck was already in Edwin's cabin, mooching off the back of a chair, when the others arrived.

Mr Deck, Dick, said Mr Taylor, and stood on one foolish leg.

A chair for Mr Taylor, said Edwin, tipping Deck out as he swung on its back legs. He's got a bad foot. There was something attractively loutish about Deck. Yate watched him move to sit on Edwin's sea chest, nearly a short man, compactly muscled with a prideful arse that he carried as if it counterhung the weight of what he toted at the front. A strange friend for Mr Taylor. Deck looked up with a sulky smile and stared Yate bold in the face.

Now Dick, how do you go? said Mr Taylor. I told your father I would keep an eye out for you.

If you see him before I do, said Deck, you can tell him I make out tolerably well.

Tolerably, tolerably. Mr Taylor beamed about the room. He ought to have got among the men earlier. Mr Denison's cabin was quite charming, more than adequate for a single man. He thought of his own cabins and their clutter of furniture and children.

I have been thinking of fathers and sons a great deal, said Mr Taylor smoothly, in preparation for my sermon tomorrow. The story of Amon and his father, Manasseh.

I've been thinking of women, said Deck.

Women too, said equitable Mr Taylor, women too. Mr Yate and Mr Denison were standing like, well, he hardly knew what they were like but it would have been more companionable if they had taken their seats.

One woman in particular, said Deck. He pulled from his shirt a piece of paper folded quarterwise which he opened and smoothed on his thigh before handing to Mr Taylor. A likeness of his sweetheart in all probability. At first the way her hair was put up and even the style of her dress reminded Taylor of Caroline, but Deck's woman had an oddly under-sized head that Taylor recognised as the mark of the hobby painter. Nothing could have prepared him for the savagery of her cleft, naked but for a horseshoe tuft of hair, her skirts turned back, her thighs plump and white with the stockings knotted over the knee. His yard twitched most shamefully. Speechless, Taylor turned the picture that Mr Yate might see but the man only craned his head a moment, clapped his hand to his forehead and lay laughing on Mr Denison's bed. Deck pinned the picture to the wall behind a curtain, laughing too. Even Mr Denison laughed, pacing a little with his hand over his mouth.

Please excuse us, Mr Taylor, he said from behind his muffling hand. We mean nothing by it. Since we can't have the reality, we content ourselves with the likeness. Even with the picture gone from sight, Taylor saw the warm gape of the woman's privates, every detail distinct, laid out like a surveyor's landscape. It was the devil's work, certainly.

You must ask God to excuse you, Mr Denison. Taylor stood to leave, Mr Yate coming after him. They crossed aft together, Mr Taylor on Mr Yate's arm.

I had expected better of Mr Denison, said Taylor who had expected better of Deck. I'm afraid he shows a very weak character.

Weak, said Mr Yate. Exceedingly weak, but he rubbed his hand across his face and Taylor thought he laughed still.

Sunday, since a high wind had set in that morning, a bank of black cloud blowing in from the east, Taylor gave his sermon in the cuddy. He preached without notes and, though the service was not as well attended as those held on the quarterdeck, the weather continuing fair, he trusted it was not unprofitable. After dinner, Yate went looking for Edwin, a pocketful of figs from the cuddy table. The captain had ordered the canvas taken in that morning and with the ship going well under reduced sail, the men were taking their Sabbath ease in the lee of the forecastle. More of a roll than he had been accustomed to the last few weeks, Yate made his way with a staggering step, one hand on the starboard railings. Piggott and Hall whittled light pieces of wood for a pair of model ships under Busby's instruction.

Each of them the same length, mind. Busby was stitching a handful of miniature sails. They've got to hang together. Four or five of the men, including Edwin with his fancy-work in his lap, sat about while the Finn read aloud from a book that must not have been fit for a Sunday because he fell off as Yate approached. Edwin came and leaned along-side on the bulwarks and the two men chewed figs and studied the sea.

I fancy your sermons more than Mr Taylor's, said Edwin, his hair buffeted about his face, sucking fig seeds from between his teeth. The low-lying clouds and distant rain brought the horizon in, the boat pitching on through its smaller world.

You shouldn't think on who delivers the message, but the message itself, said Yate.

Well, the message seems clearer to me when you say it, said Edwin with a young man's stubbornness. There was something in what he said. Yate knew he preached best when he fixed on Edwin in his congregation, that attentive face lifted to him for direction. The words came more easily, tumbling from him as if he were only their instrument. Sarah he was not anxious for but Edwin, careless and handsome, he must be saved. It was like nothing he had known before. Something like being a father, he supposed, the lung-stopping care for a son, your life distributed over a second skin nearly as dear as your own. God the Father, eternally broken on the sins of man. At times, he did not know what he last said but still the words poured from him so that he listened to himself with awe, radiant with the message and sinful distraction, the blue-grey riddle of vein that ran inside Edwin's arm or the smell of him, leaf fires and damp earth.

Sunday night, the Taylor children were not much improved, their spirits wearied by enclosure in the cabin and the renewed rolling of the ship. They called out for Mary Ford who had gone to her tea, fetching her hookpot from below at the cook's call of hot water.

Mary, said Laura in her feverish wandering voice.

Another story, said Arthur, Basil giving it again like the second bell in the carillon. Another story. Mrs Taylor looked at her husband, cast on his chair, his poisoned foot raised on a cushion.

Poor angels, she said, standing from her bunk. Her hair was in some minor disarray, the baby on her hip, red-cheeked and fractious. She went back to the children's cabin, an open book in her free hand. Basil was perhaps a little better, she thought, smoothing their thrown covers and closing the window an inch further.

Is Mary gone to bed, mama? said Arthur.

Another story, said Basil. Mrs Taylor surveyed her children. She would like to get them in a tidy house such as Mr Yate had been describing to her, fresh plastered and fenced, with a flower garden at the front and an orchard coming on. Once, she had believed she would never make the voyage but it had not been as difficult as she thought. The accounts she had heard of the monstrous height of the waves on the open sea were certainly exaggerated. And then Mr Yate's descriptions of the mission stations and the work they would be undertaking among the New Zealanders turned her head to land. Of recent days a worry was worming at her that she might land safe but one of the children pass off in her stead. This was such a heathenish fancy that she had not told it to Mr Taylor. The children were all hale enough and would be recovered from their colds soon but the baby was dwindling to nothing, a great deal thinner than she was a week ago, a rabbity look to her thin limbs and neck. She was cutting her teeth and too light on her mother's arm.

I'll read to you myself, said Mrs Taylor, and then you must sleep.

Mary reads without a book, said Basil, his look serious and considering.

This is a different sort of story, said Mrs Taylor. And Mary Ford a different sort of woman than any she knew. She sat on Laura's bunk, Basil hanging his head over the side at her, the baby unmoving.

Come, my children, said Mrs Taylor in the not quite familiar, honey-combed voice she used for reading. The winter is passing away, the spring is coming on, and the voice of the turtle is heard in our land. Will you not accompany me on my journey? Basil stared at his mother for a stretch and then withdrew his head.

What is the voice of the turtle? said Arthur after some whispering and giggling.

It's from the Bible, said his mother in her workaday voice. You remember the Song of Solomon where it says that the flowers come, the birds sing, the tree is putting forth her green figs and the vine the tender grape? Arthur leaned across Basil, thinking he might understand better if he could see his mother.

Well, that's when the voice of the turtle is also heard. Mrs Taylor smiled into his dent-chinned confusion.

But why does the turtle talk? said Arthur.

The white cat talked, said reasonable Basil.

You'll see as I go on, said Mrs Taylor and then, in a voice like Laura's, piping and with the edges of the words rubbed away, she continued, Where is our dear Mother going? Mrs Taylor's story was not received as well as she had hoped although, with a martyr's determination, she persevered.

I am going to Mount Zion, the city of the Living God, the heavenly Jerusalem and to an innumerable company of angels. If she couldn't hold the attention of her own children, she could hardly expect success with the New Zealanders, the women quite depraved and given over to temptations that Mr Yate had been too kind to detail.

You wish to know how I mean to go on my journey. I must walk for the path is drawn in lines of blood.

Blood, said Basil but he was nearly asleep. Laura had settled on her back, eyes closed, breathing heavy through her mouth. Mrs Taylor stood with the baby and saw that the boys were damply tangled, Arthur's arm out of the covers and thrown across Basil who opened his eyes and smiled, the dull, unfocused smile of sleep.

16 May, 1836

Latitude 40s, Longitude 62e

Though the sky was clear, the ship went forward grousingly, creaking over every wave and shivering sufficient to pop the nails from her bulkheads. After his noon observation, Captain Aitken stood on the quarterdeck, sextant still in hand. He stared beneath lowered brows at the high, sparkling seas as if more than any study of the sky they would tell him what was to come. The serried waves came on, the spume blowing back from their crests, their neatness runnelled behind by the broad unravelling furrow of the ship's passage. Two kinds of men are made at sea, the vaunty and the prudent, and Captain Aitken was pleased to count himself among the latter. He smelled the mineral tang of high winds on the way and reduced the sails further, ordering the topgallants doused entirely. It seemed she might yet run the gales they had been fortunate to miss around the Cape. The ship was buckish enough to keep the ladies in their cabins, though some of the gentlemen stood at the cuddy door and Parker hung off the weather taffrails, his round face a glisten of salt spray, tongue lolling like a dog's at sea.

Close to the end of the second dogwatch the wind came up suddenly, the yards creaking like teeth being pulled, and the captain gave the order to clap a reef into the topsails. The men had been half-expecting the call and were quick to settle away the halyards on deck and haul out the reef tackles. There was the usual bustle on deck as the men

jumped to their work, Mr Morris calling from the forecastle, Quick at it, and the passengers, cabin and steerage,
come above from their tea since the spectacle of all hands
at work was too enlivening to go without. Miss Button
came up with her mother and sat before the cuddy
windows, flattering her profile in the last light of the day.
Mrs Taylor could not be persuaded and Mr Armistead, too,
remained in his cabin. He was suffering from sea qualms,
according to Mr Gordon's report. Mr Armistead with Mrs
Taylor. A curtained impoliteness brushed light at Miss
Button's consciousness, a beat of faltering discomposure.
She felt herself fixed in her pose like an insect in amber. But
no, the vision of Mr Armistead and the missionary's wife
was too ludicrous, the joke bubbling seltzerish at the back
of her nose. How he had thought her a handsome young
woman, the doctor never knew. That curvature of spine
and neck. It might look well in a swan but she was a better
illustration of weak will than the crooked old man in his
physiognomic manual. He went to the cuddy door and,
sheltered from the drift of salt mist, watched Hall, one of
the ship's boys, run the length of a halyard on the deck, his
hands quite russet with tar stains.

Hall supposed he was much changed since first he came on
board for the work was second nature to him now. More
than that, seeing the foremast switch in the wind, he could
have given the captain's order himself. Better to reef now
than get called aloft after the watch had gone below. At any
rate, he must be a sailor for he did not ache for land as the
passengers did, their scurfy optimism flaking away, the
lustre quite gone from them. When the weather was fair,
the gentlemen liked to come forward and stand at the
bows, snuffling their nostrils like the few sheep that
remained in the longboat and ruining their town eyes on
the endless waste of sea. A sailor now, he would like to get

a look at New South Wales. Some of the men had been to
Australia already: Louis, Mr Morris, Pirrka the Finn,
Davis, Edwards. Mr May's brother had drowned last year
in the *Neva* as she tried to make the Bass Strait. It was a
queer place by every account. In summer birds fell roasted
from the sky and the Indians there died twice, coming back
the first time as white men, the second as kangaroos. Louis
said the ladies at the Rocks would eat him up; a tasty bit
like him didn't come their way often.

Lay aloft, shouted the chief mate from the forecastle.
Lay aloft there. Before the reef tackle had been made fast,
Hall saw Mr May and Mr Denison scrambling up the
rigging to take their places of honour at the weather and lee
earings and in the scrimmage that followed he got barefoot
over the back of Staines to stand along the foretopsail yard,
elbow to elbow as if in a taproom with Piggott and Clerk
in the buffet of air. It was a wild brotherhood to be
plunging high above the ship, the air sharp with the flap
and snap of the sail, a fist of wind down the throat. Strung
along the joltering yard with the rest of the starboard men,
Hall gripped his reef-point and, angled to the wind,
dragged it inchingly toward Mr May. The larboard watch
had taken the maintopsail but since the first mate never
went aloft they were one man short and had only just
passed the weather earing when the second mate called out
from the foretopsail yard, Haul out to windward. Down
the shrouds and backstays the men slid, the line passing
easy under Hall's calloused hands and the lock of his
ankles. At the topsail halyards, he sang out lustily, the
common pitch and roll of the deck no match for the swingle
of blunt air above.

The captain glowered a full minute at the reefed canvas
before he gave the order to Mr Morris to send the starboard
watch below. A trinkle of water falling into his hammock,

Hall slept in Cull's and when the call came for the middle
watch was glad of the jacket he had stitched and tarred from
a stretch of canvas begged from the sailmaker. The watch
went quietly enough given the gale and when Thomas Lamb
of the morning watch relieved him at the helm, Denison
slipped through the quartergalley window into Yate's cabin.
Darker than the deck where the birling white foam of the
waves threw a dimmish light, William's cabin was at first
only a smell, damp paper and cinnamon, before Denison
made out the lick of his face, bare and boyish without his
eyeglasses, his hair tousled up in a cock's comb.

Is it quietening up there? said Yate from the swaddle of
his hammock.

Blowing a gale, said Denison, made shy of a sudden by
his outdoor rawness, the tarry stiffness of his outer clothes,
his hair brined wet. He turned his back to the cabin and
shuffled off his coat and trousers.

You should have taken the bed. Denison had his bare legs
between the cold sheeting. It'd be warm by now.

We warm it quick enough. Yate crossed the cabin on
quick feet, heels lifted from the chill of the bare floor, his
skin cooling as he went, bringing to bed the gift of his
body's warmth. His only gift, he thought, not at all
troubled, even serene, his hands having the run of Edwin's
skin, the bluish white of unwalked snow, the slow bunch of
thigh muscle and his breath thickening and slowing. They
slept easily together from the first, the one curled around
the other. He had his lips at Edwin's neck, the unprotected
curve of it, the smell of old laundry rising from his shirt as
it warmed between them. Hours yet till breakfast. He
talked at the dark, though Edwin was falling into sleep,
always tired these days, ashed hollows under his eyes.
There had been a pork supper he had enjoyed once travelling through the valley of Mangakahia. Just a piglet really,
so young its hooves hadn't yet hardened. His boys killed it
for him.

Mmm, said Edwin to show he was listening. Mmh. He ruffled his fingers through Edwin's hair, its animal coarseness always a surprise. He had made a stuffing from the provisions in his canteen: bread, butter, nutmeg, pepper and salt mixed to a paste with a wild duck's egg.

Mmh. Mmh. Edwin's grunts of assent kicked into the grubbling breath of sleep but still Yate talked on of how he'd tied the piglet's nose to his tail the better to lay him in his tin plate and roasted him for nearly an hour in an iron-pot oven. He hadn't eaten better at the London Tavern. Yate's voice slowed and slurred and he slept at last, rocked against Edwin's back.

By morning, the gale began to clear. One by one the reefs were shaken out and by noon Tuesday, the topgallants were loose again, bellying before a smart breeze, the men's wet gear hanging like salted hides in the shrouds to dry. Or so they seemed to the doctor when he came up from seeing James Lyne, the atmosphere below still fetid enough to leave a stale taste on his teeth despite the blast of fresh air on deck that filled the sails and pointed all the goats' beards nor'west. It was the men's shirts in particular, their stiff salt arms and tails pegged wide, that reminded him of cured pelts. The wind forcing the water from the corner of his eyes, Dr Fowles looked hard at their buttons, their frayed cuffs and collars, until the hides seemed only shirts again. James Lyne was raving in his bed and the doctor had no inclination to lose his own hold on the material world. A peculiar case, James Lyne. The doctor did not know quite what to make of him. A solid young man by every appearance going out as a clerk to a mercantile house in Sydney, he had recently taken fits and been very subject to delirium.

A few nights previous, Lyne's bedmate, Kelly, had come for the doctor, saying James had taken a turn. In their dark poke of a berth, the ceiling beams so low and curved as to prevent a man standing full height, James Lyne howled in his nightdress, an open-throated scream as if he birthed an abomination. He sat hunched at the further end of the bed, his knees drawn to his chest, his slender, hairless calves in feminine disarray.

What is the matter, Mr Lyne? The doctor was pleased to hear the ordinary sound of his own voice. James Lyne showed the whites of his eyes. His hands fluttered like a staysail in a crosswind.

It's me, said Pat Kelly. I've fetched the doctor.

I seen old Mr Davidson, said James Lyne. Just stood there looking at me in his undershirt. The doctor waited but there was no more. Even as an apparition, Mr Davidson did not cut much of a fearful figure. The boy was clearly deranged. He quieted him as best he could with brandied milk but this morning there had been little improvement. This time the doctor had bled him, his blood coming slow and sickly. He would call on him again by evening. The doctor pinched the bridge of his nose a moment, the shirts strictly shirtlike. Next on his sick list was Mr Taylor. His foot needed consultation and he reported a boil on one of his knees, a swelling of glands in his groin and a sprain in his back. They could not be more than a month off Australia, the doctor was convinced. Land would be the best cure.

Just before midnight, Hall's watch below and as snug as could be expected, there was the tinny blast of the boatswain's whistle and the call of the chief mate, All hands take in sail. The scuttle was thrown open and one of the larboard men shouted, Save ship, save ship. Sleeping in his damp clothes, Hall was quick from his hammock but like a drunkard on the unexpected tilt of the forecastle floor, the slant of the hatchway ladder such that he could hardly make his way. Every man was above, even the idlers who were usually left to their berths at night, the cook and the carpenter, the steward and the sailmaker, called up to man the halyards. The scene on deck was horrible. With the water she was shipping and the difficulty of sparing any men for the pumps, the ship rode low and sluggish and now with the sudden gale she was almost on her beams, going forward on her side, the lee ends of her yardarms lurching into the barming water. Hall had seen nothing like it though the men were full of stories about ships turning over completely, their masts pointing fathoms deep to the seabed, a handful of men bailing into a longboat, forced to dine off each other after days of endless sea. There was more of the sea in the ship than Hall thought possible, waves regularly breaching the bows and the thigh-high water sloshing from side to side half a dozen times before it could all be got down the drowning scuppers. Mr Denison was there, a furred hat pulled nearly over his eyes and Staines grinning like a wound and Parks, was it, Parker, the quaggy old sailor travelling steerage, rolled in a piece of tarpaulin and dragging himself by the weather taffrails along of the men. Two of the larboard watch with Mr Morris were wrestling the wheel on the quarterdeck, pitched about, their feet quite leaving the deck at times, as though they broke a horse. The ship canted on a violent swell, the far yards dipped and Hall lost his footing on the high weather side of the deck, slid six feet down the slope of the deck, his bare feet in a wash of water. By his collar and a hank of hair, the Finn hauled him back. They stared at each other, their everyday faces seeming to each quite remarkable, and fought on to their stations.

Captain Aitken rose from his cabin and made the quarterdeck in his nightgown.

Hard down the helm, he roared into his speaking trumpet, a vein like a rope raised on his forehead, his skirts flying before the winds like a schooner. Hard down the helm. It blew almost a hurricane. The halyards were loosed but still there was no chance of clewing down the yards, the sails stomaching beyond capacity in the storm. Above the boom of the water and the timber's squeal and groan came the heavy knell of the ship's bell, its giant clapper worked by the yawing of the vessel. More than the sight of the men being lashed to the wheel to hold their places, the inhuman tolling of the bell quailed Hall's guts. It seemed to him the gashful sound of a phantom ship, alone in the night, her men already drownt, their souls cast off, a desperate hulk on the black waters. There it was agen, the clappered brass of the funeral.

Clew down, trumpeted Captain Aitken, or must have done because Mr Morris was shouting on the order, Clew down, clew down.

In his cabin, rocked on the sounds of the men and the struggling ship, Yate lay awake, his eyes dry with worry. He had visited Edwin in his cabin earlier that evening but they had parted without their usual prayer. Just to see the man once, the balm of him. The lurch from the hammock, the floor sooner than he'd thought and askew. In the deeps of the cabin a bright flowering and the taste of blood where he bit his tongue, falling. *The wicked are like the troubled sea, when it cannot rest, whose waters cast up mire and dirt.* He got his bare feet into his shoes and made the passage, lamp in hand, its gob of yellow light swinging wild in the woolly obscurity. Several of the cuddy chairs had come loose and tumbled between the table and the wall, their dissolute legs in the air, mounting each other and casting broken-sparred shadows. A half-kneeling scramble, Yate reached the door to the deck but it would not give. Edwin, wrecked and broken, sinking in the greenish murk, unsaved. *There is no peace, saith my God, to the wicked.* His maggoted lips and the charnel-house of his ribs washed up on an unknown shore. The doorhandle moved readily beneath his hand but the door remained fast. Lamp on high, Yate peered through the thick lozenges of the door panes, the barleyish light giving him back the room's reflection, his own distraught face, and beyond that the crazy reel of the deck and three men swept from view on the end of a rope. The door gave an inch and was flung wide on the wind, the white clamour of the deck scouring out the cuddy. Parker rolled past in a waterproof wrap, looking workaday and pleased with himself. At last, Edwin, toiling against the deck's incline, his ears muffled beneath fur flaps like the villagers at the Hikurangi pa with their savage hair long and lank and so matted that it formed two hanks over their ears like the greasy lappets of an old Billingsgate woman's cape. He could have laughed with the relief of seeing him, frowningly intent on his work in a rain of sea, but what came was prayer. He made his tottering return to the cabin, tongue honeyed with thanksgiving, at his back the plangent toll of the bell.

His wet nightgown spanking about his legs, Captain Aitken kept to the quarterdeck. He raged full as ferocious as the winds that bulged the canvas such that the yards could not be brought down.

Clew down, he shouted again though the men were giving it their best. He beat his speaking trumpet on the railings. Something must give. Pray God it wouldn't be the sticks themselves. Hall tipped his wet face to the skies as all around him the men did the same. Though the rigging still shrieked and the ship's hull rang on the ramping waves, the wind had laid off some. Hall thought the vessel lay over less for his footing was not so quavery-mavery and at last the yard was clewed down and the order given for close-reefing. One of the first to follow Mr Denison up the weather rigging, Hall saw Parker done up like a savage in his tarpaulin mat going aloft to the maintopsail with the larboard men, nimbler than he looked for a man his size and plainly practised at the ropes. Over the foresail, frapped to the yard with miles of bunt-line, the rain turned to sleet that came in shoals on the belching wind. Hall leaned over the topsail yard with his watch, clapping his numbed hands together to get back the feeling, the water black all around except where it leaped white and grey, thinking wishly on a dry hammock and a pannikin of porridge. Mr Denison was leaning over the yard-arm at the weather earing, his hat gone, his hair a wet tumble, shouting across to the men. Some encouragement by the look, his mouth nobbut a black hole. Impossible to hear anything against the storm without the man stood direct alongside. Hall looked to Piggott, as usual on the next reef-point, his nails dug into the jack-stays.

It's a life, innit? shouted Piggott. It was a woltering hardship was what it was but Hall wouldn't have traded if he'd been waged to do so.

For once the larboard men were at their halyards before the starboard watch were down and Hall heard them singing out before he made the shrouds. The gale had coaxed itself to a squall and Mr Parker, who took some personal credit for outblustering the storm, led the men in a roistering three cheers.

What the devil, said Captain Aitken, a ghost on the quarterdeck, but Mr Parker had set to thinking of his wife and went below before he could be clapped in irons, his fat neckless head framed a moment in the companionway.

The devil, said the captain, handing over to Mr Morris and took himself below. The ship was riding better, though low, and the chief mate put some men to the pumps to assist her buoyancy. They had hardly put their backs to it – *Time for us to go, ho, ho* – when Hall looked over to see an uncommon wave, sleek-sided, its creaming head near halfway up the main rigging, that breached amidships, the

poop quite lost beneath its thunderous fall of water, the
cuddy afloat and Mr Yate's window completely stove in.

It seemed to Yate at first a judgment. There was something
so pointed about it. Even as the water poured and seemed
as if it would never stop pouring through his window, the
very window that Edwin favoured for his night-time
comings and goings, he saw the neatness of its moral
lesson. He had been lying in his hammock, thinking. Or
perhaps sleeping, since when the wave breached his cabin,
the rush of water was the sound of his being dragged up
from crystalline depths. In the lamp-black dark he hung, a
bag of rude flesh, so frightened for his life that his prayers
came without spirit, flung out without hope of salvation
like a hen coop thrown to a drowning sailor. When he came
to himself, it was Edwin he thought of first, then Sarah. An
injury of sorts, he knew, but he savoured the two of them
together, their careful manners with each other in their
teatime visits to Sarah's cabin. She could speak of nothing
at all and it seemed something. When she told of their
Shropshire childhood or even her own adventures, her
stories seemed to Yate something he could lay a silent claim
to, something by which Edwin might know he was more
than the sum of himself. Still the water flooded through the
rent in his cabin. No longer the sound of his blind papers
scuffing and furniture overturning, there was only the
gulping of water as it forced its entry and the curiously
woodland effect of its pooling into his cabin. His hammock
hanging true, Yate didn't think the ship was going down.
He closed his eyes to hear the better but there was no alarm
that he could make out, no sound of anything much. The
waterfall at his quartergalley window lightened, the last
trills distinct and musical, then dried up completely. He lay
over the peaceable slosh of water, waiting.

A whinnying protest, a goat afloat or Miss Bloomfield,

and beyond that the reassurance of men, their footfall and the burl of their voices, Mr May with a lantern, and Edwin in the crack of the door, hardly able to open it against the weight of water, his eye dark with joy or perhaps only tiredness.

All right, sir? said Mr May.

All right, Mr May. He was grinning like a boy on Christmas morning. Any news of Miss Yate?

Also well, sir. Mr Taylor is seeing to her and the other young ladies. The two men had his door open and were standing over their boot tops in water, the floor gilded like an evening duck pond, a lapping of light across the walls and ceiling.

All the sleeping apartments in the poop has taken a pretty good bath tonight, said Mr May. Half the watch crowded into the cabin, Edwin's eye was dainty of his. Yate saw that he busied himself with putting in the deadlight, his back turned to the hammock, the long screws held between his teeth. His hair was wet through and thrown into points, his fingers bumbling with cold. *Many waters cannot quench love, neither can the floods drown it: if a man would give all the substance of his house for love, it would utterly be condemned.* Piggott and Hall got down on their knees, so wet a little more could make no difference, and baled up the water as it slewed from side to side. One of the able seamen, swarthy with a brigand's mustachios, waded about like a mussel man at low tide, catching at a shoe or a pair of trousers as they floated up.

Allez-oop, he said each time he secured something. *Allez-oop*.

Hope they isn't your broad best, sir, said Hall, half-laughing when a jacket came up, its pockets still spouting.

Now, Samson, said the jokesome Mr May. It was what he called the boy, once no bigger than a spritsail sheet knot but fast putting on a sailor's body. You know Mr Yate is a religious man that don't care for earthly pleasures.

I'd have thought it was sailors didn't care for pleasure, said Yate, so light in himself he might have floated over their heads even without the hammock. He was enjoying himself hugely and would have said *Allez-oop* given the chance. While we reverends dream in our dry beds, you're riding the mast in the teeth of a gale.

Ah, but you haven't seen us ashore, said Mr May. A slow wink about the room, Piggott looking around to see how Mr Yate took it and back again to the hunch of his work, his thick ear flushing meatily. Your savages are lambs in the comparison. Yate saw the men laughed only after he did. It was something like a party in his honour. Now and again Mr Taylor came along the passage and looked in at the cabin door, a lamp in one hand and a stick in the other, a man roused from a dream.

In the morning, the doctor made his rounds of the cabins to offer his professional assistance should it be required but, if he were honest, his real interest was in some colour for his letters to his wife. Apart from the letter he had given the pilot off Deal, he had been unable to get anything else to her. He had written steadily, excepting the four or five weeks when Miss Button had taken his eye. Some sixteen pages he had now that he carried with him, folded over in his breast pocket like an armour for his heart. He wrote of food mainly, sometimes the weather. Any gentle thought he had of her he wrote down at once before the hurly-burly of the day cast it adrift. On their last night together, his weak health such that all his husbandliness must be advice, he had told her that should he fail to return, she must marry again. The thrilling unspeakable thought of a second husband. She had cried in his arms until they were both quite limp with satisfaction. He had said as much again the morning of his departure, the children waving a handker-chief from the cottage window, asking that she mourn him a little but take a husband before their son put on a beard. Yet here he was, ten thousand miles from his family, the first of the cabin passengers to put his head on deck after the storm, so much healthier than before, his cough all but gone.

All the cabins below had remained intact throughout the night, a slight wash of water down the starboard companionway the only indication of the deluge in the poop. Miss Yate's cabin, likewise Miss Bloomfield's and Miss Baker's, had taken the wave, though Mr Taylor had set most to rights again. Mr Taylor was making quite a virtue of his family's having been spared.

Truly we may say God is good, he said although the doctor was not persuaded. A faulty logic, often a weakness of the religious. After all, Armistead had slept through the night undisturbed and he was playing the guardsman with Mrs Button and her daughter both. He helped Mr Taylor reposition Miss Bloomfield's bed clear of the window although it seemed it had suffered most from water leaking under the door. Mr Yate's room was worst damaged though the man himself swung in his hammock, mild as milk, unable to dismount for the fearful wrack. Half a foot of well-trampled sea slurry prevented the doctor's entry so he offered his commiserations from the doorway.

It could've been worse, said Mr Yate from his sailor's bed. Mr Denison has gone for a couple of boys to shovel the floor clear. The desk too would need shovelling, the doctor saw, and the bed. The deadlighted gloom brought his spirits low and he thought remedially of his own neat cabin, his horsehair trunk stowed beneath the bed with its handstitched coverlet and his roped shelf of natural specimens. Mr Yate was dealing with the situation admirably. To look at him, you might have thought him strung between apple trees in a summer orchard.

The following day was quieter. Mid-morning, a weak sun broke the cover of the clouds for an hour or two, the sea foam tossed about by a quibbling breeze. Captain Aitken turned all hands to unbending the old sails and putting up new ones. When two new topsails, a new foresail and mainsail, were bent, the old sails that had always seemed white as white were sent down plainly scorched and yellow. Never before used, the dazzle of fresh canvas was laid on with a complete set of new earings, robands and reef-points and, with new braces and clewlines going up fore and aft, Captain Aitken considered he had a good suit of running rigging again. The passengers were holidayish after the gale, sitting on the poop as much as they were able, their spirits lifted with the entertainment of the men running up and down the ropes, tiny dark figures against the high loft of the sky, the old sails taken down and lying jaundiced and tattered on the deck. Yate sat with his sister, watching the cut-out doll of Denison rising and falling on the rigging until he felt that his eye had threaded every reef-tackle and spilling-line on the ship. The cook had his fire going once more and the steerage messes could be seen at the galley door, collecting their pea soup and dumplings for dinner. Mrs Parker cut her husband's hair at the forecastle and then, for a couple of pig's feet, James Lyne's and Pat Kelly's. Lyne was looking a little better, the doctor thought, though he would not speak above a whisper and had a shrinking look to him as if he'd been caught lifting brandied figs from the steward's pantry. The men's hair tumbled promiscuous on the planking, a few eddying gusts against the forecastle and a wide scatter. Dr Fowles suppressed a shudder as a clump blew over the toe of his shoe.

Sydney soon enough, Mr Lyne.

To be sure, breathed James Lyne, his forehead, newly exposed by Mrs Parker's handiwork, bulging pale over his brows. Mrs Parker opened and closed her crafty scissors at the doctor.

I'd givyer a good price, Doctor, she said. Snick, snick, the insinuating scissors. He did not catch her meaning at once. Still in his shirtsleeves and removing the short hairs from his ears with a wetted finger, Parker laughed, gave the doctor a fat wink.

Ah, said Dr Fowles, one nervous hand to his curls. Not for now, Mrs Parker.

Won't git any shorter, you know, said Mrs Parker but she put her scissors in her apron pocket and made short work of her jellied pig's foot.

Yate's cabin was so gloomy after being washed out that he slept several nights in Edwin's bed, returning to his own in the hours before dawn. Edwin had finished the rope fancywork he had been working at, a shortish wide strip in the turk's head pattern, a handful of loose strands at either end, the twine fashioned in a series of interlaced squares that reminded Yate of a quilt he had seen on an American whaler anchored in the Bay of Islands. He guessed a bell pull when Edwin asked him.

Guess again, said Edwin but Yate couldn't think. Too thick for a bookmarker surely. Perhaps some nautical device.

I should have asked Sarah, said Edwin, smiling broad. He was a half-hour off his watch, sitting up, the bed so narrow that Yate must lie on his side against the wall. Its a bracelet. For you. The idea of a bracelet did not seem to Yate so very manly but Edwin was fastening it to his right arm, not at his wrist where he had thought but over his elbow, holding the loose strings taut between his teeth while he worked the piece closed. Yate held his arm upright, the sleeve of his nightshirt falling back, his chin puckered in consideration.

There, Wiremu, said Edwin. It was William's New Zealand name. They had not so many letters as the English

and must get by without. His own name would be Erewin;
William had worked it out for him.

You'll have to cut it now to take it off, said Edwin. He
pulled the blanket over William's shoulder and kissed his
eye shut.

I won't, said Yate. Take it off, I mean. He wasn't sure
how he felt about the bracelet and kept his eyes closed, listening to Edwin move about the cabin, getting ready for his
watch. His heart clumped as if Edwin had traced his turk's
head pattern directly on his skin with a needle. A woollen
jerkin for warmth and his waterproof in case it came on
again for rain. Edwin pinched out the lantern and made the
door in the dark, Yate pressing his face into the pillow's
sourness, the soft fall into sleep, like a child put to bed
while adults still move through the house.

The ship rode out the week under reduced sail, the
weather continuing rough enough that from the royal
yard the white sun rolled in the socket of the sky. Hall did
not come down directly. He clung at the yard that bucked
and tossed, looking down on the deck through the dark
ropery of the rigging, most of the sail furled and the spars
festooned with lines. Nothing like the models him and
Piggott were making with the help of the carpenter. His
fingers too thick for the delicate work, Piggott had settled
for a one-masted yacht but Hall, knowing no other ship,
made his a faithful copy of the *Regent* right down to the
binnacle and the tiny fish-davit that he had stained with
tea. Too grown for such theirselves, they were to be given
to the Taylor boys. He would be glad to let his go. With
all its undersides in view, the exposed keel-pieces and
timbers that in any ship at sea were under the waterline,
it looked a lumbering thing howsoever careful he hung it
with canvas. He turned his face to the circling horizon
that marked in every direction the limit of his sight. The

sea was blue and raked with foam, the sky cast over complete with cloud so light that the sun's disc could be seen behind, canting about like a second ship. Where the sky and sea joined, there was a slight bending as if Hall rode the highest point and everything else was a falling away from his prominence. No gull, no ship, no island but still he saw plenty. A sort of footprint in the water three miles to larboard where maybe a whale had sounded. He hadn't seen a whale with his own eye so they seemed yet fairyish creatures. They've seen you, boy, Busby had said, even if you haven't had a look at them, and gave a quackling laugh what might as easy been a cough. Low in the sky to the southeast, a thickening pelt of water meant a gobbet of bad weather before dark. Friday afternoon, they shipped one freak wave that plunged down the open steerage hatch. Saturday, they passed St Paul's in the heart of the night.

After Saturday's second dogwatch, the starboard men went below. Not yet raining, the wind blew such rafts of salt spray across the deck they were soaked to the last stitch. A miserable gang, wedged jig by jowl into the pitching forecastle, some of them changing their wet clothes for damp, none prepared to ship for sleep since every sign was they would soon be called above again. The lantern swung from its hook, its smoking, guttering light making strangers of them all. The last month of the voyage, they were down to ham oil. Hall's tarred jacket hung off the end of his hammock, streaming and ungiving as if it still had a body in it. His shirt was only wet where his jacket leaked along its seams but he could squeeze the water from his trousers. He poked about in his kit without finding anything better, chafed his feet warm with a handful of oakum. The men were readying for a game of cards, sitting in a circle around a chest that swooned and wavered under the gibbety lantern. Piggott was in, patting a space beside him to show Hall where he might sit but he had no liking for High Low Jack so waved him off, climbing into Cull's hammock with his feet bundled in his canvas hat.

The lantern swung to and tother and was cursed for a laggard, the men cupping their cards at the light, trying to make them out.

Can't hardly see if I'm holding kings or queens, said Piggott half-boastful, his tousled hair standing up like a porkingpine.

Anything's a change, said Davis. Given how this time of night you're usually holding yourself. The men laughed greasy in the swing of light, Piggott hunching his shoulders to his ears and making a show of looking to his cards.

First thing I do makin land, said Staines, is get myself a hot feed of ribs and Yorkshire pudding. The lantern tipped overhead, catching Hall in its waxen circle, the men at their cards losing their eyes in the shadowy swags of their foreheads.

If you don't take a drink first, said Edwards, I'll buy you the dinner myself. Staines laughed with the others.

Nothin wrong with a drop before dinner, he said, taking a wet-lipped suck on his pipe. Good 'nough for the captin, it's good 'nough for Mr Staines. He knocked his pipe out on his knee but it had been empty the last few days and was habit only.

The last man with tobacco, Pirkka the Finn was taking it by the hen's noseful, his smooth face behind the blue cloud drift of smoke like a gibbous moon. He held his short-stemmed pipe square in the middle of his mouth and when he breathed out every man breathed in. Staines put down a card and fished in his pocket for a pinch of tea leaves that he tamped in the bowl of his pipe.

Still playin, old woman? he said to the Finn. Imperturbable behind his smudge of smoke, the Finn toyed with one card a moment, played another. Limp as worn corduroy, the cards had lost their twank and went down silent on the wood. Edwards' game. He raked the pile to himself.

Lucky is all, said Davis. I only win if there's a wager on it.

That's not my recollection, said Edwards. Claggy with tar from who knew how many sailings, the cards were difficult to pick up. In the tropics they couldn't be shuffled no how.

Get on, said Davis, his cheeks bricking red. If you're playing, play.

I was thinking of that game you had going at Java, said Edwards, putting down his card slow while Staines yipped laughing and even the Finn smoothed his mouth with the broad back of his hand. Couple of years back, weren't it? Seems you had a bit wagered on that game. Listening large from the trough of Cull's hammock, Hall saw Davis had his mouth turned down mulpy, scowling at his fist of cards. All around the circle, the men were playing their cards in turn, faces turned expectantly to Edwards, their clothes steaming in the jouncing lantern light.

We was anchored off Schiedam Island while the captain tried to get a cargo for the homeward leg. Twelve hours' shore leave, Davis and me got into a game with a couple of boatmen, didn't we? Edwards put down a card, turned his hand palm up above the cards. His game again. The slow rake of the cards.

Anyway, pretty soon it's clear we're being cleaned out by the Javas and I bail out the game. But not Davis who always wins if he's got a wager on it. His money's long played away. Twenty plugs of tobacco he got in Sydney. There's a sigh at this, a moment's breathed sympathy for all the pleasures the men have known and lost. Even his shoes. Around the table the cards are paddling down. He's got nothing left to play. They've got no English, the boatmen, or hardly none but with some pantomime, some pointing at the sun and counting off in stones, they offer to play another round; everything they've won off Davis against the hours left in his shore leave. Two bells but still no call for all hands, the ship falling heavy down a joltering wave, Hall was fighting sleep, the smear of the lantern seen through his lashes.

He lost, a course. Davis had played out his hand and gloured about at his companions.

Watch and weep, said Staines, playing a card and calling the game his.

Now the thing of it was, said Edwards, these two boatmen who between them made a sailor look rich, turned out to be playing for China Charlie, the ship's providore at Samarang Bay. And he comes over pretty smartly with a silver tray of tea and sweetmeats for me but Davis he takes inside for hours. Returns him to the ship before night with his shoes on his feet and all his money jingle-jangle in his pocket again. All the men look sly at one another, Davis shaking his head low like a horse at a gate.

What was you doin all that while, Davey-boy? said Staines, skewering him with a look. He lit his pipe and the tea leaves flamed up and went out, a quick draw of black deviltry.

I told you already, said Davis. I was teaching him English.

I reckon you was, said Staines, dealing the next round. And learnin the Chinese for can't sit down, I bet. He enjoyed his laugh like it was a rare drop, rolling it at the back of his mouth while he looked about all the men, even trying for Hall when the lantern swung wide.

Leastways when I got home my wife was waiting for me. Davis spoke so quiet Hall thought himself the only one to hear.

What? said the Finn.

You think losing a card game's something, said Davis in an uphill voice. Pirkka comes home from that self-same trip and he'd lost his wife. His three cherry-bums calling some oyster-seller Pa.

That wasn't it, said the Finn but he dropped his cards and stood, the rest of the men scattering back, Staines growling low in his throat like a dog before his bark. Davis still sat with his cards up.

Well, that wasn't all of it, he said reasonably. With our sails still in harbour, she was showing her mutton for tuppence a feel.

Stand up, said Staines and Davis stood, looking about uncertain like a man as laid his hat aside and forgotten where. Without taking his pipe from between his teeth, the Finn bucked his great head back and smashed it into Davis' face, the blood gouting from his sideways nose, his cards falling one after the other from his hand. Davis took a step back, another, one hand to his clarty nose, bubbling blood, and the Finn took him once in the eye, once at the ear, two chops and Davis was down like a fall of potatoes.

He's not done yet, said Staines, lifting Davis to his feet as he hulluped up his hard tack and tea. Come on, man. But the Finn took up his coat and cap and went above. The clampering sound of the men's feet on deck. Three bells.

After a week of rough seas and rolling cabin, Armistead was ready for calmer weather. He woke to the new week, resolved to action. He had been led by the nose too long. All the previous week, giving the word to Gordon that he was seasick, he had loitered below, déshabillé, in full expectation of one of the ladies Button tapping light at his door. The mother probably since she was the bolder and had visited him once before. Or perhaps Miss Button with her sloop neck and her coltish sense of not knowing what to do with her limbs. Just let her come. He waited in vain,

Tuesday, Wednesday, Thursday, Friday, the only knock at his door Gordon's, that shambler calling on him twice a day to ply him with sickbed strengtheners from his private store. However Armistead clacked his tongue or pretended sleep, he could not be got rid of inside a half-hour.

Did you tell the Buttons I was indisposed?

Yes, said Gordon, his paddle of a face sprouting crimson. Mrs Button and Miss Button both.

What did they say? A pause while Gordon examined his shoes.

I don't know they said anything as such, he said at last, even a falsehood beyond him. Armistead put his face to the wall. Who could know his torment? He had been hard for days it seemed, tender beyond pleasure, and dared not lay a hand on himself for fear one of his ladies would call and he already spent. By night, he slept distracted between sheets so stiff they would have to be put overboard on arrival, the prong of his yard like a spritsail yard preventing him from turning in his bed. Then he frotted himself to the brink of madness, imagining Mrs Button's dimpled knees, and once, god help him, the two ladies giving him suck together, and spouted lonelier than a midnight whale.

Monday morning, the ship had ceased its heavy lurchings and Armistead woke to an idea as straightforward and uncrafted as the best of plans. He would ask Mrs Button to call on him. It had worked before. Or Miss Button if he fancied the change. He chose his clothes with his usual care, laying out a roll-collared waistcoat and a plain bow stock with buckram stiffeners. Miss Button or Mrs Button? He smoothed himself with attar of roses, laughing at how his problem had become so very much simpler. No matter. Whoever crossed his path first he would ask. Pomaded and cologned, he made his way above, almost cross-eyed in the passage outside his cabin in case the Button door should open and confront him with the prospect of both at once. No one in the cuddy except the doctor who always sat early to breakfast. Mr Yate and Mr Denison with their heads together in the doorway. Good mornings all round and the two men took their leave, going forward, arms about each other's shoulders. Armistead stood content and blinking on the poop, the canvas so much whiter than he had remembered, the mainsail banked over his head like a great cloud. A moment or two and Mrs Button came on deck, caught sight of him on the poop, her mouth open as if she would hie him from there, then hurried up the companionway. Too late he remembered that previously it had been with the civility of his card that he had requested she call on him.

Mrs Button, I was wondering–

You're well, Mr Armistead. She was lovelier than before. That stripping gaze and the tip of her inflaming tongue caught between her teeth.

Quite well, madam. I wish– but before he could choke his desires into an acceptable formulation, there was Miss Button coming up the companionway like a curse, all smiles and tripping along the poop on her little cat's feet.

Mama, is Mr Armistead completely recovered?

You must ask him yourself, said Mrs Button, turning to her daughter but breathing as she turned his exact wish, I shall call on you a quarter before three, so that all day Armistead was unsure it had been anything but his fancy.

A riotous romping day. After breakfast, the Buttons retired to their cabins, the missionaries below for their lessons. A strong wind from aft and though Captain Aitken paced the quarterdeck and scowled, it held. A quarter-hour more and he gave the order for a reef to be shaken out of the topsails and the reefed foresail set square. The ship muscled forward, foaming at the bows.

Another reef from that foretopsail, said the captain. Armistead sat on the poop, cosseting his hope that grew virgin and billowing as the canvas overhead. Tackles were got upon the backstays and everything that could was reeved tight and steady, the ship fair spanking across the water. Dinner was a frolicsome affair with the captain at the head of the table boasting on the fettle of his ship.

She's sweet when she wants to be, he said on a mouthful of mutton. I'd trust this bucket with my life. Mrs Button laughed, her small oval teeth showing milky in her mouth.

Oh, she said, a bucket, sir, as if there could not be a better joke. Armistead for once did not care. The damn ship could sink tomorrow if today he had Mrs Button in his cabin. I shall call on you a quarter before three, he had thought she said. She was looking at him from across the table, head on one side like one of Gordon's pet birds. Rather than think of her further, he put his face to his mutton and potato. Armistead sported himself like a handsome man, Mrs Button thought, though in truth she considered him curiously assembled. His forehead made from two distinct parts and protuberant teeth that pressed his lips forward as if he were always about to say something but thought better of it. Something unfinished about his face. She almost felt sorry for him.

After dinner, Armistead went below to his cabin, his nerves so wrought that he must lie down however briefly. Miss Button sat with her mother on the poop. A lovely girl, thought Mrs Button and was herself taken aback by her fervour. Sophie had colour on her cheeks and the cream curve of her neck was blotched with blood. Skittish, she had been giving off an animal heat since breakfast.

Are you tired, Sophie? said Mrs Button.

Not at all. She shook her head as if it were preposterous. But you, mama? Perhaps you will take a rest? Mrs Button stood and smoothed her skirts.

I will send Alfred up to sit with you. The air was white

with the ripple and pop of the wedding-cake sails and Miss Button sat beneath them quite dazzled with the world and its ungluings.

At ten before three, Mrs Button let herself into Armistead's cabin. His head came up with the opening of the door and she saw he had run himself ragged. Before he could get to his feet, she came across the cabin and took a chair alongside his.

You flatter me, madam, said Mr Armistead, a rake once more. He put his hand to her chin and leaning awkward across the arm of his chair kissed her, eau de cologne and his mopish breath. Mrs Button suffered his kissings a minute and then pressed him back in his seat, her hand at his chest. There was something doglike about him, an amber light deep in his eye that struggled after human intelligence, a patience that was wearying.

Shall we ever arrive, Mr Armistead? We were not made for the sea, I think. Mrs Button spoke inconsequentially and worked her kid slipper from her stockinged foot. Her slipper was long and thin. Lying on its side, it seemed impossible that it could hold a foot. Mr Armistead swallowed. He had never seen inside a lady's shoe.

The doctor thinks we'll land within the three weeks, he said, though everyone had heard the doctor's pronouncements at dinner. My own guess is– Mrs Button wiggled her foot in its white Lisle stocking and gave Mr Armistead a hot stare. His guess forgotten, he got down on his knees before her, his gaze tangled in hers, and took her other foot in his lap, its plump upper, the high arch of her instep through the leather like fine saddlery. As if viewed through the wrong end of a telescope, Mr Armistead was suddenly a long way off and unremarkable. He might look better in a regimental jacket. Surprising how that altered a man. There was a creak, a metallic click at the door, the startled beam of Mr

Armistead's face swinging past, and Sophie was letting
herself into the cabin, trembling and hardly able to stand,
even her mouth bloodless and unpractised. It seemed she
might faint away but she stood and looked at her mother,
half-smiling beneath her Apollo knot, her foot sliding from
Mr Armistead's thigh as he reeled away, still on his knees,
Miss Button, Miss Button, bleating. Her mouth hung open
which Mrs Button thought did not suit her. She was startled
clearly. Altogether too lovely, Sophie wore her best pair of
embroidered day gloves and, as if it were yet some error
easily rectified, consulted the card her mother had slipped
beneath her breakfast plate that morning, a little frowsed
from overuse, Call on me in my cabin at three, over Mr
Armistead's signature.

Mama, she said, with no particular emphasis.

Sophie, said Mrs Button, slipping on her shoe and taking
her tender and motherly from the cabin, an arm about her
shoulders and many kisses to her ear.

He aha te Atua? Yate began the lesson with a revision of the first catechism.

He Wairua nui te Atua, replied Mrs Taylor, *he Wairua pai hoki–*

E matau, said Yate, prompting.

E matau ana– Mrs Taylor's mind was elsewhere. She wanted concentration, she knew. Flighty, Richard called her.

Melons, Mr Yate? she said. Do melons grow at Waimate? They had not had fresh fruit for months. Or any vegetables but potatoes these last weeks. Her husband looked up from his book, his brow corrugated, as if he had come this far on the promise of melons.

Not that I know, said Yate. Not melons. He looked awkwardly at Mrs Taylor a moment, her disappointment plain. Plums though and apples. Mr Clarke was quite successful with grapes in Kerikeri. Oranges too. His mouth watered and he felt his want of manners in having to swallow before Mrs Taylor. She did not seem to mind.

And berries? she said indulgently. Anything of that kind?

Currants, said Yate, tasting them as he spoke. And raspberry canes that Mr Davis got from Port Jackson. Mrs Taylor laughed, her head lowered once more to her book, and looked up at him from beneath her cap as if she thought she might have been teased. He had been about to say strawberries of which there were very many produced at every mission settlement, eaten at Christmas with the pudding. Grown wild, they were the only remaining sign of the routed Wesleyan settlement in the Wangaroa Valley. He had come across them once among the fern on an overland trip with his boys a couple of years back. Not a shingle or board of the house remaining, not even a walking track, he wouldn't have known the place but for the wild strawberries and, after some beating about, a broken peach tree, little more than a trunk with one green pencil shooting new from the bark.

He looked at the Taylors, their unsuspecting heads bent over their workbooks, training their tongues in a new language. As Christians, they thought they knew already the impermanence of the material world but in New Zealand they would experience that knowledge newly. Nothing to be said about it for now. He thought they were making good progress in the language, particularly Mrs Taylor who seemed to have some flair for pronunciation, her husband preferring to concentrate on spelling. Though confined to her cabin this morning, Sarah was more than proficient. Of course, she had the benefit of private conversation classes. Even Edwin had picked up a few phrases, not all of them polite. *Kia titoitoi taua*, he would say, rocking the bed laughing. As they neared their destination, the Taylors became quite grasping in their desire to know more until they seemed to Yate almost as voracious as the New Zealanders. When he had first come to the country they did not want to learn anything but supposed that if they let their children attend the mission school, they would receive a payment. He smiled thinking about it. The very same thing in relation to taking a pill or draught of medicine. On recovery, likely as not, the patient presented himself at the mission settlement to claim the fee he thought owing. Now, of course, they were building roads to their villages and raising buildings so that the missionaries might come and teach them to read and write their own language. Yate gave up the catechism for the morning and instead led some drills in grammar: *te tangata; o no a ta to te tangata;*

ki te tangata; te tangata; e te tangata; i e ki te tangata. The doctor could hear the lesson from the cuddy: *ten tomato, o no a title ten tomato, keep ten tomato.* He was feeling low again, that bleak-spiritedness that came on him from time to time without warning. The Buttons kept to their cabin; even Armistead had gone to ground again. There was no one to talk to except the children, playing in the corner under the negligent supervision of the Taylors' servant. He was glad when Gordon came by, at a loose end himself, and suggested they make up a card game in Armistead's cabin.

In about the longitude of Cape Leeuwin, the ship was making good speed, such a steady wind behind her that Captain Aitken had ordered up studdingsails for the fore- and mainmasts. He stood on the quarterdeck, the sun on his back, his hat keeping the hair from his eyes. With an easy cantering movement, barely any sideways swivel, the ship went forward, handsome as ever. A small thought burst expansively in his head. A captain loves his ship always like a father loves his child, but it's easiest when she's in full sail and getting on magnificent. With the sails piled up once more and the weather steady, the men were put to getting the ship ready for harbour. The standing rigging was being tarred down, new coverings and seizings fitted, and though there was not opportunity for varnishing, the ship was being scraped back from aft to stern. Captain Aitken deliberated a while as to whether he might send down the new sails and bend the old set in their place but in the end left things as they stood. There was still Bass Strait to come. Plenty of time for recklessness once he'd landed.

Dinner was a quiet affair. Mutton, roast and boiled, and more potatoes. The Buttons had their meals sent down and, hearing Charlie and Sadler rattle their plates in the passage outside his cabin, Mr Armistead came late and hangdog to the table. Captain Aitken looked liverish at the potatoes greenly sprouting on his plate and waved his glass at the steward for more claret. Not much point in sitting down if Mrs Button stayed below. Dr Fowles tried for sociability at his end of the table, asking Mrs Taylor how her lessons were coming on.

Getting easier, I think, said Mrs Taylor, looking around for her husband who nodded through his mouthful. Where we have twenty consonants, the New Zealanders only have nine.

Nine, said the doctor. He wouldn't have imagined. It's a wonder they can speak at all. On the doctor's right, Miss Baker and Miss Bloomfield exchanged a look of uninterpretable blankness.

We've translated Genesis, said Mr Taylor at last. He had been having some indigestion and chewed each forkful fifty times before swallowing. Matthew and John.

Genesis, said the doctor with some warmth, for he had a particular theory about Genesis.

Kenehihi, said Mrs Taylor. There is no G in the language, you see, so we make do with K and the H takes the work of the S. She had said too much and blushed at her plate.

In the New Zealanders' Bible, said the doctor, what is the original sin that brought death into the world? Mrs Taylor did not quite follow his question. Gordon breathed slackly through his mouth and smiled when anyone looked at him.

It's the same as our Bible, said Mr Taylor. There is only one Bible although many translations. He had put it rather well, he thought. In New Zealand he would preach in the native language and he thought simple formulations would be best.

And the original sin is– ? Mrs Taylor saw that the doctor was waiting, eyebrows raised. It seemed he really did not know.

Adam and Eve's disobedience, said Mrs Taylor.

It was the apple, said sulky Miss Bloomfield. The others treated her as if she was as stupid as Miss Baker, locking themselves up for private lessons without her. She hadn't enjoyed herself so far and didn't imagine New Zealand would be any more to her liking.

There is a thought in certain circles, said Mr Taylor with some delicacy, that Eve was the original sinner and Adam more properly her victim. This was an idea he had been elaborating since his conversation with poor Pat Kelly, the Catholic boy in steerage. Mrs Taylor looked at her husband narrowly but he worked his upper lip and would not meet her eye.

Adam also ate the fruit, said Miss Yate.

I don't believe a fruit was literally meant at all, said the doctor, seeing his opportunity. No one paid any mind though Mr Taylor contemplated him a placid moment with a grass-chewing expression.

Adam also ate the fruit, said Mr Taylor. Regrettably so. But I am not convinced – he dared a glance along the table at Mr Yate who was swinging back on his chair, playing with his knife in an ungentlemanly manner – I am not convinced he knew it was forbidden. He nodded a couple of times, freshly persuaded of the rightness of his argument. I think it a fair interpretation to say there were many trees in the garden and Adam may not have known which was the tree of knowledge.

It was the apple, said Miss Bloomfield unmoved. Captain Aitken had finished his claret and stood to take his leave. He disliked such discussion intensely. Rather be back in the forecastle again scraping the tar from beneath his nails than idle away his dinner making over the Bible. Yate was spinning his knife over and under the knuckles of his right hand without dropping it. A trick he had learned from Edwin. It was because they were two men that they could look at each other's nakedness without shame. He wouldn't have thought to consider himself after Adam but Edwin was like the first man, beautiful and fallen.

Later that night in Edwin's cabin, he told of the cuddy conversation about Adam and Eve. Edwin was not impatient as Captain Aitken had been. He sat easily as ever, listening in his loose-necked way.

The serpent himself could read the Bible to his own advantage, said Edwin but he could see that it was not enough. I think, he continued, speaking slow and watching William's face as closely as ever he watched the surface of the water, I think we're all sinners and by the blood of Christ are saved. It was a good thing to have said. Yate took off his eyeglasses and knuckled at his eyes, smiling. There was in Edwin a work of grace, he was sure. He put his ear to Edwin's chest as he lay across his bed and listened to his underwater sounds, some deep murmur and the floating bump of his heart.

Tell me one of your stories, William, about the sinful and unsaved. He felt Edwin's breath muss his hair, his voice rumbling up through his chest.

Well, said Yate. He rubbed his hand across Edwin's trouser fronts, thinking. When I first came out I was on a convict ship from Manchester to Hobart Town. I think I told you so. The *Sovereign*. Eighty-one prisoners which was not so many. All of them women. Through the fabric of his trousers, Yate massaged Edwin's yard. Twenty-six years, he'd been then. About Edwin's age though not half so worldly. He had wept leaving London though he hadn't known he'd loved it, some ugly wet privacy wrenched from him like shelling an oyster. He'd been frightened of the women at first, their criminality but more their womanliness that seemed a rude thing, so close and crowded.

There were two of them that weren't saved, said Yate. One of them just eighteen to look at, Polly she called herself, and both of them always unwell. Edwin crabbed beneath him on the bed and crooked one leg against the wall, the cabin beginning to roll a little more as the wind slewed about westward.

They lived most of the voyage, one or other, in the hospital receiving visitors, said Yate.

Go on. He unbuttoned Edwin and cleared him of his shirt-tails.

I looked in on the sick room once and saw two of the officers giving Polly a fuck. That was all Yate had made out, one officer working between her legs, the other with his hand on himself, waiting his turn, and Polly, a handkerchief spread beneath her head, looking at the ceiling with an epicurean satisfaction. Three bangs on the hatch and the call for all hands to reef topsails. Edwin slipped out from under Yate and leaped from the bed, one foot jigged into his shoe and the fumble of his trouser buttons, his bottom lip heavy at being balked by a change in the wind.

I'm having enough trouble reefing myself, he said, as he stuffed his shirt into his trousers and, laughing, caught up his jacket, an odd limping half-run, bent at the waist. Yate could hear the men at their hatchway, their footfall and the drag of the reef-tackle. Soon there would be the chorus of *cheerily, cheerily, cheerily ho* and Edwin out on the yardarm, his jacket sleeves filling with wind. A funny thing about Polly. When the ship docked, a young man came on board and, with the chief mate's permission, chose her for his friend's wife. He would tell Edwin when his watch was below again. All the women were on deck to take the air when the young man came alongside and some were very ribald as he walked among them making his choice. It was thought at first he chose for himself but when he settled on Polly, the youngest-looking and still quite fair for all her debaucheries, he told her it was for a friend who was too busy to make the ship that morning. He described his friend to her and asked if she were willing.

I have no objection, said Polly. *Cheerily ho, cheerily ho*.
Yate heard the men sing out once more at the halyards and
pulled a blanket over his legs, waiting. Of such moments is
a life made up. I have no objection.

All week the men were kept busy at the canvas, the weather
so inconstant. A series of sharp gales swept across their
passage so that the captain let the ship scud before the wind
on bare poles, every sail downed or close-reefed under
louring skies. After the gales, a strong clear wind frequently
got aft and then the sails were squared and once as many as
four stunsails set, the ship rolling along, a fine spray thrown
over the bows as far back as the waist. Friday afternoon
after dinner the doctor sat to his letter-writing in the cuddy.
Mary Ford sat at the far end of the table, the four Taylor
children in her care. The previous day, by his calculation, the
ship had made four degrees eastward. He checked his figures
again, distracted by the troublesome game of the Taylor
boys and the incessant bawling of the infant. Their fat old
nurse, Mrs Ford, watched them unruffled, speaking now
and then to the raw-faced baby as if they had an understanding, Not happy, little one? Is it another tooth? By the
captain's account, she was a convict woman, emancipated
now, returning to the colony after a voyage home. Yes, he
was sure they'd made four degrees yesterday or close
enough. Another thirty and they would turn the corner for
Sydney. All being well, they'd arrive in just over a week and
he stood to win his bet with Armistead. Arthur and Basil
Taylor were playing sea captains with the model ships they
had been given by the sailors. Alfred Button was quite put
out not to have got one.

You could share the big one with Basil, he said to Arthur,
and I could take the little one, but he only persuaded
himself. The Taylor boys sailed their boats across the table
countless times, scouring the surface, the doctor was sure,

and roaring their captain's orders, Clew down the yards, Jesus save us.

We could play shipwrecks, said Arthur looking sly at Basil.

What's that like? said Basil.

It's when two ships smash together and the smallest one sinks and everyone goes overboard and drowns. Basil thought blinkingly a moment.

Say we play where both ships sink? he said.

And everyone drowns except one boy who gets saved by a dog, said Arthur.

We don't have a dog, said Basil. Mary Ford looked at the boys over her knitting. She had unravelled an old knee blanket of hers and thought to make each of the children a waistcoat but it was taking longer than she'd hoped. Perhaps just one for Arthur then and the rest could grow through it in turn. The doctor looked out the streaming cuddy windows. He felt himself growing unhinged with the baby's crying, her only pauses for an angry intake of breath.

Mrs Ford, he said at last. Keep the children quiet or remove them from the cuddy. That bucolic face lifted to him a moment.

They are happy as they is, she said. And after a moment's consideration, There is no place else to take them.

I'm not happy, said the doctor, testily. There was something not quite right with Laura, the young girl. She rested her chin on her hands and stared at him quite openly. Take your leave now. It was quite ridiculous that he should have to sit at the same table with the vulgar woman, let alone argue the point with her.

Then go hang, sir, said Mary Ford, her slab of a face quite untroubled. I'm my own master. She counted her stitches complacently and the doctor, discountenanced and angry, went below to write up the extraordinary incident for his wife.

Except for a very few appearances, the Buttons kept to their cabin all week. On Friday, when Sadler carried their breakfast dishes back to the quartergalley, Captain Aitken was waiting.

What's going on down there, boy? he said. It was the first time Sadler had been spoken to by the captain directly. Are the Buttons unwell?

No, sir.

Well, said the captain, bristling his beard with his thumb. They can sit to the table like everyone else. I can't have you running up and down like their personal servant.

It's no trouble, sir, said Sadler, edging his tray into the quartergalley. Captain Button had promised to split a shilling on him and Charlie if their meals were brought punctual. It wasn't worth his liver to cross Captain Aitken but he and Charlie had big plans for their shilling. Still, Captain Aitken hung about the quartergalley, crowding his great head and shoulders through the doorway.

So, he said, as if he accused him of something. What are they doing down there day after day?

Nothing, sir, said Sadler, unnerved by the interview and then, seeing the captain's eyebrows beetle together over his nose, Captain Button reads and does his papers, sir, and Master Button, sir, acts fretful bored.

And? Captain Aitken suspected he was being toyed with.

Sir, Mrs Button and Miss Button is sewing. Without a further word, Captain Aitken withdrew, half pleased to think of Mrs Button and her daughter bent to such a task. Captain Button himself was gratified by the sight. His wife and daughter had been most docile lately. Once more, it seemed he might congratulate himself, privately mind, on his foresight and strategy at settling his family in New South Wales. With the lamp pulled close to their work, the two of them sat, head to glossy head, as if in a cameo, Sophie so like her mother at that age he felt he was a young man again.

A crease between her eyebrows, Mrs Button was restyling the sleeves of Sophie's best evening dress. She had taken out the down padding and detached the sleeve from the shoulder, pinning a row of vertical pleats at one end and hazarding a tight cuff at the other.

What do you think, dearest? She lay the loose sleeve over Sophie's arm and they both sat back, admiring.

It looks well, mama, said Sophie, but I thought Mrs Runciman said that the cuff should be longer. She took up a much-read letter and sloped it to the light. You see, she writes of a full but limp sleeve and a tight cuff extending nearly half the arm beneath the elbow.

Half the arm beneath the elbow, said Mrs Button. She felt herself in the pincers of an unfamiliar patience. Mrs Runciman had written from Paris at the beginning of the year describing the bishop sleeve seen on every fashionable arm. This last week Mrs Button had given herself up to the task of making over Sophie's wardrobe. She could, of course, have employed Mrs Eylard to do the work for her. No doubt she had a neat hand and would be glad of the money. Yet there was something in the unwonted business of needlework that pricked her satisfaction, the two of them sitting close in the coddle of lamplight, their needles bright and competent, the rest of the cabin, the ship, even the insensible sea fallen away around them. Sophie was sewing a new trim on her Babet cap, a broad ribbon of an uncommon green.

It's the perfect colour, mama, she said, holding it first to her own cheek, then her mother's so that she might see the effect for herself.

It is, said Mrs Button. Very fetching. She looked fierce and tender at her daughter, still childlike about the cheeks but a lady's ear and chin. Quite how it had come about she was not sure but all Mrs Button's fresh optimism for New South Wales was harboured in her daughter. She put tiny neat stitches over her basting, joining the sleeve to the

shoulder once more. Mrs Button thought she might keep a
light carriage at Argyle. She could see herself in a china
crêpe riding shawl, some water-colour landscape winding
past. Captain Button would not think much of the idea at
first but in a new country they must all be prepared to make
adjustments of habit. She turned the dress right side out
and stroked it into shape.

What do you think, my dear? Mrs Button had a new
voice for Sophie, thick with emotion and secretive though
there were no secrets between them.

Oh, mama, said Sophie and said nothing else. Mrs
Button danced the dress lightly and remembered her first
ball, the rivalrous throat-clearing of the gentlemen, the
powdered floor and her Limerick gloves. She worried a
little at the hem.

I think Mrs Runciman said the skirts are being worn
longer, said Mrs Button.

To the instep, said Sophie gravely, almost solemn.

With a false hem we might just manage that, said Mrs
Button and sat stroking her lapful of flowered silk.

In full expectation of arriving at Sydney before the week
was out, Yate raised a purse of twenty pound for Captain
Aitken. For his own part and his sister's, he contributed
five pound. Mr Gordon, Mr Armistead and Dr Fowles
were put down for three pound each, Miss Bloomfield and
Miss Baker for one. Captain Button refused to subscribe at
all, sending a message with the steward's boy that he had
paid his passage and would pay no more. This news
arrived tartaric in the cuddy, Sadler speaking his piece and
making himself scarce. The general feeling ran against the
Buttons, Yate thought it fair to say, with Mr Taylor going
so far as to count the glasses of water sent down to them
and each evening expressing his aggravation when the
doctor prepared their diluted wine. Indeed, Mr Taylor was

frequently bad-humoured these last few days and most put out that Yate thought he might contribute five pound to the kitty.

I've put up that amount myself, said Yate. Five pound is your proportion according to the number of your family.

My argument would have been the very reverse, Mr Yate, said Taylor. His voice sounded whining in his own ear and he crossed his arms over his chest in a gesture he hoped was authoritative. The size of my family means I'm less capable of being liberal than a single man. In comparison with Mr Yate, he often felt inexperienced and boyish. Three pound would have been sufficient. More than sufficient. Especially as he had not received any marks of attention from the captain.

You must pay as you see fit, said Yate.

I will pay the five pound but I take no merit for it, said Taylor, managing to disadvantage himself twice over.

On Tuesday the potatoes failed and the cuddy passengers took their meat without vegetables. Yate had not had much chance of speaking with Edwin since the start of the week when the weather grew squally and the men were constantly on deck, night and day, wet through and dog-tired. That morning the coast of New Holland was seen off the larboard beam but indistinctly beneath a mass of lowering cloud. Tuesday night, the ship passed King Island and entered Bass Strait. Though no one could say quite how the information had been come by, everyone on board knew that Mr May's brother had gone down thereabouts last year on the *Neva* coming from Cork with a hundred and fifty prisoner women and their fifty-five children. Captain Button told it to his wife, Mary Ford told it to Arthur and bug-eyed Basil, Sadler told it to Hall who had it already from Davis. Of all souls on board, only Captain Peck, his chief mate, twelve of the convict women and eight of the men made it to King Island after the ship took an uncharted reef on her larboard bow.

And before morning, said Mary Ford with a gentle shake of her jowls, a half-dozen of the women drunk themselves dead on a puncheon of rum what washed ashore. Half the passengers could not look at Mr May, half could not take their eyes off him as he went about his work, ash-eyed as the other men but with the radiance of a Christian martyr. It was most peculiar, the fish-breakfast bones of Mr May's brother rolling the sea floor beneath their keel, his mildewed hair, salt and pepper as Mr May's no doubt, drifting weedily in the deep currents. Yate was on deck, despite the cold and the rain and the high winds that whistled in the rigging. He could not bear to sit alone in his cabin or in the cuddy with all the talk of the Buttons and Mr May's brother. At night too, since Edwin rarely came below, he was often on deck among the salt fraternity of the men. The moon was in her last quarter and so dimmed that the night before he had not been able to see King Island, only heard the change in the water as it passed on the starboard beam. The strait was filled with islands and rocky outcrops, Judgement Rock, Devil's Tower, some of them little more than teeth, the clear channel barely nine miles at the widest passage. At ten knots an hour the ship pushed forward, the wind on her quarter, topgallant sails down, the squalls so unpredictable that the men were on stand-by with the topsail halyards ready to let go. Upright and wind-whipped as any stanchion, Yate stood on the poop and tired his eyes on the rackety waves. Captain Aitken had given the order to look out for the Curtis Group and once or twice during the morning they were fancied in sight though at his noon observation the captain made them yet forty miles off. Edwin was aloft on lookout, unseen from the deck, his face to the west where Yate set his own.

By mid-afternoon, the winds had increased to a gale, the waves came up, hail rattled off the canvas and tipped onto the decks in melting drifts. The topsail halyards were let go and all hands stood by to reef. With the yards down and the canvas no longer stretched before the wind, the air was electric with the sounds of the sails convulsing about the masts. The howl of the wind and the wave, the captain screaming through his trumpet, the whining of ropes and the men's bawling and Yate still stood, hanging on to the poop railing with blue fingers. He could not have described the scene though he was awash with its sensation. The mainsail loosened, then the jibsail, the acres of wild canvas seemed any moment to shake the ship to splinters. The men put their backs to hauling but the buntlines were carried away.

Haul away, you goddamn sweeps, haul away. The captain shouted into his trumpet. His hat was gone, blown away as he'd promised Mrs Button, and his hair dripped wet over his eyes.

The lines're gone, sir. There was a sharp report like a musket's discharge and the maintopsail was blown to pieces, a hundred ribbons streaming where once the sail had been.

Let go the reef tacking. Haul away the clewlines. Captain Aitken's cheeks were madder red and he looked to swallow his trumpet. Haul, haul, haul away before you lose the mainsail, you parcel of soldiers. She'll be gone to rags. Square the foresail. He had twenty men to do the work of thirty and sweated plenty before he had the ship laid to under a storm trysail, less chance of getting through the pass by daylight than he had reckoned that morning.

Dinner was served so late that the doctor had already taken his place before the steward's boys had laid the cloth for dinner. The ship lay to in a most dangerous position, he

knew, but she was still sound and the cuddy warm. A strong
current was setting through the passage and there was the
danger that she would be driven onto the lee shore in the
night. The captain had told him so, sodden and frozen
through, come in to drink off a glass of straight brandy.
Though the captain was too agitated to sit still, the doctor
was hardly anxious at all. Hopeful would be the better
description. Though the cabin passengers were low-spirited,
some of the ladies tearful and the gentlemen on the quiet side,
the doctor looked at the steaming bowl of boiled mutton
with an appetite. The forks and knives jigged from one end
of the table to the other. He meant to put his little stock of
cash in his purse and sleep with it beneath his pillow. Even
in a shipwreck, he thought there was a good chance of his
making the shore. Tomorrow was his wife's birthday and the
doctor excused himself early. He called again on Armistead
who had been lying in bed all day, croaking about his conscience. At ten o'clock he put his head in at the cuddy to wish
everyone good night. The lamps were low, the captain
haggard with not having slept the night before. Still the
doctor burned with a kind of euphoria. He went below to his
cabin and made his preparations for the night. His pilot coat
he hung on the hook nearest his bed with a bottle of rum and
water in one pocket and as many biscuits as he could fit in
the other. Fully dressed and wrapped in his cloak, he put
himself to bed. He checked that his shoes and basin were
handy and extinguished his light. It was full dark in his cabin.
Creaking mightily as it shifted with the setting current, the
ship was going hard to leeward toward the rocks. At the first
call of Breakers ahead, the doctor would be on deck with his
iron basin which might be useful to bail the boats as the sea
ran high.

About eight the next morning, Charlie knocked on the door
with a bowl of hot water and the news that land was close

by. The doctor was up in an instant, one foot in his basin, and on deck without shaving. Mr Yate was already on the poop with Mr Denison, the latter so tired from his night watches, half a beard bluing his cheeks, that he nearly slept on the other's shoulder. The wind was still fresh but the sun shone most welcomely, the grey waters brilliant once more, foam-footed rocks and islands on every side and the ship went forward at nine knots under topgallant sails.

Mr Yate, said the doctor, strutting about the poop, actually clapping his hands together, the sound travelling distinct in the frosty air.

Has morning ever looked better? said Yate. He had been up most of the long night and was glad for the sun's warmth, watery as it was. At two, the ship had almost drifted onto Wilson's Promontory and the captain had been obliged to clap on sail despite the high wind and the risk of carrying the spars and rigging overboard. Now they sailed safe between islands, their slub limestone forms covered over with burned grass and some grey smudgings that might have been stunted trees or shrubs. From the clear sky, a roll of thunder.

Mr Yate, sir, said the doctor, tallying the scenery off the larboard side with the map in his cabin, I give you the Curtis Group, the Hogan Group, the Devil's Tower and – his finger hesitated a moment – Great Island, I think, or as some have it, Flinders Island. Drunk on the names, he resolved to say less in the hope of being appreciated more. As the ship moved forward, what he had taken for coastline resolved into distinct islands, the sea between pounding up frills of spray hung with rainbows. He went below for his sketchbook.

The following night was rougher than the last, the ship pitching more than she had the entire voyage, the sea running high and higher, waves regularly breaching the

bulwarks and a fearsome weight of water swirling dangerous across the decks before it could be got down the
scuppers. The men had been taking in sail since noon. No
sleep for the last two days, their only food biscuit and salt
beef so hard it needed to be soaked for an hour or two, the
men were running on nothing but the knowledge that
Sydney was two hundred miles off. It might have been two
thousand for all the thought Hall gave it. He was furling the
foretopsail with his watch but they were so knocked up that
it took them ten minutes just to haul up the canvas, another
quarter-hour to get out on the yards, though on a man of
war it was but a two-and-a-half-minute job or a flogging for
the last man down. The new sails were starched and stiff,
not bent long enough to handle easy. More hail. Buffeted by
cross-winds, it fell like snow, weightless, this way and that.
Hall was on the lee yardarm, the leech sleety and unman-
ageable with the vessel's reel and roll. His head was so
chilled that he couldn't make out his thinking, lost in the
bleach of light coming off the topsail. He bent over the yard
as far as he dared and saw his hand, as if it were someone
else's, scrabble on the rough canvas of the sail without
making purchase. From the sling on the lee side of the mast,
Mr Denison shouted something or leaned over, any rate, and
worked his mouth. Though biting cold, a bead of sweat ran
a line down Hall's back. Piggott was next as always, horse-
breathed and clubbing his hands on the sail to keep them
from freezing. Together, the two of them gripped the edge of
the sail, Hall bent tight to the yardarm with Piggott's weight
against his, no sensation in his fingers, only the sight of them
coming together with the canvas between. The leech was
brought up taut along the yard at last, Hall's weazened
hands scraped raw but only bleeding later in the warmth of
the forecastle, the clew handed to Mr Denison to make up
the bunt. By nine that night, the ship was lying to once
more, under close-reefed topsail and a storm sail.

SLOW WATER   265

In the heart of the night, a mountainous wave rolled directly over the bows, loosened the spritsail yard from its eye bolts, popped the seams of the forecastle, filling the men's hammocks and slop chests with water as it passed over, stoved the front of the cuddy and poured in tons over the stern. The steersman was thrown over the wheel and saved from going overboard by being winded on the mizzen-mast. Most of the men were on the foreyard, the foaming head of the wave only a little distance under their feet, and for one surging, spray-smacked minute they could not see if any ship remained beneath them. Mr Morris, himself clinging to some piece of the mizzen rigging, ordered the men to the pumps, the ship riding so low that a second wave must bury her completely. Mrs Taylor woke from one nightmare to another. Something about the soughing of the bare oaks behind the rectory and her children trapped in the branches, calling pathetic. She woke and they called still, Arthur's the only intelligible voice, Laura and Basil like a nest of mice disturbed. Before she could put her bare feet to the floor, a rush of wind and water and glass swept through the cabin, extinguishing the lamp. Richard called, Caroline, Caroline, in the dark like a child. In the children's cabin, both the stern windows, dead-lights and all, were dashed to pieces and the room quite afloat. The children screamed lustily and sobbed still when they were rubbed down and put to sleep in their parents' berths. Mr Taylor got the lamp lit and, after some delay owing to the confusion on deck, a couple of men came to fit new deadlights and bail out the cabins.

The whole day the weather continued bad, the ship drifting bare-masted with all hands at the ready. Busby repaired the spritsail yard and extra lashings were ordered for the spars, anchors and the longboat where the last sheep rattled knee-deep in the shiny droppings of its absent companions, its

miserable nostrils flexing for the smell of land. The cuddy
furnishings were ruined, the cushions grey and dripping in
one corner like a nest of slaters. The doctor took his breakfast of biscuit and boiled pork in his fingers, sitting on the
table, eating off a swinging tray that Mungo had suspended
from a ceiling beam. He breakfasted alone, Charlie and
Sadler standing by, inquiring politely after his night. Dinner
was taken the same way, boiled pork again and mutton,
roast and boiled, handed about by the steward and his
boys, but everyone sat up to it excepting the Buttons. The
gale had eased a little and under close-reefed topsails the
ship made her way more steadily. Arthur and Basil Taylor
were quite excitable with the washout of their cabin and
the novelty of sitting on the table.

We don't like a shipwreck, do we Arthur? Basil had a
piece of boiled mutton in one hand, a roasted piece in his
other, and looked serious at his older brother.

Not much, said Arthur carelessly, as if it were all the
same to him. That night he slept in the same berth as his
father, Laura beneath with mama and little Mary, Basil
with Deck. He had wanted to sleep with Deck but papa
said it had to be Basil because he was smaller.

I'm only smaller because I'm younger, said Basil and
cried on his father's resolute shoulder as he was carried
forward for the night.

At two in the morning, Sunday 12 June, the lights on
Sydney Head were sighted. Yate heard the call go up but
stayed in bed for the middle watch, Edwin curved beside
him, a smooth white tusk. Edwin had been so tired he
seemed drunk, forgetting his words and letting Yate slip his
shoes off and roll him into bed. Yate couldn't sleep but lay,
eyes open in the dark, as if watchfulness were a talent.

Sydney-o! He heard Mr Morris give the call but he lay as
before. His legs ached at standing so many hours on the

poop yesterday, the blue coast blurred on the distant horizon, then looming bold and iron-bound by mid-morning. Every cabin passenger had crowded on to the poop, the doctor pointing out Mount Wright and Mount Dromedary, Murroga River a little south of Bateman's Bay. Even the Buttons made their appearance, Captain Button standing behind his wife and daughter, a hand on each shoulder, their three faces lit to the shore like a painting of patience rewarded. Now Sydney Heads. He listened to Edwin's breathing and suffered for the first time in years an untethering, all his hopes welked down to nothing. Toward morning, the window above the bed sketched its square in light, then picked out the curtain's pattern from behind and drew the cabin's murked furnishings into daylight colour. Many feet in the passage and on deck but still he lay, watching Edwin sleep. He had no stomach for scenery.

The entrance into the harbour lay narrow between two prominent headlands, their galled cliffs rising from a mild and milky ocean. The passengers lined the sides, craning at the view, the whitewashed stone lighthouse on the southern head, and some structure at the cliff's edge, a telegraph the doctor supposed, looking for all the world like a gallows with two fellows in red nightcaps close under. Inside the heads, the signal was made for a pilot and soon a skiff came alongside, launched from Watson's Bay.

Rowed by two government men, said the doctor, or I am no phsyiognomist. The pilot he was less sure of. The first fresh face since Deal, the pilot was a narrow man and short, tight in the makings, so thin about the face that the round balls of his cheekbones stood out painfully beneath his eyes. He wore his hair close to his ears with a quiff rolled over his forehead and had a rough tongue in his head. Ordering several tacks to get between the heads, the wind contrary and the tide running against the ship, he swore at the men as easy as breathing though it was Sunday and ladies present.

Get to the devil, squint-a-pipes, he said to the Finn when he thought him slow to the bowlines. Are you waitin' for another wrinkle in your arse? He went in and out of the cuddy – five times, the doctor counted – and mixed himself a stiff glass of grog.

Let go and haul, by God. He seemed affable enough for all that. As the sails were being set to his instruction, a block dropped down on the deck between the doctor and the pilot, hard enough to leave a dent in the planking.

Never mind, guvnor, the pilot said to the doctor who had started beside him. Only one of the men's legs dropped off with the scurvy. He tipped his narrow head back at the sails. A wry mouth and a pissin' pair o' breeches'ud be too good for you, he shouted. Though the ladies turned their faces from him, they were not prepared to relinquish their view, every tack opening some green bay to their consideration, the hillside spruce with English villas, elegant and preposterous, red-legged gulls gliding high, the white wedge of their tails, grey wings black-tipped, the harbour itself beautiful, completely sheltered from the open sea and crowded with tiny islands. After some hours, the ship was worked to her anchorage off Pinchgut Island, the rattling of the cable chain playing out as the anchor was let go, a sound not heard since it had been dropped off Deal a hundred and two days previous.

Until her gunpowder was discharged, the ship was not able to proceed to its mooring in Sydney Cove. The pilot was persuaded without much difficulty to stay – Devil I will – and take an early dinner. Though everyone wanted to be away, no one could bear to leave the society of the deck for the business of crating and packing. Captain Ryan of the *Camden* called to take a glass of wine. He had brought

Bishop Broughton to New South Wales ten days earlier but had suffered a mutiny off the Cape in a heavy gale. Shaken still, he spoke no word of it until settled in the cuddy, pausing in his story to bite his thin underlip whenever the steward or one of his boys came through. For two days his ship had been worked under easy sail by his passengers.

Even the bishop took hold of a halyard at one point, said Captain Ryan pausing to chew the rare morsel of his lips. It seemed there was no question but that several of the men would be put to death and the remainder transported to Norfolk Island. Sadler came through and was treated to suspicious looks all round.

Reverend Trotter's sent a boat for Mr Yate, he said, grossly injured. Everyone had the news in an instant. Sadler went and knocked at Yate's cabin door.

Who is it? said Yate. He sat at his desk rubbing his eyes, the cabin swimming with dark shapes and lozenges of candied light. He had been writing his instructions for Edwin. Pray twice daily, on rising and preparing for bed. Remember always the corrupt character of man. Remember me, he wanted to write, remember me always.

Who is it? said Yate.

The steward's boy, said Sadler. Some reverend's sent a boat for you.

I'll be there in a minute, said Yate and soon appeared on deck in his bent black suit, hair polished, his Wellington hat in hand, made his farewells to Sarah, he would be back that evening, and went forward self-conscious under every eye. He was roped over the side, Edwin's the only face he cared for among the gaggle of men, Careful, careful, let him down handsome, and rowed up harbour.

Reverend Trotter's man, in knee breeches and a red kerchief at his throat, handed Yate a folded copy of the *Sydney Gazette*, put his back to the oars, pulled and breathed, pulled and breathed. His hair was cropped close to his pink scalp, his head knobbled like a knee. He had a chunky, well-practised stroke, the timber chuckling in the oarlocks as he crabbed his way to shore. Yate sat in the stern of the low bumboat and counted a hundred strokes before he turned and looked back at the *Prince Regent*, less impressive for his being no longer on board, smaller-seeming somehow, like Arthur Taylor's model ship. Her sails being taken in, she was all sticks and strings. The passengers who had seen him off were still watching at the railings but at this distance he could not distinguish any face in the tallow crowd nor, however much he stared and blinked, any man in the rigging. He turned his face away, looked over the shoulder of his oarsman at the glint of the copper-clad steeple of St James's Church and the windmills whaling on the rise of Woolloomooloo. Reverend Trotter's man began to blow a bit, the smell of warm milk on his breath, but did not slacken his pace, his regular hunches and stretches, the sloshful drip of water off the oars. He looked direct at Yate, friendly more than impertinent, and rowed.

How is Reverend Trotter? said Yate.

Pretty well, sir, since you arksed.

And Reverend Hill?

Not so well, sir, said Trotter's man with the same unthinking cheer. The boat rocked considerably on the choppy harbour and Yate was glad to see they nosed around Bennilong Point and the castellated stub of Fort Macquarie in to Sydney Cove, twenty or so three-masters with their pennants strippling in the breeze, a handful of jolly-boats plying to and from, the gloomy-fronted warehouses shut for the Sabbath.

The melancholy duty, said Reverend Trotter's man, pointing with his lumpish chin at the newspaper that Yate still held under his arm in a distracted fold. It was not today's paper as he'd supposed, but that of a week last Tuesday, an item marked up for his attention. *We are extremely sorry to have imposed upon us the melancholy duty*, he read, *of announcing the sudden death of the Reverend Richard Hill, second assistant chaplain of the colony, who dropped down dead in Saint James's Church last evening.*

God rest his soul, said Trotter's man like belching. Yate said nothing. Between Port Phillip on the crest and King's Wharf, the densely serried cottages and huts of the Rocks stepped irregular one behind the other up the hill, laced together by goat tracks that glittered in the weak sun.

Paying Reverend Trotter's man a shilling, which he bit out of habit before secreting in the waistband of his breeches, Yate climbed the sunken steps to the port yard and started up George Street. Four months at sea and he had lost his legs for land. The sandstone rock beneath his feet bobbed and pitched as if the whole town had slipped its moorings and sailed with the tide. Mitchell's marine store; the ship-smith; a smut of boys playing chuck-farthing outside the mastmaker's, one of them, a cockade of orange hair, scratching his balls, thoughtful and watching Yate as he passed; Mr Dawson's foundry; a ribby dog, tan and black, its rag of tongue showing pink as it licked itself under the dusty verandah of the newspaper office. On the corner of Bridge Street, Yate settled his hat – to Trotter's man, shadowing behind, he seemed to be screwing it onto his head – and made his way past the auction house that dipped and rocked as he passed unsteady, the tea merchant's drawn curtains, the bank with its three imposing entranceways. A rank wind funnelled down the street. Eddying in corners and twisting down the empty thoroughfare, the thick dust from the brickfields reddened the toes of Yate's boots and coated the glass of his spectacles. A little further, a two-horse carriage driven by a liveried servant clipped smart across the street, throwing up wings of dust, its wheels squeaking still when out of sight. After the ship, the world seemed very big though there was no Edwin in it. Past the double-storey residences with their shop fronts below, the cooperage, the darkened, empty window of the jewellers, still the scrape of a following foot, perhaps the redhead boy, until at the corner of George and Hunter, his hand checking his pocket, Yate turned to find Trotter's man making after him, a steady ten paces behind.

Mr Trotter says I was to company you. A guileless smile and a rasping rub to his cropped scalp.

To the church? said Yate.

Yes sir. So they walked not quite together but as if on the same string, Yate feeling the tug of Trotter's man behind him, barefoot and half-dressed, as he continued through town, turning east into King Street, the handsome terraced houses, double-fronted some of them with matching pots of clipped bay, several phaetons and gigs tipping by, their occupants in Sunday best showing him every gawping attention as was the Sydney custom, past Pitt Street, he cocked his head down the block at Park Street where he had taken his board with Mrs Brown, his hat tipped to a young lady out walking with her umbrella and a servant, wiping his forehead on his sleeve when she was passed, over Castlereagh Street.

Or not quite over since as he waited for two mounted officers to ride on, the tails and manes of their horses braided tight, Trotter's man waiting behind and behind him three dogs nipping a fourth into their pack, there was Mrs Brown herself in her cap and apron, her bustles flounced at the back as if she had tied on several kitchen dusters before leaving home, unchanged since last he saw her except a quarter her size again.

Blind me, is it Mr Yate? said Mrs Brown, though she could see it were. She wrung his fingers with her laundry hand though she supposed it a liberty and agreed straight off to prepare his rooms for Monday.

I was saying only yestiddy to Mrs Bibb something or other, said Mrs Brown in some confusion, throwing her apron over her face until she recovered her composure. She's well, most well. This last parenthetical as she smoothed her skirts. Your name came up anyways. As it does, she said waggingly, as it does. She'll get a shock when I say I seen you. I won't hold you here on the corner. Mrs Brown squinted brisk at the sky as if she expected a change in the weather. But I'll see you t'morrer. Her whispered shout as Yate crossed the road, trailing Reverend Trotter's man, What time shall I expeck you?

Late afternoon, I'd think, called Yate and shouldered on, over Elizabeth Street and on to St James's Church where the verger, a narrow man with jug ears where neat fuses of dark hair sprouted, darted out and seized him by the wrists.

I brung him, said Trotter's man and slipped through the entrance to the western gallery with the grin of a dog taking the best spot before the fire.

The verger drew Yate by the elbow toward the vestry door, talking all the while as if he were the man that had been at sea for months. He had a squeaking voice and a ducking emphasis to his head that reminded Yate somehow of a sewing needle. Or perhaps a dibbler. One of the few remembered toys from Yate's childhood was a wooden figurine of a bird on a stick, weighted equivalent at head and tail, that the flick of a finger could set to motion, a rocking peck that the verger had down perfect. He hadn't thought of his bird in years, the daub of red paint on its head that took so pleasingly the impression of his milk teeth. Yate studied the verger close, laying up his jut-eared, bobbing manner for his evening conversation with Edwin. It seemed Mr Hill had died in the vestry, while writing in the register the name of the man he had that afternoon buried. Further elaborations were given over pipingly as the verger steered Yate inside.

Monday evening last, Mr Yate. It's only natural you'll want the detail. Mr Hill was sitting with Mr Langhorne just

here when he laid his head in his arms on this table. With
the door to the street closed behind them and his horizons
shrunk to the vestry walls, Yate felt again the phantom
swell of the sea rocking up through his feet, the verger
dragging on his arm like a light anchor.

Mr Langhorne asked what the matter was but got no
reply, Mr Hill falling to the floor. Yate didn't need the
picture of Mr Hill's death to think the vestry sepulchral, the
very dust sliding down a single beam of sunlight that angled
in the high window seemed buried alive.

Dropped here, said the verger, his face solemnly bowed
over an unremarkable section of floorboard. Gargled in his
throat a bit as Mr Langhorne gives it, *articula mortuus*, you
know. For the wages of sin is death but the gift of God is
eternal life. Mr Mitchell was called but it was no use. The
finding was death by visitation of God. From behind the
panelled door that opened to the church, Yate heard the
officiating minister reading the commandments.

Church's full, said the verger, helping Yate into his gown.
We were hoping you might give us the sermon. The church
was crowded and close enough to suggest that it had been
full some time. When Yate entered, the congregation's
coughing and shifting ceased a moment before a whisper
ran around the eastern gallery where the subscription pews
were rustling with Sydney's best silk and *mousseline de
laine*. Landed at half past eleven, Yate climbed the pulpit
stairs at a quarter after twelve.

Yate arrived at his lodgings a good quarter-hour before his carrier, a pock-pitted fellow with a handcart he had taken on at the wharf. Park Street was looking very neat in the drizzle of afternoon sun, the evening's chill just setting in the shade. The polished windows of the Barley Mow, a couple of feckless orange dogs sniffing and pissing, the scorched race grounds at the far end where the carriageway ran into Hyde Park. Yate was seized off the street by Mrs Brown's woman, a new one, he thought, since he did not remember her crooked smile, and ushered into a small sitting room off the front hall where Mrs Brown was waiting with Mrs Bibb, the two of them soothing their expectant nerves with the toasting of many rounds of bread over the grate. For a moment all was a confusion of plates and toasting forks, Yate sidling forward with his hat under his arm, the ladies getting to their feet, crumbed and buttered, passing comment between them on his appearance, Unchanged, unchanged, I say changed for the better, but from some politeness unable to address a word to him directly. He was pressed into the best armchair, Mrs Brown's, plumply buttoned and overstuffed as the landlady herself who took Mrs Bibb's who took, in turn, a fireside stool.

I've had your room turned out, Mr Yate, said Mrs Brown as her happy friend double-buttered a fresh piece of toast for their visitor. The bedding's been aired and the windows open since morning.

Thank you, thank you. Once for the room, once for the toast, fragrant and dripping yellow. After the rancid butter on the *Prince Regent*, this seemed rich enough to make a meal. Last night, on his return to the ship, the doctor had contributed to the tea table a basket of fresh provisions he'd ordered from the pilot: milk, tea in a twist of news-paper, oranges with their stalks and leaves still attached, bread and a pat of butter made up circular and stamped with a cow. The butter had been the best thing though Sarah had preferred the oranges, taking a curl of their greenish skin to eat in private in her cabin. Mrs Bibb fussed with another piece of bread over the fire, Mrs Brown fetching him a saucer of salted radishes from the tea trolley beside her. He sat and ate, contented, the bread fatly sliced, browned on both sides with a chewy white centre.

And your sister, Mrs Bibb said, approaching with a second piece of toast, did you bring her out as you hoped?

She is this minute at Woolloomooloo with Mrs Jones, said Yate. And Edwin left on board though that was not easily brought into the conversation. Their last interview had been grave, each a stranger again, wrecked on the lonely knowledge of his own body. The Society's crates reroped and waxed, the snuff-like smell of land cutting the salt smack, Yate tasted finality in their farewell kiss, for all it would not be their last. Voyage done, it was not clear what might be afforded them now. Mrs Brown found her teapot dry and, having rung her tiny bell for a minute unheeded, shouted genteelly for her servant.

Poor Mr Hill, said Mrs Brown on seeing she was looked at.

No one can know when his time is come, said Mrs Bibb, complacent teeth in her toast and then, more sly, We heard you was to fill his place.

Nothing is decided, said Yate, fiddling at his empty cup. The woman came and went with the teapot, smiling bolder this time and showing Yate her snaggle tooth.

In the morning, Yate lay in his bed waiting for his hot water to be brought. His curtains were pulled and he watched a high square of purple-grey winter sky, a single fleeced cloud scudding past. He had known where he was the instant he woke. Park Street, alone. Edwin first, then Sarah, he would see how they were settled. The smell of bread was heavy on the landing and in the dining room a Lieutenant Fisher and his wife were dealing to their breakfast: sugared porridge, kippers, toast and marmalade, black tea and milky coffee. Mrs Brown had set a place for him but he had an impatience to be gone. He walked out and took a carriage on King Street for the wharf. Down George Street, the shop doors hung with cages of cockatoos and parrots, to the dockyard Yate rode, his heart singing as he neared the water, the clotted old bottle smell of an anchorage, a sailor lurching by uneven with a barrel of herring on his shoulder, a clutch of passengers, newly arrived, all eyes and open mouths, the harbour busy with small craft, bumboats and dinghies. The *Prince Regent* not yet alongside the wharf, Yate hired a boy to take him out.

Can do, sir, said the boy, taking his squinting measure. A couple of strokes out, he hoisted a makeshift sail so mended it appeared patchwork and they spanked across the small waves that slapped the sides of the ships moored close in: the revenue cutter, the *Prince George* and the *Tigress*, an East India Company cruiser. When Yate came up the ladder, Edwin was on deck, his face pleased and shy at their meeting.

You're back, he said, taking off his cap and replacing it.

And brought breakfast, said Yate, taking advantage of Edwin's awkwardness to look and look at him as if he provisioned himself against his absence. After he paid his respects to Captain Aitken, they sat on the poop and ate egg-glazed currant buns with Mr May who happened by.

The ship's better for having all the passengers off, said Mr May. No offence, sir. A clear run for the men is all. He ate slow with a sideways working of his teeth, a mechanical clicking at the back of his jaw, turning his bun between his fingers as he chewed. The doctor's below now. Taking a few more of his boxes off. Yate ate and nodded. He listened to Mr May talk on and watched Edwin eat, the apple in his throat going up with each swallow, and every now and then his pale blue eyes swimming up to his.

Dropped back to the wharf, Yate set out walking for Woolloomooloo, where he found Sarah quite settled at Mrs Jones's house, if a little unnerved by the visits of various neighbouring ladies who had been calling to see what she might be wearing by way of London fashion. They walked in the garden, Sarah charmed by the rasping screak of an unfamiliar bird scrambling open-winged overhead, white-feathered with a solid nutcracker beak, and the slow chuck of the turning arms of a nearby windmill.

Is Mrs Brown's comfortable as you remember it, Will?

Quite as comfortable as that, said Yate. It seemed they might be longer in Sydney than he had planned, Governor Bourke and Bishop Broughton both applying to him since Sunday to take up the position at St James's Church until it could be supplied from England. Marsden, too, was of the same mind, calling the previous night, much aged since they had last met, his eyesight severely dimmed, his wife entered upon her promised rest this October gone which he could hardly bring himself to say, staring owlish and losing the trail of his sentences. He urged Mr Yate to accept the position temporarily. Even in his grief, Marsden was happiest when he imagined he bullied someone to his bidding.

I'm invited to give the sermon at Parramatta this weekend, said Yate. Edwin was hopeful he could take leave from the ship and they would ride up on Saturday. Three days, maybe four, by Yate's calculation. They had not been

on shore together and he ached for it as other men antici-
pate landfall.

Mrs Jones's cousin is putting together a picnic party at
South Head for Saturday, said Sarah, by way of showing
she could take care of herself. She had a knack for knowing
how a person's thoughts drifted, obscure and half-lit,
beneath the smooth order of speech. It made her seem older
than she was, though she was not old. Of herself, she knew
next to nothing.

Do you see? she said, pointing as a blunt-headed bird
with yellow crest flung itself overhead, the white pinions at
the end of its outstretched wings separated like fingers.

Cockatoo, said Yate. Cockies. They sat on the garden
bench, heads back as the birds flew over, thrashing through
the foliage of the stringybarks on the hill's rise, Sarah
thinking about sounds, her brother of words, which was
the same thing.

Late afternoon, Mr Taylor sat in Dr Jeanneret's library
overlooking the street, a volume of Milner's *Church
History* open on his knee. He was well pleased with the
character of persons who had called on him that morning.
Mr Cowper, Mr Hassall who was Mr Marsden's son-in-
law, Mr Hand. Of these, he had liked Mr Hand least. A
Lutheran minister, engaged by the Society to work among
the natives of New South Wales, Mr Hand was not a pre-
possessing individual. Irregular and awkward in civil
company, he had been entertained fairly by Taylor but his
call would not be returned. From his seat, Taylor saw two
ladies pass by, parasols furled, as if for a walk in the park,
their hems draggling in the dirt, next, several dust-plumed
gigs and a water cart and after them, a man of what order
he could not say, in hessian boots, white cords and a
cutaway coat. It seemed to him from even his brief acquaintance with Sydney that there were all sorts of persons

passing as society. Dr Jeanneret had told at dinner of a gentleman grazier with some thirty thousand sheep and perhaps as many acres, regularly invited to the Governor's entertainments, who was later exposed as a transported man. Not that Mr Hand could carry such a suspicion, Taylor smiled to think it, though he was dressed like a bush settler in town for the day, his short pipe carried through the buttonhole of his coat. Mr Cowper was a more pleasant thought, with his invitation to take tomorrow evening's lecture at St James's Church. It was the best church in the colony, with a rich purse, though it might have fallen already to Mr Yate. Mr Hassall, too, had the undoubted air of a gentleman. Three boys of his own and four girls, he had admired the children exceedingly and made Mr Marsden's apologies in a most amiable fashion.

Someone came down Pitt Street with a long, careful leg, black shoulders hunched, that Taylor did not recognise at once. Mr Yate looked different on land somehow after their months at sea, as if he owned the street he walked on. Taylor himself felt as if he had yet to arrive. There was a vagueness to Sydney he found dispiriting. As if at a poor theatrical, everything tinsel and pasteboard, he could not get into the spirit of the thing. The gentlemen on horseback, no less the parasoled ladies, put on their acts while troops of wild dogs snarled under their feet and their pockets were eyed sidelong by convicts that stood brazen in the dirty streets, the initials of their barracks printed on their slops. The natives were just as implausibly got up, blown together like dry leaves on any corner, most of them in English clothes so old all colour was long leached from them. On his arrival at the wharf, he had been arrested by an old man, on closer inspection perhaps no older than him, that cupped his hand for a coin and said in an unexpected baritone, neither aggressive nor proud though it partook of both of these, All this my country. Caroline had to come and disengage him. She and the children were far more adaptable, it seemed, thriving on the expansiveness of land, the baby fatter now than it had been just two days ago. They were with Mrs Jeanneret visiting friends two-and-a-half miles from town at Glebe. Since she had their bed sawed in two, Caroline had not come to him as a wife but once, preferring now to sleep with the low fence of the baby between them. Mr Yate paused at the house next door, then came on, unlatching the doctor's gate and coming up the path. Taylor thought he might have called sooner. A Mr Langhorne had met them on landing at King's Wharf when he had expected Mr Yate, as a familiar of Sydney and his fellow labourer, to direct him to his residence. They had much in common and might yet be friends. The bell rang and Taylor sat a minute until the library door opened and Mr Yate was shown in by Dr Jeanneret's manservant.

Mr Yate, said Taylor, pleased of his company in spite of himself.

Mr Taylor. Yate eased himself into a chair and looked out the window. A fair view, he said, Taylor nodding. You read Milner, I see. And went on to tell how Mr Williams had lost two volumes of that work to the New Zealanders who used the paper for musket cartridges. Taylor smiled, laughed even, unwinding. They spoke of this and that, two men together. The Bedgoods were put up in a poor hole that ran with more rats than the ship and better accommodation must be found for them. Taylor had walked with his wife in the Government Domain and seen many plants he recognised from English greenhouses, some in full flower though he noticed in them a distinct tendency toward yellow. A pleasant hour passed, the afternoon sun falling off from the window, the room darkening until the servant came, creeping and apologetic, to light the lamp and Yate stood to leave. Five o'clock. There was a chance Edwin might come off the ship and they could take dinner together at Petty's.

I call on the bishop Thursday morning and could introduce you, he said. If you're free.

I'm free, said Taylor as if he might not have been, as if he were a man who could keep a bishop waiting. He stood at the window and watched Mr Yate go, misjudged man, hat in hand, his scalp shining shy beneath his thin hair.

The road to Parramatta was rutted and rough, water lying in deep runnels though it had not rained for days. Still Yate preferred it to the river, the steamer leaving Sydney at nine each morning but often running aground in the shoaly water, requiring the passengers to be rowed ashore. The coach was more reliable, though crowded, but in the end he had hired two horses from Barker and Hallen's stable on Sussex Street behind the barracks, a mouthy mare for Edwin that looked steady and a chestnut gelding for himself. Edwin had frowned when Yate said he would arrange horses.

Rather the coach?

I can ride, said Edwin but at the stables he circled his horse so long he spooked her into a tight round of pig jumps, arch-backed, hooves close, the liveliest she ever was. Out past the old burial ground and up Brickfield Hill, over Black Wattle Creek, four ducks rising windily from the water, finding their formation as they rose, and past the distillery, Edwin sat heavy on his horse, daylight visible between his seat and his saddle each time she broke to a stuttering canter. Himself no horseman, Yate was a neat enough rider, careful heel and steady hand. Edwin, so beautiful on the rigging, jigged along like a split sack of meal, legs wider even than the mare's barrel back, nearly going over her ears when she stopped to rip some grass from the wayside. By the time they passed the boundary stone Edwin had made peace with his animal's gait, riding loose-reined but keeping a tighter seat, once spurring past

Yate, turning and waving his hat at him, his face broken in a smile. Up ahead a rising of dust in the stillness, an iron-gang on public work, breaking rock in their yellow and greys, a red jacket supervising from the shade, the shuffle of leg-chains and the thin clink of the picks. One fellow looked up at Yate as he passed, his mouth a raw hole, not angry or insolent, perhaps hungry but not hungry either, some dumb animal emotion, his face plastered white except where runs of sweat showed the man beneath, so that it was two leagues before he could look at Edwin. The houses were less frequent now, the greater part of the way through woods, dreary and desolate in the Australian way, the white-trunked trees evergreen yet seeming bare, their leaves scanty and withered. The two men did not speak much, though they rode the last miles side by side, lulled by the leatherish smell of horse and the reeling open country. They watered at Mr Blackland's where, on account of the ladies, they took their tea in the garden, rolled bread and butter and slices of lemon cake cut thicker for the gentlemen.

Parramatta itself lay in a hollow, hardly guessed at till the last rise, a scattered place, each house separated from the next by gardens. The place of eels. Parramatta. The horses put their necks down, blowing as if they had been ridden hard and the men idled, in no hurry for company, even such as a small town might provide. Yate looked but explained nothing, the roof of the parsonage, the Maori Seminary, Mr Palmer's house, the cemetery and the two spires of St John's Church on the old river flats, the Governor's country house, the Female Factory and beyond, a straggle of blue trees lining the near river bank. He thought they would stay at Mrs Walker's inn but, calling at the parsonage, Marsden would not hear it.

Are you preaching tomorrow at my church? said

Marsden, not waiting for an answer. Then you'll stop tonight at my house. He shook his great head, belligerent and hospitable, completely bald but for a fringe of white hair over his ears. Edwin shook his hand like a gentleman, respectful but uncowed, and the two of them were shown upstairs to their rooms that they might dress for dinner.

The supper party was small. Marsden himself, of course, Miss Martha Marsden on his right hand, Miss Elizabeth Marsden, their sister Jane who had married their cousin, Thomas Marsden. It seemed Miss Martha had expected company for she served a white soup, larded sweetbreads, boiled ham and roast fowl with watercress. Edwin was dazzled by the cutlery and kept his stained hands in his lap. Since he could not see the length of the table, Miss Martha selected her father's food and cut it on his plate without affectation.

Is this your first visit to Parramatta, Mr Denison? she said, worrying a bone on her father's plate.

It is, Miss Martha. A pleasant and productive town from what I've seen. He wore an old suit of Yate's, the pantaloons a little short in the leg, and a white waistcoat. With his tact and his open navigator's face, Yate didn't wonder he caught the attention of the Miss Marsdens.

Is Thomas here? said Marsden of a sudden.

I am, said Mr Marsden agreeably. Miss Martha patted the back of her father's hand and looked to the plates of her guests.

Well, Mr Denison, said Marsden. A polite attention from Edwin and some nervous skittishness from Miss Elizabeth. I brought the first horses to New Zealand. Not every man can say as much. He forked some ham into his mouth and wiped his babyish lips. 1814 that was. The New Zealanders hadn't seen anything bigger than a pig.

Papa, said Miss Martha but Marsden slid through his

stories, an old man who knew his comforts. The time bushrangers had fired on him, the bullet hole at the back of his old gig for years after. The wife of a farmer who had conspired with her convict servant to murder her husband, Marsden made suspicious by their intimacy after the funeral.

He was thought to have died of natural cause, you see, said Marsden. From the far end of the table, Mr Thomas Marsden moaned and gave his chair his heel as if it were his horse.

Oh Thomas, said Miss Martha, sorely disappointed.

But when I had the body disinterred, said Marsden, not to be put off, there was a three-inch nail under his nightcap, driven into his brain. Mr Thomas Marsden clenched his teeth with the effort of not falling, his right arm loose among the salt and pepper cruets.

He is taking another fit, said his wife, anguished, to her sisters. Eyes rocked back in unshared pleasure, Mr Thomas Marsden was suddenly limp, slipping boneless to the carpet. It was finished. Mrs Marsden wept, Miss Elizabeth went from the room, calling for Matthew, he must be wrapped warm and put on the sofa. Edwin knelt beside the man, lifted him against his chest like a weight of rolled canvas, Mr Marsden's arm falling long and loose. It was his talent to seem in ordinary moments monumental.

Here, said Miss Martha.

Here, said Mrs Marsden and Edwin rested her husband on a low sofa, a blanket tucked tight about him. One sister chafed his wrists, another rubbed liniment on his temples, his wife hung over the back of the sofa and there being too many ladies, Yate and Edwin retired for the night, their bedroom windows hanging over the night garden and the scattered glitter of the town.

Sunday, Yate preached at St John's, many familiar faces in the congregation, some sniping at the news of his taking the chaplaincy at St James's. At the Orphan Asylum, he examined a dozen girls for confirmation, ten of them adequately prepared. In the afternoon, he lectured to the prisoners at the Female Factory who listened more attentively than the parishioners of St John's, many of them crying though the superintendent told him they would return to their habits like a dog to its vomit. The Sabbath was not much honoured. On their way to the Factory, Yate and Edwin saw three men butchering an ox that was not yet dead, others making bricks as if it were any other day. Monday, they rode to Kissing Point, about six miles journey, where Yate preached in the small church. Saddle sore, Edwin stood in his stirrups some of the way and on the return they walked a great deal, wading over their boots across streams, two bridges down some months ago and not yet repaired. On the skirts of a wood, they hobbled the horses and put their coats down inside-out, lying under the huge sky. Edwin's face was so close to Yate's that he could not see it distinctly nor did he try. A great luminous terrain it looked, a smudged distant planet, which was a truth of sorts for though he thought the world of Edwin, more often he thought him simply a world. He was talking in that slow, hand over hand way he did sometimes, as if he thought his words might not take his weight, and Yate luxuriated in not quite listening, the burr of his voice and the moon-like glint of his skin pleasure enough. These days were soured by Edwin's departure, like milk on the turn. Yate missed him already, most guttingly when they were together, knowing his contentment then as the measure of what would be his sorrow. There were no words for such loneliness or at least none that might be set against it to any purpose, that might whittle it to manageable proportion. He said nothing of it to Sarah though she was so careful with him lately that he thought she had it from him somehow. Since they had arrived at Sydney he had a different alertness to

Edwin he recognised at last as remembering, a kind of storing of the details of his person against his departure. Yate rolled his head back a little and saw himself reflected in Edwin's mild regard.

If you woke up here, said Edwin, you'd never think you were in England. The rattling of the gum-tree leaves, the loft of unbroken sky.

In New Zealand, said Yate, for he felt he must say something, it's different again. He leaned in close, eyes shut against the blur of Edwin's skin, and kissed him. The scratch of bristle on his afternoon chin. Remember. Remember too the suckling noise made in kissing, neither a moan nor a hum. The flies buzzed and bit but still they lay, heads close, some sweet smell but no flower in sight. On land, Edwin smelled of the sea, a faint briny lick coming off him now they could no longer hear the dull pulse of the ocean. Tuesday, they returned to Sydney, passing the Governor's dirty linen, coming to Parramatta under guard of a mounted soldier to be laundered. Edwin took breakfast at Yate's lodgings, returning to the ship on the promise of visiting every evening at six o'clock or earlier as his duties allowed.

Walking to Woolloomooloo with his family, Mr Taylor gathered flowers, all unknown to him except the furze mallow and nightshade. They were to dine at Mr Mitchell's. On the way, they called on Miss Yate at Mr Jones's and were introduced to Mrs King, the wife of Mr King, once Governor of New South Wales. A gracious and intelligent lady, she requested the loan of Taylor's recent sermon. Miss Yate was in the best form he had seen her, asking his opinions of the place. He preferred her to her brother which was a sorry admission. Earlier that week, there had been a meeting of the Society's Corresponding Committee which resolved that Mr Taylor should take his family to New Zealand in four or five weeks, Mr Yate staying six months longer in Sydney to supply the late Mr Hill's place. Taylor found he was mostly relieved at the decision. Mr Yate had not proved a friend, thought Taylor as his party proceeded to Mr Mitchell's. Though he had left his card several times, the man had not introduced him about nor called unless it was for his own convenience. If Mr Yate were a cold fish to all, Taylor thought he might have worn it better but he was the steady companion of the ship's third mate who had no claim on his friendship at all. This Denison had been Mr Yate's guest at the parsonage when he had gone to stay with Mr Marsden at Parramatta. At dinner, Caroline and Mrs Mitchell spoke of servants. They would need a girl at least and perhaps a man. Mrs Mitchell had a New Zealand girl, Betty, she thought she could let them have from the beginning of next month. Six pounds a year was settled and a new gown annually for good behaviour.

She will have her dresses, said Mrs Mitchell going in to dinner, for she's a diligent girl and practical.

Miss Yate dined with the Taylors at Dr Jeanneret's on Friday and afterwards the whole party repaired to the ship, now moored alongside the wharf. In the cuddy were the doctor, Miss Bloomfield and Miss Baker, Mr Armistead, Mr Gordon. They were resplendent in each other's company, mawkish with love and silent. Even Miss Bloomfield was looked on kindly. The ladies settled to their methodical pleasantries, the three men to the poop where Taylor joined them after a minute, their thumbs hooked through the armholes of their waistcoats.

Disgraceful, said Mr Armistead, a disgraceful – and was silent as Mr Taylor joined them. Taylor waited to be looped up in the conversation but the three men said nothing, standing quiet and alert.

What is disgraceful? said Taylor banteringly. He wondered that he hadn't spent more time with these men on the voyage. Mr Armistead not always sufficiently a gentleman perhaps but straightforward enough, which was to be valued in a man.

It's nothing, sir, said Mr Gordon, flush-faced.

It is Mr Yate, said Mr Armistead.

You don't know, said Mr Gordon and took his leave.

I am solicitor enough to be sure he'd have his neck stretched at home for half as bad, said Mr Armistead. You know he would, he called after Mr Gordon. A legal expression, no doubt. Taylor didn't know it and, in his awkwardness, he gave up his confidence.

To my sorrow, he said, I've found Mr Yate less than a friend. On the quiet of the poop, the muffled sails frapped tight to the yards, it sounded like a confession.

That afternoon, they visited the Museum, the Taylors and Miss Yate who looked close at every exhibit as if it were a sign for something else. Sarah enjoyed a museum, the locked wooden cases more than their contents and the hushed dustiness of knowledge constrained. She did not care to read the plaques but looked at each object to see what it said about itself. It was her experience that most things humped their own truths with them unawares. It was as yet a small collection, mostly specimens of natural history, but edifying. Taylor stood a long while before that strange creature Major Mitchell designated a Nondescript. Certainly it appeared perfect in its singularity. A great variety of the kangaroo tribe and some hideous creatures called native bears. Disgusting, Mr Armistead had said. Not disgusting but – disgraceful. Taylor stood in the museum's mothball gloom and weighed the difference between the words, the latter more public than the other, he decided. He walked home thoughtfully, he would have said, except he arrived no more sensible than before. Dick Deck was expected for tea and stayed so late he was invited to sleep the night on the Jeanneret's sofa. Everyone retired but Taylor who stayed to see to Deck's comfort.

Have you seen Mr Yate of recent weeks? said Taylor looking away and busying himself with some particular in the manner of a man making conversation.

I dare say I have, said Deck. He is that often on the ship old Jack is thinking of signing him on. Something careless about Deck as if he weren't quite tamed. He had a purposefulness to him that could seem like a lack of intelligence and a quick anger that crackled his skin. Other men's thoughts seemed to him fleas, fleet and irritating. The world was best got through by force. He punched a cushion into shape for his head and removed his boots, struggling thick-fingered with his laces. By necessity, Taylor thought, Mr Yate would have to be a good deal on the ship. The Society had sent out provisions in his care and he must supervise their unloading.

And nothing to fault in his manner, Dick?

Nothing, said Deck. His jacket was off, his waistcoat unbuttoned, but he didn't think it civil to undress further while Mr Taylor stood blinking at him. Most liberal, I would say. I took tea with him and Mr Denison last week and stopped the night at his lodgings. A closed-mouth yawn that watered his eyes. The three of us in bed to start, tighter than ticks, but so much tickling I moved to the sofa. Nothing near as comfortable as this one, he said. I'll sleep like an angel tonight. He looked pointedly at the bed he had made up until Taylor took his leave, Good night, Dick, and climbed the stairs slow to lie awake and think in the muzzled darkness, listening to the baby's hedgehog snufflings.

On Monday 27 June, Taylor sat in Dr Jeanneret's study some hours, writing Mr Yate a letter. Caroline and the children had gone that morning to Mr Betts's at Parramatta and the house was still, only his thoughts and the scratch of his pen for company. *My dear Sir, I feel I ought to give you some–* he hesitated a moment, then wrote in a strong hand, *advice.* He had spoken no further to anyone but, under his consideration, the matter had grown hard and crystalline as the passage of time presses the muck of coal into diamonds. *There are so many reports to your prejudice that I should not be acting the part of a Minister were I not to put you on your guard against them.* Although he had no false starts or rewritings, the letter had taken him more than an hour already. He sweated as if it were physical work, his sentences coming out so exquisite that it seemed nothing was unspeakable between him and Mr Yate. *Suffer him not as you value your reputation, not only as a Minister but as a Man, ever again to have a part of your bed.* Sometimes he ached to show his friendship to Mr Yate and would have gone in person to Park Street had he thought his eloquence more than paper. In his pridefulness and human weakness Mr Yate had lost his way and needed saving. *Believe me to remain, dear Sir, yours sincerely.* It was a short letter that he had by heart on finishing. He sealed it without reading it over and gave the boy a half-shilling for its delivery.

All the day, Taylor walked about transfigured, the smallest tasks falling on him like blessings. He ate a self-conscious lunch with the Jeannerets, his head heavy and filled with light like Mr Yate's glass beehive, so that he was sure his thoughts were available to anyone who looked at him. Seven years since he had been ordained, he had never truly known what it was to save a man before. Not even the afternoon coach to Parramatta could diminish his shine. He went to secure his seat with the Jeanneret's manservant, a cringing fellow who sloped away once his luggage had been stowed. Counting himself, there were six inside though the coach was built for four and a load of Irish on the outside, bawling and shouting, who stopped every quarter of a mile to drink until the journey took twice as long as it ought. He could barely keep his knees free of the lady's opposite, the coach too close to allow him the cordial raising of his hat, and the whiskered gentleman next to him of such a size that he nearly cracked Taylor's ribs each time they took a corner. Sydney dropped back, the last excited dog fell away from the coach wheels, slavering and panting, as they started up Brickfield Hill, Taylor dressed against the cold but sweating in the tight squeeze of the coach. The other passengers seemed to know each other, speaking of the five robberies on the Sydney–Parramatta Road the previous week, four men, two of them armed.

They wouldn't dare knock off the coach, said a man at the far window, his boyish chin ornamented with a tuft that he turned over and over his finger.

Wouldn't they though, said the woman opposite Taylor, in a voice used to disappointment. The houses thinned until they were one deep, lining the wayside on either side, hard-pressed by fields of oats or barley. Taylor stared from the coach, his eye turned back by the blank windows of the houses, even the stable doors shut, a toss of woodsmoke from the chimneys all he could secure for himself. He wondered what Mr Yate might be doing this minute, his letter surely arrived.

The coach pulled into Parramatta in a drift of mizzling rain, Mr Betts's gig sent to meet Taylor and have him home for tea. Caroline was tender-faced, watching for him behind the rain-smeared parlour window when the gig pulled up at the door. She thought the children might have the ringworm again. Arthur had Basil, Laura and the two little Betts, Sarah and Charles, bent to some suppressed game in the corner where the lamplight fell uneven.

Good evening, Papa, he said over his shoulder like a grave little man when Taylor came in. With the key on a belt around her waist, Mrs Betts opened the parlour sideboard, the mouse-coloured gleam of eggs, a round of butter, bread, a low tart of some sort, so the girl could fetch the tea to the table, Mr Betts going back and forth empty-handed, smiling in pleasure.

I'm not yet used to the New South Wales practice of keeping the foodstuffs under lock and key, said Taylor when he sat to the table, a reprimand in his voice though he had wanted to sound only observant.

It's not just the theft, said Mrs Betts, a nervous glance at the closed door.

Last year, said Mr Betts, one of the women assigned us nearly poisoned the whole family. She had – Arthur was listening, on his knees, blotched golden under the lamp, his eyes round, lips pressed together. Taylor placed his hand over Mr Betts's to prevent him going further.

Quite, quite, said Mr Betts, glancing back at the boy. Taylor wanted madly to squeeze the children to him, ringworm or no, Caroline also, but he sat upright at the table, his thoughts disordered still from the coach's judder, Mr Yate in his rooms, alone, Mrs Betts pouring and Caroline passing the cups, and let himself be persuaded to a second portion of salmon pie and piccalilly.

The next morning, Mr Betts's girl brought hot water and, with a modest smile as if it were all her own doing, opened the curtains on a world muffled and quiet. It had snowed in the night and snowed still, the flakes drifting from an iron sky, everything clean and new under its soft hummock, the fence posts capped with white, the barn roof, the lawn with its doubled track of footprints, the orange trees hung with frosted fruit. It had not happened before in man's memory, residents of the place for more than forty years

having never seen anything like it. All morning it snowed,
the whole town covered right to the churchyard flats, and
Taylor knew it for a sign though he did not think what it
signified. His every sensation was curiously swaddled so
that he could not say what sort of man he was. Knowing it
was a fancy, he thought he might walk out in the whiteness
and meet Mr Yate on some untrammelled field, nothing
but gratitude between them. He was gentle with his wife
and easy on his children, imagining his new fragility theirs.
Mr Betts brought the letter to him after midday and he
took it tremblingly upstairs. *My dear Sir*. A long letter,
pages and pages, and Taylor unprepared. *I should really
imagine from your Letter that you had lived all your life in
a small and very confined village where you had allowed
yourself to listen and believe all the malicious scandal*. It
was cold upstairs with no fire in the grate, the room filled
with a queer blue light coming off the snow. The paper
itself felt pestilent between his fingers. *I have no secrets –
all my words and works are open to all men. My conduct
with Denison, who I respect and love, by night or by day,
has been such as I should not be afraid for the whole world
to bear witness to*. It stopped snowing as he read, the high,
bright voices of unseen men travelling clear over the yard,
licked back and white. Taylor's faith held for half a line,
shimmered as its own mirage and was gone, a cold fist
taking its place which rose retchingly in his throat until he
could only have relieved himself by pounding Mr Yate to
oblivious meat. To think of the meals he had sat to with
that man, damned beyond hell and knowing it but eating
his almond biscuits with a narrow, anxious face, and his
wife exposed to such society. *Believe me that I take your
Letter kindly, very kindly meant. Let me know when you
are likely to come down to Sydney. With kind regards to
Mrs Taylor*. The orange trees on the slope beneath the
window shivered and threw their load of snow. Let him
perjure himself how he likes, thought Taylor, pressing his

cheek to the cold bite of the glass. I will pursue him until he has paid in full.

The following day, the snow having melted away except where it persisted in tight or shadowed places, Taylor went to Sydney, his wife gone with Mrs Betts to inspect Mr Mobbs's orange groves. He went on board the *Prince Regent* and sought an interview with Captain Aitken respecting the unpleasant reports of Mr Yate. The captain was as condescending as always, not in the least put out by his informations, brushing them aside as so much idle talk. Taylor was glad to see his low opinion of the man confirmed. A seaman, Aitken was hardened to men's iniquities and accustomed to think his own command absolute.

I wish to speak to your men, said Taylor, keeping his seat although the captain stood restless and pawed the papers on his desk. They may have further intelligence on the matter.

You'd go elsewhere if you wanted intelligence, said Captain Aitken, some faint insult larding his words that Taylor could not work out until later. Speak to them as you like but don't get in the way of the work. Taylor stood to leave and was half across the cuddy, strangely small now and desolate, when the captain called after him, My advice, Mr Taylor, and when he turned, reluctant, Leave things be.

The men had said very little to him, nothing useful, though none of them seemed to be working. He suspected they indulged him which was an uncommon feeling, their smiles broadening at his back as he disembarked. A much more interesting and profitable dinner with Mr Armistead, Dr Fowles joining them afterwards for a cigar. Mr Armistead was very worldly, Taylor supposed.

A sinner, Mr Taylor, certainly. An apostate. Mr Armistead nodded and pressed his lips shut over the jut of his teeth. But in my line of work, sir, a criminal plain and simple. Walking George Street, his head swimming with cigar fumes and some tuberous hurt, thinking of the wretched man, guilty of the grossest indecency and still smoothly superior, offering my wife his kind regards, Taylor was startled to see Mr Yate ahead, walking toward him, that distinctive hunch and narrow melancholic face. He thought to conceal himself in the auctioneer's but hesitated too long and the man was upon him, his sluggard's soul rotten and damned to eternity.

Pink-cheeked and pink-eared, Yate made his way along Pitt Street and Market Street, having left his lodgings before dinner, Mrs Brown promising to keep his plate warm over a bowl of water in the oven.

It's the water is the secret, sir, she said boastingly. It don't dry out. Cold enough that the horses' snorting breath hung in the air, he walked briskly, past the Italian goods store and the Royal Theatre with its freshly pasted hoardings, not quite humming, whistling neither, but wound up on a tune of Edwin's that had got into his head and couldn't be got out.

> O *Betsy Baker, Lived in Long Acre, Married a Quaker.*
> O *Sally Rackett, Pawned my best jacket,*
> *And kept the ticket.*

Edwin had woken this morning singing and sung as he scraped the lather from his jaw and sung at breakfast – more black pudding, Mr Denison? – and sung as he went down the street, striding quick so he'd not be late at the ship. Yate had watched him go from his upstairs window, the handsome sailor, until he saw Mrs Bibb making good speed up the street, her skirts full with the wind behind her. Now the song turned in the warm burrow of his recollection and sang itself.

O Polly Hawkins, With her white stocking,
Beats all at talking.
O Kitty Carson, Jilted the parson, Married a mason.

He did not sing but his lips twitched in places as if he might and he had such a curious stoppered expression that anyone would have thought he was making for the druggist.

Good day, sir.

Good day. It was Mr Aspinall, hurrying by, one hand to his hat, a gentleman known to him from a meeting at St James's for the propagation of the Gospel in foreign parts. A most successful meeting, attended by perhaps sixty gentlemen of rank: Marsden and Justice Burton, of course, several chaplains and most of the Government Officers and Members of Council. Prevailed upon to speak of his interview with the King, his social success was secured the following Saturday at the wedding of the Colonial Secretary's eldest daughter to Mr Harington. Edwin liked to joke that he had shaken the hand of a man who had shaken hands with His Majesty and took such a pride in it that Yate hadn't told him the King did not shake hands. Some grey thought passed over him. Not the imminence of Edwin's departure, though that wore at him like a stone in his shoe. The letter. Mr Taylor's letter. He had read it to Edwin the day it arrived and put it in the fire. Perhaps nothing would come of it. That was Edwin's conviction. He had said nothing to Sarah when the three of them went into the barracks to hear the band play. He would speak to Mr Taylor when he returned to town and make him see sense. Rumour was the greatest wickedness in the colony. Only last week the *Sydney Gazette* had published an article asserting that he himself was not an ordained minister of the Church of England, a slander corrected in Monday's *Herald*. Perhaps this matter would be as easily retrieved although he feared Mr Taylor was not an intelligent man, slow-witted and righteous, his prejudice grubbying everything he didn't understand.

As if he had conjured him, Mr Taylor stood before him, one foot on the sill of the auctioneer's doorway, the other on the street, a stump-legged apparition, green and drawn, staring at him as if he were the ghost. Yate rubbed his right arm over the elbow for the feel of Edwin's rope bracelet.

Good afternoon, Mr Taylor, he said but the man was silent. You are well, sir, I hope. How do you find Parramatta? As a young man at Islington, Yate used to examine himself in his looking glass, his face seeming not like the other missionary students, scaffolded on a reckless certitude but as yet unknowing. Mr Taylor had that look now, passive and suffering. Yate thought two men passing gave him an odd look and feared suddenly that Mr Taylor would make a spectacle of him.

My sister tells me you've been most attentive to her, he said. Do you have time to take dinner with me? Something he said pricked Mr Taylor, he didn't know what. He stopped rocking back and forth in the doorway, stood down with both feet on the street.

I have spoken with the ship's men this morning. And dined with Mr Armistead. The clipping and snipping of Mr Taylor's words reminded Yate of the haberdashery. Nothing was going as he had hoped.

Mr Armistead is of the opinion that this is a legal matter. Mr Taylor seemed to take a glaucous enjoyment in his business. A legal matter. There was a constable loitering opposite the post office, a slab-chopped brute of a man Yate was certain wouldn't hesitate to pitch into him if told to do it. The yellow and grey kit of the ironed gangs, the transports to Norfolk Island, the blood-crusted triangle at Goat Island. He would not think of the scaffold. This was a country where a legal matter might make a beast of a gentleman. The watery sun fell across Mr Taylor's bloated and bullying face, dissolving it into rods of green and grey that slipped and floated until Yate looked to the square front of the auctioneer's rooms for his balance.

I hardly think we need Mr Armistead's legal opinion, said Yate. He felt his bracelet once more for courage. I've shown your letter to Justice Burton, who advises me to take no notice of gossip. A bluff so extravagant, it was at once believable. If there is a legal action, he thinks it mine. For libel. Mr Taylor faltered, opened his mouth and closed it. He took his leave without a word, returning to Parramatta to lay his case before Marsden, Yate continuing down George Street, his blood keening in his neck, *Woe unto them that call evil good, and good evil; that put darkness for light, and light for darkness; that put bitter for sweet, and sweet for bitter*, quieting himself over a tray of gold watches at Maclehose's.

July began a nervous month that sweetened and settled as the days drew on for August with no sign of further business from Mr Taylor or his associates. Yate bought Edwin a black kerseymere suit from Wood's and took him to the theatre, a benefit, full-price tickets only, offered by the soldiers of the 4th Regiment. They were guests in the Mitchell's box and he felt the Governor's spyglasses on him when he stood for Mrs Mitchell. Yate suspected Edwin had never been to the theatre. Before the curtains went up, he was entranced with everything, the crowds on the street outside, the lights, the raked seats. He was a discreet young man, Edwin, and took his delights privately but he couldn't look at Yate without a grin, his face glowing like a covered lantern. Absorbed by the glees as if they were for his particular instruction, he sat still and attentive while the theatre clapped and called at the entrance of the young soldier who took the ladies' parts. All the following week, he sang *Darby Kelly* in the Scottish style.

Rain turned the dusty streets to mud. Park Street was particularly affected, Mrs Brown having hay put down at her door, carts and drays daily bogged to the axles between George and Castlereagh. Yate visited the sick, Mr Hook's widow on George Street, a rotten plumminess bubbling through her Rowland's Rose Bloom. He preached at the hulks and Hyde Park Barracks, the prisoners' eyes like wicks pinched out and smoking. Between rounds of marrying, burying and baptising, he attended meetings opposed to Bourke's plan for national education. He published a letter to the parishioners of St James's Church on the occasion of the approaching confirmation, printer's costs paid by Mr MacLeay, Justice Burton and Mr Jones. The pamphlet was written on the small, gate-legged table in his rooms at Mrs Brown's. *Those who would live godly in Christ Jesus must expect to suffer persecution.* He wrote in the evenings mostly, his thoughts transparent to him at the end of the day, Edwin moving about in the adjoining room. *The flesh will always be striving for mastery and the body will never cease its endeavours to subdue the soul.* Edwin was too restless a person to read though he sat, book in hand, looking out the window onto the street, the unlit comings and goings of Sydney and the house fronts opposite with their gashes of lamplight.

You know, William, he said from the bedroom. One of the wild bullocks off the *Samuel Cunard* got loose at King's Wharf the other day. A pause, Yate waiting with his head up but saying nothing. He got through the Tanks into George Street and made a havoc, as Mr May tells it.

Um, said Yate.

Captain Jack doesn't think he can get up a cargo here. We'll go to Newcastle soon, he reckons. Unbearable to think of Edwin gone from him, in the daily company of men more or less indifferent to his presence, while he himself stayed on in Sydney, halved and hollow. With his young man's mulishness, all his strengths as yet untested,

Edwin thought it wouldn't be long before they met again. Yate thought it would not be in this world. They said their prayers together and put out the lamp for bed. Quick, in the thick drape of the dark, Yate got Edwin beneath him and made him moan, his ribcage falling and rising in panted breaths, brought him to the brink of his moment but would not let him tip into it, both his hands trapped over his head, his cock standing unattended, Jesus, William, the only way Yate knew to make time slow, to tether himself to now, to here, against the spring tides of an unwanted future. Later, when his eyes made sense of the dark, he watched the back of Edwin's head and his own seed let down like tears.

The *Prince Regent* was to sail to Newcastle in ballast on Friday 5 August. Yate felt his golden days gutter to nothing like a man who burns his fingers on the last of his candle. Tuesday was their last night together. Already a little lost to each other, they slept chaste as brothers, neither wanting to do anything for what might have to be thought the last time. Yate ordered a gig for the wharf, hardly knowing how to be in Edwin's company if he was to forfeit it. The abrasive etiquette of farewells, the half-sentences and those not spoken. Yate stayed in the gig and ordered the driver home with Edwin still in sight, his bright hair lost beneath his cap. He had never cried for a man before. Mrs Brown sent meals up for two days. He could see no one, not even Sarah. Solitude was a new kind of prayerfulness. He lay in bed and burned until he had no insides but was as an animal hide, nothing but skin either side. Nothing to plumb or dredge, he could not think where faith might come from. The air darkened about him and the things of his room made known to him their artless secrets, the roundness of the doorknob slicked shiny by years of unknown hands, the bedstead spire. No longer the author of his prayer but its flayed witness, he slept through two days of unreflecting blackness and woke cleansed on Friday afternoon, a bowl of Mrs Brown's mutton broth and a letter written to Edwin on the ship.

Yate was sufficiently repaired to take up his duties again Monday though Mrs Brown would have assigned him to her calf-foot jelly charge for a few more days. The Newcastle–Sydney steamer brought a letter early in the week and she hurried it up to Yate's rooms. He put it in his waistcoat pocket, only reading it on the street as he walked to Hyde Park Barracks. *My dearest Friend, My Father, For never did I feel so acutely a separation from my friend before, and feel confident I never shall again. I was most agreeably surprised while at dinner by Mr May who came down and began making a bargain with me what I should give him for something of great worth to me. I struck my bargain for some bread and cheese, little expecting what it was, when he presented me with your Letter, which was the best meal I have had since I was at Park St.* Cranked and radiant, he was an odd sight, Mrs Brown's lodger, his head nearly wrapped in the wind-blown sheet of paper he read, feet unheeded through the dust. *The passage was delightful as far as regards the weather, but to me the most melancholy I ever made. I had nothing to employ myself about, and so gave full scope to my imagination. I walked the larboard side of the poop nearly the whole of the time, picturing to myself and fancying you were with me until I was aroused from my reverie by the well known bawling voice of old Jack, Stand by for a rope for the Pilot boat, when all my castles and churches which I had built came tumbling down, and I felt I was alone. I was on shore on Friday evening, but on a different errand to what I was the evening before, it was for drunken men, which with great difficulty I succeeded in getting off, excepting Edwards who still remains in Sydney, which makes a small number of hands one less.* Edwin wrote as he spoke, a rare skill Yate knew, though some of his New Zealand boys had it. He might have known them from their letters even if they had not signed their names. From habit, his own prose was too picked clean to carry the mess of him. *The Captain has not spoken half a dozen words to me since we left Sydney, which pleases me well, as I feel as little inclined to listen as he does to speak. The Doctor I think is getting much worse, as he scarcely leaves his Cabin, and is continually coughing. I have not spoken to him but once, nor shall I ever again be enabled to be free with him as with others. I shall often look at my directions, and apply them closely, setting the shadow before me now I am deprived of the much loved voice of the substance, and fancy is speaking to me. There is a pleasure in melancholy, I think.* Yate walked beside Hyde Park, his step light and spirit uncorked as if it really were a park instead of an unlucky piece of treeless ground, fenced around and scored through with the furrowed traces of the water carts. *Thanks to your kindness, my dear Yate, there is nothing which I stand in need of at present, excepting to be a little nearer to you where I can get a sight of you and a chat now and then.* The wind across Hyde Park was dust-ridden and drove two tears from Yate's right eye. He dashed at them with his coat sleeve and walked on until he could make out the barracks clock. *Had I time I could go on writing which would be of no use other than to gratify my feelings. Dick sends his love to you, and says he shall write you in a day or two. And now I must conclude, as the Steamer is coming down to us and I must be moving. God bless you and enable you to triumph over the malice of your enemies, which are mine also, be they who they may. My dear friend, I remain without hesitation, your unalterably affectionate Son, E. H. Denison.*

The Friday after Edwin sailed, Yate had a letter from Bishop Broughton, requesting a meeting for four o'clock the following afternoon at the St James's vestry. Detained longer than usual at Goat Island, Yate came a quarter after the hour, heart-split to see Mr Armistead and Mr Taylor at the vestry door, the one insolent, the other injured; inside the bishop and, dear God, Justice Burton.

Gentlemen, we begin, said Bishop Broughton, his lip quirking in Yate's direction though he could not look at him, his gaze flopping wide on either side, brittle and bloody as a wounded bird. None could look at him or even stand close though they were obscenely alert to his presence, a warm excitation shuddering through them as he came in. From some perverse sense that he might fall, he remained standing. They were all of a piece, Yate saw, the four of them come to some arrangement almost mechanical, its delicate sprung workings designed for his own back.

Gentlemen, said the bishop, bringing them to order. All of us know that rumours of an unspeakable nature are circulating throughout the colony. Of that matter, I can as yet have no opinion. He paused to admire the inviolability of his conviction that ticked as fatly as any pocketwatch. As a Christian, Mr Taylor saw fit to warn Mr Yate of these rumours some weeks ago. Am I correct, Mr Taylor?

My Lord, said Mr Taylor. Your Honour. I thought it my duty. I urged him to repair his conduct with Mr Denison. That was in a letter dated the twenty-seventh day of June.

A letter, said the bishop and nodded to all, his eye still skittish of Yate, standing invisible in the vestry's murky centre.

And I met Mr Yate two days later on George Street, said Mr Taylor, speaking quick at first for fear of losing his chance but soon relaxing into the importance of his testimony. He told me he'd put his situation before Justice Burton, a deferential humbling of Taylor's eye in the judge's direction, and that Justice Burton had advised him to disregard my letter as nothing more than gossip.

Mr Yate said Judge Burton was of the opinion that your letter was to be discounted? said the bishop.

SLOW WATER

305

I have never spoken to Mr Yate of the matter, said Justice
Burton and could not have pronounced his death sentences
more weightily. Mr Taylor and Mr Armistead looked
sidelong and were delinquent enough to smile at each other
in the vestry's dead aquarium light. I met Mr Yate once only
since his return to the colony, accidentally on Elizabeth
Street between his lodgings and the court house, about the
fourteenth of June. He communicated nothing to me of any
letter on that occasion or any other. Yate saw that no one
could look at him, not even the judge who, in his horse's
wig brought from England, tempered his eye every session
on murderers and fornicators. Justice belongs to those who
exercise it.

For this reason, and this reason alone, said Bishop
Broughton, I find Mr Yate guilty of prevarication and falsehood. The main accusation will be considered in due
course. He inclined his head at Yate. Before these witnesses,
I interdict you from the exercise of your public ministry. He
brought his beaked nose toward Yate, almost kindly, like a
mother bird that would stuff life down his throat. Have you
anything to add to our proceedings? All that false civility,
the tricked-up trappings of proper procedure, the loss of his
pulpit that stretched him thin with grief and the finer-
grained loss of Edwin, and among that lumber an
unexpected tinder as he saw himself broken and exultant
on the crucifix of his disgrace.

I am innocent, said Yate, the plea of the guilty man,
and because his relations with Edwin were beyond
reproach, because it was the pure luminousness of what they
traded between them that forced men to turn their heads
aside, he handed to the bishop his only certification of his
innocence, the two letters he had received from Edwin,
though before he had stumbled to the corner of Elizabeth
Street, one manged dog and then three rolling along at his
heels, he missed their anchoring weight and might have
flown over the town on the least wind, a cooling flake of ash.

At a jog-trot came a mongrel dog round the corner, broken tail after wet nose, black coat scurfy in the sun. The fur on his elbows worn down to the leather, he had a white patch over his left eye, an indulgent monocle that gave his snortings and pokings an air of business. He came on with such a purposeful sprung step he might have been making for home but circled back with the same application to smell a pile of horse dung, cracked in the heat and fly-blown, and to piss on a damp patch outside Mrs Mudie's. A small dog, young perhaps, he urinated like a bitch, half squatting and taking his weight on his front paws. Hot and straw-coloured, for half a minute the cleanest thing on the street, his water pooled neat as a cartographer's island, its estuaried shorelines holding a moment, throwing the noonday sun, before sinking damp in the dust. He put his nose to his own smell, that dog shock of selfhood, the things and places of his previous hours memorised in his stench and headily unbottled to break and mend with the present, the air flailing with the perfume of the breadcart, intimations of the countryside in the wagon tracks, resinous myrtle leaves and the bafflement of herded cattle, the high baked dome of the season coming on for summer and always other dogs, some known to him, most not, hot gullets and wormy arses. Legs braced wide, he shook his coat, the flap of his lips over black gums the sound of rags being shaken out an upstairs window. A house door opened and he turned his head as he went, flannel tongue dripping, the cool scent of inner rooms and unthought upholstery legged

on to the street by a pair of gentleman's trousers. He
sneezed the dust from his nostrils, stiff legs braced wide,
and trotted on, white-tipped tail bent and flown like his
colours.

Two miles across town from a laneway's shadowed
passage bloomed the fishhead stink of the sea so that he
jogged back to nose it, on a sudden undecided, but keeping
finally to the sun of the public roadway that ran slightly
downhill, his back feet skewing a little and throwing the
dust, the kibbley smell of ale and working men. Outside
Cribb's Hotel on the corner of Gloucester Street and Cum-
berland Lane, the Rocks, Constable Naughton saw him
coming, a slight black dog with laughing jaw.

He's mine, said Naughton to Constables Kelly and
Moore, waiting until the dog drew level, one bouncing step
beyond him, another, when he stepped out, truncheon
already raised so as not to give the alarm, and bashed his
skull just over the ear, the clean dull sound of caving bone,
the dog turning in the air to land on his side, his hide shivering its last convulsions as if already catacombed with
maggots.

Two and six, said Naughton. With one stroke. For show,
he recreated the blow, twirling his gobbety truncheon.

He's not gone, said Kelly peering close.

He is, said Naughton, scarce looking, all his warning
for Constable Kelly who had before now poached his
bounty with a breakfast egg tap, the hard work done
already. Not as brawny as the other two, Kelly made up
with cunning. He preferred a short wide plank with two
nails hammered through and wore his brother's tannery
boots to draw the dogs.

I say he's not, said Kelly, jigging the beast with his boot.
The dog's feet, one white-stockinged, ran in the dust and he
thought he was at the abattoir yard again, slavering for a

piece of lung, though his head was pulped grey and raspberry and his eye leaked down his muzzle. Naughton
coshed him twice more to be sure and dragged him down
the laneway by his back legs, his head a bloody chrysan-
themum, to throw him on their grisly cart, a glistening
curtain of flies whining into the air and settling.

And baby makes sixteen, said Moore.

Seventeen, said Kelly, contrary and correct as ever.
Reckon we'll get our forty?

It's not even two o'clock, said Naughton. Easy as pissing.
The three men stood and smiled in the slim shade of
Cribb's, a block up the street a couple of freckled mongrels
sniffing under each other's tails and running toward them
shoulder to shoulder.

Past midnight Yate stood at Mrs Macquarie's Chair
looking back over Farm Cove, the moon in its first quarter
wobbling below in the dark, flaking apart in white scales
on the unseen movement of the water then binding itself
together. The cabin passengers had been quite gone on
moon-watching despite the captain's warning them
against it. A tropical moon hanging full and heavy like a
blood-streaked yolk would have them all on the poop
singing and sighing though Yate hadn't seen the point till
now. Remote the moon and cold but these last months it
had been his sun. Some voices behind him, laboured with
drinking, a man and a woman, a grunt and the snapping
of shrubbery, perhaps two men and a woman. He did not
turn or even start at the noise behind him, grown so like
a ghost he was at least in the night uninhabited by human
fears. The jellyish moon found its shape once more, broke
open and scattered like a shoal of silver fish. One night,
late August, three men had stopped him at the wharves to
turn his pockets out, strange fellow wandering about in
his reverence's weeds. He looked at them and said only, I

have nothing. Even then he had not been fearful of loss or violence, only of being obstructed in his way, anything left him pinned to his ceaseless night wanderings of the town. Let go, he was never bothered since and had come to think of himself as invisible even under the magnesium blaze of the moon.

Down past the Governor's stables Yate walked, the quarter moon on his shoulder, the old lime kilns, a light still showing at the upstairs window of the water bailiff's, the slap of water on the hulls of the blackened ships at their moorings, the *Prince Regent* back from Newcastle since the second week of September, trying to get up a cargo off Campbell's Wharf. It could have been any ship now Edwin had signed off and taken lodgings on Castlereagh Street.

I couldn't leave you to them, William, he had said and set his jaw as if they might quarrel on it. So much what Yate wanted, he was only relieved. I'm coming off, said Edwin and that was the end of it. It's my name too, you know. The last more a rhetorical point since few people had Edwin's name and in most stories he was the third mate or, for those who had even less sense of a ship's rank than what two men could make together, simply a sailor. Edwin's rooms at the rear of Mrs Campbell's house were ungenerous and lacked aspect but he inhabited them with a seaman's ingenuity and looked sufficiently at home there for Yate to think some-times that they might, when all this had been got through, establish themselves in some new landscape within walking distance of each other and lead unremarkable lives of comfort and virtue. Yate's shoes were almost through at the soles but he had lined them with blotting paper rather than stop at Wood's for a new pair. It might be half-one, his watch left at Mrs Brown's when he came out to walk empty-pocketed. Up Harrington Street and the crooked lanes of the Rocks, pushed out of line by the straggle of

huts and cottages that grew where they stood, the night
thickened with lights and voices, the seamen taking their
rum in the drinking houses and one getting rid of it outside
Ellen Riley's, groaning it up beside the steps, hands on bent
knees. Still the shaly sound of the sea, louder in the dark,
and two men pissing against a wall or showing their cocks
in their butcher's hands as Yate passed unseen, carrying his
hat on account of the warmth, his neckcloth loose. He
would have liked to leave off his jacket altogether and his
waistcoat, and walk in the night half-dressed as Dr Fowles
had when the ship was becalmed.

Kent Street was moon-bleached, the house fronts grey and
grey-black, Yate's own skin when he looked at it brought
out paperish. At the back of Bathurst Street, a screwed-face
man in a ragged vest clanging on an iron bell that set the
dogs' noses to the sky and a clutch of speculators come
from nowhere to stand lonely beneath the smoking lamp of
the night auctioneer hammering down his first lot, five
cases of stolen tea. On he went at the same dreamer's pace,
his breath coming raw up Brickfield Hill, till he crossed
over on Goulburn Street, down Castlereagh, the scrubby
end near the cattle market and the old gallow grounds, to
sit two hours on a darkened step in the lane, watching the
dead window of Edwin's room at the back of Mrs
Campbell's. Like a poultice, the bone-coloured light pressed
on his bare head, drawing out all manner of thought that
could not find its tongue by day. He would have liked the
clarity of nakedness. The native women had stripped Mrs
Fraser of her clothes when the *Stirling Castle* was wrecked
on a northern reef, the newspapers reporting this as a barbarism though he wondered that it might not have been an
instruction. In a land so vast it hid its revelations in plain
view, he might have liked to be taken up by a tribe of men
who made their home by walking, the promise of illumi-

nation shimmering beyond the last fenceline. Barred from the St James's pulpit through the workings of the man that now hoisted himself into it each week, he had come to learn it was the wordiness of prayer that weighed men to the world. Chafed by cuff and collar, his thighs rubbed tender in his trousers, his clothes, like his words, were an irritation to him. He was no longer a gentleman in frock coat and top hat such as Mr Taylor, Mr Armistead, Bishop Broughton and Mr Marsden with their letters and their hearings and the resolutions of their committee that he return at once to England which he had thought to do at first only let the *Elizabeth* sail without him, staying to clear his name that daily grew more soiled and strange to him. As if it were a disguise, he would throw it all off and go into the desert with his rope bracelet, his absurd white shanks and pastry skin that couldn't take the sun rather than be marked by Mr Armistead who, by Edwin's account, had tickled a statement from Mr Morris for the price of a bucket of ale.

The day after Mr Yate's licence had been revoked, Mr Armistead had taken the steamer for Newcastle on the advice of Justice Burton, to record the depositions of the sailors against Mr Yate. Thinking the *Regent* might sail any day, the bishop gave him a dispensation for travelling on a Sunday. Hall was at the masthead with his slush bucket and saw Armistead spuffling down the waterfront, his pompousness dragged behind him like a great black balloon, and before the man had picked out the *Prince Regent* among the tilt of vessels, his arrival was all over the ship. Armistead set up his papers in the cuddy and interviewed the men one after the other until the room stank as it never had on the voyage, unwashed armpits and tainted milk crotches. It was often necessary for him to rest his nose in his handkerchief. The captain insisted on being present and tried Armistead's Christianity with his interruptions. First summoned was Mr

Morris who went with a glance behind and beside him, Mr May with a wink to his men that a gentleman oughtn't try and roister a sailor on his own ship, I'll give that legal advice for nothing. Next Lamb, Davies who was gone for a longful while and the Finn. The joke was never as good coming out as going in. Though his bucket was half full yet, Hall came down to the forecastle where the men gathered, rubbing their noses with the backs of their hands and hitching their trousers. They stood facing the same direction like sheep on a windward slope, watching the cuddy door.

What does he do in there? said Staines, as if it were a complaint against them all.

He asks questions, said Mr May, and writes down the answers.

I an't being written down, said Staines in his grunnying voice but he went easy enough when he were called. The cook was sitting in the dark of the galley when Hall pushed the door an inch open with his shoulder, a bottle and glass before him though Mr Morris might have looked in any minute.

Mr Armystead's here, said Hall, hearen stories against Mr Yate. Staines says he'll string him for a sodomite. The cook drank and nodded. He's taken the men one after one, said Hall but still Louie said nothing, seeming his own man, all his skin for himself. What'll I say? He squeezed his whale tooth inside his shirt and waited.

Whatever you like, *matlo*, said the cook and it was like falling again, that time off the jib-boom, his brainpan as blank as the sky.

Hall was never called. Armistead didn't know the men's names and when the captain stopped providing them, he assumed he had heard them all out. He hadn't enjoyed the success he had hoped, the men grinning and stupid, quick to agree to whatever he put to them and shy of anything else.

Were you aware that Mr Denison visited Mr Yate in his cabin by night?

Yes sir.

Visited Mr Yate often? Armistead's voice sonorous and ready for the courtroom.

Yes sir.

And were you aware that Mr Yate visited Mr Denison in his cabin also by night?

Yes sir.

Anything else improper in Mr Yate's conduct?

No sir.

Were you aware that Mr Yate's language was not always that of a gentleman? A harder question for most, half saying yes, half saying no, Mr Staines stumped and reddening until he finally said, I think I'm aware of a gentleman's language, sir. Weathered men, their sleeves still rolled, they stared at him then the captain before answering and agreed or disagreed without conviction, like children who couldn't tell right from left. Packing his papers away, Armistead thought Mr Morris would come to an understanding, given the right circumstances.

You haven't heard Mr Denison yet, said Captain Aitken.

Don't intend to, said Armistead.

And you haven't heard me. The two men looked at each other, hating. Record that I say it's nothing but envy, Mr Armistead, that spreads such reports of Mr Yate.

Envy is a sin, said Armistead tying his pages, but not a crime, I think. He was tired of having thick-clothed simpletons as company and promised himself he would speak to Justice Burton of his career. Staying overnight at Hutson's Hotel, he suffered himself to drink for an hour with Mr Morris at The Sailor's Rest, a portside tavern, crowded and joyless, the ceiling resined yellow with tobacco smoke.

I couldn't count the drinks I've had here, sir, said Mr Morris in spiritous good humour. Only usually I lose money to the ladies – he bunted his chin at a couple of unlikely slatterns with dirty hems and rouged cheeks – not make it off a gentleman. He shook his head to clear it and signed his name while the words still crawled.

Yate stretched his leg in the laneway, the square of Edwin's window still dark though the sky lightened, no longer full black but bluing in the east, the stars in that quarter fast fading. Edwin walked the streets with him mostly, the two of them eating up the night with their shoe leather, speaking of anything but this. One or other would send a note and they met on the shadowed side of Hyde Park but the previous evening the boy had returned empty-handed, loitering in the doorway, still hopeful of a penny, Mr Edwin's not abart, sir, and Missus Campbell says she don't know where he's at, not been his mother. The pair of them had walked every street more than once though they seldom noted where they went, their unhurried conversation the only orientation either needed.

I came home this afternoon, Edwin said one night, to a seashell and some kind of dried seed-pod I think was Sarah's doing. She had called on Yate after dinner so he thought Edwin's guess likely. Mrs Campbell says if I'm to be a collector she'll have to increase my charges. Sitting now in the lane beneath Edwin's window, Yate remembered how he had heard Edwin smile in the dark beside him. Sailors are not collectors, he knew. They are always casting off, casting off, scraping their hulls clean of the barnacled stuff that other men gather to themselves. He fixed his eye on the window until it pulsed light and dark with his staring. Sometimes nothing more than his presence could draw Edwin from sleep to the glass as the full moon draws the tide high up the beach. Several times now, while he waited without expectation, Edwin had woken and drawn back his curtain so that they looked at each other frank and unregretful across the tin rooves of Mrs Campbell's out-houses, the recognition so precise it made a science of them. Once, though Yate didn't know it, Edwin had stood alone over the empty laneway, curtains wide, his candlestick of a torso drawing the light to him, and frigged himself and wept. Day coming on, there was yet no sign of Edwin. They would dine together at Mrs Brown's at noon. Yate stood stiffly, his feet pinched from resting, and made his way to Park Street, a flop-eared dog his slouching company.

The days were difficult. Cramped in his rooms long hours and subject to rude attentions when he ventured without, he fretted and wrote endless letters. *My dear Sir, I do not really know how to begin to write to you at all, such a wonderful change has come over me, and so different a creature do I feel to what I was when I saw you.* He had no ease during the day and wrote to the authorities and every man of his acquaintance proclaiming his innocence, demanding the public hearing at which he might meet his accusers directly and clear his name. Bishop Broughton, a man who tried his patience beyond endurance, would not convene his court nor hand the case to the Colonial Secretary's office but kept trying to worry his evidence into something of substance. Under his instruction, Marsden had written to Mr Clarke and the missionaries at Waimate asking after Mr Yate's reputation there and requesting the native boys be interviewed about his conduct with them. In August when he stripped him of his licence, the bishop had promised Yate he would inform him within twenty-four hours what action would be taken but now he no longer replied to his letters. Yate's friends called with kind advice. Mr Harington, Assistant Colonial Secretary, was sure the whole affair would blow over. A storm in a teacup, he said in the library after dinner with the ladies sent to the parlour. He cut a look across his brandy glass at Mr Yate who sat unsmiling.

Not surprising, he supposed, since Marsden and now that bluster of a bishop had their teeth in him and if they couldn't take a bite then neither would they let go.

I've written to Busby at New Zealand, said Harington after Yate had sat a silent minute. Told him to get together some written support from there, a character reference, something of that sort. My report's with Mr Macleay and I expect the bishop will be called off you soon enough. Lie low a few more weeks and we'll laugh of this by Christmas. He drained his drink and took up Yate's untouched glass. Truly, William, don't worry. Harington glanced at the library door. He was getting impatient for the ladies. I told you last time when Mr Jones and I visited the ship the main evidence against you was contradicted by Mr Morris himself. First mate or not, he couldn't keep his story straight. When we were finished with him, he didn't know if he was Arthur or Martha. He champed his lips on his napkin. In the meantime, stay clear of young Denison. That's the best advice you'll get today. Mr Harington often sent his carriage, Mr Jones or Mr Mitchell did the same, but the last of the day flaring orange on the skyline was always Yate's relief, the matted tumble into black. Sarah came, mornings and afternoons, bringing always some cipher of the world, a spiky red flower that Mrs Jones called the bottle-brush, a bag of almonds and French plums, three Turkey figs for Edwin. She was rumoured to have taken fits when she heard the news, but it was so perfumed and petticoated by the time it came to her that she had not understood it for a slander until William explained it. Even then, she was untroubled. She had a letter from Mr Taylor that she threw away, begging her to consider him her brother.

As if I were short a brother, she said and laughed despite it all.

She had been spared the bishop's investigation though she would have liked to tell how on the voyage Mr Taylor had felt obliged to shun Mr Armistead on account of thinking him an adulterer. Preliminary to any formal tribunal, the investigation stretched for days which Yate found trying, no witnesses called but those who spoke badly of him and many questionable affidavits read out by Mr Armistead. Nothing from Mr Gordon who thought him maligned, no statement from Captain Aitken or the Buttons, Edwin unrepresented. Yate sat for the most part silent, nothing said in the vestry that was not written down by at least half a dozen persons, Marsden grumbling that some of the most influential persons in the colony maintained his friendship still. His solicitor, Mr Chambers, was in attendance and leaned mumblingly into him, They haven't a case, sir. All talk, no case, although Yate's chest clutched in fearfulness, a man who had been a Shropshire boy. In his counterfeit sorrow and his best waistcoat, Mr Taylor tilted his deferential head at the bishop, the magistrate and the judge in turn. He testified that Mr Yate and Mr Denison had made repeated visits to each other's cabins though Yate had told the bishop plainly he was in the custom of sharing his bed and pitied those who thought it improper.

Considering their disparity of rank and education and moral deportment, said Mr Taylor, nibbling his teeth, there was an unbecoming intimacy between Mr Yate and Mr Denison. I saw Mr Denison tickle Mr Yate once in passing him on the deck.

Hardly a crime, said Mr Chambers in his crumbly voice. A crime. Yate could hardly make sense of the word. It was difficult always to remember Edwin when others were speaking of him. Grubbing after him, they missed him entirely, their own coarseness coming off on him. The bishop, the judge, Marsden himself, like dull poultry clucking and scratching over what might have been obvious to anyone, Edwin's limited education, his minor rank, without considering how much more miraculous these made his finely worked accomplishments, his grace, his humour, his capacities for transformation. Yate sat hunched beside Mr Chambers, a very specific ache he associated with Edwin's absence bending his shoulders forward over the cave of his chest. Mary Ford had been dug up on Fort Street where, to Mr Armistead's surprise, she kept a house and three servants. By her affidavit, she had seen Mr Yate with his arms about Mr Denison's neck. Also Deck's. The doctor testified to the same familiarity of conduct between Mr Yate and Mr Denison. Mr Armistead had even laid hold of Mrs Parker somewhere and taken her statement that the boatswain had declared in her presence that if Mr Yate had taken the same liberties of language with him as he did with the other sailors he would have knocked him down. This was read out with the relish of a swung punch. The gentlemen gave the ladies' evidence with particular tenderness. Mr Langhorne said his wife had called at Mrs Brown's lodgings and seen Mr Denison with his head in Mr Yate's lap. From Marsden, his neck thrown like an old bull's, the two men had slept together at the parsonage in preference to sleeping singly, though he hadn't known it at the time, and Martha had observed them holding hands beneath the dinner table, Mr Yate eating several pieces of meat off Mr Denison's plate.

I didn't see it for myself, he said, red and blowing, my eyes not being what they were. Mr Taylor said that liberties had been taken by the two parties, Mr Yate giving presents to Mr Denison, a suit of clothes, the sum of twenty-five pounds, a gold watch, a dressing case and who knew what else.

On one occasion, said Mr Taylor who had forgotten it in the courteous excitement of bloodletting, I went down into Denison's cabin and was shown a naked person, a picture that is to say of nakedness, a naked female figure. He gobbled his breath and looked to the bishop. Mr Yate only lay on Denison's bed and laughed when I reproved him. There was a silence as Mr Taylor looked at his shoes before the scratching of several pens scored the close hung air of the vestry.

I have two letters, said the bishop, from Mr Denison to Mr Yate. Among the papers in front of the bishop Yate looked for his letters but could not see them.

I want them back, he said to his solicitor, Mr Chambers nodding.

On their tone and character, said Bishop Broughton, I shall offer no observation. It was the bishop's habit to make a virtue of his restraint all the while implying that, should he unleash himself, it would go the worse for Mr Yate. That being said, a tighter grip on his waistcoat buttons, they prove to my satisfaction that Mr Denison is not a person whose education and acquirement could recommend him to Mr Yate as a companion. Their speaking of impropriety and indecency Yate bore with animal patience but that they would presume to speak of companionship, of the friendship between men, he could not bear.

These letters, said the bishop, squeezing his eyeglasses off his nose and looking about the unfocused room, appear to me to manifest an absence of all religious earnestness and even the ordinary respect which every person in his station should pay a clergyman. He gave up a sigh as if it were a prayer, eyes raised to the vestry ceiling, and adjourned for the day, the gentlemen deferring their black carrion huddle until Mr Yate and Mr Chambers had left, the violent broad day beyond the churchyard and all the unprotected hours before night.

Against her every expectation, Mrs Button was enjoying New South Wales and expected to for as long as Captain Button did not remove them to Argyle. Newspaper reports

of bushranging in the district had persuaded him more than
she could that it was tactical to remain in Sydney.

At least for the season, said Mrs Button though her
husband thought only of the six men robbed between
Sutton Forest and Bargo Brush, a pistol snapped at one
fellow for three pounds and his boots. At her persuasion,
he had signed the Governor's book at the porter's lodge so
they might be eligible to attend the balls at Government
House but his preference was to sit with the papers reading
the police news which is how he learned of Mr Yate's
disgrace. *A series of documents has been forwarded to us,
in reference to certain recent proceedings, originating in
the alleged improper conduct of a Missionary on the island
of New Zealand. We hardly know how to deal with them
– yet they are of a very interesting nature. On the one hand
we find charges of a most revolting nature (supported by
evidence wholly uncontradicted) preferred against a Christian Minister, by a gentleman of respectability; while, on
the other, we are opposed by that very natural reluctance
which every well-directed mind must feel, to give credence
to statements which, if true, would reduce the individual of
whom they were made, to a state of moral degradation
which we dread to contemplate.*

The case is not as grave as has been made out, said
Captain Button over the *Sydney Herald* one morning to his
wife who gaped a little because she thought their way to
Argyle lay clear though he only referred to the business
with Mr Yate, an anonymous subscriber writing to the
editor to declare that he had read all the documents relating
to the case and, convinced the accusations were false, only
wished they might come before a court of justice so an
impartial jury might proclaim the missionary's innocence.
When the Captain had gone on his afternoon's business,
Mrs Button showed the newspapers to her daughter.

Is it Mr Yate? said Miss Button, rubbing her newsprinted
fingertips together.

I believe it might be, said her mother. And I think *a gentleman of respectability* is meant for Mr Armistead.

Oh mama, said Miss Button, made uncertain by the recollection of his cabin door swinging open and her slow-witted scramble to make sense of the scene, something there she had not got out yet. What's he said to have done?

Can you not guess? Miss Button read again and made a very pretty speculation, whispering in her mama's ear and blushing.

Nothing half as bad as that, my dear. Mrs Button smiled though she could have laughed. It's when one gentleman uses another for a lady, she said and went to lie down an hour. Miss Button read the papers again slow, not sure what she had learned. Her mother would tell her anything but much remained for her to explain to herself. The thing about Australia, she thought, was that nothing stayed in its right place except by force. Convicts rode the streets in carriages and took their women to the theatre. She wasn't sure what it meant for a gentleman to be used as a lady, giddy imaginings of Mr Armistead crouched to Mr Yate, caressing his shoe in his lap. Mrs Fraser had been used for a black lady which was a terrible shame. It was Mr Denison, she supposed, though he was nothing like a lady.

The days were dry and hot, by afternoon the morning's heat radiant from every surface, the barrack walls and roadways, life feeling very much like fate between the squeeze of the city's hot breath and the indifferent ball of the sun. The ladies wore white and floated behind the glazed darkness of upstairs windows or walked a little in the evening as the sun wore itself away, their imprudent bodies insistent on sensation, skin unfurling like perfumed night flowers. By day, the streets swarmed with red dust, the watercarts being hardly seen. Up York Street came a

cart wobbling and squeaking, its far wheel loosened and
rolling elliptic, one witless white dog yammering in its
trace, a gutter of dried blood caked to the tailboard, Constable Kelly weighting down the tarpaulin and beating flies
from his face, the hams of Constables Naughton and
Moore wedged together at the front. The cart stopped
outside the police yard. Kelly dropped the tailboard and
threw the tarp from a malevolence of dead dogs, snarling
and sleeping, legs branched to the sky, several snouting in
a corner after a forgotten stink, others taking the bloat,
barrel-bellied and close to comic. He tried to shovel them
off but they were melted together under their coat of flies,
one monstrous dog with forty chests, striped and brindled,
yellow and black, with seventy-nine eyes and forty gore-
stumped tails. Nothing but breath keeping them light, in
death they were each a man's weight. Swung from the cart
by the legs, they fell heavy, black and liver, lion-ruffed,
golden, muscled across the shoulder, face gone to a clag of
blood, seal's head, tar ooze from the arse's neat pucker,
speckled, white eye patch, three-legged. Moore got down
with a brace of tails in his basket and had them arranged in
a semi-circle on the grass plot in front of the station before
Naughton came out with a police officer, a desk man by the
look of him, a frayed head like a chewed-down pencil and
soft, underwater hands. He glanced at the heap of dead
dogs, counted once, then twice, the harvest of tails, thirty-
nine, forty, making it five pound even and authorising the
promissory note.

Friday, mid-November. Yate lay on his bed, the light from
the street pulsing red and orange through his eyelids. He had
written to the Colonial Secretary's office once more and
again to Bishop Broughton but after several weeks had no
reply. Lately even Mr Harington was not returning his calls.
He could not count the letters he had written from his

rooms whose walls grew warm as a body, his signature growing unfamiliar as if he forged himself. He could write no more nor read. Prayer was impossible, the scrape of a bucket in a well gone dry. He couldn't sleep. The air in his room grew close, twice-breathed. He put on his shoes but stood hesitating at his window, the respectable heads of Sydney making their unimpeded way beneath bonnets or hats as if they had no thought of him. Mrs Brown's woman was shuffling about on the landing with a broom. She didn't smile at him any longer but watched as if she were studying him for something. He took all his meals in his room or in Mrs Brown's front parlour and the woman could hardly lay a tray before him. It was hours before night and he thought he must walk or grow mad in his rooms.

The street was another sort of madness. People spoke of him as he passed or he imagined they did. At any rate, they did not speak to him except one or two who offered their greetings as credential to their level-headedness and did not wait to hear his response. Once as he had passed the watch house at Clarence Street by day a gob of sputum was hawked at his feet that he did not know for sure was meant for him but rolled and lay dusted red like a piece of Turkish confectionery. He wore his hat low and watched his shoes appear and reappear, avoiding the main thoroughfares, up Bathurst Street and along Kent. By day, he didn't care for the fashionable throng on George Street nor chance the lonely wastes of the Domain. He preferred the dubious streets of the Rocks where he was not the only business, a crooked gentleman in black with his hat worn low.

Along Kent Street he went, measuring out the city in strides. In the light of day he saw nothing, the steady tick of his feet coming and going and the dark halo of his hat brim. The grocer's wife had kept a caged parrot that she spoke to in a cackle, *Hel-lo Mar-tha*, though in the seven years of his apprenticeship he never heard it talk. Every day now thoughts of his boyhood washed over him unbidden. A tow-headed boy he had been, so near-sighted his world clung close and inwrought, falling away at the margins in smears of blurred colour, the dumb complexity of things half seen. Recollected, his childhood was made the same, intricately worked, detailed to the last button. He saw himself at fifteen, rolling the vaporous kegs of vinegar from the storeroom or, younger, holding his father's finger as they walked the river bank, rooks rising in the updrifts, a spider's nest wound around three bent reeds, his paltry life unmarked as the scoop of sky that birds traverse as they like and was swiped with wonder that he had grown to be a man in a distant country and was pursued for an apostate, that same near-sighted boy still staring through his eyeglasses which tidied the whole world to his view, the land falling away to the bright plane of the harbour and a three-master sailing in from the heads. *My soul waiteth for the Lord more than they that watch for the morning: I say, more than they that watch for the morning.* The Psalms were his consolation though previously he had found them a little weak-backed. He was changed utterly, he knew, because like the weave of his clothes Isaiah had grown too coarse for him. *How is the faithful city become an harlot!*

On the Rocks he went between the clanging crowds like the clapper of a bell until on Gloucester Street, on a broad open space of hill, a small girl dragging a dirty string got in under the brim of his hat and looked at him frank, her mother looking too when he tilted his vision uphill a little and behind her a further man sitting on the grass with his sausage-curled wife, their children clustered close and open-mouthed, a man selling cockles in lemon juice, the scent of crushed grass drawing a dog on by the nose, a clot of butchers still in their aprons, three gingerbread ladies, arms linked and laughing, a skipping boy threading a line of children through the throng, the bruit of talk but no word distinct, ranks of people, dozens and dozens of them all looking at him with blank expectation. One man before many he stood and was humbled in his skin and fearful though he knew the day of judgment would bring many before the one. He took off his hat and the press of people fell silent, those that were sitting stood. The knack of preaching lurched in him like a barrel shifting unseen in a ship's hold and he readied himself for some gaseous word to float up, something plain and uncorrupted for these people with their home-hewn sins, their plastered bricks and gardens of carted soil. It would be a biblical event though he didn't know if he was to survive it. A cry went up, a single tribal cry that eased a hundred throats, satisfaction and disappointment webbed together. There was to be no speech. A man stepped forward, grim with a face like crumbling masonry, a leader of some sort no doubt with a collective duty to discharge though the crowd paid him no special attention as he came on and shouldered past, Yate turning as the man continued downhill, the surprise of a further crowd behind him, the backs of their heads turned to him, all facing as he did now the gaol yard below where the form of a man, attended by a minister and the executioner, transformed the dark spars of the gallows from monument to instrument. For a gooseflesh moment, Yate thought it was Mr Taylor but it was only Mr Cowper, one hand on the condemned man's head while the executioner wound him about with rope as if pinioning his arms were another kind of care. Yate would not watch the bag being put over the man's head and climbed the hill, blood-drained and terribly mindful of the leechlike stares that stuck to him as he passed, until halfway up the steep and rocky footpath of Argyle Street he heard the exultant shout and milked his own neck with a distracted hand.

He stumbled on as if lost in the bush, as if each house front,
like each flayed, flesh-coloured eucalypt trunk, could not be
distinguished from the last, walking in loops though always
with the delusion of pressing forward. His hat still in hand,
the city was a wide place, a raw open sky overhead and the
rake of the streets to the sea, the gentlemen in their polished
carriages and a couple of labouring men with a handcart
sliding thoughtlessly away from him as dust motes in the
sun. Two constables outside Mr Aiton's public house on
Clarence Street slapping their knees and clucking their
tongues for a fine white dog that stood in the yard, his
polished black nose sampling the world beyond the gate.
The dog leaned forward, head and curly chest in the street,
and then came crouching to fawn at the men, beating the
dust with his tail plumed pink. Two truncheon blows that
Yate felt at the back of his skull and the dog was dragged a
little way from the house, one constable pocketing his
collar, the other severing his tail before they hurried away,
one man looking hard at Yate as he went with silent
whistling lips. Yate walked toward the corpse and bent
gingerly over it as though he might be savaged by even a
dead dog. A handsome animal though his tail was gone and
treacle welled in the dent in his head. At the body before the
flies, Yate thought he might ground his current of sadness
by touching the wiry hair of the dog's ribs but his usual
squeamishness about the dead prevented him. How faith-
fully they resemble their living selves. His shoes clear of the
leaked blood, he squatted to peer into the eye that lay open
under the sun, his own head bulbous and shrunken in that
velvet curve while small and receding fell away the mad
world over his shoulder. It was a vision of something, a
cloth ripping in the temple, and he was running in the full
glare of day, his hat in his hand, mouth open and unquiet,
not concerned for, not knowing even, the spectacle he
made, the disgraced man running the length of George
Street hatless with his neckcloth skewed. At Castlereagh

Street, he hung a few minutes on Mrs Campbell's railings before knocking at her door.

Mr Denison, said Yate.

And who shall I say is callen? said Mrs Campbell, for she supposed that was how fighting insults were dished in society. In Edwin's upstairs room, Yate cried at last as if he were not more than a boy, a swelling grief for all he had lost and all he had left to lose. Edwin held him as he wept, William, William, you're here now, and bathed his face when he was done. He settled Yate on his bed, stroking his head in his lap.

I've been thinking, he said shyly, when we go from here, perhaps there'll be a position for you somewhere as ship's chaplain. Yate looked through half-closed eyes at the underside of Edwin's chin, a ship's chaplain, the neat turn of an ocean cabin, what of Sarah, and slept a dreamless stretch.

Early December, Mr Harington received an extraordinary letter. *My dear Sir*, wrote Mr Busby, *I sincerely sympathize with you in the revulsion of feeling with which you will receive the intelligence that the wretched man whom you have cherished as a friend, has been beyond all doubt for many years in the habitual practice of a crime which God has above all others marked by a display of divine vengeance in this world.* Not as encouraging as he had hoped, Harington read on untroubled. He had it on the authority of a clerk tight with the Crown Solicitor's office that unless the offence could be proved to have taken place *per anum*, as the legals put it, nothing could stick. His own carriage ostentatious at Yate's Park Street address, he had staked his public name on the man. *I understand that he is ascertained to have made not fewer than 60 persons the instruments of his unnatural lust and it is to be feared has added to the Catalogue of their former crimes this worst of*

all which was never before heard of amongst the natives.
The natives. He had not thought to consider them. At
worst, he imagined buying off a couple of discreditable
sailors. But sixty natives put rather a different light on the
affair. The stupidity of the blasted man. Sixty. Sixty. Was
such a number even plausible? Harington arrested himself
in the arithmetic to review his situation. He could speak
with the Secretary this afternoon and set up a meeting with
Bishop Broughton, or better go softly via Marsden, before
the week's end. Sixty. It worked out at a little more than
one a week for a year. Not out of the question, he supposed
and went to tell his man he was no longer home to Mr
William Yate.

Marsden's sight was fading but he thought he hadn't lost
his senses yet. From his study window, he watched his field
of cows, their necks low for the December grass, still
greenly sweet. He held a magnification glass without which
he could not have made out a word of Mr Clarke's letter or
the six native depositions against Mr Yate. He ran the glass
over the page once more – *taking his departure for
England, unwilling to commit to paper the disgusting
details, the abominable practice* – before marking his place
with his thumb.

   Here it is, Mr Taylor, he said but did not read the passage
aloud. Taylor sat opposite, hands clasped and held between
his knees, a churn of sensation in his stomach such as he
had before stepping up to the pulpit to speak. If he understood Mr Marsden correctly, Mr Yate's guilt was
established beyond question. The missionaries at Waimate
had apparently burned the unfortunate man's possessions
and even, it seemed, shot his horse. Taylor wondered
whether shooting a horse could be considered quite Christian. No denying there was something bracing in such
barbarism.

That the abominable practices of the individual in question began soon after he came to the land, read Marsden in a scriptural voice. That every station in which he visited has been polluted by them. That they were carried on at the native villages which he visited and even in the road to those villages and shocking to relate, Marsden rubbed his eyes and moaned low like a calf for its mother, that he introduced to Christian Baptism the very natives who both before and afterwards were the misguided partakers in his guilt. He could not bring himself to look at Mr Taylor. Catching a lick of sun on his glass, he twirled it so that a flock of yellow lights flew about the walls of his study, flattening across his bookshelves, leaping forward to skim Mr Taylor's forehead and put out his eye in a golden haemorrhage.

I'll leave you to make copies for the bishop and the Colonial Secretary's office, Mr Taylor, said Marsden, head down, awkward to look another man in the face after what he had just read. Perhaps you'll lock the door until you are finished.

Taylor turned the key and had an instant's proprietary pleasure in taking charge of Mr Marsden's study and the square of landscape beyond the window, the old man's felted footsteps diminishing along the passage. He tweaked his trousers and sat to the desk. Mr Yate was ruined. There could be no doubt. If there was a flare of happiness in him, and he was moral enough to allow there was, then it was a very proper jubilation such as Moses must have felt when he drowned Pharaoh's army, six hundred chariots and horsemen buried beneath the Red Sea. He read first the deposition of Pehi, certified as a true translation by Mr Clarke, Mr Williams and Mr Davis. *He said to me, Unbutton your trousers. I said to him, For what purpose should I unbutton them? He said to me,* Kia titoitoi taua.

(The meaning of this expression is an act of most gross obscenity committed upon one another, each holding the penis of the other in his hand.) I said to him, We shall be caught by Mr Davis's daughter. He replied, In the evening, come to my home. In the evening I went. On my arrival the fire was burning in his house. I entered. He said to me, Stand there. He said to me, Wakatoratorangia te te. (The passage which follows is too obscene to admit of translation.) I went to him three times. Beyond belief. He put the papers down, gravely shocked, stood and looked about him without seeing anything, registering only the blare of light from the window as he turned. *Once at Pateretere, when we went to bathe. He said to me, A woman will not appear quickly for you and me. Let us go and bathe. He pulled off his trousers. He called to me, Come down into the water, I'll break your head with my penis.* He had not thought of the mechanics of Mr Yate's sin, enough that he had conducted himself indecently in full view of the cuddy, that he had favoured a sailor with his attentions. Mr Clarke wrote that he might have furnished a hundred such confessions, were there time and need. He had competent witnesses who could come to Sydney to give evidence, one or more of the missionaries accompanying them as interpreters. Toataua's deposition. *He laid hold of me and dragged me by my hand into the tent, and we titoitoi. That ended there.* Samuel Kohe's. *He said but as for me my wife is this, a hand. I went to him three times before my baptism and since my baptism I have been many times, more than I can count.* Philip Tohi. *When we were at Paihia there was a Committee and we went to Kerikeri in the boat. We were called to fetch food for the rowers of the boat. He told the men to stand before him, to unbutton their trousers that he might see their — . He was very merry.* That a man could do such things and still have the shape of a man seemed impossible. Yet here was the evidence. He copied with care, knowing that every sentence undid Mr Yate a little more, piercing his skin to let

the corruption run until the man could not hold himself
together.

That night Taylor sat against his pillows in bed while
Caroline put up her hair. She was to be delivered in five
months and was content, full of floating secrets. Truly the
heart of man is deceitful, he thought. There was Mr Yate,
all those mornings in his cabin, instructing them in the New
Zealand language which harboured words that could not
be translated into the decency of English. That long narrow
face that had suckled on another man. His fingering for his
place in Caroline's book. He looked at his own uninnocent
hand and closed his eyes. His wife watched him in the
mirror, her mouth spiked with hairpins. In his nightgown
he looked a sad cruel boy.

Are you well, Richard? she said, holding her pins a
moment. She looked at herself in the glass. In her condition,
other people were a struggle. She seemed larger than
anything else, not only her physical increase but more
important, grander, brighter even as if she drew the world's
colours to herself. Sick at first, each morning curling back
on the day like a yellowish rind, she was strong again and
sentimental enough to feel a kinship with Mr Marsden's
doleful ewes, their new lambs, all leg and tail. Richard
looked over her shoulder, a reflection seen in clouded
water.

Mr Yate is utterly ruined, he said.

Utterly? A hairpin arrested in its jab.

Unspeakably.

With Sarah and Edwin, Yate embarked on Captain
Crawford's *Ulysses* on the fifteenth day of December.
Feeling had turned against him. He sensed it as surely as a
sleeping sailor knows the change of the tide. There was to

be no public case against him, however he implored Bishop
Broughton. Marsden was agog that Mr Yate had the
effrontery to take his passage with his companion in
disgrace and prayed daily for Miss Yate's spiritual well-
being.

We are not so righteous as to forget her in our prayers, I
hope, Mr Harington, he said, his dim eyes groping for the
man's face.

Quite, said Mr Harington. Though why the fool hadn't
run at the first opportunity he'd never know. Still, his information had it that the administration preferred to let him
go. For all the missionaries's poking about, not one native
boy would attest to being taken from the rear. Lucky for
him, it seemed William's tastes lay elsewhere.

Edwin, Yate and Sarah: the three of them were the only
passengers which was as well since they recognised in themselves a perfect society. There was, Yate thought, an
algebraic harmony to their company, the robust engagement
of three, that did not survive intrusion. When Mr Mitchell
called with a bucket of green-veined gooseberries and his
wife's best regards, they came apart like a card trick. In the
light of nothing warmer than civility, they were ordinary
people only, with habits and laughable affectations, the
work of being themselves hatefully visible like the under-
parts of a dry-docked ship. Sarah fussed and fretted. Edwin
was made awkward, knees and ears, like a boy strung up on
his growing pangs. Hating Sydney, Yate was impatient to
haul anchor, not for England, that indifferent country, but
to be again a society afloat on a world of water, answerable
only to the eye of God that was the sky itself over the
brawling ocean. The Ulysses was a tidy enough ship though
Edwin was happy to find it deficient on several accounts.
The standing rigging needed work, for instance, and the
second mate was more of a seaman than the first.

That can lead to trouble, Edwin said, unconcerned. The
men always know right down to the greenest boy. He was

not used to sailing cabin. There was no cuddy but a tight room off William's starboard berth that Sarah called the parlour, its low ceiling ribbed with rafters and a thick-glassed window giving on to the upper winches of Mr White's warehouse. Captain Crawford was lading whale oil and Edwin preferred to stand on the poop, the men rolling barrels across the planking, the brisk salt air overwhelmed with the effluvium.

Edwin supervised the loading of their effects. Yate saw him going easily between the carters and the men, nursing against his chest the deal box of bulbs that would never reach New Zealand. That was the thing that grieved him most, to be forbidden the country he loved, Waimate the one place that made a natural sense of him. Whenever he thought of New Zealand, it was always a homecoming, the ship anchored off Paihia and Mr Williams's boys rowing out for him or at Waimate, returning from one of the outlying villages, Selim eager for home, leaning into his reins, his boys running effortless beside the horse, pulling on their clothes when they came in sight of the mission, the English steeple and the three hip-roofed houses strung along the rise above wheat fields that rippled at evening like a grass sea. And this time his imaginings were curlicued with the thought of Sarah, attentive to her own projects, the infant school and the village women, the end of her day the end of his and the unlicensed addition of Edwin, new minted as when first he saw him off Deal this February gone, master of a schooner trading up and down the New Zealand coast. Hard to think of the bulbs shuffling in their chaff in leaded darkness.

Still the ship did not sail. Each morning brought again the slow-whaling windmills on the skyline, the roofs and

streets of Sydney, like the disagreeable feculence that bobs
about a ship becalmed. In the grip of a fright that every day
tightened its pincers on him, Yate was fearful of everything:
any carriage that came down to the water or any dark-
suited gentleman who walked the dock; the expectant
afternoon skies; the tall stretch of the windmills; the
thoughts that crabbed the inside of his skull. All these
boiled down more mundanely to his dread of being separated from Edwin, to know him in the world but be
without him.

If I'm taken from the ship, said Yate but did not learn
how his sentence finished for Edwin froze like a bird-dog
on point and would not hear him through.

No one's taking you, he said as if his assurance could
prevent it. Yate soothed himself by making a Christmas
pudding. On the parlour table, they grated suet and stale
bread, the fat slippery-soft in the heat, Edwin taking a flap
out of one knuckle and sucking the blood from it. Yate cut
thin strips of peel from a lemon and an orange, the citrus
cutting the waxy animal smell that filled the low parlour. A
frown concentrated Edwin's eyebrows over his nose as he
cored and chopped an apple. He worked carefully until he
had the trick, taking a pleasure in his own handiness. It was
the same when work was going forward, Yate remembered,
that pleased self-absorption, his philosophic habitation of
the task. The same in bed. A vision of Edwin attentive and
frowning over the business of his rope-callused hands
flooded Yate's cheeks with blood. He measured the milk
over the bowl, his head bent and cooling. Edwin caught the
last of Yate's blush and tracked in his mind the possible
causes.

Do you think we'll have our pudding in harbour or at
sea? said Yate.

At sea, for sure, said Edwin slow and coming up with
nothing.

Here was Sarah in her bonnet, footweary from town and crowds. She had been to Alexander Andrews for dry fruits which she unpacked onto the table, Patras currants and pudding raisins, Valentia almonds, English walnuts, white Jamaica ginger, two nutmegs and a quill of cinnamon. Nothing as gay as her harvest though she kissed her brother, ate a piece of chopped apple and let him scold her for it. The newspaper had published a piece about him that morning, Mrs Langhorne had told her, meeting by chance on George Street. Sarah hadn't read it herself but Mrs Langhorne had been most adamant that it called for William to be removed from the *Ulysses* and tried before a jury on the evidence of some sixty affidavits, newly arrived from New Zealand. William was untying the packages and exclaiming, his hair at the back of his head grown thin where he couldn't see it. Altered by her fresh knowledge, she did not know where to put herself, how to look him in the eye, or Edwin either. Nothing in all of Mrs Langhorne's poison had turned her so much as one degree from her brother but, alerted now to his danger, she was so impatient to be gone she would have hauled anchor with the men if it had seen Sydney slip away faster. She had not been the least sympathetic, Mrs Langhorne, her eye dipping into Sarah's basket and coming out superior. Stolid in triumph and shrill as if the family horse had come in at the Yass races. Or as if she were the horse itself, four-square and thick-hocked, thought Sarah, not much practised in cruelty.

Any news of our sailing? she said, the break in her voice giving her away. A quick relay of glances that laced them together, light and sure as a net. Edwin to her, a frank rope-testing stare; William to Edwin, the flip of a soldered fish turning fleet against the current; her own gaze falling to the table with its mess of half-unwrapped supplies and coming up again, replenished, to mesh with William's, stubborn, proud, frightened, a boy again.

We can't know what will come of this, said Edwin which,

of course, was always true but it nearly brought her tears on, being said so kindly, his sympathies as usual tilted at hers. Yate poured a glass of barley wine, a glass of stout and a handsome measure of rum over the chopped fruit and spices, his world shrunk to the three of them but still seeming a magnification, and each stirred in turn, standing to counter the weight of the pudding batter, their hopes, like their anxieties, buoyed on the muzzy fumes that wreathed their heads.

Sir, Mr Yate, how do you do, my friend? This is my speech to you. There are two things in my heart at Waimate this day, light and darkness. Mr Clarke tells me you are alive in England. How do you do, Mr Yate? I have a daughter now, Mere, by my wife. Mr Davis teaches me to turn shoes at the blacksmith's shop. You are not dead. There is much I wish to show you but you will never come to this place any longer, Mr Clarke says. He says the devil rides you.

One night before Mere was born their mouths were all full with your name, Mr Clarke, Mr Davis and Mr Williams. We were called in one after one to Mr Clarke's parlour. Many of your boys said nothing but with Toataua and the others I told all the truth because I loved you best. I told how you taught me in your study at night, showing me in a book your England country and all the sea between. I said my catechisms that I had learned from you but their pens did not work for that. They hooked our words from us like eels and wrote down only what they chose. Mr Davis read to me what I had said but it was only pieces like the remains of a feast after the men have eaten. He wrote my name after although you know I can write my name for myself.

Your horse was shot and all your belongings burned. You will not come back here. Mr Williams is gone to Turanga and Mr Taylor has taken his house. He cries in the night since his son is dead, Arthur Taylor. Going to his mother in Te Puna, he fell from his horse and was dragged in the road until he was dead. Mr Taylor's boys brought him back to Waimate on their shoulders and all the boys from the school came out and cried to see him.

King William is dead also but Queen Victoria has written a book to Mr Williams and Mr Busby that she wants to be a friend to the New Zealanders. All the chiefs have a feast at Waitangi, put their names on the book and call three cheers. I write to you that you may know about it. Wiremu Hau and Reweti Atuahaere from Waimate put their names in the book at Waitangi and the Queen's man, Kawana Mr Hobson, brings the book to Waimate. Six more chiefs put their names in the book at Mr Taylor's house.

On one of the days of November, in the third week of it, on the Tuesday, I begin to write this speech to you. My pencil is not so fast as my mouth. Some men say that the mission men asked Mr Hobson to come here, and now Mr Hobson will call for the soldiers and take away the land and everyone who put his name on the Queen's book will be her slave. Sir, Mr Yate, listen to my thoughts. I think Queen Victoria is our friend and protector. Mr Clarke says so. He says you live now in London, the village of the Queen. Speak my name to Queen Victoria and tell her we are sitting here in peace.

When my words were written and my name put down by Mr Davis I said to Toataua and the others that writing is lies. It travels too far to be truthful. My slate that you had given me I threw away. To Mr Clarke I say that I will go to England to see Mr Yate and look upon his face once again but my heart is resting in Waimate with my wife and daughter so I send my words only.

Mr Clarke says no more about you. Mr Davis will not say your name. You are a ghost of this place. Everyone is writing books to everyone and everyone is writing his name. I tell my daughter this story which is written down nowhere. Once there was a man of God come to us from England, my friend Mr Yate.

From me is this, from your boy Philip Tohi that you called Piripi, written with my pencil at the Waimate, to Mr Yate. This is all my speech to you. This is all.

'Yate returned to England in December, determined to clear himself, but was dismissed by the C[hurch] M[issionary] S[ociety] on the confusing grounds that he had refused an investigation into the allegations. He made extensive, but vain, efforts to force the CMS to reopen his case.

Because of the taint Yate was unable to obtain work. Nevertheless he sustained his relationship with Denison, which he always protested was innocent. Finally in 1846 powerful evangelical patrons obtained for him the position of chaplain at the abandoned St John's Mariner Church at Dover. He worked with seamen until his death there on 26 July 1877.'

Judith Binney,
The Dictionary of New Zealand Biography
ed. W. H. Oliver (Wellington: Allen and Unwin, 1990)

Acknowledgments

Although a work of fiction, *Slow Water* has drawn heavily on historic material, both archival and published. Important documents for the project are three shipboard diaries, *The Journal of Reverend William Yate, 1833–45* and *The Journal of Reverend Richard Taylor*, both held at the Alexander Turnbull Library, Wellington, and Fowles's *Doctor's Diary during a Voyage to New South Wales* held at the Mitchell Library, Sydney. I have also drawn on Yate's own book *An Account of New Zealand and of the Formation and Progress of the Church Missionary Society's Mission in the Northern Island* (London: Seeley and Burnside, 1835).

Judith Binney's 'Whatever Happened to Poor Mr Yate?' *New Zealand Journal of History*, October 1975, vol. 9, no. 2, pp. 111–125, remains the best historical reconstruction of the Yate scandal and was my invaluable guide to the relevant archives. Unless taken from newspapers of the day, all italicised passages in the Sydney chapters are taken from documents held either in the Colonial Secretary's Correspondence at the Archives Office of New South Wales or the Church Missionary Society papers at the University of Birmingham – the latter reprinted with copyright permission from the CMS.

For further details of life at sea in the 1830s, I consulted *The Journal of a Voyage to Australia in the Bark Amelia Thompson, Captain William Dawson, 1839*, by Reverend John Jennings Smith; Juanita Minter's *The Ship North Briton: Voyage to Australia: The Diary of David Melville* and *Steerage to Australia: A Diary of John Sceales' Voyage on the North Briton 1838/39*; Jean Main's *The Barque John: A Voyage to the Land of Hope, Gravesend to Adelaide, 1839/40*, all held at the Australian Maritime Museum, Sydney. George Bayly's *A Life on the Ocean Wave: Voyages to Australia, India and the Pacific from the Journals of Captain George Bayly 1824–1844* (Melbourne University Press, 1998) was also a source for several fictionalised scenes.

My project was greatly assisted by the generosity of Philippa Bassett, the special collections archivist at the University of Birmingham; Barbara Browning of the Ephemera Collection at the National Library of New Zealand; Rodney Burke, the curator at Te Waimate Mission House and Phil Parkinson of the Turnbull Library. I am grateful to Te Tumatakuru O'Connell for the Maori translations that appear in the opening section. Thanks also to Terri McCormack and Ann Standish for archival and library research and to Hannah Robert and Elizabeth Nelson for their clear-headed transcriptions of Dr Fowles's diary. Finally, many thanks to my friend Ange Wither for fact-checking and general sleuthing.